The Black Dragons

RICHARD A. HACKETT JR.

The Black Dragons

For more information about the author and other novels or books he has written, please visit the author website at:

www.rhackettjr.com

The characters and events in this book are fictional, and any resemblance to actual persons or events is coincidental.

Acknowledgements

This book was written for my son Trey. The character of a man is not about what he professes to be in his life, but how he lives it out, how he responds to adversity, and who he lives it for.

There are many secrets hidden amongst these pages that I hope you discover, but the most important thing to remember is that God is amazing, friendship is priceless, and love is always worth it.

I love you.

A special note:

All proceeds from the sale of this book go to support **Sea Mercy**, a non-profit organization dedicated to bringing free health care to the remote islands of the South Pacific via a floating health care clinic.

To learn more, please visit their website at:

www.seamercy.org

Facebook:
Sea Mercy

LinkedIn:
http://www.linkedin.com/in/richardhackett/

Chapter 1

July 30, 1777

"Boom!"

The cannon blast shook the frame of the massive French frigate *Indiscrete* as it sailed north, struggling to distance itself from the fort and island they had just departed. James had arrived at the island accompanied by his best friend in a British vessel of war. Now he was returning home without him in a French vessel of war, and the pain of the loss tore at his very heart and soul.

James Thornton held the railing and steadied himself, matching each roll of the sea with his legs, as the wind carried the white smoke from the recently fired cannon across the deck. He watched as the island continued to grow smaller and smaller with each passing moment. He tilted his head upward and saw the sailors scrambling across the rigging of the masts and out along the yards. As they were tying off and securing the sails, the wind seemed to fight against their every effort. James watched as the wind pulled against the hemp ropes that were tied to those massive sheets of canvas stretched across the blue sky above him. He felt the ship groan as if in protest as it sluggishly responded to each new gust.

Through the creaking and groaning of the ship, the popping of the sails above, and the splashing of the waves below, he could hear the officers yelling orders in French across the wooden decks and high into the sails above. Then on cue, a hundred men responded to the orders and glided across the yards and rigging. James did not understand the language of the orders, but he recognized the duties being performed and was impressed at their dexterity and grace as they moved across such deadly heights. His eyes drifted down to the deck of the ship and across the deadly row of massive *18 pounder* deck cannons pointing outward. Each cannon had a large wooden plug secured into the muzzle. He saw a vast array of ropes tied across and around each cannon to secure it to its mounts and blocks to prevent it from rolling backwards and crushing one of the crew. He had seen the damage this vessel and its cannons could do in battle and was happy to find that his circumstances now had him standing on the other end of those cannons that could deal out such death and destruction.

The warm, moist air was blowing across the deck bringing with it that sweet smell that he had grown to love, as it was carried to them from the nearby island. As he glanced back toward the fragrant island that was fading in the distance, memories of the events that lead up to this point came rushing back to him. He inhaled deeply then exhaled as he remembered and allowed himself to relive their last year together. It had been a year filled with the tragedy and suffering of war, but also one filled with more incredible joy, purpose and excitement than he knew most people would never experience in a lifetime.

In spite of those recent powerful memories, his mind and heart could not stop thinking about the friendship he had with Bode King, and how they had come to share it together their whole lives. That relationship started in 1758 when he was seven years old and living in Edenton, North Carolina. His father, Colonel William Thornton, a British army officer, had hired a new foreman to help run the plantation that he had recently purchased eighty miles west of Edenton. From his earliest memories, James' father had always been creative when planning for his family's future, but buying the plantation struck many as an outlandish notion. Even though he had no experience in running a plantation, he made the decision to purchase it from a fellow officer and friend after visiting it on his most recent return home. His mother was initially aghast at the idea and the purchase, but after several days and long nights of endless discussions, they had come to an agreement. From that moment forward she not only supported his purchase, but she made his dream her own as well. One of her only requirements was to hire a man to manage and run the plantation during his many absences as a result of his military responsibilities with the British army. Most recently, the British had fought in what seemed to be endless battles with the French and their Indian allies who were constantly attacking the northern colonies. Understanding her concern, Mr. Thornton spent a great deal of time interviewing who he felt, and what others said, were the best plantation foremen in the area.

His father was also looking for a man of character who could oversee his family during his absences as well. A man's character was not something his father would take lightly in his search. The man he settled on, and eventually hired, much to other plantation owners surprise and consternation, was a man named Elijah King. His father introduced Mr. King to his family and a few days later, at the insistence of his father, Mr. King brought his family over to their home and in turn introduced them to the Thornton's. James remembered being excited to see that Bode, who was Mr. King's oldest son, was about his same size and age.

James was very curious and hesitant as he looked at the boy across from him, both seemed to be watching and wondering about each other. From a distance, they were sizing each other up based on the simplest and most innocent of criteria, until their fathers called their names for introductions. James, as he was trained by his father to do, held out his hand to shake the young Mr. King's hand. At first, Bode just looked at the hand that was outstretched before him, almost as if he was confused. At the nudge of his father, he finally reached out, and cautiously grasped it and then shook it and smiled. James shook back and returned the smile as well; he could not have known at the time that they would become life-long friends.

Their new home and plantation was over eighty miles up the Roanoke River, almost due west of Edenton. "Way out in the middle of nowhere" as his mother would say, during her visits with people living in nearby towns. The Thornton and King families, along with the thirty-nine newly hired workers and their families left Edenton. The entire party traveled as a group and either rode or walked alongside the nine wagons that were loaded with supplies, tools and seed for their new life.

For James, all the preparations and concerns of their new life were secondary compared to the thrill of the travel and the possibility of adventure that it held. The fact that he had another young boy his age, living on the same plantation, was a huge blessing in his mind. James could not wait to test the waters with Bode. As simple as friendship requirements can be for seven-year-olds, the ten-day, eighty-mile journey provided plenty of time for them to learn that they were more alike than James could have ever dreamed. From the outset, they were inseparable as they talked and laughed and played the whole trip.

Upon arriving and surveying everything, it was evident to their parents that the massive plantation was in a horrible state of disrepair. However, Bode and James thought they had found heaven. At every opportunity, once they had finished with their chores, Bode and James would spend their free time running through the open fields, wading and fishing in the nearby river, exploring new lands. They spent their time arguing and fighting, laughing, dreaming, and building a very special. A friendship that James would discover later in life to be a very unique friendship.

While some of the workers began preparing the fields for planting, others were either repairing or building the needed structures that were required to house the crops and families of the plantation. James and Bode found themselves in a unique age category, as other children were either younger than James and Bode and were tied to their mothers during the day, or they were much older and were busily engaged in the heavy labor requirements of the plantation. Those first few years they were too young to be tasked with any major responsibilities, while at the same time they were too old and energetic to be bound to the house. The two years that followed were the most glorious years of freedom that two boys could ask for, and they took full advantage of them.

Although there was plenty of free time, life was not always just fun and play. James' mother, Charlotte, had been a school teacher before marrying his father and every day she would invite all the children living on the plantation, which included the Thornton and King families, to the little school house that had been converted from an old shed. She would teach each of them according to his or her age and skill level. James at first was very concerned for Bode and the other children from the plantation, for most of the children had never been taught to read or write. James recalled how strange it seemed to him that most did not seem to even want to learn. But, in spite of their resistance, his mother was determined and persistent with Bode and the other children. With James' encouragement and help, Bode and the other children gradually, not only caught up, but to James' frustration, Bode was even challenging him in their studies. In many ways, it was Bode who became the teacher. Bode was always very bright and hungry for knowledge and he learned very quickly.

James could not remember much about the first few years at the plantation, except for the fun he and Bode had, and that his father was often away at war. He did know that with Mr. King's guidance and supervision, the plantation continually grew larger and more profitable, as new fields were cleared and planted each year. The growth also required the hiring of new workers and their families to handle the additional crops and harvest schedules. As James' mother would always say, 'God is truly blessing our efforts' and Mr. King was always the first to agree.

As more workers and their families arrived on the plantation, the same challenges faced their children as they started school. They would come into the classroom with big fearful eyes and it would often take weeks to get them to participate in any activity, but eventually the other children, who had already worked through their own fear of school, would help them to learn and laugh along with everyone else.

At every chance available, he and Bode would dive back into the imaginary world in which they were brave soldiers, noble pirates, or world explorers. Side by side, the pair battled countless enemies, armed with stick swords and broom handle muskets and fence post cannons, with their brave troops right behind them. In every adventure, just at the moment when defeat seemed inescapable, the pair would find a way to extract a victory in the face of over-whelming odds. Together, there was no army or foe that they feared nor any who could ever stand against them.

James smiled at the memories but his heart was pensive at the thought of how naive those boyhood dreams had been. Personal experience had been an exacting tutor and the costly lessons he had learned was that war and battle were only glorious to those who directed it well removed from the battle lines. To the soldiers and citizens caught up in the egocentric plans and decisions of emotionally disconnected and power hungry leaders, war was a brutal, destructive and a horrific waste of human life. James shuddered and tried to shake the flood of memories that at times were unstoppable. There were the sights of unspeakable acts done in anger, the smell of smoke and death, and the sounds of firing muskets and exploding of cannons. The screams of dying men, the insults and challenges shouted across the field of battle, the blood that flowed unceasingly, and the helpless and emptiness he felt watching the life fade from the eyes of his dearest friends. James' father had always said that war brought out the worst in men, but he had also told James that it could bring out what perhaps is the best qualities of mankind; bravery, courage, sacrifice, loyalty compassion, mercy and faith. James had seen these too. As of yet, he still did not know how to separate the memories but he some how knew that to preserve his sanity and the true nature of who he was, he needed to learn how to focus on what was good while never forgetting the evil that surrounded the rectitude that rose above it.

"Excusez-moi!" A voice from behind James momentarily pulled him from his reverie and back to the deck of the French frigate. Standing behind him was a young French sailor trying to coil a section of rope that James was standing on. James smiled and stepped aside and the young man quickly completed his task, stepped away from the area, and smiled. "Merci." James once again nodded back. He looked across the deck, as the alacrity of the sailors seemed to be slowing now that their ship was on a secure tack with the wind. James knew that a sailor's life was not an easy one and the cost of the freedom of the sea was great deal of time absent from family and home.

"Home," he mumbled to himself. The idea of it seemed so far away as he thought about his own family. He stepped back against the railing and scanned the horizon off the starboard side where he stood, and then glanced back at the island again. Although James loved the memory of his childhood, he never remembered life on the plantation in North Carolina as being an easy one either. He remembered that his father was gone so often during the early years of his life, with duty calling him to the defense of the colonies and to lead the troops as required by his position. He was so happy when he finally retired from the British army as a Colonel in 1763 so he could spend more time with the family. Whether it was his youthful lack of understanding or a testimony to his father's humility, it was not until later in life that James learned that his father was actually a highly decorated and well-respected officer, a reputation he had earned while fighting in the French and Indian Wars from 1755 to 1763.

During his father's military years, James remembered months would pass, and once more than a year, without his seeing or hearing from him. In those times he was grateful for the ability to work under the tutelage and guidance of Mr. King, as were the other workers that were learning the business of growing and harvesting cotton, corn and tobacco. Mr. King was the most kind and patient man he had ever met, always taking the time to explain the reasons for doing things to James and Bode, not just barking orders at them. The kindness and patience of Mr. King greatly influenced and helped develop James' own character as a man.

From 1758 to 1775 his father and Elijah King, mostly Mr. King during his father's military absences, grew the plantation from their immediate families and the original thirty-nine workers into one of the largest cotton, corn and tobacco plantations in the state, eventually employing over 350 workers by 1775. For James, there was always hard work and long hours, more so the older he got. There were always challenges that had to be faced with every new season and every new worker and family added to the plantation.

James took a deep breath, shook his head at the memory, and was grateful that he was too young to understand most of what was going on around him in the early years. He credited that innocence to his youth and to his parents' hard work in protecting that innocence for him and his other siblings for as long as they could. As with many things, the loss of innocence is often a casualty of age.

James glanced back from the island at the sound of movement behind him and saw a young Negro crewman stumble and fall to the deck of the ship. Members of the crew had purposely overloaded him with rope and gear, and several of the French sailors began yelling something at him in French and laughing at his situation. James could see the embarrassment on the face of the young boy and immediately bent down to help him up, and help carry some of the rope and gear for him to his destination. A French sailor said something to James, causing the other sailors within hearing to laugh, and James turned and locked eyes with the man. It was clear to not only the man who had commented, but to all the other men that James did not find the situation funny. Moments later the smile fell from the man's face and the laughter from the rest of the sailors in the area stopped. James pointed for the young boy to lead on and walked behind him, carrying the rope and placing it where the boy indicated.

"Merci." The boy said and smiled at James as he headed back across the deck of the ship. James nodded and smiled at the boy and watched him disappear into the hold. James took a moment to glance around the deck of the ship, but none of the French sailors seemed to be willing to look in his direction. The interaction with the young boy brought to mind another moment in time that he and Bode had shared when they were younger.

It was during his twelfth year, in 1763. A man and his son had come to visit their plantation and to speak with his father. It seemed to James that he was there to complain about how Mr. Thornton was running things, for as he and Bode came into the house, he could hear the other man yelling in the other room. As they watched, they saw the man's red-headed son, perhaps a year or two older than James, with his ear pressed against the door listening. Not quite sure what to make of the exchange between the fathers in the other room, James and Bode walked up to the boy standing outside the door. James first introduced himself, the boy reluctantly shook James' outstretched hand, and then James introduced the boy to Bode. Bode reached out to shake the boy's hand as well, but in a strange awkwardness for all three of them, the boy turned cold toward Bode. The boy refused to even acknowledge Bode as his face steadily grew more stern and angry. The apparent anger was first expressed toward James and then toward Bode. James remembered looking at Bode and seeing something in Bode's countenance that he had never seen before. In response, Bode lowered his hand, shifting his eyes to the ground and stepped back and became silent.

The boy suddenly turned back toward James, grimaced and unleashed a barrage of angry words at him. "You're as big of a fool as your father is. Slaves should remain stupid and untrained for anything but pulling cotton and cutting tobacco," he yelled at James. "You don't know it, but you and your whole family are a laughing-stock to everyone!"

Slaves? Laughing-stock? James still could not understand the reason for the boy's anger, and then he suddenly thought he understood why the boy was so confused and angry.

"Oh, Bode is not a slave. He's my friend," James replied, hoping to reverse the awkward situation that was developing. James was stunned to see the boy look back with so much hatred on his face that James almost melted under his gaze and his next verbal barrage.

"He's a stupid Negro slave, and he belongs outside with the rest of the animals!" James knew that Bode would never tolerate such words from him or anyone else, and was actually looking forward to hearing him return the insult to this stupid redheaded boy. However, when he turned to see how Bode would respond, he was shocked to see him instead turn away with his head down and walk toward the front door. The boy's sinister laughter followed Bode out the door and down the steps.

James could not believe it. He and Bode had fought dragons and giants and all sorts of foul creatures together, they had even fought each other. There was nothing that Bode feared, so why had he turned and walked away from this arrogant boy and his insults? His heart raced and his anger started to boil at the thought of what this boy had done to his friend. He turned to hear the laughter of the boy again and the venomous words still flowing from his mouth.

"That's right… you run nigga boy! Run back to the…" The boy never saw it coming, nor did James realize he had thrown the punch that landed squarely on the boy's mouth before he could finish his last words. James was not sure why he swung at his mouth, perhaps it just seemed like that was the source of the problem and the quickest way to stop it. The next three punches landed just as solidly and squarely on the boy's nose and cheeks in spite of the boy's best efforts to protect himself from the smaller aggressor pounding away at him. His last punch landed with such force that it dropped the boy to the floor at James' feet where he began screaming and crying for help at the top of his voice.

As the door flew open and the two fathers came running out, there was James standing over the red headed boy with his fists clenched ready to continue the assault.

"James!" his father yelled and James, recognizing the tone of his father's voice and the trouble he was now in, looked over at his father. With blood flowing from his nose and lip, the boy crawled out from under James and ran whimpering to his father's side in tears.

James could not remember the exact words that were exchanged. He did know that the two men spent the next few minutes listening briefly to each boy's explanation of the event that unfolded, with both taking their stand in support of their boy's actions or words. Both were very upset and neither man backed down from his position on the matter.

He did remember his father suggesting strongly that the man and the boy get on their horses if they both wished to avoid further injury. The man continued to shout curse words at James' father, using words that James had never heard before, as he dragged his still whimpering son off to their horses.

"I will not forget how you treated us here today Mr. Thornton!" The man sneered at them across the courtyard.

"Nor shall I ever forget how you and your son treated me, my son, and my friends in my own home Mr. Johnson," he replied. James and his father stood on the porch and watched them as they rode off down the road. Once they were out of sight, his father bent down and asked him if he were hurt. James, realizing that he had not done so earlier, took a moment to evaluate his condition.

"My hand hurts," James said, finally relaxing his clenched fist and shaking his right hand as his father chuckled.

"That often happens when you hit a head filled with nothing but rock, son," he said and smiled at James and then stood up and shook his head with a faint smile as they walked back into the house. "Try as we might to soften the contents, I've found that it rarely changes what goes on inside the other fellows head." His father paused and sighed as he glanced out a window in the direction of the two riders. "Although I must say, I was really hoping for the opportunity to test that theory on Mr. Johnson's head." They both smiled and his father ruffled James blond hair and continued, "Don't tell your mother I said that or we will both be in big trouble." James smiled and looked up at his father as he thought through the words he had shared.

"Am I in trouble?" he asked, and his father returned a gentle smile.

"Yes, but I promise the punishment will be light. I can't have you beating upon every person that visits us that does not agree with how we run things here. It's always better to show restraint to an enemy when possible, than to rush into battle in anger." James nodded at his father's words and then thought about Bode. He was still very confused by Bode's behavior.

"Father, why did Bode let the boy say those things and just walk away without standing up for himself?" he asked. His father thought awhile before answering.

"Because Bode proved to be a lot wiser than either of us when it comes to showing what restraint looks like," his father said, but he could tell that James did not understand his meaning. "James, Bode knew that striking that boy, no matter what the situation might have been, would have created a world of trouble for him, his family, our family, and the plantation." His father looked at his son. "That's why I am so proud of you. You were willing to stand up for your friend in a difficult situation, even though he could not have." He smiled and put his arm around him. "I need to learn to do that more as well," he said. Looking through the window toward the nearby house where Bode and his family lived he saw Mr. King standing on his porch as if he were trying to determine a course of action.

When James went to visit Bode later that evening, Bode's father seemed very upset about the event. "I'm sorry about what happened at the house young James." Mr. King had said to him as he stepped into the house after being invited in. "These kinds of things rarely turn out well and I sure hope this does not bring trouble to all of us." James nodded.

"Father does not seem that concerned, but thank you." He looked around. "Is Bode here?" he asked and Mr. King seemed to hesitate a moment before answering.

"Yes, but he's feeling pretty bad about things… mumbling something about feeling like a coward for not standing beside you," he replied and smiled.

"Father said it was actually for the best and that Bode was very smart and brave to leave," James said confidently and then was almost embarrassed by his next words. "I was just wishing he saw how I got the better of the bigger kid." He smiled sheepishly, and then there was laughter from the back room and Bode stepped into the doorway.

"I only went far enough away that the boy could not see me, but I did see you punch him out," he said smiling from the doorway. "I would have come back and helped you if he would have gotten the upper hand on you… but you socked him so good!" He laughed and they both smiled as James puffed up with pride.

"Best punch I ever threwd… threw." James said confidently and they both laughed again as they reenacted the fight and the punches that were thrown, while Mr. King shook his head as he watched the two of them.

"Mr. King, can Bode and I spend some time outside together?" James asked several minutes later. Mr. King seemed to consider it for a while.

"I don't see how a little time together before bedtime could hurt anything," he replied and Bode and James jumped to their feet and raced for the door, stopping to grab their hand-carved wooden muskets and swords as they headed out onto the front porch and nearby fields. They never went anywhere without them and James, as always, had brought his with him and had set his beside Bode's before he knocked on their door.

They played for a long while before they returned to Bode's home. They sat on the porch in silence for several minutes watching the last of the sunset.

"That must be hard." James said, breaking the silence that had crept into their time together.
"What?" Bode replied.

"Having to walk away from someone who needs a beating for what he is saying." Bode seemed to think long and hard before finally answering him.

"You make it hard." He said sadly.

"I do? How do I make it hard?" James replied defensively.

"You and your family are different. My dad and mom say it as well. What's more, you don't even know it." Bode responded and James seemed to contemplate Bode's words.

"Is how we are... bad?" James asked cautiously.

"No. But it..." Bode seemed to be trying to gather his thoughts, but before he could answer, the front door opened and Mr. King came outside and sat down with the boys. Apparently he had been listening in on their conversation.

"Actually, the word I used was 'special' James, not 'different'. Your family is very special to us and to the other workers. What Bode is trying to say is that it can be confusing for us. Our lives here, all of the lives of the workers here, are far different... no, far better, than any other place we have been before."

"How then is that bad?" James asked again.

"It's not, you knucklehead." Bode interjected and then shook his head and rolled his eyes.

"Watch your words Bode," Mr. King stated sternly and gave Bode a look that made it clear he was serious. He waited until Bode nodded before continuing. "It's just that we end up living two lives, one while we are here and a whole different one when we leave the plantation for supplies. Sometimes keeping the two straight can be challenging, in fact deadly if we are not careful," Mr. King ended.

"I'm sorry; I didn't know that." James answered Mr. King.

"I know, young James, which is what makes you so special to my son and why your family is so special to my family. We are treated no differently than anyone else is treated." James just nodded at Mr. King's kind words, though he did not understand the deeper meaning behind it all.

"It's also why the hired workers work so hard for the success of the plantation here. Because they know this place is special and they, like your father and mother, don't ever want it to change for them."

They sat quietly on the porch in deep thought watching the sunset and the darkness slowly creep in around them before James broke the silence.

"I don't want to ever be like that boy and his father Mr. King. I hope I never become like that as I grow older." James seemed hurt by the thoughts and Mr. King put his arm around James.

"I hope you never become that boy either James. I also hope your father stays safe, for I do not know what we would do without him." Mr. King said.

Even though he knew his father was a soldier in the army and that it was a dangerous profession, the thought of his father being killed had never really crossed his mind before. The reality of the thought suddenly scared him. He knew that Mr. King had run the plantation while he was away before, and that they would be able to make things work if needed again, but he didn't know what he would do without his father.

James learned later that his father was contemplating that very same thought following the recent altercation and was writing his unique ideas down on paper and preparing to put a plan in motion, a plan that would not only changed the operations and workings of the plantation, but the very destiny of both boys.

Chapter 2

The following week, after twenty-six years of service to the crown, James' father announced that he would be retiring at the end of the year from the British Army. The British officers and officials above him were very disappointed and even angry at the decision and tried very hard to dissuade him. The only way they would accept his resignation was if he accepted the position of British Regional Protector of North Carolina. This would put him in charge of the surrounding militia, should there be a need to defend the territory, and it would keep him active in the British army and still partially under their direction and control. Feeling he had no other option, and knowing the negative influence the British officials could inflict on the operations of the plantation should he decline, he eventually agreed to accept the position. He viewed it as a stepping-stone to his and his family's freedom.

The new assignment sounded very important to James, but his father had laughed at the title. He said that it simply meant that he was to direct and lead former officers and soldiers that were now living in the area who were either too old or too fat to fight. The men of the local militia would meet twice a year, his father said, "to determine who was fit enough to lead should a war break out" and they would sit around guessing what their troop strength might be should a "call to arms" be sounded for all able-bodied fighting men. His father knew that such a force would be untrained and ineffective in battle.

During his father's last years of service he had become very disenchanted with the British Army and with his experiences with those officials in charge during his career. He often had shared in detail with James and Bode the ineptness and arrogant thinking of many of the officers with whom he had served. He even took the time to explain the exact situations or decisions that they had made that cost good soldiers' lives, inflicted damage on the colonists, and the waste in time and money such arrogant thinking costs. His father also shared with them stories about great officers whom he had encountered, but those stories seemed to be far fewer in number.

On several occasions James had even overheard his father speaking with his mother about the challenges and abuses the British were inflicting on the colonies and Indian tribes. Although he rarely discussed it with the family, his father seemed to grow more and more frustrated and angry with the British as the years passed. He would never speak about those feelings in public, nor join in on any discussions with local leaders who were feeling more and more frustrated with the taxation and control that the British were extracting from the colonists. The decisions that were made by the English crown were made without ever consulting those that it was being required.

The "plan" for the plantation that his father had written down and discussed with his mother and Mr. King, was actually very simple and was put in motion on his 13th birthday in 1764. On that day, his father had returned from his regular trip to town to sell goods and barter for supplies. On this occasion, one of the wagons carried a large crate, several small wooden barrels and several small boxes that needed unloading. James noticed that the crate required several workers to move it into the house, and the smaller boxes were very heavy for their size. The two barrels did not appear to be heavy, but they stored them in a nearby locked shed instead of in the house.

James watched as his father spent the next week building a wide and tall cabinet just inside the main room of the house. He kept the crate on the floor next to it. As James watched and fetched wood as needed for his father to cut and sand, despite his best efforts, his father would not answer questions about the cabinet or the crate. As James started to see it come together, he eventually figured out what it was that he was building. As his father was sanding a final corner of the cabinet, James walked in with his father's musket that was usually stored in his parent's bedroom, positioned it in one of the ten slots within the cabinet, and then stepped back to look. His father stopped sanding and looked at the musket sitting on the shelf, perfectly fitting the slot it sat in.

"It's going to look pretty nice, father," James said and backed a little further away from it to get a better look.

His father looked up at the musket and then back at James; then he stepped away from his sanding efforts and stood next to his son and they both admired the cabinet.

"I guess it will. It looks rather lonely though wouldn't you say?" His father said and James nodded.

"Is that what's in the crate over there?" he asked his father, who looked over at the crate and then back to his son.

"Yep." Then there was a long silence before James spoke again.

"Does mom know?" He asked in an almost whisper.

"Yep," he replied.

"Is she happy about it?"

"Nope," he replied, and they both took a deep breath.

"That's a lot of muskets." James said with a smile.

"Yes it is," his father replied.

James leaned over and whispered to his father, "Can I have one?" There was a long silence before the answer.

"We'll see… we'll see."

The next day his father opened the crate and one by one removed the Kentucky Long Rifle muskets and set them in their slots in the cabinet. James and Bode thought they were the most beautiful muskets they had ever seen. His father told them that they were long rifles and that they were very accurate and could fire a bullet a greater distance than his shorter-barreled musket provided to him by the British army.

"Why do you have so many?" Bode asked James' father.

"That will be made known in due time Bode."

James had overheard his mother and father speaking the following evening from his room. She was very concerned about the money he had spent on the muskets. He already had several Army-issue muskets and pistols, why the need for so many? But his father mumbled something in reply that he was unable to hear. The next day he saw Mr. King and his father in the main room looking at the muskets and drinking tea. Mr. King kept nodding and then shaking his head at his father's words as James quietly moved closer to the door.

"I hear what you are saying, William, but I'm not sure it's a good idea. I think it might cause more harm than good. The slave owners are not going to like it when they hear about it," he said, as he took another sip of tea.

"I know, but I don't think we have much choice. With the war with the French escalating, I fear I may be called away and the plantation left unprotected." After a long silence, Mr. King stood up from his chair and set down his cup of tea.

"I'll speak with our best thirty men based on your request and we'll see how they respond." James' father stood and patted Mr. King on the shoulder.

"Don't worry, Elijah, there is a soldier hidden inside all of us just waiting to get out." Mr. King raised an eyebrow.

"William, that is what worries me the most. They love this place and respect your family; I just hope they can keep things in perspective."

The following weekend Mr. King and James' father had assembled about thirty of the men from the workforce in their front yard. Most were young men, but there were a few older men from among the more junior workers. Bode and James sat on the steps and listened as his father began to speak to the men gathered before him.

"Gentlemen, it has come to my attention that I may be called away for duty in the near future. The defense of the plantation in my absence is of great concern." The men looked back and forth at each other as his father continued. "You need to understand that an enemy of the plantation is not always a foreign power bent on conquest. Indeed it has been my job to keep such powers at bay, but more often than not the enemy is a group of bandits preying on the innocent, or a roving band of Indians seeking revenge, or even a disgruntled neighbor who does not agree with how we do things here." He let the last words sink in a moment as he looked out over the planted fields, barns, and houses of the plantation and then turned back to the men.

"With everyone's hard work, we have built one of the most successful plantations in North Carolina, and as you know, our laborers are treated very differently from those of any other plantation. This difference creates a discomfort among the common folk of the nearby towns and plantations. I'm sure they would like to see things here changed and returned to what they feel is normal, but I refuse to let that happen and I ask you to stand with me, to defend what we have built." The workers mumbled in agreement and nodded their heads as his father reached down and grabbed a handful of soil and let it crumble out of his hands.

"This is not who we are, but it is where we chose to live. Those who desire to either harm us or change this way of life and what we believe should know that we will not surrender our land or beliefs without a fight, nor will we fear them or embrace their beliefs." He could see the men fidgeting more and more as his father spoke to them. "So why have Mr. King and I asked you here today?"

He walked over, picked up a wooden club and a sharpened pole, and turned back to the men. "I know you are all brave men and you know how to use a club or a stick to defend yourself and your family should the need arise, but these weapons are no match for a musket, pistol or bayonet." Mr. King handed James' father a musket. He turned, aimed and fired at a large melon that was sitting on a post fifty yards away. As the gun roared and the smoke escaped the barrel and flash pan, the melon exploded. His father continued speaking to the men while reloading the musket. "As you can see, the musket enables a man to remain protected at a distance while engaging an enemy. You can fire from a window, a doorway, from behind a tree, rooftop, wall…" He primed the flash pan, added the powder, shot and wadding and drove them down with the ramrod. "As you can see, with the proper training, a man with a musket can become a deadly opponent." He slid the ramrod out of the barrel and placed it back into the storage cylinder. He then turned, raised the musket and fired again at a melon sitting on a post next to the former one with the same results. He turned and handed the musket to Mr. King.

"Men, you just saw two shots in less than a minute. That means two very surprised enemies will not have an opportunity to harm you, your family or anyone else on this plantation." He walked back to where they sat and stood almost within their group.

"My desire and hope is to take those of you who are willing and train you how not only to use a musket, but to understand how to work together as a fighting force to defend this plantation in a time of need." He let the idea sink in as he stepped back to where he was before and turned to face them. A voice coming from the back of the group of men was the first to speak.

"Folks are not going to like this Mr. Thornton," a voice replied and his father looked through the crowd until he recognized who had spoken.

"I know Jeremiah, that's why we are going to keep it a secret for as long as possible," he replied. Then another voice spoke up.

"How long does it take to learn to shoot a musket Mr. Thornton?" one of the younger men asked with a smile which James' father returned.

"It depends on how well you listen, follow orders and how much you are willing to practice, Samuel. I know you are a good worker, so I would expect you to be able to load and fire a weapon somewhat accurately at close targets in less than a month."

"I'll shoot and practice as much as you'll let me." He laughed and the some of the other men laughed and agreed as they patted him on the back. One of the older men, who was the plantation veterinarian stepped forward holding his hat.

"How many are you looking to train Mr. Thornton, because I want to be one of them?" He said with all sincerity and all the other men spoke up wanting to be included as well. His father reached over, patted the man on the upper arm, and smiled. "I appreciate that Doc." He then turned to the group of men and raised his hands to calm them down so that he could speak. "My desire," then looking at Mr. King he corrected himself, "Our desire is to train all of you. Our challenge is that we have only 10 muskets to work with, so we will need to train in shifts of ten men. While 10 are shooting, the other twenty will be working the fields as usual. Once a week we will train as an entire unit in marching, maneuvers and defensive positions and formations." There was much excitement and bravado from the men that had gathered and the energy kept climbing. His father sensed the moment and then nodded to Mr. King.

"Listen!" Mr. King raised his hand to quiet the group. Once they calmed down, he continued. "You need to understand several very important challenges that go with this opportunity. You must keep it secret for as long as possible. A Negro man or worker trained to shoot a musket is not a thing to brag about. Even once you are trained, you should not speak about it or profess your ability to anyone outside the plantation, or you may create a great deal of trouble for yourself and your family. You need to understand that this is both a blessing and a curse, so accept the offer only after you've put a great deal of thought and prayer into it." James' father stepped forward and added to Mr. King's words.

"Should you decide not to participate, please know that Mr. King and I will not look with disfavor on you or your decision." At these words, there was seemed to be some quiet discussion among the men.

"For those that choose to be trained, I expect the same attitude from you toward anyone here who chooses not to train or you will be asked to leave the training," Mr. King explained and heads nodded. There were mumbled agreements throughout the group. As silence fell over the group, Mr. King stepped forward.

"I would like to know by the end of the day tomorrow of your decision. Simply come by my house and let me know. If you have questions or concerns, we can discuss them. Thank you for coming."

The men dispersed with some of the younger men asking the older men what they were going to do, or what they should do. Several groups of younger men were already practicing their imaginary shooting technique as they walked away. Mr. King turned to Mr. Thornton.

"Well, it looks like you might have your plantation militia. God help us." He smiled at his friend.

"God already has Elijah. I just hope this is what He wants for us as well." Mr. Thornton answered.

The following evening, the news came in that of the thirty men invited, twenty-six had chosen to be trained. The four who declined had expressed deep concern for their families and any retribution that might come from such training. On the third day, his father took the men into the house and showed them the muskets. He told them that the first and most important step in learning to be a soldier was to understand discipline and teamwork. Each man was given a long hickory stick the length of a musket. James remembered Mr. King joking that he wished that more of them had chosen not to be trained so he would not have had to cut down and carve so many sticks.

For the next four weeks all the men did was march in formation and practice defensive battle positions with their hickory muskets. At the end of the four weeks, they were broken into two groups of thirteen. His father had purchased three more muskets for the training. Over the next three months, his father and Mr. King trained the twenty-six men to load and shoot the muskets, while they continued to work on their battle formations and defensive positions. Mr. Thornton had often commented to James that many of them were excellent marksman, but now he was surprised at how quickly the men had learned formations and defensive positions as well. It seemed the camaraderie of working together in the fields and the special honor of such unprecedented training helped to bond them in spirit and purpose.

The plantation militia continued to work and train together all that year and their confidence and pride grew with every month. James and Bode would train with them on every occasion, marching drills, assuming defensive positions, and mock loading and firing of their own hand-carved muskets.

The following year his father acquired an additional fifteen muskets, so that each member of the plantation militia now had his own musket. His mother and Mrs. King were also busy with some of the wives of the workers during the year, for they had secretly been sewing together unique and handsome uniforms for the twenty-six men. The jackets were made of thick double-stitched charcoal gray cotton with reinforced shoulder pads for the rifles to rest against while standing or marching. The pants were black cotton with a gray stripe running down each side. Each uniform had a black leather belt with smaller leather pouches attached to the front and larger leather containers on the back. The front pouch held a powder flask, shot bag and wadding and the back pouch held a musket ball worm, extra flints and a cleaning barrel snake.

At the end of the year, they threw a grand graduation party for the twenty-six men. His father and Mr. King gave each one of the men his own musket to keep at his home so that they could be ready at a moment's notice to defend the plantation. The second gift to the men was from his mother, Mrs. King and the other women who had made the uniforms and belt kits, designed and sized specifically for each man. Jokes were made that some of the uniforms had to be redesigned many times to keep up with the well-fed men. There was much laughter and singing and storytelling of the past year of training. James would never forget their shock and gratitude when they were given the muskets and the uniforms as their graduation gifts. The uniforms and gear were worn with pride during training sessions. Every young boy aspired to be a "militia man."

James remembered that the next year rarely saw his father at home, for his military duties required his presence in the north, consulting on securing and fortifying the northern colonies and the new French territories acquired during the past seven years of war. Before he left, he instructed Mr. King to continue to train a new group of militia each year. The previously trained militia, with Mr. King's guidance, would train the new militia. During the brief time his father did come home that year, he spent a great deal of his limited time with the militia, sharing with them his experience on the field of battle.

With the plantation's success, the need to hire additional workers also allowed more and more potential militia to be trained. Pride of being part of the militia had overshadowed the fear of such training. The following year, when James and Bode were fifteen, they were deemed old enough to train with the next group of militia. There were now over fifty, trained militia at the plantation. James and Bode would be part of the 3rd group of twenty-five men, raising the plantation number of men at arms to seventy-five. The boys had both trained and practiced with the initial two groups as youngsters, and both had been taught how to load and fire a musket, but they had never officially been trained due to their age. They both excelled in the training and they quickly became the key leaders of their group. At the end of the training, they were given their own muskets and uniforms and at 16, they were both asked to train the next group of twenty-five men to join the militia. Looking back, James could see that his father had purposely positioned him and Bode to be perceived as leaders by the men in these two militia groups. As they came to be treated as leaders by others, they trained and taught their two groups with an even greater fervor and pride. To give the trainees more experience, Bode and James would pit the two groups, the 3rd and 4th groups as they were called, against each other in movements and formations. They would confiscate all the ammunition (just the lead balls) and use only powder and wadding to emphasize the reality of fire and the importance of speed in reloading. Although a few of the men resented the intense training, most of the men were young and unmarried like Bode and James and they enjoyed the idea of being viewed and trained to be the best two groups in the militia. Seeing the results of their dedication, his father began transferring men from the 1st and 2nd groups into the 3rd and 4th so that the entire militia could be completely unified and further refine their skills.

By the end of the fourth year, there were 100 trained militiamen and each one had been given a uniform and musket as a gift of honor. Although there were more men on the plantation who wished to be trained, they were informed that all further groups would not be provided with muskets and uniforms.

Because of the purchase of so many muskets by his father, the local British authorities became suspicious and summoned James' father to an inquiry. He carefully explained his reasons and, for the time being, they withdrew their objections but stipulated that he was not to purchase additional muskets. James' father learned later that most of the suspicion and pressure on the British authorities was being generated from the surrounding plantation owners who used slaves. They feared the idea of training and arming former Negro slaves and workers, and they worked hard at every opportunity to discredit and undermine the development of the plantation militia.

It was decided that the militia would continue training and any new men would be added as a reserve squad. Although the other plantation owners and citizens were aware of the 100 muskets that were now residing at the plantation, the actual number of trained militia was to remain a well-guarded secret. Mr. King had stated many times that if it had not been for Colonel Thornton's incredible reputation as a fair man and loyal and decorated soldier, the disgruntled citizens would have used force to remove the muskets. His father felt that the 100 muskets in the hands of trained men was the real reason that gave them pause to such an action.

In that fourth year his father spent a great deal of time talking with and teaching his son and Bode all he knew about the army, about defensive and offensive tactics, and about fortifications (defending and attacking), about troop morale and training, and in addition about the use of cannon and how to defend against them in battle.

Every night James would sit by the fire and listen to his father telling stories about past battles, wars, leadership and understanding the characters of men. James would share the stories with Bode the next time they saw each other. His father was very perceptive and patient with his son; he always seemed to know just how far to go before James was not following what he was saying, periodically doubling back to make it a little simpler for him. Later, he would tell a related story to help James to think critically and increase his understanding. James realized later that his father was trying to share with his son and Bode everything that he knew on the subject, in the event something were to happen to him.

The plantation continued to thrive and grow, experiencing only one bad crop year because of a hurricane that had swept through the area. Although the storm took its toll on the plantation's buildings and crops, because their plantation was located further inland, it actually fared better and sustained less damage than the coastal plantations.

In 1768, the members of the plantation militia were each given a pair of fitted black boots and a black side fold hat to add to their uniforms. Like the uniforms themselves, these were only worn during training exercises, and never worn as standard clothing around the plantation. The men looked very impressive in their uniforms and you could see and feel the confidence and pride of each man as he stepped out to take formation each week.

Chapter 3

James was told he was somewhat handsome and pleasant at eighteen years of age, however, when it came to courting the young women of the area, James found himself rejected and perhaps even despised because of his family's position against slavery. Although he tried to court many of the young women in the area, he rarely got beyond an introduction once the young woman's parents were notified of his interest in their daughter. Through the pain of rejection and judgment, James understood to a small degree what Bode, his family, and the other Negro workers had experienced most of their lives. In a way, he was grateful to at least understand and relate to the emotions that were common to them. Bode would simply laugh when James would tell him how things went on his date or attempted date, and he would remind James that he brought this on himself. Bode on the other hand seemed to have his pick of the young women at the plantation, and it seemed as if all of them liked him. Bode, only seemed to like the ones that didn't like him, or that played as if they didn't like him. James never could quite understand Bode's reasoning, but it made it so they had a lot less time to spend together working or training with Bode chasing after the other young women.

James' two sisters were growing up fast and both were beautiful. He knew that potential suitors would be calling on them in a few years. He hoped they would not be hindered in finding a great husband as a result of their choices as a family. His brother Andrew, the youngest of the family, was nine years old and seemed to need his big brother to play with all the time, as he had not yet found a friend at the plantation like the friendship that Bode and he had forged. James would always try to encourage him to play with other children his age, but although Andrew would play with the other children, he really only wanted to spend time with his big brother.

At eighteen, James was assigned to lead the team of wagons into town to make the sale and transactions for the plantation. After many years of accompanying his father, James felt proud to be trusted to conduct the trades and purchases for the plantation. Mr. King would always travel with him, but James always had to conduct the transactions for the majority of the merchants would not deal directly with Mr. King. Mr. King would prepare James before each transaction. He would tell him exactly what and how the particular buyer or seller would try to work a deal, what to watch out for, and how to walk away from a bad one. At first he felt as if he was making a lot of mistakes that were costing the plantation revenue, but it was only on the smaller item purchases or sale, for the bigger item prices like cotton and tobacco were generally pretty much fixed. The key was to get your cotton to the markets early for the best pricing and their plantation was always one of the most efficient. Tobacco on the other hand required a great deal more care and timing with regards to harvesting and curing it for maximum flavor and value. Both the cotton and the tobacco harvesting and curing was something that Mr. King and the workers were very good at, and the quality of the Thornton Plantation's crops generally resulted in strong revenue each year.

James would always stop and talk with the daughters of the shopkeepers and vendors, who were close to his age, making an effort to speak to the fathers as well. He felt his chances might be better with one of the city families than with one of the other plantation owners since they did not employee the large number of slaves that the plantations did. He came to realize that he was not sure if he would even want to marry a daughter of one of the plantation owners, for he suspected that the two very different philosophies would be a source of constant frustration and tension in the marriage. With every visit to town, James could feel the growing resentment towards his family and the militia. Like yeast working its way through the dough, he could feel the hatred working its way through the people.

Toward the beginning of 1770, James' nineteenth year, two men came to visit Colonel Thornton and his father asked James to join them in the discussion. His father introduced them as Mr. Ronald Paxton and his plantation advisor, John Baker. Mr. Paxton had fought under the leadership of his father during the French and Indian wars and he was there now asking for assistance. He and his family had built a plantation thirty miles to the west of the Thornton Plantation and it had grown into a profitable business. During the last two years, the plantation had been raided at harvest time. The masked bandits attacked at night with an overwhelming force of between thirty and fifty armed men, stealing and pillaging. Each season, a large percentage of their cotton crops were stolen, hauled off in wagons while the family was held at gunpoint.

The day following the raids, Mr. Paxton had ridden to the nearest town and requested assistance from the local authorities, but the authorities were never able to find who was behind the raids, and if they did know the ringleaders, they were unwilling to divulge or act on the information. Mr. Paxton suspected that they must know the party behind the raids as it seemed that the bandits knew just when to raid the plantation, for each time they waited until the very day after cotton was bailed to attack.

James' father questioned the man, and based on his answers it became evident that he and his family were not popular with the locals. They came from a well-to-do family and the Paxton's had purchased some of the best ground in the area, and had hired some of the best workers in the area. Some had come away from the other plantations. But they also, like the Thornton's, abhorred slavery. This seemed to agitate the local populace greatly.

He explained that each year the number of bandits attacking had increased and so too had their cruelty. During the first year's raid they only pillaged their crops and threatened him and his family. This last year; however, they had murdered three unarmed Negro workers as examples, and threatened the remaining workers and their families with a similar fate if they did not leave. Many of Mr. Paxton's Negro workers took the threat very serious and immediately left the plantation. Others waited until the majority of this year's cotton harvest was complete, and then left. What was more concerning to Mr. Paxton was that he had heard from those in the area who were friends to his family, that there was a rumor that this year's raiding party was bent on totally destroying the Paxton plantation and running off all the workers and even killing the Paxton's themselves if they resisted. The man was obviously very concerned for his family and for those that have remained loyal to them, so he was here making a desperate plea for help.

Mr. Paxton told his father that he had heard about his militia and was hoping he might be able to assist him, further, that he was willing to pay to cover any costs or labor challenges that might be incurred. His urgency was great for the harvest time was nearly completed and they would be bailing the cotton this week.

His father invited the men to stay the night and rest their horses. He wanted to use the opportunity to talk it over amongst them. He gathered Mr. King, Bode and James together to discuss the situation in greater detail.

"Do you think this might be a ploy to pull men from our plantation?" Mr. King asked.

"Anything is possible, but I've known this man for many years, he would not be one to betray a friend. I had also heard about his losses from prior years, so I know his story to be true." He responded.

"This could cause quite a ruckus out there, seeing armed Negro soldiers and all in uniform?" Mr. King interjected.

"Yes it could." His father replied. James looked over at Bode who seemed in deep thought as well and then leaned forward in his chair.

"Correct me if I am wrong, but the feeling that I think we're all getting is that the thieves are local citizens. How far are we willing to go to prove that point?" James said to his father. His father nodded and looked back at his son.

"You mean how many men are we willing to put at risk? Well I've learned never to send a smaller force where a larger force was needed to succeed. You either commit yourself fully to the victory James, or you withdraw." His father answered and then seemed to think some more in silence. Then he stood up, walked to the window, and looked out.

"Mr. King, I would like to commit the 3rd and 4th groups to assist Mr. Paxton in the defense of his plantation and to ensure that his crops are delivered safely to the market for sale. I will need James and Bode to each lead the 3rd and 4th groups respectively, and I will personally oversee both groups. We will be short handed here on the plantation, so I will need you to stay and keep things running smoothly during our absence." James listened and watched his father transform from a plantation owner into the Colonel role with confidence and ease. Mr. King glanced at his son and James who each smiled, and then stood up to face James' father.

"How soon would you like to have them ready Mr. Thornton?" Mr. King replied.

"I would like the men to be ready to march at the earliest opportunity if possible Mr. King."

"I will notify them this evening and have them ready to march first thing in the morning. I anticipate a 3-day march to the plantation. Mr. King, would you ensure that each man is carrying enough food and water for 5 days and enough powder and bullets for fifty shot. That should be more than sufficient for what we are hoping to accomplish." His father said and then turned to the two boys. "I'm selecting your units because they are the best trained in the militia, something I know that you are both proud of. They have been trained to follow your commands, so you will need to be strong, courageous and confident as you lead them."

"Yes sir." They both stood and replied together. His father walked over to the almost empty gun rack and opened a drawer. He reached in, pulled out two pistols, and handed one to each boy.

"This will be the only thing that separates your identity as leaders from the other men, so wear them proudly." His father said and both Bode and James were stunned by the gift as they held them in their hands.

"Thank you father." James said proudly.

"Thank you Mr. Thornton" Bode replied as well, but Mr. King started laughing in the background.

"What is it Mr. King." His father seemed perplexed.

"The only thing?" He exclaimed. "That might be the case for Bode, but I'm guessing the blond hair, fair skin and blue eyes on James might be another potential difference." He laughed again, as did Bode and James.

"Well put Mr. King." His father smirked. "Any other tidbits of deep knowledge you would like to share before you head out to prepare the men?" He raised an eyebrow and smiled.

"No sir." Mr. King replied and then tried to hold the smile in, but couldn't and started to laugh again, which started the boys laughing and eventually his father joined in as well. In looking back on the moment, it was a testimony to his father and the mindset he had toward men and soldiers. He did not see color, but instead he saw only the character or the rank of the man.

Later that evening, both Bode and James traveled through the workers area to meet with and encourage the men as they prepared for the journey. For the most part, they seemed very excited. Each of them was busy laying out their uniforms, oiling their muskets and preparing their packs. Those not invited from the other groups seemed almost disappointed, or perhaps was it a guarded relief that was on their faces.

After they had finished visiting the men, Bode and James talked late into the evening as they discussed the men, the journey and prepared their own packs. They had both been trained with the pistol, but it seemed different now that it was their very own to keep. They tried to determine what was the best place and way to carry them, but eventually they just tucked them into their front belt and smiled.

"That pistol really makes you stand out from the rest of the men." Bode laughed as he finished the last of the sentence. James put his hat on.

"Yeah, but once I cover my blond hair, you won't be able to tell us apart." He seemed serious, but they both started laughing. Then Bode became serious for a moment.

"My guess is, the majority of the fire will be coming your way in anger at you for being white and leading Negroes, so try to keep your blond head and blue eyes out of their sights." Bode said and then there was silence as they continued packing. "I mean I don't really care if they shoot you, it's just that I've invested a lot of time into training you and would hate to have to start all over again with some other 'slow to learn' person." Bode said without a smile.

"Yeah. I know what you mean." James replied in the same serious tone. Then they both smiled as they finished up. Bode stood up and stretched.

"I'll see you in the morning." Bode said as he headed for the door and James nodded in return.

"Hey!" James called out to Bode, who turned and came back into the room and looked toward James. "Are you nervous or excited?" James asked and Bode seemed to think about it a moment, then shook his head.

"Just scared." He said and then smiled as he left. James thought a minute and then realized that the strange feeling in his stomach might just be fear. He headed downstairs and saw his father, Mr. Paxton and his assistant standing near the hearth. The four of them spoke late into the evening discussing the plan and their commitment to assist them with the defense of their plantation and crops. They guessed that the timing of the attacks corresponded with Mr. Paxton's request to hire the wagons from the nearby city to transport his harvest to the city for sale. The thieves would steal the rented wagons from the farm, use them to transport the stolen crops to their destination, and then leave them scattered by the roadside in different locations around the county over the days following the theft. It seemed suspect that all of the wagons were returned following the raids.

Part of their plan was to march the majority of the militia, forty men, off the main road to the outskirts of the plantation with the guidance of Mr. Baker, with the remaining ten men of the militia marching with his father and Mr. Paxton. They wanted to march the smaller group of ten militia past the city to let anyone that may be watching know that there would be a defensive force in place to protect the plantation and hopefully dissuade the guilty parties from repeating the offense again this year.

James hardly slept at all that night and woke early to find his father already awake as well. After eating breakfast, they formed up as two groups in the courtyard. They watched as ten men of the militia, along with his father and Mr. Paxton began their march toward his plantation. The men looked admirable in their uniforms with their muskets over their shoulders as they headed down the road following the two men on horse. Since his father was the regional commander of the British militia in North Carolina, James' father had given him specific orders to carry with him should he be stopped by any regional leaders. The orders simply stated that James, Bode King and their force of forty men were ordered to meet at Mr. Paxton's plantation to assist and repel with all available force, any and all bandit raids upon his property. He was to await Commander Thornton's arrival with his ten men. It was dated for that day and signed by his father and the seal of the royal army was pressed into a circle of wax on the inside of the orders. His father told James to share the "orders" only in the event that a British officer stopped him or should a larger or apparently hostile force set against them out of fear or concern generated by their force passing through their area.

As they prepared to march out, his mother slipped something extra inside his pack and gave him a kiss on the cheek.

"Be careful and take care of your father." was all that she said. His sisters and little brother stood on the porch and waved and yelled 'goodbye" as they marched out of site. The second group took a road to the west that Mr. Baker, Mr. Paxton's assistant, was familiar with. That road met up with a back road that ran beside a river that led to the Paxton plantation.

The first evening, the men were definitely tired and most had blisters on their feet from wearing the militia issued boots. Some of the older men who knew how to cook heated water in small pans and then mixed various ingredients that they had brought with them into it, making a delicious smelling stew or soup to the envy of the rest of the men. Others simply broke off some bread and cheese and washed it down with water. The men laughed and sang as they cooked or rested and after a short meal they set out their bedrolls and lay down to sleep. Guards were posted on 3-hour shifts in case there was any trouble that wandered into camp.

Morning came too soon and the men slowly slid their boots back over their blistered feet, gathered up their equipment and formed back up for the second day's march. The older men showed the younger men a few tricks they had learned about packing and carry items so that their hands were always free and the load was evenly distributed on their backs. Some of the boys had the "know it all" mindset at first, but after watching others apply the lesson, it was not long before they were leaving their pride behind and taking the strain off of their backs.

The second and third day's march went very slowly once the group left the road and began traveling along the back trails in order to avoid being seen by any locals on their approach to the Paxton plantation. Several times dogs could be heard barking, but neither the dogs nor their masters came out to see what was garnering their attention. It was evening when they eventually arrived at the plantation. The men were housed out of sight beyond the main barn in a tobacco-curing shed. The Paxton's had sent down drinks and food for them and they learned that James' father and the other ten members of the militia had arrived earlier in the day. Early the next morning, James, Bode and James' father were escorted around the plantation to survey the land to scout for the best defensive positions. That afternoon, while the three of them discussed defensive strategies, the workers began baling the last of the cotton and Mr. Paxton rode into town to schedule the rental of additional wagons to transport the cotton. Although it was business as usual, it was assumed by James' father and Mr. Paxton that the ten uniformed members of the militia were seen marching on the road toward the Paxton plantation, and hoped that that alone would be enough to dissuade the bandits from raiding the plantation this year. If not, then the other forty-armed men would hopefully put a stop to the raiding and those behind it once and for all.

James' father oversaw a group of men who constructed a defensive barricade made of the very same chest high cotton bales they had committed to protect. They stacked two bales in front to act as the main wall, and a single bale behind the front two so that the men could stand on it in order to gain additional elevation over someone coming at them. It was laid out in such a way to keep any attackers from either running through the barrier, or attempt to flank them, without first stopping to take down the heavy bales or climb over them. As far as defensive material, he knew the cotton bales would offer some concealment for his men and stop any musket balls from passing through and striking a man, but it could make for an awkward platform to stand on should a confrontation ensue. They boarded up the back doorway into the barn where the cotton bales were stored and formed the main defensive wall across the front entrance of the barn. A group of eighteen men would serve as the visible central defense of the plantation. It was composed of James' father, Mr. Paxton, his sons and son in laws, and ten members of the militia that had traveled with James' father. The group, by itself would pose serious obstacle should the bandits attempt a direct attack on the barn. The remaining force of forty men was positioned outside the plantation. The plan was to surround, surprise and engage the attackers should they once again raid the plantation. The men had agreed that should the show of force fail to prevent hostilities, running off the raiders was not enough. The bandits would regroup and come back once they learned the militia was gone, or attack the wagons along the way where mounting a defense would be much more difficult.

The plan was to have James' father's group engage the bandits and hold the attention of any attackers converging on the barn's defenses. Bode and James would each lead a group of twenty men around the right and left flanks of the attackers in an attempt to encircle them and force them to surrender. Should they choose not to surrender, then the three pronged attacked would enable them to bring deadly fire upon them from three sides. The effect of the attackers being caught in such a cross fire would be far more devastating than just the single line of fire from the makeshift barn defenses. The high fences and smaller stone buildings of the plantation created a funneling effect so that there was really only one way for the attackers to approach the barn in force without crossing very difficult terrain and James' father had designed the defenses accordingly. The flaw of the defensive plan was the danger of either of the smaller groups being engaged separately by the whole bandit group, the smaller group would be out numbered. James' father did not feel the bandits were that well trained or organized enough to perform such a coordinated maneuver and that the element of surprise would work in their defending force's favor.

It was not until the fourth night that the attack came. The rented wagons were to arrive the following day to pick up the baled cotton harvest. As they guessed, the bandits were also aware of that fact and came that night. It was almost midnight when James heard the first musket shot come from the main barn. The men were ready and quickly got to their feet and primed the charging pans on their muskets with fresh powder. Knowing speed was essential; the men left their packs and bedrolls and wore only their uniforms and ammunition belts. James nervously smiled at Bode in the darkness and then at the other forty men as they prepared to split up into two groups.

"Be careful and make us all proud. Stand your ground and protect the man to your right and left. If we do just that, we will be victorious." He then quickly shook Bode's hand and he and his twenty men ran to take up their position on the right flank.

His father's goal was to try to fire a warning shot, then attempt to stall the attackers for as long as possible by offering to negotiate; allowing Bode and James the time they needed to move their men into their flanking positions. If that failed, it meant the attackers would fire the next volley of shots and James and Bode and their men would need to move even faster to get into position. Negotiations must have occurred, for it was several more minutes before another musket shot was fired, then another. Within minutes there was a continual stream of shots being fired. The sheer number of shots being fired made for bad news as it sounded like there were a whole lot more men firing, which meant that the size of the raider force was larger than they expected. This was a worst-case scenario. The thought only made James worry for his father's safety and run even faster down the trail that would lead them to where they needed to go to reach the position to begin the flanking attack.

The sound of musket shots had a steady and unrelenting rhythm by the time James and his men reached the flanking position. In the darkness, they quickly formed up into a line that allowed for five feet of space between each man. The goal was to not bunch up, but not get too far away from each other should the fighting get close. James also wanted to be able to yell orders to his men from the middle. As they began moving forward, the sounds of the firing muskets gradually grew louder and the flash of light could be seen with each burst of shot fired in the darkness. As his men came across the first open area, they ran into a group of five wagons with slaves, young boys, and even some women sitting on buckboards as if watching a show. At the sight of the militia moving upon them, they screamed in terror and jumped off the wagons and ran downhill away from the battle and the sounds of the muskets. From what James could see, none of them were armed, or at least none of them stopped to fire a shot at them as they fled dropping whatever they had been carrying to speed their exit.

James and his men kept moving forward in unison toward the sound of the battle. James halted his men at the first sight of the enemy, whose silhouettes were outlined by the flash of their muskets and the dim light cast from the torches that they used to assist them in reloading their weapons. James formed a line with his men and then raised a war cry and his men quickly joined in. The sound of his twenty men was not deafening or horrifying by any means, but by the stunned looks on their opponent's faces, you would have thought the devil himself had appeared at their backs. They all stopped firing and turned to look at the armed men they now faced. James and his men were within seventy-five yards of them when they had halted and lined up and on his command they raised their muskets and aimed at their targets.

"Drop your weapons and surrender immediately!" He yelled and at first it appeared that the twenty plus men that he could see were going to do as he commanded. But then a fool from the right broke the strange silence and yelled, "Kill'em boys... They're just slaves!" and he raised his musket and fired at James. The sound of the ball whizzing past his right ear brought James back to the deadly reality of the moment. He could see the other bandit men now had a renewed sense of courage and were turning and preparing to direct their fire at James and his men. James then did what he felt was the only thing he could do. He raised his own musket and yelled "Fire!"

James briefly thought about aiming at a man whose musket was loaded, but for some reason he instead took aim at the man who had shot at him. The man had made the mistake of standing in front of a torch that the bandits had brought along to aid in their reloading, which made targeting him in the darkness much easier. He squeezed the trigger and the roar of the fire and smoke erupted from the barrel. The flash at first hid the result of the shot, but as his eyes adjusted again to the darkness, he could see the man stumbling backwards as if trying to catch his balance, then drop down onto one knee and slowly falling onto his side. The steady roar of the other twenty muskets to his right and left and the flash of light that each musket gave when fired revealed a scene framed in billowing smoke and death as he saw that several of their shots had found their targets. He and the militia quickly began reloading as they watched their opponents trying to recover from their barrage and determine what they should do next.

Another man, huge in size, came running down the hill toward them carrying a cutlass in one hand and a musket in the other screaming racial obscenities toward them. James focused on getting his musket reloaded in time, but the man was quickly closing the distance between them. He could see that other bandit men were once again starting to gather their courage to charge after the man as he ran toward James and the militia. He glanced over to see his men were also struggling to get their muskets reloaded in time, but what made the situation worse was that he could see that there was an ever growing fear in their eyes the closer the man got to them. He knew panic and flight were only a moment away and that he needed to act quickly. James finished loading his musket but knew that the man would be on them before he could prep and fire, so he stepped out into the charging man's path and drew his pistol and fired almost point blank at the man. The musket ball hit the man squarely in the chest and abruptly halted his forward movement and the hateful and obscene words as well. James then primed and raised his musket and shot the next closest man coming down the hill.

"Prepare to fire!" He yelled over his shoulder as he stepped back into line with his men. Those few who had finished reloading were raising their muskets to await his order. The majority of the men charging down the hill slowed considerably after witnessing the two men die in front of them. James' deadly order and the raised muskets were suddenly all that were needed to first halt and then reverse their wild charge. As more and more reloaded muskets were raised and aimed at them, they seemed to realize the danger of the situation. As they stood there trying to decide what to do, another battle cry and volley issued from across the field of battle. James knew that Bode and his men had engaged as well. James decided to take advantage of the moment.

"Drop your weapons and surrender, or you will be fired upon!" He cried. Within those last moments, the last of his men had completed reloading and now twenty muskets were aimed at the fifteen men before them. One by one, the men began dropping their weapons. Two in the very back of the group choose to run, but James did not give chase as they were heading toward Bode. For a moment James was unsure of what to do, as he had not thought about what to do in the event of taking prisoners. He realized he needed to get things quickly under control and his men back into the battle to help Bode.

"Sit down on the ground with your hands on your heads." He ordered. The group of raiders began to obey his words. "Group 1," James called, "gather the weapons and guard these men. Shoot anyone who tries to escape. Groups 2, 3 and 4, form a line and follow me."

James guessed from the sounds of men screaming and yelling that the bandits were in full retreat. The only avenue of escape left to them was a desperate run now down the middle of the three militia groups. He quickly ran his men to block that avenue of escape. There was sporadic musket fire, but the more common sound was his men yelling, "Surrender or we will fire!" as they ran into various bandits trying to escape the ever tightening noose of the trap. Within the next half an hour, they had rounded up over thirty prisoners.

Just before dawn, they divided the main groups into small patrols and searched by torchlight around the plantation looking for men in hiding, or wounded men that needed attention. The militia confiscated over fifty muskets and twelve wagons, including their teams of horses. The prisoners were gradually all moved to the barn to prevent escape and to make it easier to keep an eye on them. The wounded were brought to the Paxton's porch and were treated by Mr. Paxton's family and workers to the best of their abilities. The dead were gathered and brought to a second barn where they were covered with large canvas wagon tarps.

At first light, Mr. Paxton had his workers expanded the search to include not only the areas of battle, but the surrounding area in case someone had wandered off wounded and needed attention. All told, there were twelve dead and fourteen wounded bandits. The militia and Paxton plantation staff fared much better, with eight wounded, six of which were from the Thornton militia. Fortunately, none of the wounds were life threatening, but James remembered that his father instructed the men to reveal any wounds they had received for attention teaching him that even the smallest of wounds can turn deadly if not treated properly.

As the workers went out to search the area, the militia once again took up defensive positions around the plantation and with extra men positioned at the barn in case the remaining bandits or their families returned to start the fight again. Other guards were positioned to prevent the prisoners from escaping.

Later that morning, James' father and Mr. Paxton began to interrogate the prisoners, man by man. At first the prisoners responded arrogantly and refused to answers questions, but when they overheard James' father began discussing where to setup the firing squads to carry out the punishment for their crimes with the men, they were quick enough to betray the ring leaders behind not only this attack, but the prior attacks as well. Each man's confession and statement regarding their involvement and who else was involved were written down. James' father then required the men to sign the document. As the confessions unfolded, it became clear that there were many influential residents and leaders of the city and surrounding area that were involved, including the head of the local protection authority who had stated that no one who participated in the raid would be prosecuted. James was shocked at how cruel even common people could be and how willingly they would participate in such horrible activities when there were no consequences for such actions. They learned that the ring-leaders behind the raids were two brothers, Thomas and Sidney Corzine. Thomas owned a large plantation and Sidney was a wealthy merchant and the chief cotton buyer for the surrounding area. Although they both strongly opposed Mr. Paxton's stance on slavery, the truth of the matter was they wanted to acquire the Paxton's land. The brother's plan to acquire the plantation was simple and cruel; to use money and hatred to enlist the populace, and fear and economics to drive the Paxton's out. They would then come in and secure the plantation.

During the interrogation, they learned that over eighty men had participated in the previous night's attack, double the men involved in the prior year, and that they were all men from the surrounding area. Many were considered 'good people' by the Paxton's and James could see that they now felt deep shame and regret for their participation. Many could not explain their choice to participate, other than it had been the talk around the area and they had gotten swept up in the frenzy of the Corzine's rhetoric. Others, who had participated, had very clear reasons, as the Corzine's had fanned the flames of their hatred. James' father was surprised and saddened to learn that the Corzine's had used the militia as their ultimate rallying cry and justification for the attack on the plantation. They even offered a bonus to any participants who killed any Negro militia or free worker. Everyone they interviewed had known about the ten uniformed Negro militia members, but they had no idea of the other forty.

As expected, toward the afternoon, family members of the prisoners began to arrive looking to ascertain the fate of their boys and husbands who had not returned home. None were allowed in with a musket and each person was searched before being escorted onto the plantation. There were several occasions when the militia spotted people trying to sneak onto the plantation. However, they were driven off with verbal warnings, and several times muskets were fired above their heads to make the point, for James' father had made it clear that there had been enough bloodshed.

With careful questioning, Mr. Paxton was also able to determine who in the area was not involved in the plot. Once the innocent were established, he sent the bandits family members to contact those individuals that were not involved and to invite them to the plantation to assist in the matter. Although many came, James' father selected seven of the men not involved in the plot, who were prominent, well-respected citizens, to act as a confession board. Each prisoner was lead before the seven men and their confession was read out loud for them to hear and to confirm the accuracy of the confession. They were asked to swear an oath of peace to the Paxton family and they were also required to apologize to each family member. James' father made it clear to each of them that if they were ever involved with such crimes again, the militia would march back and imprison those involved and their lands would be confiscated.

The punishment for the surviving half of the Corzine brothers was more difficult to administer. Thomas Corzine had been killed in the skirmish and James learned later that he was the big man that he was forced to shoot in the initial confrontation. Although Sidney Corzine did not participate in the attack, he was the financial arm and driving force behind it. He and the local protection official were arrested and were to be put on trial. James' father made it clear to those families whose husbands and sons were now either dead or wounded, that Mr. Corzine and his illegal ambitions were to blame for their family's loss, not the Paxton's. James' father strongly recommended that Mr. Corzine compensate those families for their losses and also repay the Paxton's for their last two years of stolen crops. As immediate compensation to the Paxton's and in lieu of formal charges against those who participated in the attack, the weapons and ammunition confiscated from the prisoners were not returned, nor were the wagons and horse teams of those who brought them. Mr. Paxton did offer the option for the prisoners to repurchase their wagons and horses at the going rate, but held firm in his stance that their muskets were forfeit.

The families of those who had fallen in the battle were allowed to claim their dead and the bodies were removed from the plantation for burial. There was much crying and wailing at the deaths, and sadly, even threats of revenge directed toward the Paxton's, and James' father and the militia, as they left with their dead.

They stayed three more days until things had settled down enough for them to begin the return to their homes. The whole demeanor of the militia, including Bode and James had changed. The battle, with its fear and death, had hardened the men, yet it also instilled a sense of inner pride and confidence in them in what they had accomplished. There was a renewed sense of respect for each other and for the danger of battle. They had performed outstandingly in both Bode and James' eyes, and his father too, had raved about their performance. The three wounded men could not walk, so they were put into one of the captured wagons that Mr. Paxton had included as part of the payment for the militia's help. In spite of Mr. Paxton's insistence, James' father would not accept any money from Mr. Paxton, but after much discussion, his father did agree to accept forty of the fifty captured muskets and a wagon and team as payment. They both seemed happy with the final agreement.

Mr. Paxton and his family were very grateful for their assistance, gave them food, drink for their journey home, and sent them off as heroes. James and Bode could feel the pride in their men and even within themselves as they marched away from the plantation and down the road. In front were twenty men in formation with his father leading them on horse, followed by the wagon and then the remaining men following in perfect formation as a rear guard.

When they arrived home two days later, his mother and the families of the militia were there to greet them. The members of the militia that had remained to guard the plantation and the plantation's workers were there with warm embraces and cheers for the men. The whole plantation community gathered for a time of celebration replete with food and ale and the people laughed and talked late into the evening as stories of what had transpired. During the evening, his father and Eli came up to where James and Bode were standing as they watched their men interact with everyone. James could not put it into words at the time, but they were different than when they left.

"They left as farmers, but they returned as soldiers." His father said, summing up what James was trying to articulate, and James thought that was an accurate observation. "So have the two of you." James' father continued as he looked at Bode and James and patted them on their shoulders. James thought about how the militia, his friends, had stepped in harms way for a plantation family that had been persecuted for their beliefs, their workers, and the deaths that they had witnessed as a result of that intervention. He also thought about the attention they had now called to themselves. *What would be the result of this?* James wondered.

"Was it worth it father?" James asked and his father seemed to contemplate his answer.

"When it comes to friendships, it is always worth it. Sometimes we see the result of helping a friend immediately; sometimes it comes later in life when you are in need. But a friendship that is not worth protecting at your own personal risk is really not a friendship." His father replied.

"But the men of the militia were not friends with the Paxton's, is it right for us to place them in danger for our friends?" James asked and his father seemed to contemplate the question before answering.

"James, there are times when we chose to stand and fight for a friend, and there are times when we chose to stand and fight for a belief. It would be a sad day if a man refuses to take a stand when both are present." His father said and looked at James. "The Paxton's were our friends, but they also believe in what we are doing here as well. One or both were reason enough for all of us to offer our assistance." His father ended. James felt a new clarity as to why the militia was formed and what criteria they would apply to make decisions on its use.

The yeast of hatred toward the militia was quickly working its way through the population after assisting the Paxton's and James could tell that his father was very concerned. Within a few short weeks the truth of what took place at the Paxton plantation had turned into a cruel rumor of how the militia had supported an uprising of slaves. As a result of the rumor, plantation owners and local leaders began demanding that immediate action be taken to stop future atrocities from occurring again. It was not until the local British officials traveled to the Paxton plantation to determine the truth, and then to each concerned plantation owner that the danger of action abated. James' father and Mr. King wrestled with the perceived danger of the militia and initially felt there was little they could do to stop it, but then discussed at great length how to win the hearts of the concerned plantation owners that hated them without putting the lives of the militia and their plantation at risk.

Following the Paxton encounter, many requests were made of his father to utilize the militia for various purposes across the state, but his father accepted very few of them. Most of the requests were frivolous, self serving and petty in nature, others were clearly a political test of James' father, his allegiance to the Crown and the purpose of the militia; some requests were just, but far beyond the ability of the militia to succeed. In the winter of 1772, James' father accepted one request and called the militia to action. He felt it had a high potential for danger, but if handled carefully and wisely early, he felt the risk would far outweigh the danger and would keep the colonists and local Indians from going to war with each other. Having fought with and against the North American Indians, James' father knew the dangers and cost in human life of such an unnecessary war. The local Indians, during a difficult and cold winter and in retaliation for further encroachment onto their lands by colonists, began raiding some of the smaller plantations and farms in the area to acquire the food they needed to survive. James' father dispatched emissaries to the tribes telling them that they were bringing aid. With what basic supplies they could part with, James' father, James and Bode and one hundred-members of the Thornton militia accompanying him, marched into the Indian lands and delivered the needed supplies. Colonel Thornton then negotiated a tentative peace while making it clear that any attacks in the future on plantations within the protected areas, would bring war between their peoples. Although no shots were fired, the militia had performed perfectly in its appearance as a highly trained and disciplined fighting unit, impressing upon the Indians the seriousness that such a threat of war carried with it.

Sadly, much like the Paxton plantation encounter, it did not take long before the facts and results of the Indian negotiations changed from a successful and peaceful solution, into a rumored alliance of the Thornton militia with the local Indians. The apparent goal of such a rumored alliance was the complete overthrow the British rule in North Carolina and the armed rebellion and destruction of the local slave owners. Apparently the Thornton plantation with their slave army would then rule the area, either killing or enslaving all the white population. Mr. King was very concerned by the dangerous allegations and what it would mean for the plantation, however James' father seemed more humored by it.

"Apparently, they have discovered our plans Elijah." James' father exclaimed and Mr. King just shook his head.

"This is not something to joke about, William. All of our lives are at risk if this rumor grows." Mr. King replied with a serious tone. After a brief moment, James' father let the smile fade from his face.

"Elijah, I understand the dangers that we face and that we have done nothing to deserve such lies. I also know that as long as we stay together and do not give in to fear, that none of these plantation owners have the courage to take action against us. Only the British army has the strength and ability, and we will never give them cause or reason. So I say let them sow their lies amongst themselves. I would rather have them love us than fear us, but fear is a good deterrent until then." James' father said and smiled. Although James could see that Mr. King understood his father's position, he had a difficult time embracing it.

Chapter 4

It was also becoming very clear that the locals were not excited about the growing strength and success of this "Negro" militia and would voice it regularly through many official channels. These concerns would eventually work its way through the channels and get back to James' father. One thing always proved true with the locals, whenever trouble came, they were always quick to recount their objections and accept and embrace the militia... that was until the danger or need for them was over.

His father was careful to instruct and train the workers and the militia to understand the long-term impact of their actions and the pride and rarity of being a part of such a militia. In spite of the bitterness from the locals, it made the militia even more eager to volunteer for the thankless jobs when the need called. But that was about to change.

In the late spring of 1776, on a cold rainy day, a British officer on horse and accompanied by twenty British foot soldiers arrived at the plantation. Their arrival caused quite a stir among the militia and workers and James could see that his father was concerned as well as they marched toward their house. James' father sent Bode to tell the militia to remain inside and not to arm themselves, which would normally be the standard response should armed men approach the plantation.

As James and his father watched them approach, James could see that the British soldiers were fully equipped and the officer was wearing a full dress uniform to impress. He was a very heavyset man with a bright red wool jacket, buttoned and wrapped tightly around him with a cloak over his shoulders.

"I know you." James' father said to no one in particular as he looked through the window toward the mounted officer. He then turned and nodded to James and stepped out onto the porch to greet the officer and his men. The officer and his men were glancing about as if expecting trouble or something hidden on the plantation.

"Colonel Wentworth, it is good to see you again. I believe it was in Trenton that we last saw each other." James' father approached the officer who slid slowly from the back of his horse. The stiffness of a long ride on horseback was evident as the man and his large body adjusted to not only the ground under his feet, but to the new angle that was required of his legs in order to stand straight. As he seemed to stretch his body, he handed the reins to one of his men and then walked with a stiff limp of fatigued muscles toward his father. They shook hands and the officer smiled.

"Yes, I do believe it was in Trenton Regional Protector Thornton." He replied to his father in formal acknowledgment of his father's military title. James' father suddenly turned toward him.

"James, this is Colonel Robert Wentworth. Colonel, this is my son James Thornton Jr." James stepped forward, shook the man's outstretched hand, and said, "It's a pleasure to meet you Colonel."

"The pleasure is mine, young master Thornton… Pleasure is all mine," he said with a smile and would not release James' hand as if he was looking for something hidden behind his eyes.

"He looks just like you William," he said as he turned back to his father and released James' hand. "I'm guessing he has the same spirit as well from what I can see in his eyes and the firmness of his grip." He smiled back at James and his father nodded with a smile.

"I'm working hard to train him to avoid the mistakes I have made in life Colonel; fortunately he got his mothers intellect so he learns quickly." He smiled at his son, who seemed entertained by the banter between the two men.

"What brings you to these parts Colonel?" James' father asked and then continued, "If you and your men are passing through and need a place to stay for the evening, you know you are always welcome here. We can provide food and comfortable lodging for you if you have need." His father offered to the British officer, who smiled and looked back at his men and then back to his father.

"Well William, the answer to the first part of your question is 'you and your men'." He said and an awkward silence filled the air as his father raised an eyebrow and nodded. "As far as food and lodging, this might take a few days, so I'm grateful for the offer and I will compensate you accordingly." It was almost on queue that Mr. King, who James had not seen approach nor noticed until this moment, stepped from behind James and his father and headed toward the twenty British soldiers.

"Sir," Mr. King said, addressing Colonel Wentworth, "Might I escort your men to one of the closest covered barns where they can put their packs and bedrolls down and dry out by the fire; then we'll see if we can't find a hot meal for them?" Mr. King said to them with a smile and held up one arm as if motioning for them to head toward a nearby barn. The soldiers looked very interested in the offer and James could see that their clothes were soaked from the rain. They simply turned toward their Colonel to await orders. Colonel Wentworth nodded his head and the men quickly fell into line behind Mr. King as he walked them toward the barn.

"Colonel, I know your desire is to stay with your men, but we insist that you stay at our house with us. We can make up one of the guest bedrooms and stoke the fire and put on some hot tea to take the dampness and chill off." His father said to the officer. James could see the relief on the officer's face from the offer, but he did not accept and held up his hand and shook his head as if to say no.

"My place is with my men…" he started to say, but his father interrupted him.

"No, we insist you stay with us." The officer nodded and thanked them. James realized that the whole interaction was an informal way of allowing the officer to avoid the colder barn accommodations, while at the same time to save face in front of his men.

James stepped forward and offered to take the officers horse and stable it for him. The man at first seemed confused, and then realized that there were no other servants around and that James was the only one to give his reins to. Colonel Wentworth removed his saddle bags and a large pack and then handed the reins to James. James nodded and smiled as he took the reins and headed for the barn with the horse in tow.

"Thank you James." The officer said over his shoulder and headed toward the house with his father. His limp seemed less pronounced.

As James led the horse toward the barn a barrage of thoughts and questions ran through his mind. The "you and your men" response from the officer to his fathers question as to 'what brings you here' was very concerning and he could see that it was concerning to his father as well. Were they in trouble with the crown? Was Colonel Wentworth going to disband the militia and confiscate their weapons? He was not concerned with the twenty men that were here should problems occur, but he knew from his father and from his many stories that they would return with a full regiment or two should they not get their way on this first visit, or worse, should the visit turn violent. He knew the British would return and kill or capture the men and his family, carry off the other workers, and then burn down the plantation to prove a point. If things were bad, he knew his father needed to be very diplomatic during this situation.

James was happy to see Bode waiting for him in the stables and the two of them quickly removed the saddle and brushed down the horse as they discussed the situation at the house. James shared with him the words that the officer had spoken to his father and his own thoughts as to what they might mean. They both knew this was a very serious situation and that all that they had worked so hard to build was at risk. James was already preparing for and counting the losses before he knew what was truly going on.

Bode seemed to recognize the character flaw in his friend and looked directly at James.
"I think the best place for you to be is in the house with your father, learning what it is that they are here to do." Bode said and James looked at Bode and realized that he was actually trying to void going back to the house, and that Bode was right. Perhaps he subconsciously thought that 'not knowing' was somehow better. He nodded and patted the horse on the backside as he walked around it.

"I'll finish up here, but you better get back to me quickly with an update if you hear anything." He said and smiled at James and then continued. "I'll stick around the barn so you can make an excuse to check on the horse and then fill me in. Agreed?" He said and smiled again.

"Agreed." James smiled back and headed out the door and toward the house trying to figure out where he should go that would enable him to overhear the important discussion without seeming to eavesdrop.

As he came through the front door he could see the officer and his father sitting down by the fire and his mother pouring tea into the cups held by each man. She looked up and saw James walking past the door.

"Would you care for some tea James?" She asked and James at first was not sure how to respond, as he was hoping to listen in on his father's conversation with the officer from the other room, but as he looked toward his father, he saw him nod toward him.

"Yes. Thank you mother." He replied and stepped into the room where his parents and the officer were. The officer had taken off his cloak and heavy wool jacket, but James could see that the man still looked rather heavyset even without it.

His mother set the teapot down on a plate that rested on the end table near the three men. "I'll go see to dinner for you and your men, Colonel." She smiled and excused herself.

"Thank you, Mrs. Thornton, that is very kind of you," the officer replied.

The next half hour was filled with shallow discussions about where they had marched in from, the people that the officer had met along the way, and if the colonel had any news on certain officers and people of influence that his father knew and was concerned about. The colonel, who asked similarly polite questions, answered all James' father's questions graciously. There was an awkward moment of silence as if both men had gathered enough information on each other and now the only course remaining was to move into far deeper and more relevant matters. The officer took the opportunity to change the direction of the conversation.

"William…" The informal conversations had allowed the formality to shift to a more personal level. "…tell me about this militia force that I have been hearing so much about lately." He asked and sipped his tea as he looked at James' father and awaited his response.

"Is this the issue that brings you all the way out here, Robert?" James' father asked. The colonel nodded and set his cup down.

"It has caused quite a stir and drawn a great deal of attention to you, William. I'm not sure how much of what I hear is true, but many of the people with whom I have spoken with on the matter are very concerned about what you are doing and what your goals might be." He said calmly, but in a far colder manner than before.

"What is it that they are saying that has caused such concern?" His father asked. The officer seemed to pause as if determining if he should pursue the line of discussion he was considering. He took a deep breath.

"I have found no cause to believe what is being said, but I'll share with you the accusations of those opposed to your actions and direction and then you can shed a little more light on the matter." He said with raised eyebrows. It was more of a statement than a question. His father nodded in agreement with an upturned hand for the officer to continue.

"As you may have heard, the colonies are becoming more and more obstinate toward the crown and there is a growing seed of rebellion sprouting up in the northeastern colonies." His father nodded in agreement, although this was news to James. The officer continued, "It is being said that you are building a militia force to support such a rebellion should it occur." The officer motioned toward his father as if to say, "your turn". James watched as his father ever so slightly shook his head from side to side and frowned.

"Whether I have agreed with the policies and orders of the Crown or not, I have spent my whole life defending the crown and its colonies from aggressors. What sentiment grows against the crown in the north had nothing and continues to have nothing to do with the reasons for the creation of this militia. The force on this plantation was not only created to protect our land and our neighbor colonists from local aggressors, but to support the crown and serve it as well. If you can share with me one situation in which we have involved ourselves that proves otherwise, I would like to know of it and respond accordingly," his father said. The colonel just stared at James' father as if trying to see into him and then answered.

"William, in every situation that has been reported, you and your militia have represented the crown admirably. I think the question to ask is why do so under the banner of your militia instead of the crown? Is it for personal gain and prestige?" His father seemed stunned by the statement, set his teacup down, and leaned forward in his seat as if to whisper something to the officer.

"I was charged by the crown with the creation and leadership of a military force of volunteers to defend and protect the North Carolina colony. The truth be known, the crown has been too preoccupied with other more important ventures to provide the needed military support or supplies in order to facilitate such a request, or to create a strong enough military force of volunteers to do such a job. Robert, I resigned and retired from that commission because the men appointed in the primary cities to facilitate such a plan have their interests rooted only in their individual cities. Those cities already have an established militia and a military presence, but they neglect the protection of the outlying plantations and farmers." His father leaned back in his chair and stared at the fire a moment. "I have no interest in rebellion. My interest is right here on this plantation and with my friends. I learned from leadership and from the Bible that when much is given, much is expected. Whenever I have been informed of a need from a plantation or town which the defended and fortified cities would not fulfill, I have offered what help we could provide," he said and then suddenly laughed. "Their gratitude lasted about 5 days before they wanted us to take our dead and wounded out of their town." He then turned back toward the officer. "What else are we dealing with?" he asked.

The officer seemed to think about what James' father had said and then continued. "Why the Negro workers, William? Why not use the surrounding citizens and colonists for your militia?" he asked.

"Distance and training. You cannot ask someone who is trying to grow crops and protect his family to travel several days by foot on a regular basis to train and practice with a group. Yet you and I both know that without that training, any such militia force does not have the discipline needed, and in battle is only good for one volley before they break ranks and flee. The men on this plantation train weekly as a unified force. They have now seen battle; they have looked down the barrels of muskets and learned to stand their ground and to protect their fellow militiamen. More importantly, they want to be part of this militia; they volunteered to be a part of it, and they are proud to be a part of it. We both know that such an attitude is a rare and valuable character in a soldier," his father concluded.

After a long pause, the officer interjected what was on his mind. "I have heard that your men fought well in every situation… Almost as well as a British soldier would have," he said.

"They should," his father said. "They were trained in the same fashion." His father seemed proud of the statement, but James remembered that his father had told him that the training the militia received was different from that which a typical British soldier received, "More relevant to the times and weapons," his father had said of their training and maneuvers.

"That is somewhat hard to believe," the colonel said with a smug look.

"Why is that?" His father responded, even though he already knew the answer before he asked the question, but he wanted to hear the man say it.

"William, they're Negroes and there have always been problems in trying to incorporate them into our ranks," he said as if it was a statement of fact.

"No Robert, they are men. Just like you and I are men. The problems you say we encountered were from never treating them as such during their training. I'm talking about the non-Negro officers and the men." James' father let that sink in a moment before he continued. "They are all treated the same here and they have just as much opportunity to lead as the next man does." The silence could have been cut with a knife as both men both turned to look at the fire.

"So is this just a fact finding mission, Robert, or are you here to deliver specific orders or demands to me?" his father asked, breaking the silence. The officer at first frowned, but then smiled.

"William, you were always one to cut to the chase as quickly as possible," he said to his father. "So be it. You have restated your loyalty to the crown and I believe you. Now knowing that to be true, I have come to request the use of you and your militia for the needs of the crown," he said with a mischievous smile on his face. James looked at his father who sat silently and looked as though he were contemplating a chess move that had no opportunity for victory in it. As they sat there in silence, James played the various discussions through his mind and realized that the officer had cleverly influenced his father to state his loyalty to the crown, the loyalty of his militia to the crown, and their ability to be on par with the soldiers of the crown.

"Is this a request Robert, or an order from the crown?" his father asked. The officer seemed to think a moment before responding.

"I would prefer both sides view it as a 'request'." He finally replied, but James knew that meant it could very easily be changed to an order if the request was rejected. His father reached for the pot of tea.

"More tea?" he asked and in response to a nod from the colonel, filled both cups. James was amazed that his father remained calm during the exchange as he watched him set the pot back down on the end table.

"Specifically, what do you seek?" He asked the officer as they both sipped their tea. The colonel set his cup back down on the saucer and folded his hands on his lap as if satisfied.

"William, as you may or may not know, the French and the Spanish have kept the crown very busy in the Caribbean. We have had to increase our presence there in order to protect our short-term and long-term interests. The past ten years have seen us wrestle away and then lose several of the southern string of islands to the French. We recently landed and captured the smaller city fort on the eastern side of the island of Martinique from the French and the plan is to resupply it from England with supplies. We plan to land a sizeable army there next fall, then march across the island to capture the more important western fortress from the French. If successful, we will control the whole island." He said.

"So how does that apply to my militia?" his father asked the obvious question. The officer seemed a bit uncomfortable delivering the next bit of news.

"Our losses while securing the smaller fort were considerable in men, supplies and ships. Much heavier than we anticipated. As you can imagine, the need for men and supplies is most urgent at the moment and the replacements and supplies from England may not arrive in time or in sufficient numbers. We need a temporary solution until the fall, or the gains will be lost."

"So what is your plan for my militia?" his father pressed the further.

"We have three armed vessels currently anchored in Edenton. They have taken on about 150 British soldiers and colonial conscripts stationed in the northern colonies. The men and the ships are fully armed and gathering final supplies before heading south. When I heard of you, your trained militia, and their exploits, I came to secure their participation in this endeavor. They are much needed and will be used to defend the fort from French counterattacks until the arrival next fall of the main force. Next fall you and your men will be released from duty and transported back home," the colonel said without emotion. His father slowly stood up from his chair and walked over to the fire and with the toe of his boot kicked a stray ember back into the flames. James could tell he was deep in thought and watched the officer intently looking at his fathers back for some signs of non-verbal feedback. The officer suddenly broke the silence.

"In further thought William, since I have been assigned to lead this resupply, I do not see the need to have you lead the militia. With proper introductions, I will ensure that they are taken care of during their service to the crown and pay you accordingly for the loss of your slaves," he said to James' fathers back as he watched it go suddenly rigid. His father mumbled something into the fire, which the officer tried to make out.

"I'm sorry, say again?" the officer asked and James' father turned around to face the colonel.

"I said they are not slaves, Colonel Wentworth. They are free men who happen to work for me and I cannot simply order them to fight for a cause not their own," his father replied. The officer at first looked surprised by James' father's words, and then seemed to change direction with his thinking.

"Well, if they had no problem following you on these other military excursions, they will follow your wishes on this one as well." he replied and looked at James' father then, frowned as he saw him shaking his head. The colonel's eyes tightened and he rose to his feet, "Then I will personally conscript them into service and compensate you accordingly for your losses." He walked to the fire and then turned his back to it. "I need the men, William, willingly or otherwise, but I would prefer you gave them to me willingly," he said. James' father responded.

"Either way, their time will be hard, their food poor at best and their accommodations horrible compared to the royal soldiers. That is how it is for Negro soldiers in the royal army, Colonel, and we both know it." He stared at the colonel, who after a few moments looked away from him.

"I will do my best to ensure they are treated fairly and fed properly, William. You have my word on it."

"It is not your word that I'm concerned about, Robert; it's the men holding the various levels of rank below you that will make their lives hell. They are the ones you do not see or hear when you are away. I know and you know that to be true… we have both seen it in the past." The colonel seemed to at first be offended and then settled down before answering.

"In war, there are many greater atrocities committed than what you speak of, William, and you and I have seen them committed in the past as well." His father looked at the officer and calmly replied.

"Neither are acceptable, but the ones I speak of are against our own soldiers, not the enemy. They deserve better than to be treated worse than dogs."

The silence between the two men created a chill in the air that could not be removed by more wood on the fire or another cup of hot tea. It appeared that neither side was going to acknowledge the request of the other. The officer finally broke the impasse by walking over and refilling his cup of tea.

"William, I will give you until the morning to think it over. If I do not have your support and the support of the militia, I will conscript them by orders of the crown and things will go far tougher on them than if they came willingly." He walked toward the exit of the room toward his bedroom and then turned back to face James' father. "William, if you think that remaining silent and not assisting me with the selection of the men will make things more difficult, I will simply conscript double the number I came for, but will pay the same for their services. I'm sorry it has turned into this, but I was hoping to see a lot more loyalty to the crown." He turned and saw James still sitting in the back of the room and nodded toward him. "Good night gentlemen and thank you for the tea and the warm fire." He then walked down the hallway and they eventually heard the door to the downstairs guest bedroom close behind him.

James watched his father continue to stare into the fire, obviously deep in thought as he contemplating all that had just transpired and the difficult decisions that he now had to make. James tried to wrestle with the same challenges that his father faced, but could not come up with a sound solution. He knew his father did not want the militia to be sent without his guidance and protection, but he also knew that at fifty-seven years old, his father was not as young as he used to be. After a long period of silence, James finally interjected as his stood up from his chair. "Perhaps we should take a walk and speak with Elijah and Bode on this matter?" His father seemed almost startled by the words coming from behind him and turned to look at his son. At first he just stared in the direction of his son and then nodded.

"I think that's a good idea. I could definitely use a few good friends around to help think through this." He smiled at his son and then they both turned and headed for the door, stopping briefly to grab their coats.

As his father stepped through the door, James caught a movement in the corned of his eye and looked across the room to see his mother sitting in the darkened dining room next to the kitchen. He knew she had heard the entire conversation and was now fighting through the same worries and concerns that James and his father shared. He knew that her thinking would be far different from theirs, as she loved and cared in a deeper way that only a mother and a wife could. He could not see her face, but he knew she could see his. He smiled and nodded his head as if to say it was going to be all right, but he knew this evening and the next few days would not turn out well for anyone. He knew she loved his father so much and lately had expressed her concern more and more about his health. She had enjoyed the plentiful and consistent time with him these last few years since his retirement from the army. James wished he could say something to reassure her, but nothing came to mind as he closed the door behind him.

Chapter 5

As they stepped off the porch into the growing darkness of evening, James mentioned to his father that Bode was at the barn waiting for him. They stopped briefly by the barn to add Bode to their company, and then continued over to the King home to meet with Bode's father. Bode could see the consternation on the faces on both the Thornton's and knew from the years of friendship and experience that the best course of action was to wait until they were all together to talk about it. Elijah was waiting on the porch of his home when the three of them emerged from the darkness. No words were exchanged as they approached; they just stepped up onto the porch and followed Elijah into the house, where each of them selected a chair and sat down around the table in the kitchen area. Elijah turned up the wick on the lamp so that the faces of each of them could be seen clearly in the increased light. He then sat down and turned to James' father.

"I take it things did not go well with the officer," he said as he then shifted his eyes away from his father and looked at James. James just shook his head and remained silent.

Over the next half hour, James' father accurately recounted his discussion with Colonel Wentworth. When he finished, he turned to Elijah and Bode as if to gauge their reactions.

"I'm so sorry to have gotten us into this mess. Elijah, I should have listened to your advice and warnings early on. My pride got the better of me," his father said. Elijah seemed to reel back as if stunned by his words.

"You're sorry?" He questioned, his voice lightly raised. He stopped and then started again. "You're sorry for giving these men the self confidence and pride to stand face to face with any foe? For giving them a glimpse of what life and freedom is truly suppose to look like?" Elijah seemed to grow in size as he continued and held out his hands. "William, we all knew there were risks in this course of action. No one was forced to pick up those muskets, or to form those marching lines, or to step into harms way. We each chose it, and I'm confident that every one of those men out there would do it again every time." James could see Bode nodding his head at his father's words. "William, in my shame, I was more concerned that these men could not succeed; that they were not of the same caliber and character of white soldiers. You on the other hand believed in every one of them. You believed in my son and me and in our friendship. Your creation and training of this militia helped me overcome my lack of faith in my own people. That is something of value that I can never measure, but I will treasure it forever." Elijah and Bode both had tears coursing down their faces. James realized that his eyes were watering as well and he had to swallow hard. "William, whatever might come of this situation, please understand, I will never harbor ill feelings toward you and your family, but only deep admiration and gratitude. We, the four of us, and every member of this militia will tackle this challenge just like we have tackled every other challenge that we have faced, with faith in God and faith in each other." Elijah stood up from his chair and held out his hand to James' father, who after a brief pause also stood up and shook his hand then embraced him with each man patting the other's back. Bode stood up, walked around the table, and embraced the two men as well. Not wanting to feel left out at this rather emotional moment, James stood up and joined them.

After switching around and taking turns embracing each other individually, the men gradually found their seats again.

"So what do we do, William?" Elijah asked James' father, who seemed to think for but a moment before sharing a plan that he seemed to have already been formulating.

"My guess is that they assume we have a one hundred-man militia, since that is the largest force we have used, not the current 150 men that we have. My goal is to negotiate that number of men to be committed down as much as possible, but I'm not sure how successful I will be, as they seem quite desperate for soldiers." His father glanced at Elijah and Bode and James as if seeking their thoughts. Elijah spoke first.

"Who will be leading them?" he asked, which was the question that was on James' mind as well.

"I will," his father said, "for without a white officer who will stand up for the militia, the militia will be mistreated and mishandled by the other white officers and soldiers. I won't let that happen." James looked at his father's rugged frame, and knew that it had seen its share of wear and tear. James recalled the picture in his mind of his mother sitting in the dark fraught with concern. James did not know how to say that he believed that his father should not go without sounding disrespectful to his father. Elijah apparently did not have that same concern.

"You're too old, William." He smiled and then continued. "The mind and heart are willing, but the body is weak." He laughed, but James' father did not seem to see the humor in it. "It's time to pass the torch William," Elijah said.

"To whom?" his father replied. The words hurt James and caused his pride to rise up inside of him.

"I'll lead them." James said, as he somehow overcame the fear of going someplace far away for a long time and in the middle of a battle. Elijah smiled and nodded, but his father shook his head.

"He's not an officer. They will treat him just like the rest, maybe worse in some ways because he cares for the men," his father replied as if to end the discussion.

"Make James an officer and the leader of these men. We know that he already is in their eyes. He will protect them as best as he can. He is mature, smart, tested in battle, and has been trained by the best." Elijah smiled at James' father and paused. James' father glanced at his son and saw James looking him right in the eye and nodding his head in agreement with Elijah's words. Elijah continued not providing James' father with a chance to come up with a rebuttal. "James will need someone he trusts and who can communicate with the men to be with him as well. That's why Bode will go with him and you can also appoint him an officer of the militia." James looked over at Bode who at first seemed to be in deep thought, then started to smile as he looked at James.

"Someone has to keep you out of trouble." Bode said, and they both smiled. Somehow having Bode with him eased James' inner fear and his courage grew.

"We both lead the best trained groups of the militia, so we can take care of ourselves," James said, and then interjected. "Well, Bode's group is a distant second, but he's trying real hard." James said sarcastically and then smiled as Bode reached over and punched him in the arm. The four men laughed and the mood lightened dramatically.

As they realized the dangers and difficulties they faced, the men adopted a more sober mood as they continued to speak at length about their future leadership roles. They then went to the homes of certain prominent men of the militia to speak with them and their families. Finally, they called a very late meeting with the militia in the large tobacco barn near the workers' quarters where they shared with them what was unfolding on the plantation as a result of the request of Colonel Wentworth. James' father and Mr. King were as candid as possible when speaking to the men about the dangers, the risks to their lives, the possible treatment and conditions that they would encounter, as well as the leadership positions ascribed to James and Bode. They talked about soldiers' pay (which was a good wage for their families and would be paid in advance) and about how they would take care of workers' families should something happen to them while they were away. His father also told the men that anyone who did not want to go based on family or health reasons would be transferred to another group and exchanged for a soldier that chose to go. Much discussion and interaction ensued; the majority of the 100 trained men were willing to go but there were those who were not. When the meeting was concluded, they had formed the men who would depart into four groups of twenty-five men each. The 1st group was to be led by James, the 2nd group by Bode, and the 3rd group led by Joseph Hope and lastly, the 4th group was to be led by Robbie Hanson. The goal was to convince Colonel Wentworth to select only the first two groups, but they also needed to be ready just in case the British officer pushed for more men. They had to change out three men from James' 1st group, and four in Bode's group. The 3rd group needed twelve men changed out, while the 4th group was left mainly unchanged. Each group was given specific orders for the morning and then they all headed off to sleep.

Bode and James remained after the meeting, as did Elijah and James' father. They tried to figure out what their fathers were talking about, assuming that they themselves were the subjects of the conversation. Eventually they resigned that their fathers knew more about the situation than they did and they walked quietly back to the edge of the fields. The rain that had fallen all the prior day seemed to have drained the clouds revealing the stars and the partial moon. The fields suddenly came alive before them. It was the middle of planting time and James though about the amount of work and great care that was needed to eventually bring the crops to market.

"It's hard to imagine not being here for a planting and harvest." James said to Bode, who nodded and thought about the hard work compared to the threat of war and dying on some foreign island.

"Do you think it will be as bad as your father says for all of us, being a part of the British army?" Bode seemed very concerned as he asked his question and James could tell he was looking for a real answer, not a funny quip. Deep inside James was glad Bode had said "all of us" knowing that each man would probably receive his own share of abuse for the role he would play. He nodded.

"Yeah, but were not alone. We'll all have God and each other to help us through it until we get home."

James remembered the Bible verse, from the book of Proverbs chapter 17, verse 17 that his father had shared with him about his perspective on his friendship with Elijah. He shared it now with Bode as they prepared to go in separate directions for the night.

"A friend loves at all times, and a brother is born for adversity."

"Bode, that is a perfect scripture for us and to share with our men. Although I wish you were not to be put in danger, I'm glad you will be with me and our men with us," he said and shook Bode's hand and patted him on the shoulder. Bode became serious and after a moment began a quote from the first chapter from the book of Ruth. *"But Ruth replied, "Don't urge me to leave you or to turn back from you. Where you go I will go, and where you stay I will stay. Your people will be my people and your God my God. Where you die I will die, and there I will be buried. May the LORD deal with me, be it ever so severely, if anything but death separates you and me.""*

James was impressed that he could quote so long of a scripture from memory and wondered why he had taken the time to memorize this particular verse. As they stood together, he thought about the scripture and wondered how true it could turn out to be. There was an awkward silence and then a smile crept onto James face.

"Great. I talk about brothers and you chose to share a scripture about two women. I'm deeply disappointed and maybe a little concerned, Mr. King." James tried to be serious, but could not hold back the smile.

Bode at first tried to explain it, but then simply said. "Well, the woman Naomi in the scripture reminded me of you. She was always complaining and faithless." He rebutted and smiled and then they both laughed and headed to their homes. There was much to do before the sun would rise and as he looked up into the sky he could see that most of the clouds had moved on and that the stars and the moon were shining brightly.

The next morning, right at dawn, James' father sent James to request of the still sleeping Colonel Worthington, to survey the troops who had mustered and were waiting for him outside. The colonel quickly put on his uniform, freshly pressed thanks to James' mother, and stepped into the hallway where James' father was waiting. James could see that the officer seemed confused and was still trying to shake off the effects of the deep sleep from which he had been awakened. James turned and went out the door ahead of the other two men and took up his position in front of the four groups of twenty-five men that had formed in their respective ranks, in front of the house. Each group had five lines of five men with one additional man standing in front of each group.

Although he had reviewed them several times already, James wished he could somehow review them one more time before the officer stepped outside. As he glanced toward the men, the sun had risen above the tree line and it was illuminating the men before him. The barrels of their muskets and the gray and black uniforms were pronounced in the morning light, and the overall impression was impressive. He was so proud of them and he smiled briefly at the men, then cleared his face and turned around in time to face Colonel Wentworth as he stepped onto the porch with James' father.

As the officer stepped forward from behind his father, James could see that the Colonel was surprised by the sight before him. On queue, James gave the order, "Attention!" and he heard the sound of 100 men responding to the command as they lifted their rifles from having the butts resting on the ground to their shoulders in a brief series of clean and professional looking moves, all of which seemed more synchronized than ever before. The officer remained silent as he stood on the porch and looked out over the lines of men before him as if counting them. He then stepped forward to the edge of the porch steps. From behind the colonel, James' father said clearly to the officer.

"Colonel Wentworth, may I present for your review the North Carolina Central Militia." James' father stepped up next to the officer and looked down at James, who stood in front of the four groups. "Captain Thornton, would you please introduce yourself, your officers and your men to Colonel Wentworth for inspection."

James responded loudly with a "Yes sir!" and stepping forward toward the base of the stairs and rendered his salute to the colonel.

"Colonel Wentworth, Captain James Thornton at your service, sir." James awaited the officer's review and response before continuing. The Colonel turned to James' father as if to say something, then decided against it and slowly went down the porch steps, stopping in front of James. He stood there for several seconds longer before finally responding.

"Captain Thornton, would you please introduce me to your men." He then returned the salute to James. James knew that by acknowledging his rank, the Colonel had given his approval of it. James made a quick soldierly turn to face his men and walked toward Bode.

"Colonel Wentworth, may I introduce Lieutenant King, my second in command and leader of 2nd Group." Bode saluted the Colonel, who once again stood in front of Bode for several seconds before stepping closer to Bode as if to whisper to him.

"How much do you love your men soldier?" He asked Bode and Bode did not hesitate with his answer.

"I would die for them, sir." The officer nodded his head and stepped back to stand in front of him, then returned Bode's salute.

"Lieutenant King." He said and then followed James to the next soldier.

"Colonel Wentworth, may I introduce to you 2nd Lieutenant Hanson and assistant leader of 1st Group." The officer acknowledged Lieutenant Hanson's rank and then they repeated the introductions again with 3rd Group lead by 2nd Lieutenant Smith and 4th group lead by 2nd Lieutenant Hope. During the third introduction, James saw that the twenty British soldiers were now dressed and moving into formation twenty yards away from 1st Group. They seemed confused and nervous at the sight of the black and gray uniformed soldiers that seemed to have appeared and formed up from nowhere.

The British officer walked back to where James' father was standing at the top of the porch steps and then turned back around to face James.

"Captain, can you demonstrate some of your men's marching and battle formations for me?" James hesitated a moment as if trying to organize his thoughts, then stepped forward.

"Colonel, may I request the use of 1st and 2nd Groups only for your demonstration? 3rd and 4th Groups have not been thoroughly trained, sir." James watched as the officer surveyed then men of 3rd and 4th groups. It was evident (and secretly deliberate) that their formations were not as sharp as the other two groups, they also seemed much older and their uniforms did not fit as well. The officer turned back toward James.

"Why have they not been trained to the same level, Captain?" he asked sharply.

"Sir, this is a plantation and these men make up the majority of our workers. They are in the fields working during most of the daylight hours, as are those who lead them. What free time we did have, we spent primarily with the 1st and 2nd groups." James replied.

"Did not the other two groups join you in other operations Captain?" the officer asked, knowing full well that they had.

"Not to their shame in any way sir, but they were used primarily in secondary support roles, sir. 1st and 2nd groups are the more battle tested groups." James did not feel comfortable stretching the truth on this matter, but they needed to play the charade if they were to avoid losing all the men to the British Colonel. The officer seemed to think about it longer and then gave in to the request.

"Very well Captain."

James turned and surveyed the men before giving his first set of orders. "Leaders of 3rd and 4th Groups, march your men to a position next to the British soldiers."

"Yes sir!" Both Smith and Hope shouted back and barked out a few preparatory orders. It appeared that chaos ensued as the men of 3rd and 4th groups bumped into and tripped over each other as they marched to the open area next to the British soldiers (something they were told to purposely do the night before). During the transition, James could see the British soldiers snickering among themselves at the sight of the unorganized two groups. James glanced at the British officer and could tell that he was very disappointed with what he saw. Once the men of 3rd and 4th group had reformed next to the British soldiers, James waited a brief moment before starting the demonstration with 1st and 2nd groups. James stepped in front of his men and began to speak.

"Men, we will be implementing a quick march to the end of that fence line," James pointed to a fence across a field readied for planting, "where you will form a two-level skirmish line and load your weapons and then fire on my command. You will then execute a staggered skirmish line retreat when ordered. Lieutenants, are we clear?"

"Yes sir!" Both Bode and Robbie Hanson shouted in response.

James gave quick orders to reform facing the fence line that they were to defend. When the order was given the men marched and turned with precision at each order until they were lined up facing the desired fence line that was twenty yards away. James moved to stand at the center between the two groups and barked another set of orders that put the two groups in a fast run while maintaining formation across the twenty yards. When they arrived at the fence line, each group spread out twelve men across and two men deep and began loading their muskets. Even with the quick run across the field, the men were loading quickly and presenting arms at the ready.

James issued an order and the front row of men in 1st group dropped down to one knee while the back row of 2nd group stepped forward aimed over 1st group's heads. "Fire!" James yelled, and smoke and fire belched from the muskets. James barked another order that sent 2nd group, who had just fired their muskets, retreating at a dead run fifty yards back toward the house to reform their skirmish line. 1st group, who had been previously kneeling, stood and took aim and awaited orders. As the retreating 2nd group arrived and formed their skirmish line, they immediately began the process of reloading their muskets. James, who was still with 1st group, gave the order to fire, belching smoke and fire from their muskets. James and 1st group immediately retreated towards 2nd groups newly formed line.

As James and 1st group reached 2nd group, 1st group continued on past them, forming a new skirmish line fifty yards closer to the house and started the same reloading process. James stopped to join 2nd group who had completed their reloading and were now ready to fire. Again the muskets roared and belched their smoke and 2nd group turned and ran fifty yards past the now waiting 1st group behind them, with James stopping to join the front line group.

They repeated the fighting retreat maneuvers until they reached the initial starting point, in front of the house. James issued another set of orders and the men reformed in their original 5 by 5 groups in front of the steps as the thick smoke from the muskets drifted across the field. James could see that the men were breathing heavily, but they held their positions and had followed orders almost perfectly. James was very proud of them. He turned and walked toward the waiting British officer for further instructions. The officer and the twenty British soldiers were obviously surprised by what they had just witnessed, as there was no longer any snickering coming from any of them. The British officer walked forward to stand in front of James, who was once again standing at attention.

"At ease, Captain. I must say, your men performed admirably. They consistently reloaded in less than one minute, they held their formations, and they followed your orders promptly. I'm very impressed." He walked past a now relaxed James and stared at the men a moment.

"Have they trained with bayonets?" He asked James. James walked up next to the officer and stared out at the men before him.

"We have trained with the formations for bayonets, but because we use long rifles, we cannot put the blades onto the muzzles and still fire effectively," James replied, "Although not as deadly, we have trained to strike with the tip of the musket which has the same reach as a bayonet on a shorter standard rifle." James answered and the officer nodded and then raised an eyebrow.

"Why select the long rifle Captain?" the colonel asked James.

"They have a longer range and greater accuracy, sir. They are a little slower to load, but we have found the range advantage to benefit us greatly," James answered.

"Are your men good shots, Captain?" the colonel asked James with a smile, who responded.

"Sir, pick any five men from these two groups and they will hit a standard gourd three out of five times from seventy-five yards." The officer seemed at first surprised by the boast, but then laughed.

"Captain, after what I saw this morning, somehow I believe they would." He moved toward the house but turned back to address James again. "Captain, you may dismiss your men. Please join us at your earliest opportunity." He then spoke to James' father, "Shall we retire to the house to discuss things further?" James watched as his father nodded his head and motioned with his arm toward the steps and front door.

"I believe my wife has a delicious breakfast waiting for you Colonel." He said.

James waited until his father and the colonel had entered the house before giving the orders for the men to return to their homes to await further orders. He shook each of the group leaders' hands and asked them to convey to the men how proud he was of them and that he would keep them informed of further news and plans. As the men withdrew, James looked over to see the twenty British soldiers still standing in formation as the Colonel had neglected to issue orders to them before leaving. James walked over to the apparent leader who stood looking straight ahead. He was shorter but older than James and James saw by his insignia that he was a corporal. He hesitated a moment, then went ahead with his hunch.

"Corporal, your men are dismissed. Retire to your bunks and I will make sure that breakfast is delivered shortly." James turned as if to walk back toward the house, but stopped as he saw that the man did not respond to his command. He knew he was being tested, so he turned back and stepped in front of the man. "Corporal, is there some confusion with my order?" he asked the man who now seemed in an internal battle as to what to do.

"No," he replied and then hesitated before finally saying "Sir." James stared at him a moment longer.

"I understand how odd this might seem to you. I did not intend that my men and I would be called into service with you either. However, if there is to be discipline and order, chain of command and orders will be followed, or there will be consequences. Are we clear?" The man briefly looked James in the eye and saw that he meant it.

"Yes sir!" The corporal responded and saluted James, who at first looked past him and at the rest of the men. He then stepped back and returned the salute to the Corporal, who issued the necessary orders to his men to return to their bunks.

James took a deep breath as he returned to the house. He noticed movement to his left and as his eyes shifted he saw Bode leaning against the side of the barn, remaining out of sight. He had watched the whole interaction between James and the British corporal. He grinned and shook his head and made a silly looking salute toward James as if copying the corporal's salute. James just motioned for him to go away, shaking his head and smiling back at him. He realized that as always, Bode was there "just in case" something was to go wrong.

The discussion with the British officer went as well as could be expected during the morning and into the late afternoon. There seemed to be a sense of urgency with the Colonel that helped to force compromises that might not otherwise have been agreed to. As James' father anticipated, the Colonel requested all 100 men, but James' father pleaded the premise of intense financial hardship for the plantation if all 100 of his workers were to be conscripted. With spring coming on and additional fields needing plowed and planted, trying to make due with 50 less workers seemed daunting enough, let alone losing 100 of them. James' father also pointed out the value of fifty well-trained soldiers who would not need training and the additional resources that would be required to lead and supply 50 untrained men. The British Colonel eventually withdrew the request and settled on the 50 men of 1st and 2nd group.

His father then set about the negotiation of payment for the services of the men during the estimated 12-month tour of duty. Although he tried for full British soldier's pay rates, he knew that would be difficult. They settled on a slightly lower rate for the regular militia, but the officers were to be paid their full rates. Colonel Wentworth definitely struggled with the idea of James being given the rank of Captain, as his age and experience did not justify it. But his father insisted that James' rank needed to be high enough to protect his men from the prejudices of the leaders within the British army.

The Colonel eventually agreed to James' fathers terms and seemed to grasp the need to protect such a unique militia from the abuses of the established views of the military and its officers. He seemed to have even grasped the long-term possibilities of the potential uses of similar local militias that his father was trying to convey. Colonel Wentworth issued the financial notes to James' father to negotiate as needed with the authorities for compensation and the orders for distribution of the monies to the families of the militia workers. Despite the fact that the men would be receiving less than British regulars, the promised soldier's pay was actually higher than a worker's wages. Although the risk was substantially higher, this helped to alleviate some of the financial concerns the soldiers had for their families.

The Colonel made a final and key decision that was strongly supported by James' father; the men of the militia were to keep their current uniforms, and not wear the British standard foot soldier's uniform. The Colonel and James' father both felt that there would be less chance of the men being split up or divided and integrated into the other troops "as needed." As veteran field commanders, both men understood the value that the men held as a unit. They knew that there would be some difficulties with leadership and support logistics, but perhaps less of a chance of the other more concerning issues of harsh treatment and poor care. James agreed with the decision to retain their own uniforms and identity as a group but requested documents that would support the Colonel's acknowledging the ranks of him and his officers. The Colonel agreed and was even willing to provide an insignia patch to add to their uniforms that would be recognized and respected by the British soldiers in support of their concern.

Once they had come to terms on the final agreements, the proper paperwork was prepared and copies were given to both James and his father should a need arise that required them to prove formal military attachment to the British army. James and his father were well aware that any higher ranked official or officer than that of Colonel Wentworth could rescind the provisions they had agreed to, but it was the best they could do. Colonel Wentworth requested that the militia depart the following morning, but James' father was able to gain them an extra day to prepare and say their goodbyes to their families. All work was suspended for those two days and a big, goodbye party, was thrown by the Thornton's and everyone was invited, including the British soldiers.

James spent most of those two days with his mother, father and younger siblings. The moments with them suddenly seemed so valuable, compared to just a few days ago. He tucked the younger siblings in, told them stories, and answered their many questions. He wiped their tears and told them that everything was going to be all right and that he and the militia would be coming back before they knew it. The late evenings and early mornings were spent with his father and mother. James' father tried to pour all the wisdom he had shared with him the past years of James' life into those two short days, perhaps frustrated that he had not shared more.

"I should have taught you more about the use and defense of cannon in battles." James' father would state and then shake his head, yet James remembered all the hours his father had spent around the hearth teaching the two of them about the use of cannons and how to defeat them. James just nodded and pretended it was all new and just relished the time he was able to spend with his father.

His mother on the other hand talked more about manners, and proper clothing for each type of weather, and even hygiene for him and his men. She was trying to, not only help him and his men avoid sickness, but also to influence the higher-ranked officers he would encounter. He loved her so much, but never felt he had said it enough. His mother gave him a thick leather-bound notebook, requesting that he keep an ongoing journal so that he would never forget his travels and the events that she somehow knew would be of greater value than he could foresee at the time. She said doing so would help him through difficult times as he could look back on the good events when bad ones seemed to be all that he could see. He thanked her deeply and promised to do so.

James watched as other men said their goodbyes to their wives, fiancées, or girlfriends and James felt sad that there was no one besides his family for whom he had such deep feelings. In looking around at the party, he had to chuckle at Bode, who had to find a way to say goodbye to several young women whose affections he had won, each of them wanting to give him something for him to remember her by. After one such goodbye, James and Bode were walking back to the cider bowl while Bode was trying to find an empty pocket in which to put a scarf that had been knitted for him by one of the young women.

"You're going to need a wagon just to carry all those forget-me-not gifts you've been given," he smiled at Bode, who just gave him that big smile.

"I'm hoping that you will carry some of it tomorrow until we get out of sight, then we can hand it out to some of the other guys." James looked at the scarf and thought about some of the other items he had seen Bode carrying with him.

"Do you even remember who gave you each item?" James asked and Bode at first nodded, then shook his head and seemed perplexed.

"I did at first, but not anymore." First James, then Bode started laughing at his response.

That night, at the party, James' father asked Robbie Hanson, the new leader of James' 1st Group, to step forward. He was given a pistol that had been recently acquired by his father, and a large quantity of shot. In addition, he was given a cutlass and scabbard to hang from his belt to help distinguish him as a leader. It was evident that Robbie felt much honored by the gifts as he held and examined them. James' father said that he wished he could also give one to each leader of ten, but there were only a few left. Robbie had practiced firing a pistol with James and Bode as part of their training and excelled with it, but until now only Bode and James had been issued one personally. It was the same with the Cutlass; basic training was given, but only Bode and James had really been trained by his father on how to use them effectively in battle situations. Luke was happy for Robbie and had known that his father was going to give them to him this evening, so he was prepared and enjoyed the joy and pride that were reflected in his friend's eyes.

The party was concluded in the early evening so that the men could pack, get their rest and be ready to march out in the morning after breakfast. The day before the women had prepared a bundle of food for each man to carry with them on their two-day march to the port where the ships were waiting. The bundle consisted of dried fruit and nuts, fresh bread, cheese, jerky and sweet cookies and hard molasses candies.

In addition to his main uniform and food bundle, each man carried his musket and fifty rounds of main shot. He also had matching powder flasks, musket cleaning tools, wadding and flints, a belt knife or cutlass, a bedroll, a change of clothes, a black wool cloak, toiletries, and a variety of personal items that consisted of anything from gifts to an assortment of small musical instruments. Additionally, James' pack had a notebook, writing implements, and the set of orders that Colonel Wentworth had provided him. It was late into the evening before James felt he had packed his kit properly enough to allow him to sleep without thinking he had forgotten anything. He wished he could have taken a Bible, but it was far too big to carry in his pack.

Chapter 6

The morning was foggy when they awoke. By the time breakfast was over, the sun had burned through the fog. The men formed up in formation outside the main house. The group of twenty British soldiers had also formed up at first light and was waiting for their Colonel to arrive and issue the marching orders. James was surprised to see a loaded wagon also waiting outside with Elijah King sitting atop the buckboard smiling at the men as they formed up into their two groups of twenty-five.

James had said one more goodbye to his mother and his two younger sisters, Cynthia and Madison, and the littlest of the family, Daniel. It seemed strange to think that he would not be seeing them for over a year. He glanced at the plantation from the porch and knew that he would be missing the sights and smells of planting and harvest seasons, something he thought he would never have to experience. He knew it would be a difficult year with so many of the best workers gone, but he also knew that his father would be hiring new full-time and part-time workers with the compensation he had been given for the fifty-three trained men who were now ready to march away in service to the crown.

Bode and James walked over to where Mr. King was sitting on the wagon and looked as though they might take a peak under the canvas, but before they could reach for it, Mr. King stopped them saying.

"We're going to sell a few things while we are in town and pick up some new supplies while we're at it." Then he winked at the two young men he had poured so much of his life into their raising. James and Bode both suspected that something else was afoot, but they trusted the wink and the man who had given it and left the tarp and the mystery underneath it as it was. The families of the departing men had gathered around the fields and lined the road leading out of the plantation.

After about ten minutes in loose formation, and with the men waving to their families and friends in the crowd, the door to the main house opened and the unit commanders barked quick orders that brought all seriousness back to the men who rapidly reformed their ranks and came to attention. Colonel Wentworth, followed by James' father, stepped out onto the porch and stood there and both seemed to "take in" the men before them. Colonel Wentworth was in his officer's garb and James' father was in his old British uniform, something James had not seen him wear in many years. James' father had insisted on traveling with the militia as far as the departure city in case there were any additional needs. Three workers from the plantation each led a horse from the stables and delivered them quickly to the front porch. Last night James had asked to walk with his men, but both James' father and Elijah felt that being on horseback would present a much more powerful image of his rank and authority once they arrived in the city. Bode, of course, had given James an earful all night and teased him about being lazy.

James stepped forward and nodded to the two men.

"The troops are ready to depart upon your order, Colonel," he said and held his salute as his father had trained him to. The officer looked at James and nodded and returned the salute.

"Very well, Captain Thornton, prepare the men for marching; we shall leave immediately." James ordered the twenty British troops to the front of the column, followed by Bode's group of twenty-five, then James' group of twenty-five following at the end of the column. James and his father agreed that they preferred the appearance of the British leading them instead of it appearing that the militia was being driven toward the city. Once the troops were in position, the three leaders mounted their horses and rode to the front of the column. James spun his horse around and gave a "Forward march!" to the troops who started to march in step down the road that led through plantation, with men and women workers who were waving and cheering them as they passed by. The little boys ran alongside the column all the way to the edge of the property line, where they stopped and gave a final wave and called their goodbyes to their fathers and brothers as the militia marched past. James' heart felt heavy at the thought of these men being away from their families and children. James knew how his own heart felt at the thought of being away from his mother and father and his sisters and brother, how much harder it must be to say goodbye to a wife and child, he thought.

As they traveled further from the plantation, the sun broke above the trees and warmed the bundled men as they marched in loose columns of two abreast down the road. As the morning miles passed by, James would regularly pull his horse to the side of the road and allow the men to march past. He nodded to the British soldiers and specifically to Corporal Higgins with whom he had the initial leadership confrontation at their first meeting.

"How are your men, Mr. Higgins?" The corporal glanced up at James and nodded.

"Excellent sir," he replied.

"Please let me know if your men have any personal needs that require us to take a brief pause prior to our scheduled times," he responded back to the corporal.

"Yes sir, and thank you sir." The corporal finally looked up and into James' eyes when he replied. James just nodded and smiled.

The next person James saw was Elijah King sitting on top of his wagon. James walked his horse alongside him for a while, at first in silence, and then he spoke softly. "I know I don't have to ask this, but please take special care of my father and mother while we are away."

Elijah turned to look at James and smiled. "I will, James. I know I don't have to ask you this either, but please take care of my son while you are away." James nodded and glanced over his shoulder to see Bode and his group marching behind the wagon.

"I don't think I could have done this without him." James said quietly to Elijah, who replied without looking at him.

"Yeah you could. It just will be a lot easier for you with him there." James nodded.

"But it will be a lot harder for him and the men than for me," James added and Elijah shrugged his shoulders.

"Not at long as you're there." Elijah looked back at him and seemed to study the young man sitting on the horse next to him. "You've grown into a good man, James." He hesitated and then smiled, "Early on, I had my doubts." He ended and gave that unique throaty laugh he always made that sounded as if was coming from deep in his belly. James chuckled with him.

"Yeah, I was a real handful growing up. I'm glad you and your family were always there for me, Elijah."

Elijah looked at James a moment, almost as a father looks at a son. "Me too, James. Your family has been very special to me and mine. We will miss you and Bode and the men more than you know." They rode in silence for a while before James finally mumbled softly without looking at Elijah.

"Any chance of finding out what's in the wagon?" Elijah just kept his eyes forward and responded.

"Nope." Yhen he just smiled without turning to look at him. James nodded and smirked.

"Yeah, kind of figured as much." James replied.

"Never hurts to ask," Elijah responded calmly.

A short time later, James pulled his horse to the side and let the wagon pass him. As the next group of militia marched toward him, James dismounted and led his horse alongside Bode. "My legs sure are tired sitting on this horse these past few miles," he said almost to himself as he kidded Bode, knowing the past three miles of marching were far more tiring.

Bode turned his head and gave him one of those, "real funny" sarcastic looks and then shook his head. "Yeah, I can't imagine the pain you must be experiencing," he said sarcastically. James acted hurt.

"Hey, it was not my idea to ride while the rest of you walk," he replied. Bode at first didn't respond and then said.

"Just don't let it go to your head." James looked back at Bode with an "I'm shocked that you would even say such a thing" look, but knew what his friend meant. They walked in silence for a while.

"Have you ever been on a ship?" James asked Bode, who shook his head no, but then added.

"The only stories I have heard are from the other workers who had been on one, or had heard of those traveling on one. Not pleasant stories to hear." James looked over as if trying to understand what he had meant and Bode recognized the look and clarified. "They were slave ships, and the people were chained or shackled with little food or water, or even places to relieve themselves except where they laid." James' face seemed to express the vision in his mind and Bode saw it.

"Yeah, let's hope for a better situation for us."

The three-day march to Edenton was relatively uneventful with the exception of a few rain showers and a somewhat dreary and wet sleep on the second night. The first night they were able to sleep in a nearby plantation barn. The initial interaction did not go well, as the British soldiers were welcomed by the plantation owner and invited to stay in their various barns, but the militia were asked to remain outside the plantation. James was happy to see that Colonel Wentworth took a stand to support the militia and demanded the same services from the plantation owner for the militia as was offered to the British soldiers. The owner obviously consented to his wishes, but it proved the point that James' father had voiced earlier on the fair treatment of his militia. The Colonel stood up for them this time, but James wondered, would he do so again in the future?

On the third day, as they approached Edenton, the men could see the masts of several large vessels jutting above the tree line in the distance. As they crested a hill that overlooked the city, they had a better view of the ships anchored in the harbor. There were two larger vessels and one that looked slightly smaller and thinner in size than the other two. James could also see that it carried fewer cannons than the two larger ones. He hoped he and his men would have the opportunity and luck to travel on one of the larger ones.

The column halted briefly just outside of the city to allow the men to freshen up their uniforms and tighten their formations. Colonel Wentworth requested that Bode (Lieutenant King) and 2nd Lieutenant Hanson join him at the front of the column. They then marched into the city and past the various fortifications. As they passed, the troops manning those positions simply observed them silently, with most of the attention focusing on the black and gray clad militia. At Colonel Wentworth's signal, James ordered the column to halt as a British Captain on horseback rode forward to meet Colonel Wentworth just outside the front gate of the city. Colonel Wentworth introduced James' father, then moved his hand toward James. "This is Captain Thornton of the North Carolina Militia. In his command are Lieutenant King, and 2nd Lieutenant Hanson." The British Captain seemed to ignore the introduction of Bode and Hanson, and instead looked at James as if sizing him up before nodding his head in James' direction.

"Captain, I'm glad you could join us." Neither man saluted the other, so James simply nodded back.

"Glad we could help," James replied and the British Captain turned back toward the Colonel.

"Colonel, may I escort you into the city?"

"Yes Captain, please issue the orders to load any final provisions and supplies onto the ships, as I intend to sail our fleet with the tides first thing in the morning," Colonel Wentworth replied.

Their march into the city created quite a stir, the word of their arrival seemed to spread quickly, as more, and more people proceeded to line the streets to see the militia march past.

James could hear the mumblings and even some of the words being whispered among the citizens while riding at the head of the militia column, just behind Mr. King's wagon. None of the words he heard would have encouraged a man, so he and his men did their best to ignore them.

James looked ahead and saw two men who had stepped almost into the street as if waiting for the militia to come within range of them. James could see in their eyes and faces the evil that they were preparing to spew forth from their mouths once the militia had marched near them. Whether it was to avoid a dangerous situation or simply his anger welling up inside him, he decided to act first and galloped his horse to where the two men were standing, walking it right between them and forcing them apart. There was something intimidating about a horse stepping closely to where you were standing and he took advantage of that to speak to them.

"Gentlemen, I would suggest stepping back from the road to avoid injury." Without waiting for the heated reply he expected to come from them, he turned his horse in place, causing the rear of the animal to swing around forcefully, sending the nearest one in a quick retreat from the street and back onto the side of the road. The other man was pushed into the street and was left standing in the path of the oncoming horses pulling the wagon. He quickly and somewhat awkwardly ran to the other side of the road. James looked over at him.

"Please take more care next time, when crossing the street." He added and he kept his horse between the first man and the militia as they marched past.

The rest of the march through the city was relatively uneventful. When their column came to a halt in front of the dock area, the men initially stood at attention. Once the dust settled, they were ordered to stand at ease as they awaited further orders. The Colonel, the British Captain and James' father dismounted to meet with several other officials near the wharf area. While James rode around the militia to appear as if he was inspecting them, when in fact he was just trying to keep the growing number of citizens from approaching too closely to them. After he felt he had established the "no go" area, he dismounted and handed the reins to Mr. King who was still was sitting on the buckboard of the wagon.

"I'm guessing I won't be able to take my horse with me on this trip," James smiled as Elijah held the reins while James replaced the bridle with a halter and lead rope and tied it to the side of the wagon. Although he preferred riding a horse long distance to walking, the first few minutes after getting off a horse took some time to allow the knees to adjust.

About an hour after their arrival, a man dressed in a flowing white shirt, with a black jacket and black pants and boots was walking with James' father and they approached James and Bode. James' father smiled and stretched out his hand toward his son.

"Captain Ryan Donovan, may I introduce you to my son, Captain James Thornton and Lieutenant Bode King of the North Carolina Militia." James stepped forward to salute the Captain, but the smiling Captain Donovan instead offered his hand to James, who reached out and shook it.

"Captain Donovan, it is a pleasure," James said and Captain Donovan just stood and stared at James and smiled and then finally spoke.

"You're young for a Captain, but I see leadership in your eyes," he said out loud to no one in particular and then seemed to return to the moment. "Captain Thornton, the pleasure is all mine." In addition, he gave James' hand one more good shake before letting go and turning to introduce himself to Bode.

The captain seemed to hesitate as his eyes surveyed Bode. "Lieutenant King, Colonel Thornton speaks very highly of you. This must be as awkward for you as it is for me, but I'm happy to have you and your men traveling with my crew and me. I will do my best to ensure your safety and dignity." He then reached out his hand toward Bode. Bode nodded and grasped the Captain's hand returning the shake. James could hear the Irish accent coming from Captain Donovan, not too strong, but clearly evident.

"I appreciate your words and understanding Captain," Bode replied, which seemed to catch the Captain a little off guard. Captain Donovan held Bode's gaze a moment longer, then turned to survey the militia standing near the docks for several minutes before finally turning back toward James and Bode.

"Gentlemen, I have the pleasure of delivering you and your men to a beautiful island in the Caribbean on one of the fastest ships in the private fleet," he boasted and signaled with his hand toward the water and walked them toward the edge of the docks. The two bigger vessels were closer to the docks and the smaller one was behind them a little further out. James tried to follow the direction of his hand as the Captain continued offering the praises of his ship, and at first he was excited that it was one of the larger vessels. However, he soon realized from the Captain's description and the berating of the other two ships that his vessel was indeed the smaller one of the three. Knowing next to nothing about sailing vessels, James interrupted him and asked the obvious.

"What makes it the fastest in the fleet?" The Captain at first seemed hurt that he had not been allowed to finish his story.

"Water lines and sail, my young Captain." He smiled and then continued, "A bigger axe does not make for a better tool for cutting wood. Instead, it is the width and sharpness of the blade head and the amount of force that moves it forward. That is what allows it to split through any wood before it more effectively. It is the same for a fast ship." He pointed to the bow of his vessel, "See how sharp her bow is? It is designed to cut through the water, not push through it like the other two vessels must do with their wide bows." James could see his point, but he also saw the larger masts of the other vessels. Captain Donovan saw James' eyes surveying the masts, "Ahh! You think that more sail will remedy that problem? That is very observant of you." He again smiled at James, "But your thinking is flawed. Just like the man with the dull axe thinks he only needs to swing the axe harder to achieve the same results. It helps, but sharpening it works better." Captain Donovan then shrugged his shoulders, "Unfortunately, ships are not axes that can simply be re-sharpened once they have been built. What you see is old and new British philosophy anchored before you, the old with those two ships and the new with mine. They offer a false sense of security behind their guns and size, but they are often doomed in a race or when outnumbered."

James was not sure how to respond as he surveyed the three ships at anchor, for he preferred his men being on the bigger and heavier armed ships, but he granted acceptance to the concepts that the Captain was trying to convince him of. He once again thought about the size difference and then reality struck him.

"Is there actually enough room for my men and the supplies on your ship Captain?" James asked. Captain Donovan laughed and patted James on the shoulder.

"It will definitely be tight, and your men will have to take shifts in the sleeping cots, for they already have us with a full load of supplies." James frowned at the Captain's words. Once again reading his expression, the Captain replied. "Fortunately, it's a straight run to Martinique, so we will not have to suffer too long under such conditions." James winced at the thought of being packed in the hold like firewood in a shed and recalling Bode's story of the slave ships, "sounds wonderful," he commented wryly. The Captain once again laughed and slapped James on the shoulder as if he were an old friend.

"You'll be glad you are on my ship once we are out to sea my friend - you'll see - you will see." James wondered what he meant as the three of them walked back toward the waiting militia where his father and Elijah were standing and speaking to some of the men.

The next hour was spent covertly unloading the wagon and directing its contents into the waiting longboats of Captain Donovan. James could now see that it was baked goods, dried fruit and nuts, and a variety of salted meat from the plantation storage sheds. Captain Donovan was careful to keep the contents secret to avoid having to redistribute these few luxuries to the other two ships. Once the supplies were loaded, the men of the militia seemed eager to get aboard the waiting ship, but Captain Donovan kept telling them to treasure the solid feeling of the ground, for they would be on the water a long time, longer than they would desire.

During the loading of supplies, James' father had purchased all of the city's available bread and cheese. He even hired a local citizen to create a large cauldron of delicious beef stew for the men to eat prior to boarding the vessel. Potatoes, corn, beef, and peas were the mainstay of the stew and coupled with the bread and cheese, each man had enough to fill his kit cup twice. Captain Donovan, who had been invited, along with the longboat crews, to join them, was speaking with James' father. As James and Bode were walking up to them, they both overheard him say, "You know that there's a good chance that most of that meal will be in the ocean by the end of tomorrow morning?" James father and Elijah smiled and nodded.

"I hope most of it will have been digested by then, but either way we wanted them to have a great meal to remember before they start on sea rations." James and Bode looked down at the buttered bread they held and took another bite just as James' father turned to see them standing there listening in. He waved them over to join them.

"How bad does it get?" James asked his father as they stood alongside the men.

"Sea sickness?" he asked and James and Bode both nodded at the same time as they chewed their bread. His father turned to Captain Donovan who took a deep breath and exhaled as if thinking.

"Well, some have described it as repeated attempts over a several-day period to turn yourself inside out; others empty their stomachs and seem to be over it. Pray for the latter, but never fear, for although you feel as if you will, few die of it." Captain Donovan smiled and raised one eyebrow as he looked at the heavy butter James had spread across his bread.

The last of the stew and bread was consumed just before sunset and Captain Donovan issued orders for the men to form into groups of ten and climb aboard the longboats that would shuttle them to the waiting vessel. There were many handshakes, goodbyes and thank you's exchanged between the men and James' and Bode's fathers. Bode, after taking a long walk with his father, gave him a hug, then shook James' fathers hand, and boarded the first longboat heading to the ship. James supervised the loading of the final four longboats while standing near his father and Elijah. Elijah gave James a hug and said, "Take care of yourself James, and hurry home." James smiled and nodded.

"I'll be sure to take care of Bode," he said as Elijah stepped away to leave him and his father alone.

The two of them stared at each other for a long while before Colonel Thornton stepped forward and put his arms around his son.

"I'm so proud of you. Please be safe and know that we will be praying for all of you." He stepped back putting his hands on James' upper arms. James could only nod his head, but could not say anything because of the emotional lump that was stuck in his throat. His father then continued, "Be the good friend to Bode and your men that you always have been, no matter what the situation might be. They need you to be the conscience of the other officers if they are to get through this." James again nodded and managed to finally clear his throat.

"I know" was all he was able to get out. His father continued to hold onto him.

"I love you son." He finally said and then let go and stepped back.

"I love you too. Tell mother, Cynthia, Madison and Daniel how much I love them when you get home… and every day in case they forget." His father nodded and smiled; now his father seemed to be the one who was choked up.

James turned and stepped onto the last longboat that was waiting for him and glanced back to see his father and Elijah standing next to each other on the dock. The sun had set an hour ago, but the twilight that remained created a perfect silhouette of the two men that he would never forget. Although he could not see their faces, he smiled once more and without looking back he turned toward the direction of the awaiting ship.

Upon his arriving at the ship, James could see the militia walking all around the vessel like young children exploring a cave or building. There was much talking and laughter from the men as they would pop up from below decks and look over the railing at James and the final group of men arriving. Wearing a big smile, one of the men leaned over the rail and said to his friend sitting in the longboat next to James, "Willie, you ain't gunna believe this!" Then he laughed and disappeared behind the railing as two of Captain Donovan's crew reached over the side of the ship with two long poles, and pulled the longboat next to the ship, and holding it there. After passing their muskets to the waiting men, one by one they climbed the wooden ladder onto the deck of the ship. James was the last up the ladder and the first person he saw was Bode waiting for him. "Attention!" Bode yelled and every man stopped in place and saluted James as he stepped onto the deck of the vessel. James returned the salute to Bode and the men.

"At ease gentlemen." The overly formal interaction seemed awkward to James, but he knew the importance of it and played along. Bode smiled again.

"Welcome aboard Captain."

"Thank you Lieutenant King," James replied and saw that Captain Donovan was standing just behind Bode. "Captain, would you do me and my officers the honor of an official tour of your ship?" James asked and Captain Donovan bowed slightly.

"Most definitely." He proceeded to escort and describe to James, Bode and Robbie in great detail the various levels and rooms of the ship.

Over the course of the next hour, by lantern light, James learned that the ship was composed of three levels: the deck area; the gun and crew deck, which was one level down; and the hold, which was at the very bottom or keel of the ship. The hold was the largest area, but it also had very little room as it was packed clear to the ceilings with boxes, sacks, barrels and crates of various sizes. The crew deck had a much lower ceiling and required you to duck your head as you passed through certain areas. Toward the back of the ship, or the "stern" as Captain Donovan pointed out repeatedly, was where the kitchen and officers quarters were located. James, Bode and Robbie were escorted to a single small cabin that had three separate beds built onto the angled wall of the ships hull and two small compartments one larger than the other on the right side of the door and a single small table on the left side of the door of the cabin. Their three packs/kits had already been dropped onto the bottom bed, leaving the upper two open. They saw their three long rifle muskets leaning against the closets.

Captain Donovan stood at the doorway as the men surveyed their room. "I would suggest waiting until the morning light to get to know the main deck of the ship. It will also give you a chance to see my crew in action as we prepare to depart. If you would excuse me, I have some last minute preparations to address." He made to leave and then turned back, not with an 'I forgot to tell you' look, but with a look that said he had suddenly made a decision about something. "I would like to invite you and your officers to join me and my officers for a drink in my cabin later this evening if you are available?" James was surprised at the invitation, not that it was extended to him, but that Bode and Robbie were included. He glanced at his two friends who seemed to be waiting for him to give them a signal on how to answer. James looked back at the cabin and nodded his head.

"We would enjoy that very much, Captain. Thank you." Captain Donovan smiled and ducked under a beam and headed down a dark hallway toward the back of the ship.

The three of them, with the dim yellow-tinged light of their lantern, now hanging from a hook in the ceiling of their cabin, looked at each other and surveyed the small room that they shared. Bode broke the silence first. "Why don't we put Robbie on the top bunk, since he's smaller; I'll take the second from the top, and James, you can have the bottom one. Robbie and I can share a closet." Robbie grabbed his pack and started to put it into the smaller of the two closets. James interrupted his efforts.

"No, you two take the larger closet. If anything doesn't fit in yours, put it in mine. None of us has very much to worry about." Robbie looked to Bode for direction, who simply nodded and Robbie moved his pack and kit to the larger closet.

"I'm not sure if I'm more nervous or excited about all of this," James shared with his two friends. "This is all so crazy and is such unknown territory for me. I'm not sure how to view all of it," he shared openly with his friends. Bode and Robbie both nodded in agreement, but Bode responded first.

"I agree, but we need to keep our heads and discipline in front of the men and, maybe more importantly, in front of the crew of the ship if we are to keep things as... well, as positive as they currently are." Robbie nodded in agreement and tossed out what was also on his mind.

"Yeah, I'm not sure how to act tonight. Drinks with the Captain and his officers... that should be interesting."

James smiled but then seemed to get serious. "When you walk into that room, you need to know that you have every right to wear that uniform and to have that rank. Wear it proudly and confidently, or they will see through you and no longer respect you." Robbie seemed stunned at James' words, but then he nodded in agreement. James smiled and smacked him on the shoulder. He then turned to Bode. "You on the other hand, try to remember that you are NOT a General and act accordingly." He smiled and Bode gave one of those 'I'm not?' looks and they all laughed. They spent the next ten minutes putting the few items they had with them into their closets. They fashioned a double tie down that allowed their muskets to lean against the side of the closet without falling over or banging into each other. They tried to figure out if they should carry their pistols and cutlasses or leave them in their rooms. Based on the fact that Captain Donovan was not armed, they decided that leaving them in their room was the better thing to do.

As James was getting ready to visit the men on the crew deck, one of Captain Donovan's Lieutenants interrupted him in the hallway. "Captain Thornton." James turned to see the young man waiting for him with a held salute, which he returned so the man could continue. "Captain Donovan asked me to let you know that there has been a meeting called on the *HMS Ames* for the officers -" he hesitated, "um, just you, Captain," he ended the request, almost embarrassed by the correction. James had a good guess as to why it was just him.

"When is the meeting Lieutenant?" James asked the nervous man.

"Umm, right now, sir. The Captain would like you to meet him at the longboat launch when you are ready." James nodded and turned back to his cabin to gather his hat and jacket, and for on a hunch, he grabbed his cutlass. Robbie and Bode had heard the interaction in the hallway, so there was no need for James to explain. They just helped to gather his gear and make him as presentable as possible. They tried their best to straighten and smooth the material, then gave up and sent him on his way out the cabin door with a "good luck" from Robbie and a "don't forget to come back" from Bode. James nodded nervously and looked back at Bode. "That all depends on the size of the room they offer me." followed by a smile.

As James reached the main deck, he could see Captain Donovan waiting by the rail for him with two of his officers fully dressed. As James looked at the two junior officers, Captain Donovan read his thoughts.

"I'm sorry James; they made it quite clear that only you were requested." He motioned to the ladder down, "Shall we go and pretend to put up with them?" he said with a smile and James spun around and began to climb down the wooden ladder and into the longboat.

As they rowed over to the *HMS Ames*, James saw that Captain Donovan also wore his cutlass, but his men did not. *'At least I got one thing right'* James thought. As the longboat pulled next to the *HMS Ames*, even in the darkness, it was clear that it was a much larger vessel than Captain Donovan's ship, *The Dragon*. By the light of the lanterns hanging from rods over the deck, he could see that only a few people were waiting for him as he climbed the ladder to the deck. Seeing Captain Donovan behind him trying to maneuver up the ladder in his uniform, James was glad that his uniform was simpler and allowed for greater ease of movement compared to the British ones. James reached the deck and turned to see a corporal who was standing at attention with his hand held to the corner of his brow in salute.

"Welcome Captain Thornton," he barked and James returned his salute and stepped to the side so that Captain Donovan and his officers could gain access to the deck.

"Welcome Captain Donovan." The Captain returned the salute.

"Good to see you too, Jimmy." The young man seemed to glow with pride that Captain Donovan recognized him.

"Colonel Wentworth requests that you join him, and the other officers in Captain Joyce's cabin." Captain Donovan motioned for the corporal to lead them. "Follow me sirs," and the men fell into line behind the corporal, with Captain Donovan and his officers and James bringing up the rear.

As they wound their way down the stairs and into the lower deck, James could feel the difference in room and headspace with this vessel, although he still had to watch his head at times. As they approach a closed door at the end of a long hallway, James could hear talking and occasional laughter coming from the other side. The corporal knocked before entering and then stepped aside to allow the four men to enter behind him. Looking past Captain Donovan and his two men, he could see the heads in the room turn toward the door. Colonel Wentworth was the first to step forward. "John! It's good to see you; we thought you'd never make it." Captain Donovan shook the outstretched hand.

"It is good to see you again, Colonel," and then he turned to his two officers as each stepped into the room. "May I introduce you to Lieutenants Biggs and Peterson." The colonel stretched out his hand with less fervor than he had with the Captain and shook each man's hand. James was next in and it seemed to go quiet for a moment as nearly every eye in the room landed on him and surveyed his uniform. Colonel Wentworth broke the awkward moment.

"Welcome Captain Thornton." He said and then turned to the rest of the room, "Gentlemen, and to the majority of you that are not," there was a courtesy chuckle from most, "may I introduce you to Captain James Thornton, of the North Carolina Militia." In spite of his concerns, there seemed to be an actual kind and sincere tone to their hellos and welcomes and he was handed a tall glass of red port by a nearby lieutenant. The smell of alcohol was definitely strong in the room, most of which was coming from the Colonel's breath as he was speaking to James.

The Colonel seemed to have a need to continue his introduction. "In the midst of running one of the largest plantations in North Carolina, Captain Thornton has managed to train many of his slaves to not only march like British soldiers, but to fight like them, quite impressively I may add." There were some less than excited hurrahs and few "well done good man" from them as James nodded and smiled in appreciation as he leaned over to whisper into the Colonels ear.

"What workers?" The colonel seemed confused and shouted out loud to him.

"My men are not slaves Colonel; they are free men, hired workers." He at first was trying to say it somewhat quietly, but the noise in the room dropped quickly and it briefly sounded as if he were yelling. The colonel seemed confused and then James' statement jogged his memory.

"Right, right, they are "workers", not slaves - sorry dear boy." He mumbled the last part and winked at the other officers, who chuckled and either returned the wink or toasted him. James was definitely bothered by the interaction, but was not sure how to handle it correctly.

James glanced over to see Captain Donovan staring at him. When he saw that James had finally seen him, he motioned with his hand to stay calm and smiled. The group of men continued chatting for a few more minutes. Although several men had come up to him to talk, he could tell that it was more out of curiosity than camaraderie or even mutual respect. James noticed that the majority of the time they spoke, they were glancing at his uniform and the questions were never very deep in nature.

About fifteen minutes later, Colonel Wentworth called them to silence. "Gentlemen, since we are all now together and properly introduced, let's clarify our roles and plans before we sail out in the morning."

"Hear! Hear!" were the responses and everyone moved to take his assigned seat; James was surprised to see that there was even one saved for him. Not counting himself or the colonel, as he scooted his chair in and looked around the table he counted three naval captains, three army captains, and ten lieutenants.

"We have three vessels in our fleet: Captain Simmons's HMS *Ames*, Captain Clark's HMS *Bradford*, and Captain Donovan's British Fast Merchant, *The Dragon*. All are outstanding vessels and have outstanding crews." Colonel Wentworth glanced down at some notes that were on a sheet in front of him before continuing. "The *Ames* and the *Bradford* are carrying the much needed food supplies, along with powder and shot. The *Ames* will also carry the seventy British soldiers from the New York regiment, led by Captain Williams, and the *Bradford* will be carrying two forty-man contingents of British soldiers, one from Massachusetts led by Captain Kirkland and another from Virginia led by Captain Jameson." There were a few toasts lifted as the news was shared. The colonel continued as he glanced again at his notes. "Due to her faster speed and shallow draft, *The Dragon* is assigned the dangerous duty of carrying the majority of the powder, shot, muskets, and weapons for our new Fort in Martinique. She will also carry enough food for her crew and the fifty North Carolina Militia led by Captain Thornton, who have already boarded *The Dragon* earlier this evening." Again toasts were offered to the two captains. When James heard the contents of the Dragon's cargo they carried, he could not help thinking that they were sitting on a floating powder keg. He made a mental note to tell his men upon his return to stay out of the hold with any lanterns or tobacco pipes. Colonel Wentworth's voice brought his attention back to the meeting.

"At last report, the French Caribbean fleet had been driven off in a hard fought battle that, although a victory for us, proved very costly to both sides. Much of our fleet has departed for England to refit and resupply and await fresh troops for the final push in the fall. That means we will need to be as stealthy as possible to ensure that these supplies arrive." There were mumblings of agreement and acknowledgement, with Captain Simmons offering the lone voice suggesting that they just "finish the frogs off" should they run into the French along the way. There was growing vocal agreement from the other captains and officers in the room in response.

There was an excitement spreading through the men, even James felt excited about the thought of defeating the French in battle. James looked over at Captain Donovan and saw that he was the only one not voicing his agreement or even nodding or smiling, but instead, sitting silently as the voices and excitement continued to grow at the glorious thought of engaging the French. He finally interjected with a raised voice.

"How many here have engaged an enemy ship of the line before?" He looked around the room and no captain or officer raised his hand or confirmed his question. "I have," he finally stated. "That means just one Captain out of three knows what it's like, and he is captain of the weakest vessel." There was more silence in the room, but there were icy stares from Captain Simmons and his men directed at Captain Donovan as he continued, "Gentlemen, we are not a fleet of first, second or even third rate British ships. We are two sixth rate vessels and one that does not even land on the classification chart as a fighting vessel."

There were more mumblings as to how much better British training and ships were compared to the French vessels, before Captain Donovan continued. "Coming from one who knows, believe me when I tell you that we do not want to engage even a single French vessel who is above our rating. Their bigger guns will tear us apart before we can get close to them."

Over the increased grumbling of the officers, Captain Simmons voiced, out loud, the various tactics that were to be used to overcome such disadvantages and even used examples of British victories to support them. Captain Donovan raised his hand to quiet the growing rebuttals.

"I am not questioning the bravery of anyone here; I just do not wish to die as a result of someone's misplaced bravado," he continued without looking at Captain Simmons, "If we are forced to fight, we will fight and give a strong showing to the enemy, no matter what the odds might be. But as someone who has fought against evenly matched French ships of the line, and even Spanish warships from an armed merchant vessel, I must tell you that purposely engaging them is not wise. My advice is that unless we encounter French Frigates, who will be faster than the *Ames* and the *Bradford*, our advantage and success will be in the speed of our ships, not in our guns or our training. The supplies and the men we carry on our vessels are too important to have them sitting at the bottom of the sea or pressed into service by the French." There was silence by the time he finished and the earlier excitement was quelled. Bravado was suddenly absent from the room.

Colonel Wentworth finally broke the silence. "Captain Donovan offers some sound advice based on experience that we should heed. These supplies are extremely important, so our focus should be on delivering them to our forces on Martinique, not building our fighting resumes." He turned and nodded to Captain Donovan, "Captain, as the commanding officer of this fleet, I will be relying on your experience and wisdom to guide us in these matters." Captain Donovan nodded and raised his glass to the Colonel, but James could see that Captain Simmons was not happy with the leadership choice the colonel had just made. The meeting wound down quickly after the exchange and each group of officers began leaving to go and make final preparations for the departure in the morning.

As they headed back to *The Dragon* in the longboats, James could see that Captain Donovan was in deep thought and tried to cheer him up. "You may not have made any new friends back there, but I think you imparted some wisdom to a few of them." He could see Captain Donovan's smile and nod in the moonlight.

"A famous general once commented to an upstart prince that 'battle is only glorious to those that have never fought in one,'" he said softly but sternly. James thought about the quote and remembered the aftermath of the battle at the plantation. He knew the Captain was right. The memory that haunted him the most from those encounters was the wailing and distraught families of the dead men that had unwisely taken part in the attack on the plantation. They had come to gather their husband's or son's bodies for burial and their lives were forever changed.

"James, I believe you know what I mean." Captain Donovan's words brought him out of the reverie. "Do you know what I was looking for when we first met?" Captain Donovan asked him. James shook his head in the dark. "No." Captain Donovan smiled and thought for a while, gathering his words.

"I was looking for the eyes of battle in you. I look for them in every man that I meet. Your father has them." He suddenly chuckled, "Captain Simmons does not have them. He is brave and fearless, but he has no idea what it is truly like. When the time comes that he is required to face it, he will either rise to the occasion or panic." His next words seemed more somber as they poured out in the darkness, "James, I have learned that the eyes of battle have many looks to them and it is important to recognize those eyes before you go into battle with that man." The brief silence that followed had James thinking about what Captain Donovan saw in him, but before he could ask, Captain Donovan continued, "There are the eyes of deep sadness due to loss of dear friends. There are the eyes of confidence that comes from surviving a battle or being victorious in one. There are eyes of fear that have learned the extreme danger of battle. There are eyes of numbness that comes from seeing too much battle and death. And then there are eyes of hopelessness that have witnessed death in battle, assuming that they are next and stumbling toward it." James watched the captain turn and stare toward his waiting ship as the sound of the oars pulled them closer to it. He waited several strokes of the oar until the question burning in his mind was too strong to hold back. "So what did you see in my eyes?" he asked. The captain turned back toward James.

"A healthy combination of sadness, confidence and fear; which is the combination you want to find in a good soldier. You have not seen so much that you are numb to it, or convinced that you are destined to die from it. Keep that balance and your chances of keeping your men and yourself alive will increase dramatically." James somehow felt better, but also strange as he thought about it.

"James, don't dwell on it very long. Just know that I'm glad to have you and your men with me." The praise brought a warm reaction to James. Considering the whole interaction this evening with the other officers, he felt very happy that he was traveling with this Captain.

As they again boarded *The Dragon,* this time in the dark, Captain Donovan stopped at the stairs leading below deck and asked James, "I will see you and your officers in twenty minutes as planned?"

"Yes, sir." James said. He was surprised that they were going to have another meeting after the other one.

"I'll send one of my officers to escort you shortly." The captain said and he and his men turned and headed down the steps in the dark hull of the ship. James stood on the main deck in the darkness and saw that there were militia men sitting all over the ship, talking and laughing, or singing softly to themselves and anyone close enough to hear them. He took a moment to walk down the outside of the deck to speak to each man. A young worker named Billy was lying on his back on a crate and staring at the sky. James stopped to look up and saw the moon and stars, obscured in a few spots by the clouds floating through the sky.

"What are you thinking Billy?" he said without looking down from the sky. He could hear movement on the crate as Billy shifted around to see who was speaking.

"Hey Mr. Thor - Captain. I didn't see you standing there," he said and then shifted to look back at the sky before answering. "I guess I was wondering if the stars will look different in the area we are sailing too? I've kinda gotten used to them the way they are, sir, and I've never been that far from home." James nodded. "I've never been that far from home either, but I'm pretty sure the stars will be the same, just moved a little in the sky." James smiled and looked down at the deck and felt the sway of the ship from a swell that had managed to slide into the bay enough to touch the ship.

He gathered his feet beneath himself and headed toward the next group of men who were talking somewhat seriously while sitting on the heavy rail toward the bow of the ship. When they saw James coming toward them, they jumped down off the rail as if readying to salute, but James stopped them. "At ease men. No need for such formalities when it's just us."

"Yes sir." They both said at the same time and then smiled. James looked at both of them in the dim light of a nearby lantern.

"Is everything ok?" He asked them. They looked at each other for approval and then Jack answered.

"Were just a little concerned sir - when we get to our destination - just not sure how we will be treated." James started to say something but Jack interrupted, "We know you will do everything possible to make sure we are treated fairly, but if the rank above feels different, then things can change pretty fast." Spence interjected. "We just don't want to get stuck digging ditches or latrines, when there is fighting to be had." James was surprised that they felt more of a desire to fight than to play a support role for the British Army. Jack nodded in agreement. "We are trained and ready, James; we worked hard to be ready; don't let them take that away from us." James nodded at them.

"If it is in my power, I won't let them." He smiled and patted Jack on the shoulder.

As he looked around, he saw those men who had overheard the conversation he had just finished with Spence and Jack were all suddenly in agreement and wanting confirmation from him on that matter.

"Does everyone have his bunk location for tonight?" He called out across the deck and received a large number of "Yes sirs" from them. "Does anyone need anything?" James asked loudly enough for most of them to hear, which was followed quickly with many "No sir" answers from the majority of the men in earshot of him.

There was one response that was different. "More stew!" came from Tom Nance, who was one of the youngest men in the militia. James smiled as most of the men laughed at his request, "If my memory serves me correctly Mr. Nance, you ate twice as much as anyone else, and now you want more?" James asked in mock surprise at the young man. Several of the men chimed in and proceeded to expand upon James' observation with their own humor. As the ribbing settled down, James decided to quit while he was ahead, "Good night my friends!" he called out and heard many "good night" variations from them as he headed back to the stairs and entered the second deck area, feeling his way along the dark corridor to his room.

As he opened the door, Bode and Robbie were sitting in their bunks and cleaning their pistols. They both looked up. "Hey James," Bode tossed out quickly and spun his legs to hang off the side of the bed. James looked at the pistols in their hands.

"You two planning on staging a mutiny or something?" he asked jokingly. While Robbie chuckled, Bode just ignored James' humor. "One of Captain Donovan's men said that weapons rust quickly in the salt air, so to be sure to keep your weapons clean and oiled." He smiled down at James and continued, "I went ahead and also told the other men."

Robbie was always the energetic type and a stickler for details, so to have taken it upon himself to "pass the news" as it was gathered was not a big surprise. As James hung up his cutlass, he saw that his pistol and musket had been oiled and cleaned while he was gone. "Hey, thanks for the cleaning!" he said as he picked up his pistol and examined it.

The sudden knock on the door reminded James of the invitation and who was doing the knocking. "The Captain wants to keep his invitation to join him," James said, and reached over and opened the door. Sure enough, the young officer was standing there.

"Captain Thornton, Lieutenants King and Hanson, the Captain would like to know if you are ready to join him and his officers in his cabin?" Bode put his pistol down on his bed and stepped down onto the floor. Robbie slid off the upper bunk and they all reached for their jackets at about the same time in an effort to get ready. Robbie let Bode grab his first and looked around for a cloth to wipe the gun oil off of his hands. Not having the time to even remove his jacket, James stepped outside with the ship's officer to give Bode and Robbie more room to dress.

"Petty Officer Sanders? Is that correct?" James asked the young ship's officer.

"Yes sir." He replied somewhat nervously. James nodded and then explained, "I'm afraid their not being ready is my fault lieutenant, I did not head directly to my cabin when we arrived so they only learned about the reconfirmed meeting just as you knocked." The young officer smiled and nodded, but seemed unable to find the right words to respond.

First Bode and then Robbie stepped out of the cabin and they all followed the young officer to Captain Donovan's cabin. Their escort knocked once and the door was opened, flooding the dark hallway with bright light. "Gentlemen, come in!" Captain Donovan called and they stepped into the large cabin with a table in the middle of it. It was still a small room compared to home, but for the ship, the amount of room was impressive. Captain Donovan shook the hands of each man and reintroduced his officers to Bode and Robbie. Lieutenants Biggs and Peterson were standing just to his right and an older, but husky Midshipman named Richards was next, followed by the Chief Petty Officer Sanders.

During the next few hours, as they ate a light meal, they learned that Samuel Richards was the expert gunnery captain, "One of the best in the fleet" Captain Donovan professed. Captain Donovan explained to Bode and Robbie that *The Dragon* was known as a fast merchant vessel, armed with twelve cannons and was loaded with food supplies, powder, shot and weapons destined for the British fort in the Caribbean. He added that the quarters on the vessel would be very tight and cramped and the conditions would be trying at best and, if they encountered foul weather, horrendous. They had joined with two other vessels three days ago, who had been waiting for the arrival of the militia before departing on the final journey. The other vessels' crews had remained ashore until earlier that morning when word first came of the militia's arrival on the outskirts of town. Then they were quickly boarded, which was why they did not see any other troops in the city.

They learned that the port and fortress where they were heading was on an island called Martinique. The fortress they were going to man and resupply was recently wrestled away from the French after a lengthy blockade followed by a costly battle. The captain further informed them that sickness had proved to be an even greater enemy than the French, as more soldiers had lost their lives due to illness while waiting to disembark than in the actual battle. The fort had been re-supplied at that time with most goods, but the troop numbers left to defend it were low in number and naval protection was minimal. The majority of the fleet had returned to England in order to refit and bring back the additional troops that would be needed. The militia turned out to be a much needed, albeit a temporary, solution to a much larger, long-term problem for the British.

After one last toast, they excused themselves to their various cabins. Robbie and Bode both were too excited to sleep, and continued talking into the night. James, on the other hand, either from the numerous glasses of port, or the gentle swaying of the boat, could not keep his eyes open and soon dozed off to the sound of his two friends talking and laughing.

Chapter 7

The thumping sound above him and the shouts coming through the hull of the ship and through the door woke James with a start. Spinning in his bed, instinctively placed his feet on the floor of the cabin. He tried to get his bearings and leaned over to look out the small round glass window that was used for lighting for signs of trouble. Only the sight of a still distant dawn could be seen pushing its way into the sky, driving out the darkness. The cool breeze felt good as it crossed his face and filled the cabin. With the available flint, he relit the lantern in the cabin and slowly started to get dressed.

"What's happening?" Bode asked as he watched James get dressed.

"I think it's just the Captain getting his vessel ready to sail, but I'm going to visit the deck to make sure," James replied. "You're welcome to join me if you wish." James could tell that Bode was exhausted, but he also knew that he would not want to miss anything special, or have to hear about it later from James. Bode nodded as he swung his legs around, climbing down out of his bunk and onto James'. As they both dressed quickly, a steady banging sound started reverberating through the ship, coming from the bow area. They exited their cabin, both smiling as they saw that in spite of all the noise, Robbie had not made a sound or moved a muscle.

The two friends stepped out onto the deck, the growing light of dawn revealing a flurry of activity. Most of the militia had slept on the deck last night, and, while some were still trying to do so, many were now helping the various crewmembers to either pull rope, move items as they were directed, or just trying stay out of the way. The crew of *The Dragon* was scurrying about on the deck or climbing in the rigging above. James looked across the bay and saw little activity on the other two ships.

Standing on the deck, James realized that the banging noise that they had heard was the anchor chain slowly being pulled onto the ship and then being secured to the bow. The moment it broke the water, the bow of the ship began to turn slowly toward the mouth of the bay, almost as if the ship knew where it was suppose to go. James realized the gentle breeze coming from the west was causing the bow of the ship to spin around as the anchor in the stern held them in place.

"Captain Thornton and Lieutenant King!" The voice of Captain Donovan rang across the deck. "Good to see you up so bright and early. Sorry for the noise, I just hate to have some snobby 'admiral wannabe' beat me out of a mooring. We have orders to lead this fleet, so by the heavens, we will do exactly that." He smiled, as his men's actions seemed to gain speed at his words. "Prepare to drop the jibs and the staysails on my order Mr. Biggs. Mr. Peterson, prepare to hoist the stern anchor." Captain Donovan walked to the center cargo hold port and called down the hatch. "Mr. Richards!"

"Aye Captain!" A voice responded from below.

"I would like to have a cannon blast from our starboard side announce a "good morning" to each of our partner ships as we pass them by on our exit." He started to walk away, and then turned back to clarify. "No shot Mr. Richards, just noise." Captain Donovan clarified his order with a smile.

"Aye. Guns two and three on the starboard side will be ready and waiting for your orders." The voice responded from the depths of the ship almost sounding disappointed. James noticed that most of the crew that he could see in the fading darkness was smiling at the exchange as Captain Donovan walked back to where James and Bode stood.

"Nothing like the roar a cannon fired off your port side to get the heart beating and wake the mind from its slumber." He smiled and patted Bode on the shoulder as he passed by. "Mr. Peterson!" he roared and nodded to where Lieutenant Peterson stood waiting. He in turn, nodded toward the men surrounding the capstan before them. They slowly began to turn the massive winch. One man called time to keep rhythm, coordinating their movement as the four men pushed against the crossbar. The clacking sound of the ratchet and the same thumping sound that James had heard earlier began echoing through the ship as the chain links came through the deck opening and then disappeared into the belly of the ship. James felt the ship move backwards as it was pulled toward where the anchor rested on the floor of the bay, and then it slowly stopped the backward movement as the anchor broke free from the bottom.

Captain Donovan then nodded to Lieutenant Biggs who then barked an order to the men aloft in the rigging. "Staysails and jibs! Quickly now!" The crew in the rigging suddenly released the lines and unfurled what seemed like oceans of white sail and the slight breeze that James had felt earlier began to dance across the cloth until they were one by one pulled tight. James watched in fascination as the sails became rounded masses that no longer danced about, but stayed firm and solid as if you could walk across them. James could feel his body shift from the gradual movement of the ship as it was being pushed along by the gentle breeze. The unfamiliar creaks and groans of wood and rope pulling against one another at first had James concerned, that something was going to break any moment, but he soon realized that it was just the ship talking and letting those who were traveling on her know that she was responding to their direction.

"Mr. Sanders, kindly take us thirty yards past our friend's port side as we depart, avoiding any fowling of our rigging with theirs if you would." Captain Donovan walked toward the elevated stern deck where Mr. Sanders was standing next to the wheel of the ship.

"Aye sir." Mr. Sanders replied and corrected his course as instructed.

"Mr. Richards!"

"Aye Captain, starboard guns two and three are ready." The distant response came from the bowels of the ship.

The ship gradually gained speed as *The Dragon* closed the distance with the two much bigger ships moored between it and the entrance of the bay. They were big and beautiful as the growing light of dawn shed its light on them.

As *The Dragon* approached the port side of the *HMS Bradford*, James could see there were only a few crewman scurrying about amidst the still sleeping British and Virginia troops who had chosen to spend the night on the cooler deck of the vessel instead of below. As *The Dragon* came alongside of the *Bradford*, Captain Donovan yelled below.

"Say good morning Mr. Richards!"

A loud "BOOM!" sounded across the water and echoed around the bay. James felt the concussion of the cannon through the decking of the ship and watched as smoke rolled out of the starboard side of the ship. The majority of the men sleeping on the deck of the *Bradford* jumped to their feet, sat up in shock, or fell onto the deck from where they were lying. A loud cheer echoed from the crew of *The Dragon* as they passed by the port side and headed toward the *HMS Ames*. Watching the stunned and shocked faces as they stumbled around trying to figure out where the enemy was, Bode and James could not suppress a chuckle. Curses could be heard across the water, which only confirm the effect of the surprise and made the crew cheer even louder. Although the total surprise factor was no longer there, they gave the same "good morning" cannon blast and cheer as they passed the port side of the *HMS Ames*. They could see Captain Simmons, partially dressed standing on the stern of his vessel acting as if he were in complete control of the situation and were ordering his men as needed. James could see through the charade that there was total chaos on the deck, no sense of control or organization in the momentary panic.

"We will see you and the *Bradford* at the entrance of the bay in an hour at high tide Captain Simmons!" Captain Donovan yelled across the close expanse pointing toward the bay entrance. Captain Simmons nodded and barked a few more orders to his men. James smiled again as he saw Colonel Wentworth stumble out from his cabin below, partially dressed and onto the deck to see what all the cannon fire was about.

"Good morning Colonel!" Captain Donovan yelled and waved. The colonel nodded back and quickly headed back inside.

An older man stepped out from the stairs leading up from the lower decks and called to the Captain. "Your plans for breakfast sir?" Captain Donovan looked around at the various members of the crew and the militia now pouring out onto the deck from below to see what was unfolding. Captain Donovan did not respond immediately, but instead watched the growing swells of the ocean as they headed toward the bay entrance and the rolling and swaying of the ship. He looked at James and Bode, who were both trying to hold onto the railing near them and then answered the older man.

"No sense in wasting good food, Mr. Jensen. Let's let them all get their sea legs and stomachs before we feed them too much. Maybe some bread for the sailors?" The older man looked around and smiled, then nodded and waved as he returned down the stairs and into the belly of the ship.

As *The Dragon* headed further and further out of the bay and into the open ocean, Captain Donovan called for more sail and speed. James was amazed by the power and beauty of the sailing ship and the way that the crew danced through the rigging and across the decks as each order was given. As they broke from the entrance and into the open ocean, the gentle swells turned into what felt like deep ravines and mountains. The gentle rocking of the deck gave way to steep rolling and it became extremely difficult to maintain balance when walking across the deck. James saw that the crew of *The Dragon* moved up and down and across the deck without hesitation, whereas the men of the militia were stumbling, falling or holding on for dear life.

James watched as more of his men went below decks, only to come back out a short time later with a completely different look on their faces. Within an hour, there were many of his men at the railings emptying their stomachs. Some failed to make it to the railing and spewed their contents onto the deck of the ship, where the stench would drift around as the wind carried it, adding to the sickness of the rest of the men. Members of the crew would take a bucket or two of seawater and splash the floor near the mess, causing it to wash over the edge of the railings and into the ocean. Between the smell, the sound of his men hurling, and the continued rolling of the ship, James' stomach was also groaning and he thought about going below to lie on his bunk, but Captain Donovan, as if reading his mind, shared a little wisdom with him.

"Keep your eyes on the horizon, not on the deck. Let the wind blow across your face and learn to feel the movement of the ship and to counter it with the weight of your body. It will take a little time, but eventually your body and mind will adjust, or hopefully it will. That is unless you want to get the whole 'emptying of the stomach' thing over much quicker. Going below will speed it along."

After clearing the entrance to the bay they sailed north for about thirty minutes. Orders were given and sailors scrambled across the rigging and they turned the ship south and headed back toward the entrance of the bay that they had left. The sun was above the water and so much more came into view as they watched the coastline pass to their right. James could see the masts of the *Ames* and the *Bradford* coming out of the bay entrance, and in perfect timing they joined the other ships and continued sailing south with *The Dragon* leading the way.

For the rest of the day, as they would for the rest of the week, the three-ship fleet hugged the coastline as they sailed south. James managed to hold down the contents of his stomach until that evening, when he finally went below decks to his cabin. The fact that most of the crew either had been or was in a similar situation, when his turn at the railing came there were few who felt the need to comment on it. Bode was seasick too, while Robbie seemed immune. He slept the day and evening away as he and Bode took turns visiting the railing. It was not until the start of the third day that the motion sickness began to fade and James was able to hold down a solid meal. Only Bode and a few others continued to fight the sickness for another three days before it finally subsided enough for them to eat something substantial.

Those first few days James spent the majority of the time on deck watching the crew work, listening to the Captain and his Lieutenants give orders and observing how the crew responded. He continually asked a great number of questions of the Captain and the crew in an effort to understand what was happening around him. Captain Donovan seemed to appreciate James' interest and began explaining things before he would give the order, and would tell a story that would somehow relate to it. James learned to see the beauty of sailing and the majesty and power of the wind and the waves. He watched as the water began to gradually change from the darker blue to a lighter blue.

Several other ships could be seen in the distance as they sailed along, but they all seemed to turn away from them as they approached. Captain Donovan would explain to James the type of ship they were, identifying them based on the mast and sail configuration. Two of the ships were merchant vessels and posed no threat to them, one could have been a small pirate or raiding ship, but it was clearly no match for their three vessels.

By the end of the week, Captain Donovan announced that they were off the tip of Florida and would be heading southeast into open and more dangerous waters as they crossed the shipping lanes to reach the islands. He pointed out that the chances of encountering more vessels, enemy included, would jump dramatically from here forward as they traveled in these shipping lanes. The crew seemed to understand and watches and lookouts were doubled. Signals via flags were sent to the ships that followed them, urging them to put on more sail and to trim the sails that were up for maximum effect. Captain Donovan seemed to read the invisible wind and currents innately as they navigated away from the sight of land and into the deeper ocean.

James was learning enough about sails and sailing that he noticed something that seemed odd and asked the Captain about it. "Why are we not putting up full sail?" Captain Donovan smiled at James' awareness.

"Because our ship is much faster than theirs and we would leave them behind if we did. Also I don't want to overwork my crew tacking back and forth to cover the same ocean. Rest assured if I see any sails on the horizon, we'll put up full sail."

James and Bode built a great friendship with the captain and befriended the 150 crew members of the merchant vessel. Both of them were determined to learn as much as they could about sailing and navigation, as well as the background of Captain Donovan. The captain was a former British privateer and he shared many captivating stories during dinner and on watch about his many adventures and actions in the Caribbean in his youth. He knew the waters well and preferred a fast ship with fewer guns to a slower, larger vessel that was armed to the teeth. The other two ships were of the latter style (more room, but slow). James could see that Captain Donovan in his frustration was constantly cutting sail to allow their slower companions to keep up with them. He listened as Mr. Sanders cursed the ships following them for their poor sail trim and sail choices.

"Their taking the lazy man's path to sailing - get us all killed, they will." He mumbled to no one in particular.

The next several days they watched dolphin dance in their bow waves, flying fish skim across the water, and spotted large sharks off the port and starboard sides. It was a different world out on the water, a world that Captain Donovan loved and James was growing fond of. Unfortunately, with the good came the bad, as the heat and humidity were overwhelming during the day and if it were not for the breeze rushing through the open door and hallways during sail, their cabin would resemble an oven more than a room. There were days when the wind would barely push the ships along, and then days when the sails were trimmed way back, as if they were trying to keep the spars and masts from breaking. James found life on the sea to be strange but exciting.

It was early morning on the twelfth day after leaving the mainland behind, that an alarm was sounded and all hands went on high alert and full stations. As James and Bode stepped onto the deck they could see Captain Donovan looking through a telescope on the port side of the ship toward the east. James could see that the "enemy in sight" flag was already waving for the other two boats to take warning and appropriate action.

As James and Bode climbed the stairs to the aft deck where Captain Donovan was standing, the Captain lowered the telescope and turned to speak to a sailor behind him.

"Four French ships of war. Put up full sail." The young sailor dug through his box to find the various flags he needed and then strung them together and hoisted them aloft. "Maybe they will finally start sailing to their full potential," Captain Donovan chuckled as James turned to look toward the east and saw the barely visible white sails far off in the distance. "Nothing to worry about at this time, as the wind does not favor them and it does favor us. We should be able to pass far west of them before they can use the wind, although they will be behind us," he added as an afterthought.

"What kind of ships are they?" James asked after a few minutes.

"Hard to tell for sure at this distance, but I would guess third to fifth rate French ships. All of which are far more than we want to engage, nor allow to get closer to find out more." He smiled back at James. He seemed to hesitate at first, but then continued. "My only concern is that they are spread far apart, which often means they are trying to cover a great deal of ocean, as opposed to staying in tight formation."

"How is that bad for us?" James asked. Captain Donovan took a moment before answering.

"It means they are in the hunting mode, not defensive mode. It could mean that they are expecting us." James hesitated, trying to frame another question. The Captain somehow saw it coming and answered before the question was asked.

"The fort only has two sources for supplies James: England and the colonies. The colonies are the closest, so they would expect help would come from there first and they would build a plan to thwart that first." He turned to Mr. Sanders at the wheel. "Two degrees more to starboard."

"Aye Captain." Mr. Sanders replied and adjusted the wheel.

"If it were just our ship and the supplies, were not so urgent, I'd angle us to the west and beat it out of here. Unfortunately, we do not have the time, the speed, or the supplies to make such an escape. Our only course at this time is to push south and hope we are not entering a trap."

As the day progressed, the four ships slowly angled toward them just as Captain Donovan expected. Two vessels stayed to their northeast, while the other two were angling to pass behind them. Although they were many miles away, the angle closed the distance from where they were first seen. They still seemed so far off to James, but he knew they were on the same wind direction now and the distance between them was a matter of which vessels were faster.

As night brought darkness, Captain Donovan ordered the lights on all three ships doused except for a dim low hanging stern light on their vessel for their other two ships to follow. He changed course to angle away from the pursuers and gain the wind advantage. When morning came, they saw that they had succeeded in putting the pursuers in disadvantaged wind, but the pursuing ships had quickly adjusted their courses and once again they were closing the distance. It was clear that the French ships knew the destination of the English vessels, for two of the ships began to take up a position to their northwest flank. Captain Donovan told them that they were two days out from their destination, and at the rate they were sailing, they should be able to make port before their pursuers could catch them.

"If we cannot make the port, two of our three vessels are doomed, maybe all three." He said quietly.

The next morning found the four French vessels closer than before and there was a flurry of orders and suggestions being submitted by the other ships as the concern for their situation grew. Ideas that ranged from "Have one ship turn and fight to buy more time for the others" to "try to close and board the other ships using the extra fighting men that were on board the various vessels". Captain Donovan put a squash to all of them, stating over and over to stay together and sail for the port, or fight through to it if necessary.

Just as Captain Donovan felt that they would be able to make it to port before their pursuers, three separate sails could be seen to the south between them and the island. As they continued on course toward them, the distanced quickly shrank, indicating that those ships were either anchored or sailing toward them. Captain Donovan continued using his telescope to survey the three ships in front of them and the four behind them. He observed that one was a second rate French ship with eighty guns; the other two were French Fast Frigates carrying thirty-six guns. The second rate vessel was holding the middle, while the two frigates were each holding the outside edges of the port entrance. He also noted that they only had enough sail up to maneuver in order to better their firing lines as needed.

Through flag signals, Captain Donovan made it clear once again to everyone on the three ships that their only option was to stay together. They would not get through unscathed, or perhaps at all, but their best and only chance was to force through the line on the port side at full sail, pray that they make it past the initial broadside and keep sailing through to the entrance of the port and inside the safety of the fort's shore batteries. Based on the constant signals coming from Captain Simmons on the *HMS Ames*, Captain Donovan knew that the Captain was second-guessing his orders. James was ordered to prepare his men to fire at any enemy vessel that was within range of their muskets and to fight off any enemies trying to board their vessel. James had them in full uniform and ready as they closed in on the port and the enemy before them.

The Dragon was carrying mass amounts of gunpowder and a massive full broadside from any of the French ships would likely detonate it. Accordingly, Captain Donovan directed the *HMS Ames* to take the lead position, followed by the *HMS Bradford* and then *The Dragon*. As the port came into view behind the three opposing vessels, he could see what appeared to be a small British fleet of two vessels anchored inside the gun-protected harbor. The good news was that it was evident that the island fort still belonged to the British; the bad news was that the British vessels would not be any assistance until the three incoming ships were inside the harbor.

As they approached the three massive French vessels in front of them, Captain Donovan's greatest concern was realized as he watched Captain Simmons go against the orders and the agreed plan. Instead of cutting between the Frigate and the second rate ship to the north, he instead turned his ship to engage the Frigate to the south; Captain Clark turned the *HMS Bradford* and followed.

"You fool. You have given up our wind and prevented us from entering the port." Captain Donovan said coldly and could only watch as the two slow vessels in front of him sailed into the enemy's guns. "Full sail Mr. Peterson!" Captain Donovan yelled and the crew reacted on cue as more sail was dropped from above and lashed down. James could feel the vessel pull forward under the additional sail. Captain Donovan seemed to be scanning the enemy vessels looking for an opportunity or a mistake that would allow him to save *The Dragon* from the same deadly trap into which the other two ships had sailed. Fortunately, for the crew of *The Dragon*, such an opportunity presented itself.

The French frigate turned to block the escape of the British vessels and keep them inside the trap, but in doing so, lost the speed of the wind position. As if on command, Captain Simmons turned the *HMS Ames* back toward the port and the waiting broadside of the second rate ship and the French frigate's guns. The wait provoked a horrible feeling, a knowing that the guns would fire at any second and cause damage to the British vessel whose guns, few as they were, were not in position to fire due to the angle of the vessel trying to slip past. As the *Ames* came into the waiting broadside barrage, the roar of the French cannons was followed almost instantly by the sound of timber being torn apart and the screams of dying men drifted across the expanse. James watched, as the *Ames* came apart as the cannon shot from the French broadside passed through and out the other side of the *Ames*. Seconds later the main mast fell to the starboard side and into the water. He was stunned by the destruction that the cannon balls caused to the British vessel. He knew that few could survive such a massive onslaught and was horrified at the thought of their own vessel passing under those guns.

To James' surprise, the waiting French frigate did not fire at the *Ames*, but instead waited for The *Bradford* to come into its range. The *Bradford* was in the process of trying to pass as close to the Ames as possible to keep the second rate vessel between them and to gain as much distance as possible from the frigate. In doing so the Bradford crew did not plan on the mast of the *Ames* falling in front of them. The ship became entangled in the fallen mast and its rigging and the vessel lurched as it came alongside and fixed to the *Ames*. The two disabled British ships and the three French ships now completely blocked off the entrance to the port. Captain Donovan sighed heavily at the sight before him and knew the battle was over.

"Hard to starboard Mr. Sanders! There is no room left for us to sail past." He glanced over his shoulder toward the four French vessels behind him, then to the carnage before him and finally, back to the French frigate to their port side. "Let's try to live to fight another day. We can do nothing but die with these other ships if we stay." James watched as *The Dragon* suddenly angled sharply to the south and in line with the bow of the frigate that was still waiting to fire on the *Bradford*.

"You can't have us both!" Captain Donovan yelled to the French captain across the water. As if on cue, the French vessel fired on the *Bradford*. Although the effects were not as devastating, it was clear that the words Captain Donovan had shared with the other British captains, about the destructive power of a warship, were true. Their ships were no match for a French ship of the line. The *Bradford's* guns returned fire and a cheer went up from the crew and men on *The Dragon*, but as the smoke cleared, the cheers faded, as the volley seemed to have little effect on the French vessel.

As *The Dragon* turned toward the open water, James could see that the other French frigate was putting on sail and the second rate vessel was moving to come across the bows of what remained of the *Ames* and the entangled *Bradford*. When James glanced back at the other frigate, he saw that the sails were still flapping as the vessel tried to come around into a more favorable wind. Captain Donovan stepped to the railing on the port side and watched the French frigate, currently 200 yards away. At this speed they would narrowly miss the bow of the enemy ship.

"Mr. Richards!" Captain Donovan yelled.

"Aye Captain!" came the response from below.

"As we come to bear on the Frigate, fire into the upper decks." James could hear the movement and activity below the decks, as the pre-loaded guns were being primed and re-positioned to fire. James watched as the sailors on the other ship were climbing about the rigging as if trying to coax the vessel to take on more wind. Then James realized that it was time to act and stepped to the center railing.

"North Carolina Militia, to the rail and fire at will at any and every target in sight and range." James yelled and watched as either the men moved to the railing, or those on the railing raised their muskets and took aim. Captain Donovan nodded and smiled.

"The sailors are our greatest concern." He said to James.

James realized that without their sailors, they would have a harder time putting on sail. He turned to his men. "Aim for those in the masts!" James called out the order and saw several men adjust their aim.

At about one 125 yards out, several musket shots were fired from the deck area as the North Carolina militia's long rifles came into range. Each soldier immediately stepped back, began reloading as another stepped forward, and took aim. James was proud of their courage in spite of the situation before them. The musket fire became heavier as they approached the bow of the French ship and several sailors on the frigate fell from their high positions to the deck below. The death of their crewmates and the unceasing sound of musket fire sent the French crew diving for what cover they could find. As *The Dragon* passed in front of the bow of the frigate, one by one her cannons below fired. Although damage could be seen as the metal balls passed through the French ships sails, the vessel remained unscathed.

"Too bad we had preloaded the cannon balls instead of chain shot," Captain Donovan mumbled, "or the damage would have been much greater."

The men of the militia, moving aft, continued to fire as they gradually moved further and further away from the frigate until they were out of range. The frigate they had fired upon was slowly turning with the wind and the sails were coming to life. The other frigate had put on full sail and was coming around the back of the *Ames* and *Bradford*, while the second rate was now broadside to the front of both ships.

"Don't be a fool, Clark. Strike your colors," James heard Captain Donovan mumble as he glanced back at the scene unfolding. *Was there anyone who remained alive on the Ames that could have performed such a duty*, James wondered. Moments later, the Union Jack was being lowered from the *Bradford* and the doom of the pending broadside barrage was avoided.

Captain Donovan glanced at James and shook his head. "They were doomed the moment they broke line." He yelled out to his men, "Take note, a lack of discipline will kill you every time! Trim that sail Mr. Baker." James had heard his father repeat those initial words many times.

"What will happen to the crew and men of the *Ames* and *Bradford*?" James asked Captain Donovan as he continued to survey the various vessels pursuing them and barked orders as needed. He finally stopped long enough to answer.

"Those that do not die of their wounds will have a very uncomfortable time in the hold of the ship until they are transferred to a prison ship, moved to a shore prison, or ransomed. That is the fate of the officers and soldiers on board this vessel. The sailing crew will either join or have a worse go of it in a prison," Captain Donovan said in a rather distant voice and then turned toward James. "A slightly better fate than death, I'm told." He smiled ever so slightly.

The initial wind advantage and the fact that they were under full sail long before the following ships, enabled *The Dragon* to put several thousand yards between it and the two vessels that were chasing them. It seemed as if they were going to pull away and leave them initially, but soon then the two frigates seemed to match their speed and settled in behind them. James would glance up at their sails and then back to the frigates. Captain Donovan once again read James' mind. "They are fast frigates James. Although we are more maneuverable, we cannot outrun them. The one further behind the other will eventually replace their damaged sails and catch back up." James nodded. "Should I prepare my men to prevent boarding?" The merchant captain turned and smiled. "The only way they will get within gun range of us now is if I make a dreadful error, which I rarely do. We will have a very difficult time shaking two of them, so depending upon their persistence, we might be in for a very long chase."

His words proved true as they spent the next two weeks playing cat and mouse with the two frigates. After the first week, they had to go to half rations as their supplies were dwindling. The two frigates took up positions far apart on *The Dragon's* stern that made slipping away difficult. The weak wind also made cutting away in the dark nearly impossible, and morning light would find them within sight once again or closer to their pursuers. James noticed that they had swung past the same series of islands to the far south of them twice before heading north again. Twice they performed this maneuver, each time following the same track, which seemed strange to James. When he asked Captain Donovan about it, he simply smiled. "All in good time my friend."

By the end of the second week, supplies were running very low. Because the fleet commander wanted to make sure the powder and guns had the best chance of 'getting away' should they be engaged at sea, they had put them on the faster ship, which meant there was plenty of powder and guns, but it left very little room for food supplies. Captain Donovan calculated that they had less than 1 week left on the bare bones rations the men were currently allotted.

"Today we will either succeed or fail in our plan to escape these annoying French vessels," he said to James as the sun was beginning to break free of the horizon in front of them. As always, the French vessels were shadowing him on his flanks and the early morning found the sun positioned directly in their faces. Breaking from his normal routine, Captain Donovan ordered "hard to the starboard" as if to escape the one vessel as they approached a small island to their east. James saw that the French vessel was closing quickly as he took advantage of the angle *The Dragon* was taking and was closing within gun range. There was a frantic movement of men on the French vessel, as they seemed to also realize the opportunity that was at hand. Guns were being run out and prepared to fire on the British ship.

The Dragon had a better firing angle, which brought their guns to bear on the French vessel, but James knew that they were too far out to reach them.

"Let's keep their attention on us Mr. Richards. Give me a staggered broadside," he yelled below.

"Aye Captain!"

First one, then two, then each of the successive six cannons on the starboard side were fired. All the shot fell just short of the French vessel, whose crews could be seen cheering and jeering at their failure. The early morning sun lit the enemy vessel in such a powerful way that it was a most awesome sight to see the sails and crew in such bright detail. The angle was closing and both crews knew the moment was almost at hand. James could not figure out why they were not turning away again from the vessel and turned to ask the captain, who simply held up his hand.

"Just wait Mr. Thornton, we have a surprise waiting for them." As if on cue, the French vessels suddenly jolted and careened at an odd angle and the bow of the French vessel came up out of the water as it climbed onto a hidden reef just below the surface. The sound of timber grinding against stone, ropes snapping and creaking, and even the groans of men could be heard as it was carried by the wind to their ship, all of which were soon drowned out by the cheers of the men on *The Dragon*.

"Such a beautiful vessel. It always helps to know the waters better than your opponents, Mr. Thornton." He patted the young Captain on the shoulder and turned to listen to the cheers of his men. "The second Captain won't be as gullible; he sails with much more experience."

The second French frigate at first continued the chase, but to Captain Donovan's surprise, it turned back to assist its fellow vessel. The cheers went up across their ship as the Dragon left the frigates behind. The Captain turned toward James and said, "Let's go buy some supplies so we can feed this rabble of a crew." More cheers rang out from the crew and militia. "Mr. Sanders, let's pay a visit to the Dutch harbor of Christiansted on St. Croix. Plot a course that will take us there at the earliest opportunity."

"Aye Captain," Mr. Sanders replied and began looking at charts and adjusting the direction of the ship.

"How far away is St. Croix?" James asked the Captain, knowing that supplies were very low.

"About 4 days sail from here." He went on to explain that because the Dutch were neutral, they would sell them the supplies they needed, though he really hated dealing with them.

Chapter 8

It was amazing how quickly an enemy could change. One day it was the French frigates, now the threat they posed was the furthest thing from their minds; their new enemy was hunger. They dragged a very small net behind the boat and managed to catch a few flying fish and one strange shaped fish that were added to the watery soup for flavor. Other than that, the food rations had been exhausted.

It was exactly four days later when the sight of the island that they were aiming for was seen on the horizon.

"St. Croix! And supplies," Captain Donovan yelled the first part and softly spoke the second as he scanned the horizon for signs of sails and was happy to note that none were present. As they approached the port city, Captain Donovan also noted that there were two small merchant vessels anchored inside the harbor to the west.

"Nothing we need to fear or worry about," Captain Donovan said with a smile as he used his telescope to survey the fort and the flag flying above it.

"Captain Thornton, I will be sending you and a few men in with a list of supplies that I would like to see purchased for the ships stores. Mr. Sanders will see to it that you have enough coin to get our basic needs covered. If need be, feel free to negotiate the exchange of powder or shot for additional supplies," he said to James and patted him on the back.

"You're not going?" James replied. Captain Donovan smiled and shook his head, "I'm afraid I do not have the best reputation with the Dutch. My history is a little tainted and although they would not recognize my ship, they might recognize my name. So I would suggest not mentioning it," he said as he turned to Mr. Sanders at the wheel.

"Anchor us just outside the range of their 32 pounders, Mr. Sanders, with our bow facing with the wind exiting the port."

"Aye Captain."

"Captain Thornton will signal us when it is safe to enter the Gallows Bay harbor for the supplies."

They immediately ran up their proper flags requesting safe entrance into the harbor for supplies and a counter flag was raised in response. They fired one cannon to announce their presence and the fort fired a single cannon in response, acknowledging them. The sails were reduced and *The Dragon* slowly worked its way through the channel entrance, past the dangerous coral heads and into the protected area behind the reef. Captain Donovan guided his vessel masterfully and dropped anchor north of the fort. The sky was clear and the temperature rose as the ship sat motionless in the harbor.

As the crew scurried around to tie off the sails and lower the ship's boat into the water, James could see how the lack of food had affected everyone. Whether sailor, militiaman or officer, they were all lethargic and thin in appearance. As he looked at the town of

Christiansted, he could see the main fort, as the prominent landmark, sitting in front of the town. Built with yellow bricks, it was very obvious, as were its size and strength. Captain Donovan also pointed to two smaller side forts that were positioned on the island cay in the harbor to the west and on a point that overlooked the entrance into Gallows Bay from the east. The city itself sat at the base of a series of low rolling hills that seemed to flow down to it, with the reef and bay protecting the approach from the sea. The white buildings behind the fort could be seen, several of them two and three stories high. It was a beautiful city and fort, well protected.

"This is the headquarters of the Dutch East India Trading Company, where sugar and spirits rule the trade items," Captain Donovan said and the crew hooted at the word "spirits" and ribbed each other.

"Aye, if you would be so kind as to go real heavy on the spirits negotiations for us, Captain Thornton," someone from below deck shouted up at them and more laughter could be heard from the various parts of the ship.

"Any preference?" he asked.

"RUM!" they all shouted in unison, which caused James to laugh and shake his head.

"Rum it is," he replied as he carefully stepped down the ladder and into the waiting longboat, where Bode and six of Captain Donovan's men waited at the oars.

James and Bode were dressed in full uniform and wore their pistols and swords at their sides. Captain Donovan felt is was best that they not bring their muskets. The men began to row the longboat to the fort and then angled toward the wharf that could be seen to the west of it. James could see the heads of the soldiers looking down from the main fort and from the two side forts as they rowed into range of their guns. As they passed near the eastern most of the two forts, James and Bode could both see that the guns mounted on the ramparts of the two smaller forts were not 18 pounders as Captain Donovan had remembered, but 32 pounders. Of even more concern was, as they passed by the front of the main fort, they could see that the guns stationed there were 48 pounders, not 32 pounders. He glanced back at *The Dragon*, estimated its distance from the three forts, and realized that *The Dragon* would be within range of all three should the Dutch gun crews decide to fire on them. He debated turning around to warn the Captain, but knowing the Dutch were neutral, there should be no danger.

As they approached the wharf, a group of ten Dutch soldiers and one Captain were waiting with muskets at the ready. James nodded and then saluted the lead officer, who was medium height and build. He had blond hair and his uniform was rather extravagant for the heat of the day. "Captain, I'm Captain James Thornton and this is Lieutenant Bode King of the North Carolina militia. We are requesting to purchase supplies for our vessel and crew of *The Dragon*." James stated as he held his salute. The Dutch officer walked around the longboat and then stopped in front of Bode and proceeded to look him up and down.

"What kind of supplies are you needing, Captain." The officer finally answered with a heavy accent without returning the salute. James lowered his salute.

"Food, water and if possible, rum for the crew," James replied as the officer continued to look at his and Bode's uniforms.

"North Carolina Militia. From the British colonies?" he asked and James nodded. "You are a long way from home Captain," the Dutch officer snarled at him.

"Yes sir. It has been a long and difficult journey," James returned. He glanced around to see a large number of the town folk coming out to see and hear what was transpiring.

"You and your lieutenant will follow me to the fort for further discussions." He turned and walked away from the two men. James nodded to Bode and then motioned to the six men in the longboat to remain here. He and Bode followed the officer with four of the Dutch soldiers walking behind them, while the other six soldiers stayed behind with the longboat and crew. James glanced again at the town up close, the people lining the streets, and the impressive fortress that was on a rise across the long grassy yard with palm trees dotting the area. He could smell food cooking as it drifted down toward them and his stomach growled.

As they approached the fort, he could see an iron door was standing open to the south and a cobblestone path that led up to it from the town, its closest buildings 200 yards away. As they left the open grass and stepped onto the path, James took a moment to survey the fort as they approached it. It had wide open spaces all around the fort and he could see they had five smaller 9 pounder cannons mounted on each of the corner towers of the fort with a gun crew standing near them. If they were loaded with grapeshot, it would make for a very deadly approach for any army trying to take the fortress. As his father always trained him to do, he tried to grasp and remember every detail of what he saw and he could see Bode also taking it all in. The group stepped through the iron door to the fort and entered a small courtyard where they were met by an additional ten soldiers, with their muskets held ready, but not aimed.

"Captain Thornton, you will join me and meet the commander while your lieutenant waits here," the officer stated and turned toward the doorway leading into the inner fortress. James first turned to Bode, nodded slightly to him, giving a quick wink that it was okay, and then followed the officer. James was surprised how much cooler it was behind the brickwork of the fortress as they weaved their way through the corridors. As they entered the inner courtyard of the fortress, he could see the gun crews of the large 48 pounder cannons at the ready and all of them were aimed at *The Dragon* sitting in the harbor, although it did not appear that the crews were fully manned.

They crossed the courtyard to the east wall where there were several offices. One had several citizens standing outside as if waiting. A slightly older gentleman with a younger boy, who was a younger version of the man, stood just outside the door as if waiting his turn. James nodded and smiled to the gentleman and the boy, who could only be his son, as he approached the office door.

"Wait here." The officer commanded, leaving James standing in the sun as he stepped inside the office to await the acknowledgement from a rather rotund man who sat behind a desk. It appeared as if the large man was busy writing something, or at least wanted James to think he was busy. James could see the insignia on the extravagant uniform was that of a commander. The man's face was heavily powdered and hidden beneath a white wig. Standing to his right was a Negro girl who was fanning him in an effort to fight the heat of the day. It seemed surreal to James as the scene reminded him of the plantation owners and buyers that he encountered in his own country. He could feel the hunger and the heat weakening him.

He glanced back toward the older gentleman and his son who were still looking at James. The two reminded James of his own father and himself when he was a boy, when they had gone into town to sell their cotton and tobacco. They looked like plantation owners.

"How is the harvest looking this year?" He asked them. The man seemed at first taken aback by his question, and then seemed to relax.

"It will be a good year, God willing." he replied in perfect English. "Are you a farmer?" He then asked James and James nodded and smiled.

"Yes, my family grows cotton and tobacco on some of the prettiest land in North Carolina. God has blessed us with many good years, but not being there, I'm not sure how this one will turn out."

The fact that James and the older gentleman were speaking casually instead of waiting in nervous respect and anticipation seemed to bother the commander, causing the man to finally look up from his paperwork, first toward James and then toward the officer. The officer leaned down to whisper in the commanders ear, who observed James while the officer continued to converse quietly to him. When the officer finished speaking he stepped aside and the commander looked at James.

"Captain of the North Carolina militia." The commander behind the desk called out to the room in general. His accent was less than the officers.

"Yes sir." James replied and saluted. The commander simply nodded and dismissed the salute with his hand as if it meant nothing to him.

"What brings you here to Christiansted, Captain?"

"Supplies sir. French warships chased us from our destination and we thought it best to resupply before heading back to North Carolina," James replied.

"What makes you think you can purchase supplies from us? Are you trying to sneak into my harbor and attack us?" The man said suspiciously, his expression matching his question. James was confused by the response, but ignored the tone.

"No sir. It is my understanding that Christiansted is an open port for trade and supplies. We gave the courtesy announcement well outside the port entrance and a signal was returned. Our vessel is not a warship, but a lightly armed trade ship. We anchored within reach of your guns as proof," James replied calmly. The man suddenly became agitated and raised his voice.

"Are you mocking me, boy?" James was surprised at the man's unprovoked anger and James looked him in the eyes and tried to read his intentions, but could find none.

"No sir." James finally responded and the man started to chuckle.

"Are you aware that the Dutch and the French recently signed an alliance and trade agreement for the Caribbean?" he said with a smile. James' stomach knotted at what that meant. The Dutch were at war with the British and *The Dragon* sitting in their harbor was fair game to be captured or blown out of the water. He tried to think fast as he thought about his friends anchored in the harbor.

"No sir, I was not aware of that. Whether we desire it or not, those of us in the colonies are at the mercy and orders of the Crown. We are not here by choice, but were ordered to leave our homes and families and are looking forward to returning to them. I would hope you would understand our situation." He said calmly.

"It does not sound like you are all that excited about serving the British?" he probed.

"I'm a farmer by trade sir and a militia by choice. When orders are given by those above me, I'm required to obey them whether I like them or not." James said. The man seemed to contemplate his statement a moment.

"Well said, Captain." The big man smiled as sweat dripped down his powdered face. He pushed himself away from the desk and walked to where James stood outside his office.

"Here is what we are going to do." He smiled and chuckled. "Although I do not need to be, I'm going to be gracious to my enemy and give you two options. One is you can surrender your vessel to me without a shot being fired." He seemed to wait to see how James would respond. "I didn't think so. That leaves us with the other option, which is what they call a fighting chance." He chuckled again as did the officer behind him. "I am going to give you 15 minutes to get your ship out of the harbor before I open fire on it." His smiled faded as he glared into James eyes waiting for some reaction or panic. James thought about reaching for his pistol and taking the man hostage or just killing him, but he knew he would be dead in seconds as would Bode and his friends in the harbor. He knew the only option he had was the one given.

"So your response to our proper etiquette signals and requests was to mislead us into sailing into your harbor, knowing by our actions that such news had not reached us?" James asked, knowing that he would be questioning the commander's honor. The man seemed to fester in his anger at James' observation and the Dutch captain shifted his stance, obviously not happy about how things transpired.

"I like to think of it as oversight on our part, which is why I'm even providing you with the second option," he snarled back.

"So I'm guessing buying supplies is out of the question?" James asked sarcastically and raised his eyebrows. At first the commander and the officer seemed stunned by the question, then what seemed like a gentle movement inside the man turned into outright laughter.

"You are very funny Captain. No, I won't sell you any supplies after all, that would be aiding the enemy." There was more laughter, but James noticed that the Captain did not seem to find the exchange as humorous as his commander did.

"Your offer is very kind Commander. When will the 15 minutes begin?" James asked to buy some time as he continued thinking the best course of action. James knew it would take that much time just to row back to the ship, let alone sail *The Dragon* beyond the range of the guns. Unless the men on those cannons were terrible shots, *The Dragon* was doomed. The commander laughed again at his question as if he were really enjoying James' predicament. He then stopped and starred coldly into James' eyes.

"The moment you step outside this fort, Captain Hendriks will start counting." The commander said coldly.

"Thank you sir." James stepped back and saluted the man, who surprisingly saluted back. James then turned to the older gentleman and his son and smiled.

"My apologies for the intrusion on your business interaction," James said and the gentleman smiled and nodded.

"May God grant you speed, Captain," the man replied kindly in almost perfect English. The statement seemed to irk the commander and he dismissed the man as James turned to leave.

As James was escorted by the officer back through the fort, he saw the commander turn and head to the stairs leading to the main guns facing the bay, confirming that he meant to follow through on his threat to fire upon their ship. When James re-entered the smaller courtyard where Bode was waiting, he conveyed their situation to him and the soldiers around them that could understand English.

"I just learned that the Dutch and the French have signed an alliance against the British. The commander of the fortress has given us 15 minutes to get back to our ship and clear the harbor guns or he will fire upon us." James informed Bode, and he could tell that Bode grasped the impossibility of success, but understood the urgency. James turned to the Dutch captain.

"Would you be so kind as to notify your men here and those by our longboat, not to shoot us as we make our way to it in great haste?" James asked. After a few seconds, the Captain stepped outside, signaled to his men standing by The Dragon's longboat and crew, and then turned to James again.

"The next time I see you, I expect you will either be in chains or dead." He stated coldly.

"Neither sounds very pleasant," he replied and turned to Bode. "Shall we?" he said as he shifted his sword to the side and repositioned his pistol so that it would not fall out as they ran. Bode nodded.

"Captain, you may begin counting." James said as he and Bode dashed at top speed toward their longboat and the surprised men standing by it.

James immediately yelled across the courtyard to the six men on the longboat to prepare to push off. As they ran, they could hear the laughter from the men on the walls and at the door of the fort behind them. As they came closer to the longboat and crew they could also hear the laughter coming from the townsfolk to their left. James felt embarrassed and weak, but the thought of his men being blasted apart by the fort's guns pushed him further and faster than he would have thought himself capable in these circumstances. He looked up to see that the men on the longboat were already pushing off the dock and running out the oars as the bow angled to face *The Dragon*. One man held the stern to the wharf and as Bode and James got close, he pushed off. Bode was faster by about ten feet and jumped across the short expanse landing on the far edge of the stern and propelling the boat forward with his weight and momentum which increased the distance from the shore. James in his weakened state barely cleared the stern and avoided straddling the tiller, landing ungracefully in the middle of the longboat. His arrival not only added to its forward momentum, but it also knocked a few of the oarsman to the side.

"Row hard, we have less than 15 minutes to clear the guns," he yelled as the men began pulling on the oars at their best rate. Bode climbed over James' prone body and grabbed the tiller to direct the angle of the longboat. James rolled over and got back to his feet trying to catch his breath.

After a few seconds of thinking, James took off his hat and began waving it and his other arm to get the attention of Captain Donovan on *The Dragon*. Although he felt it was dangerous, James pulled his pistol, fired a shot into the air, and started motioning for the ship to leave the harbor at great haste. The signals and urgency must have worked, for James saw the men of *The Dragon* drop sail almost immediately as if they had been waiting on the cross beams for such an order. In spite of the rowing and his heavy breathing, he could hear the anchor chain being raised in the distance. James had been counting in his head to try to keep an idea as to the time they had remaining until the cannons fired.

"Turn us to the starboard and aim for the entrance, for we will not catch her before she leaves but we can still try to make an escape," he ordered.

James glanced back to the fort and the city and could see the townsfolk were now lining the wharf area, laughing, whistling and hooting. He was always amazed at how cruel people can be at times: while his men were rowing for their lives, the people were laughing at them. He glanced up at the fortress main gun area and could see the commander looking out at the bay. Glancing back at *The Dragon*, he could see that many of the sails were already filled and the ship was starting to pull against the anchor chain. He knew that it would make pulling the anchor up harder, and that it increased the risk that the anchor chain would catch on any coral heads below as it dragged along the bottom. If that happened, it would be over for all of them. In his head he had now counted to 12 minutes and they were still several hundred yards from *The Dragon*. He could tell that the men were getting very tired of rowing and the longboat was slowing. With a groaning creak, *The Dragon* suddenly took flight as the anchor broke free from the bottom. James glanced back at the fortress and could see the commander speaking with the captain, who had now joined him on the ramparts, and was pointing toward *The Dragon*.

The men on the guns suddenly scrambled as if they were making ready to fire early. If anything, James knew he had been counting faster than normal, so to see the crews moving to fire stunned him. "You gave your word!" he yelled as loud as he could toward the commander standing near the guns. He glanced back at *The Dragon* and could tell it had moved almost a full boat length through the water since his last glance.

"Boom!" "Boom!" Echoed across the bay and the screaming sound of cannon balls passing over their heads could be heard. He saw one ball pass through the aft sail structure, tearing down some rigging, while the other smashed into the aft part of the ship.

"Boom!" "Boom!" "Boom!" in rapid sequence followed the previous two shots, except this time to James was elated to see that they all fell into the water either directly behind or far to the port side of the ship. He glanced back to the fort and could tell the crews were re-positioning the last three unfired cannons. He realized that they must have been positioned and aimed to hit the ship where it was anchored, they did not expect to have to adjust for a moving target. He could see the crews of the previously fired cannons begin swabbing out and reloading the recently fired cannons.

"Go girl go!" James yelled as *The Dragon* continued to pick up speed as it raced for the entrance of the bay.

"Boom!" Another cannon ball passed overhead, and skipped off the water and struck the side of the ship, causing minimal damage. "Boom!" Another cannon ball landed in the water behind it. "Boom!" another shot tearing through the rigging and passing out the other side. James saw that one of the men had stopped rowing from exhaustion. He ordered him to take the tiller as James took his seat and started pulling on the oar as best he could. Bode replaced another man whose strength was spent.

"Rest awhile, then relieve another, as needed," James said between pulls on the oar. Because of his position, all James could do was watch the fort and the activity taking place there and pray that *The Dragon* and her crew were moving quickly to safety.

"Boom!" "Boom!" to James' surprise, the fort on the eastern point had decided to join the battle. He heard the sound of a cannon ball hitting wood and knew that did not herald good news for the ship. Although the 32 pounders were smaller, they could still tear through the hull of a ship with ease. A strong gust of wind suddenly passed by the longboat and headed perfectly toward *The Dragon*. James thanked God and prayed that it would propel the vessel forward even faster.

A long, rumbling roar suddenly issued from behind him and his initial fear was that all the powder in *The Dragon's* hold had just exploded, but then realized *The Dragon* had fired a broadside at the small gun battery fort to the east, the one that had fired on them. James pulled his oars even harder, glancing to his left to see the cannon balls striking all around the small fort. James glanced over his shoulder and was surprised at how far *The Dragon* had traveled since his last look. Looking back to the fort, he estimated that they were quickly moving out of range of the bigger guns. No sooner had those thoughts rolled through his mind, than the "Boom, Boom, Boom!" of three 48 pounders from the main fortress fired and the sizzle of them passing overhead could be heard. He waited for the terrible sound of cannon ball meeting solid wood, but instead heard the tearing and popping of fabric and lines and the splashing of water as the three cannon balls either missed or passed through the rigging. He knew that it meant danger for the sailors in the masts, but it meant a little more time for the ship to pass further out of the bay and beyond the reach of the guns.

James glanced again over his shoulder and saw that they were still several hundred yards from *The Dragon* and the distance between them was growing rapidly. He also knew that the strength of the oarsman and himself was fading. Although he assumed Captain Donovan would wait outside the bay for them, he did not know if they had the energy to make it.

"Steady strokes gentlemen." He said as he tried to keep the strokes of the oarsman together and their minds from the pain and exhaustion.

"Boom! Boom!" Two of the big guns roared from the fort, except this time there was no sizzling sound as they passed over; instead, the water erupted to the port and starboard side of their longboat, almost swamping the vessel. James glanced over at Bode and saw that he was also drenched, but unharmed, as were the rest of the men.

"That was refreshing and just what I needed." He laughed out loud in an effort to calm himself and the oarsman who now had panic in their eyes. Inside James was both terrified and angry at the same time. The near misses caused a surge of energy to course through him and the other men. Together they pulled harder and deeper on the oars in their hands. He saw the same reaction it had on the others. Seconds later a gun from the small fort fired and the ball struck so close to the longboat that it not only shattered an oar, the force of the impact ripped it out of the man's hands, leaving his fingers bloody and his arms hanging limply at his side. He could see the shock and pain growing on the man's face as the blood flowed from his fingers and the feeling came back into his numb limbs. Dazed, he seemed to be looking for the missing oar that was in his hands only moments before.

"It's ok, we got it. Sit back and rest," James said trying to calm him, but not letting go of his oar or losing time with the stroke command from the man on the tiller.

Then it was over. The only noise was the sound of their oars weakly dipping and pulling on the water, the creak of the oar locks turning with each stroke and the moans of the injured man. First one, then a second man suddenly stopped rowing and just fell forward onto their oars, pulling them out of the water. One began sobbing. With only three men rowing now, James asked the one that was not sobbing to switch positions with the man on the tiller. At first he did not respond, but after a few moments, he raised his head and slowly stumbled over and switched positions. With two rowing on each side, they were able to make a little progress, but not much in their increasingly weakened state. His arms, shoulders and back ached and cramped with every pull of the oar, and when it seemed that he could no longer continue, the man on the tiller spoke dryly and faintly. "Help." James looked at the man and saw that he was looking past him. James turned to see the other longboat from *The Dragon* carrying a full crew of 12 men rowing toward them. *The Dragon* had made it and had sent help to the foundering crew.

As the boats came together, several men stepped across to assist in moving the injured man to the bow of the longboat, while others took positions vacated by the exhausted rowers.

James looked back toward the fort and for the first time felt hatred burning inside of him toward the two Dutch officers and their men. Between the running, the rowing and the lack of food, he felt as if he had nothing left and simply closed his eyes and let their rescuers take them back to *The Dragon*. Bode slid to the middle, sat down next to James, and leaned back against him.

"Thank you Lord," he mumbled and James nodded.

"Yes, thank you."

Although most of the original crew was rested enough by the time they reached *The Dragon* to climb on board with great difficulty, two of the men needed the assistance of a rope and pulley to get them onboard. Captain Donovan and most of the militia were there as they were guided to a crate to sit on. Immediately, a cup of broth with actual fish meat in it was given to each of them to drink. James did not even question it; he just drank the broth and chewed the chunks of meat. It was heaven and within a few minutes he could feel the energy returning to him as the ship rose and fell on the swells of the sea.

"That was the worst job of negotiating I have ever seen!" Captain Donovan said and then chuckled, as did most of the crew standing around them waiting to hear what happened.

"It appears I asked for too much rum," James responded and the men standing nearby laughed and patted him on the back.

"At least he's got his priorities clear," Mr. Sanders said and the crew gave a hurrah.

James spent the next thirty minutes explaining exactly what had transpired in extreme detail for the Captain, his officers, Bode, Robbie and his key militia officers and men. Bode also related what he saw and heard while waiting in the courtyard. Captain Donovan took it all in, nodding occasionally and asking additional questions for clarification while they spoke. James and Bode learned that the few cannon shot that had struck *The Dragon's* hull had not caused extensive damage or injury, but that several sailors who were in the rigging above had been injured, one severely.

"They definitely had no idea that you and your men could get your ship moving and out of the range of their guns that fast," James stated with pride. "Truth be known, I did not think you could either. I think his plan was to pound you until you struck your colors."

"It definitely pleases me to think that we really infuriated that over-stuffed peacock and avoided his chains. Once anchored, I too saw that the original 32 pounders had been replaced with 48's, so I kept the boys upstairs in the rigging just in case we had to move quickly, knowing that we were in range. Your warning was all we needed. We're very fortunate that he was so arrogant and overconfident, or he could have quickly torn us to pieces." At the end, the Captain asked that they convene in his quarters for further discussion.

"Mr. Sanders, take us to Buck Island on the eastern end of St. Croix. I want them to be able to see us, but keep well out of their reach." He ordered and Mr. Sanders nodded.

On the way to Captain Donovan's quarters, James and Bode stopped by their cabin to change clothes. As they approached the door, they could see that it was no longer attached, but instead a piece of sailcloth hung from the top of the doorframe. As he moved the curtain, he saw that the middle bunk was missing and in place of it was a series of makeshift planks nailed into place against the hull. James turned to look past the door and saw the round indent on the inner wall of the ship. As Bode and he stood there looking in silence, Robbie came up behind them.

"Oh yeah, one of the cannon balls fired from the fort came right through our cabin, through the door, and lodged against the wall of the galley. Made quite a mess, wood splinters everywhere, but nothing in comparison to the mess it made in the galley. It hit so hard that every pot, pan and utensil that was on the starboard wall was thrown clear across to the other side. The cook, you should have seen him; he was very upset." As James and Bode stood there in silence listening to Robbie, the young man slid past them and into the cabin to grab his jacket for the meeting. "Glad I wasn't still sleeping." He added.

As they stepped into the room, they could see that luckily their lockers had not been hit by the cannon ball, although they were definitely worse for wear from the flying debris. As they opened them, all their gear was essentially as they had left it. James and Bode changed their shirts in silence, put their jackets back on and headed to Captain Donovan's cabin.

Chapter 9

June 27, 1776

They spent the next several hours discussing the encounter with the Dutch, their supplies, and their limited options. They all agreed that their first priority was to gather enough basic food supplies to sustain and feed the nearly 180 crew and militia. When they had arrived at Buck Island and had dropped anchor, Captain Donovan ordered two longboats and crew to go to shore; some to pick coconuts and others to drag the ship's net in the shallow waters for fish. In addition, he stationed several of the militia with loaded muskets on the railing with the instructions to shoot any turtle that came to the surface. The other crewmembers that were either not repairing the damage from the cannon or standing ready in the masts looking for other ships on the horizon were to be on the railing with fishing lines and hooks.

Captain Donovan knew that even with all their efforts in motion, they could not secure enough supplies in their holds to get them back to North Carolina, but that they could at least try to regain their strength and maintain it while anchored. After Captain Donovan had almost every person on the boat working on at least one task, he asked the senior officers to meet back in his quarters. Once they had all convened again, he stood up, walked to the window, and looked out toward St. Croix.

"Gentlemen, we are now at war with the French, the Dutch and the Spanish, which means there are no available ports of call for us to make to buy the supplies we need. I'm confident that all friendly ports are also under blockade," he stated and then hesitated as he continued to look out the stern window. "At least that is what I would do if I were in their position and, because of that; I feel we only have two options available to us if we want to survive." The men sat anxiously around the table to hear the options as the Captain continued. "Since we are now at war with the Dutch and find ourselves sitting in their waters, we are free to raid their vessels or lands as opportunities present. We need to be able to feed almost 200 men for several weeks to get back home. It's more than likely that we will have to change course to avoid confrontation, which will take considerably more food than a straight run. I for one have no desire to repeat our past experience of trying to make that run with minimal supplies, should we be chased around the Caribbean again." He turned to the window and looked out before continuing. "With no vessels currently in sight for us to engage, that leaves us with the only option of raiding the plantations and unprotected cities of St. Croix." He moved back to stand behind his seat as he scanned the room.

James thought about the townsfolk laughing at them as they ran and rowed their way toward death. He thought about the Dutch captain, the commander and his men and the way they treated Bode and him during their visit. His mind then went to the kind gentleman and his son who were simply farmers or plantation owners. It seemed so wrong to think that now they were going to be "pirates" that would inflict suffering on innocent people it did not sit well with him. Captain Donovan seemed to read James' concern.

"What's on your mind James?" he asked. James took a moment to organize his thoughts.

"Captain, after what we have just gone through, I have no love for the soldiers or citizens of Christiansted, but I'm a farmer by trade and the thought of us raiding an innocent farmer and his family, taking all that they have worked hard to save. Well, it just seems wrong." James replied and Bode and Robbie both nodded in agreement. Captain Donovan hesitated a moment, then said, "It's called war James. Unfortunately, the innocent always seem to suffer more from it than those who do the fighting. I don't like it either, but I don't know that we really have any other choice to gather supplies, unless you can think of one."

Minutes passed as James worked through every detail that he could remember about the main fort, the smaller forts to the east and west, the hills and trees behind the city and fortress, and the city itself. He thought about what his father had taught him about cannons and overcoming them and their fortifications. He leaned forward and picked up a charcoal stick to write with, drawing the best map he could of what he had seen and remembered, while the rest of those in the room sat quietly watching. He started with the land, then the three forts, then the city and the surrounding area. Everyone at first was silent as he continued to sketch the layout as he remembered it, with Bode adding or correcting a few items. Then the Captain spoke up as if to stop the direction he was taking.

"James, I know you're angry and would like to get a little revenge on the Dutch officers, but if you are thinking of attacking the fort with a small group of militia and a merchant vessel, it's suicide." James had almost completed his quick sketch as the Captain finished. He took one more look and then reached over and circled the east fort.

"Not the main fort, but the east fort," James said and just as he finished, a musket fired from the deck just above them which was followed quickly by a cheer from the crew. A loud splash could be heard as someone dove over the side. James at first was concerned, but then saw the Captain smile.

"Looks like we'll be eating turtle stew tonight," he said and smiled, then nodded to James and pointed back to the map. James collected his thoughts one more time and then looked around the room at the men sitting at the table before him.

"The amounts of food supplies that you say we need are sitting in the warehouses of the Dutch East India Company in Christiansted. As you said, we would need to raid three, four or maybe more plantations to get enough food to feed our men for the journey home. That's four or five days of planning and lingering around this area, which gives the enemy plenty of time to grasp our purpose and to either hide the food or prepare a defense against us at each location. I'm guessing we don't have that much time available." Captain Donovan nodded in agreement.

"It won't be long before French or Dutch vessels chase us out of here, maybe hours," he replied and then nodded for James to continue.

"Okay, let's assume our plan is to raid the town of Christiansted instead. When I was in the fort and when we were rowing in and then back out, all I could do while rowing was watch the gun crews on the main fort as they loaded and fired at *The Dragon*. The gun crews were having a very difficult time," he said and then paused a moment. "At first I thought it was just that the 48 pounders were bigger than the 32s and harder to handle, but in looking back on the situation now I think the problem was that the wall openings for the cannons were too small; they were built for 38 pounders. Not only are the 48s heavier, but they had less room to turn and angle them." James looked up at Captain Donovan, but saw the confused look staring back at him.

"How does that relate to the east fort?" Captain Donovan asked. James realized he had not explained completely all that he was thinking and tried to rethink how best to do so.

"Look, the openings on the main fort for the 48 pounders are designed to protect the city and bay from enemy vessels, not a land attack. That means that because of the design, which is even made worse by the larger size of the 48 pounders in the small openings, the guns can't be turned enough to even fire upon the east fort, or at least the majority of them can't. But the 32 pounder cannons on the east fort, which, by the way, are sitting on a higher elevation than the main fort, could be spun around to fire on the main fort." He paused and then added. "We can fire at them, but they can't fire at us." James waited for it to register with the Captain, who seemed to be working through all the various angles before finally responding.

"What about the west fort. If we took the east fort we would be open to their field of fire," he pointed out, but James had already thought of that.

"From a moving ship, your broadside accurately hit the east fort on the way out of the bay. If your cannon crews were able to fire several of the 32 pounders at the west fort first from a stable platform and higher ground, I'm guessing they could take out those gun crews quickly while the other crews fired upon the main fortress," James answered.

Captain Donovan sat quietly working through the various options and dangers. "With 9 pounders aiming at you and your men, how do you plan to take the east fort?" he asked James.

"At night," James said. "We take it at night, and then reposition the cannons under the cover of darkness. Then at first light begin the bombardment of the main fortress and west fort." James watched until the Captain nodded his head before continuing. "Under the cover of darkness, we will take the militia, along with five of your gun crews, and scale the walls of the east fort with ladders."

"The main fortress will send reinforcements once they hear battle," the Captain interjected. James nodded. "I expect they will and in fact, I'm counting on it. I'd rather fight them in the open than attack them behind their protected walls. Including the gun crews, I'm estimating there are twenty men at the east and west forts, and perhaps ninety men at the main fort," James said, but the Captain shook his head.

"You're planning on going against 100 or more trained Dutch soldiers with your 50 militia?" he asked and James shook his head.

"No. I'm planning on using overwhelming force against twenty soldiers at the east fort and then defend from a fortified position whatever they send our way from the main fort. Meanwhile your men will bombard the main fort and west fort into submission." James watched the Captain shift his eyes back and forth across the drawing and then tapped his finger on the bay entrance.

"At first light, I can sail into the harbor, staying outside the reach of their guns. This will keep them from turning all their guns on you and keep their troops behind the fortress walls out of fear from both of us," Captain Donovan offered and James nodded.

"When that happens, the militia will march in and take the city and the supplies we need, load them up on captured wagons and bring the supplies back to the east fort. We can shuttle them back and forth on the longboats right before their eyes and there's not a thing they can do about it. Then we sail home." James concluded.

"Unless they want to come out from behind their walls and attack us while we are raiding their city," Bode commented. James had already thought about that possibility.

"Again, better to fight them out in the open than while behind their walls," James replied.

Captain Donovan sat quietly staring at the map before him, dancing his eyes from the east, to west, back to the main fort and then to the city over and over. "So you never really take the main fortress?" he asked James.

"No, we just bottle them up in it," James replied.

"Very risky, James, but you might be on to something." James looked over to Bode, who smiled and nodded his approval of the idea.

"I don't know about the rest of you, but I'm hungry and tired of eating watery fish soup. So when do we go?" Bode asked. Captain Donovan was the first to respond. "We need at least a day to get our strength back, fill our bellies and regain our courage," Captain Donovan stated and James nodded in agreement.

"They need to see that we have left the area or they will be ready for us," Bode added.

"We could sail out late tomorrow afternoon, then turn back and drop the men off at night as close as possible to the city, but far enough away that we can still go in under the cover of darkness," the Captain replied.

"Captain, where do you think would be the closest and safest place to do that?" James asked.

"I'll have to review my charts, but we should be able to get you pretty close. It will take a few trips back and forth from the ship on the longboats to get you all ashore, but we can make it work. This will either be a huge success, or we'll have a whole lot fewer mouths to feed, if any." He said sarcastically. James smiled and nodded, knowing that what he said was true.

The rest of the day they rested, ate what food they were able to scrounge from Buck Island and its reefs and drank coconut milk, and then rested some more. Several groups went out fishing with the net, some continued fishing from the side of the ship, and one more turtle was shot by one of the militia. The turtle and fish stew was a welcome relief from hunger and the crew recovered their sagging spirits rapidly. The next morning, it was much the same except that the militia focused on preparing and cleaning their weapons. Bode pointed out that there were plenty of muskets packed away in crates in their hold and that it might be a good idea to carry two with them (their own long rifle and a spare British standard musket with a bayonet attached). It would not only allow them to use their longer range muskets initially, but would give them an extra shot before having to reload and a bayonet to use should hand-to-hand fighting ensue. Captain Donovan and James both thought it was an excellent idea and broke open the crates distributing the muskets, to both the militia and the gun crews.

Later that afternoon, Captain Donovan and James spoke to the entire crew and militia on the deck. They discussed their situation, the options that they had considered, and the final choice that they had made and why. They discussed the roles that each group and man in that particular group would be playing. They talked about timing and the importance of stealth. They talked about how they were going to make the short ladders that they would use to breach the walls of the east fort and how they would carry them. The gun crews were briefed on what they needed to do, and how best to do it quickly. One suggested that they bring additional powder, since it tended to be in shorter supply at fortresses than cannon shot. They agreed to each carry two loads of extra powder and wadding, as well as some extra firing tools just in case. As their final act before departing, as uncomfortable as it was for the Captain and most of his crew, they prayed, with Bode leading them. Bode prayed for a long time, praying for each aspect of their plans, for each man to be brave and courageous, for those leading them to lead with the same courage. He asked for God's forgiveness for the actions that were in front of them and the potential harm that would be caused to their fellow man. He prayed that they would be great examples of Godly men, not vengeful, bitter or angry, but faithful and confident. As he said "Amen", a silence hung over the boat, and then the militia began to sing a spiritual song together.

The Dragon was anchored less than five miles northeast from the city of Christiansted, and the Captain was sure that they could be seen and, in all likelihood, were currently being watched from the shoreline or from the hills above the city itself. There were no ships sighted that day and the ship was repaired now as well as conditions allowed. They weighed anchor and dropped their white sails for all to see. They left the windward side of Buck Island and sailed to the north as the last of the sunset faded into darkness. It was a clear night, but Captain Donovan assured them that the partial moon was not scheduled to rise until later that evening. Once it was dark, they turned The Dragon back toward St. Croix and to the small shoreline for which they were aiming.

It was almost midnight when they reached Punnett Bay, just over two miles east of Christiansted. They lowered the two longboats and quickly delivered James and 1st Group onto the beach. Once landed, they immediately searched and secured the area and waited for Bode and 2nd Group to be ferried next and then finally the five 5-man gun crews carrying their pistols, muskets and powder.

They immediately headed west toward the city, staying in close formation and hugging close to the shoreline to maximize their speed of travel and avoid the thick jungle foliage. They stopped briefly each time they found a young gumbo-limbo tree. The tree was easily recognized by its dark red bark, and the men cut the necessary ten-foot poles and cross bars, and then quickly roped them together as practiced to create their crude ladders. The gunner crews took turns carrying the three ladders as they moved down the beach while the militia took the lead. They circled around a small lagoon that they encountered to the north east of the city until they reached the sand point that jutted out into Gallows Bay. There they took a moment to survey the city and the forts with Captain Donovan's telescope. The moon had risen in the sky and although it made it a little easier for them to see, James knew that it also made them easier to be seen.

James surveyed the fortresses. He could not see any lights coming from the east or west forts, but the city and the main fort still showed signs of activity. They saw two houses between them and their path to the east fort and decided it was best to hug the eastern side of the stretch of land in case dogs were in the area. They moved quickly down the stretch of land, marching along the edge of the inner lagoon again, until the angle of the terrain started to climb in elevation, the sign that they were getting close to the east fort. They moved carefully through the trees and up the hill until they could see the edge of the east fort, where James quietly halted the men and they all stood silently looking and listening for any signs of movement.

It was so quiet that James began to feel that they might be walking into a trap and he even considered calling off the attack, but then thought about the limited supplies and the long journey ahead of them and remembered that they had little choice but to continue. He could see two 9 pounders aiming in their direction and knew that if they were loaded with grapeshot and primed to fire, he and his men would be decimated should a trap be sprung. James tried to minimize the possible effect of the cannons by ordering his men to approach the fort in five separate groups, to avoid bunching up and making easy group targets for the cannon. Three of the groups carried the ladders. Bode and his men stayed back in case it was a trap and were ready to charge forward if needed.

His heart beat so loudly that he was sure the men around him could hear it as he moved across the open space toward the fort, expecting any moment to see a flash and explosion and to feel the grapeshot raining down on him, but nothing happened. Once they were at the walls, they quietly placed their ladders at the spots James had pointed to upon their arrival. He knew that he was easier to see with his lighter skin, but it was a little easier for the men to see his movements and signals in the darkness.

James was first up his ladder and as he got to the roof edge he could hear heavy breathing just above him. He signaled for the others to hold and waited for an angry face to suddenly pop up and a pistol or musket to be fired into him, but again nothing happened. He slowly raised his head above the edge of the wall and looked at the gun emplacement. Four 32 pounder cannons faced outward to the bay entrance. He could see there were three men sitting in three different chairs in three different spots on the open landing. Each of them was either holding a musket across his lap, or had one close at hand. The position of the ladders had put his men right next to two of the men, but the third one was across the landing from them.

He prepared to signal for his men to make the attack, but suddenly the squeaking noise of a door came from below near the front of the fort. They all froze in place and tried to see who had made the noise. Looking down from his vulnerable place on the ladder, he could see that Robbie and his group of five men were closest to the noise and saw them immediately move closer to the wall to remain hidden. Then there was the sound of footsteps on gravel that moved gradually away from the opened door and to the side of the path. James watched as Robbie and his men raised their muskets to fire, but then suddenly moved forward toward the sound.

James waited to hear the sound of musket fire, or scuffling, and was ready to leap over the walls to attack, but none came. The next moment one of Robbie's men came back to the ladder, motioned, and whispered that the door was open. James signaled the remaining men on the ground to go with Robbie and charge the door while the three of them at the top of the ladders would secure the men on the gun deck. They waited until they heard the sound of his men charging into the room below, then they leapt over the brick wall, knocking away or grabbing the musket within reach of each man, putting a pistol or musket in the faces of the men. Surprisingly, one of the men still did not wake up, but had to be nudged awake so he could surrender. Robbie came up the stairs to the gun deck and signaled with a smile that everything was secure. The assault had gone far better than James had dared hope.

James descended the rampart stairs and met with Robbie. He learned that the door was opened by a soldier who had come outside to relieve himself instead of using the bucket inside that they were suppose to use. When the man finished and turned to head back in, Robbie was there with a pistol aimed at his face. He took him prisoner without saying a word. The Dutch troops had been sleeping when they charged into the lower rooms of the fort and James noticed that most of the Dutch soldiers were still trying to figure out who these black clad soldiers were and why they were even here.

James stepped out the front door and whistled softly across the open area. Seconds later he saw Bode and his men come across the open area, followed closely behind by the gun crews. The fort was far too small to hold the fifteen prisoners and the seventy-five men in their group inside, so James ordered two teams of five men, led by Robbie, to stay with the prisoners. He assigned the twenty-five gunnery experts to working on repositioning the four 32 pounders to face the main fort and the west fort. While four gun crews were working on that, he had one crew load the two 9 pounders that faced inland with grapeshot in case of a ground assault on the fort. Bode and James and their forty men moved toward the city and positioned themselves in the tree line overlooking the road to the city. Should the main fortress send additional troops or a large force to the east fort, they wanted to have the best firing position on them.

One of Robbie's men broke into the food storage for the east fort and distributed its contents to the militia and sailor gun crews. For the Dutch troops staying in the eastern fort, it seemed that bread, dried fish, jerky and rum were the options. The food was passed around to fill the empty bellies, but the rum was held back. James needed the men sharp for what was to come next. The food did not go very far, but it was enough to replenish their energy. They took shifts resting as the cannon crews worked on positioning two guns each toward the main fort and the western fort and repositioning the wheel blocks to keep the kickback from rolling them across the roof when fired. Robbie took the fifteen Dutch muskets that had been seized from the prisoners, made sure they were loaded, and laid them on top of the gun deck to be used should the fort be attacked.

Just before dawn, one of the militia from Bode's group came quickly and quietly to James. "There are soldiers coming," he managed as he caught his breath. James carefully peered through the firing slot in the north wall in the direction that the militia indicated. A seven-man Dutch contingent marched - or a better description would be that they strolled - toward the fort. Bode and his men had taken up positions on either side of the road and James watched as Bode and his group literally swarmed the Dutch soldiers from the side of the road as they came between them.

"Drop you weapons or you will be shot." Bode said in English whether the Dutch understood him or not was another question. There was a tense moment of hesitation by the Dutch soldiers, but then any semblance of bravery disappeared and common sense won out. The soldiers laid down their weapons. One carried a kettle of warm stew and another carried two baskets filled with loaves of bread. James made his way to Bode and his men, and ordered two groups of five to search, bind and escort the prisoners to the fort. He detailed two men to distribute the stew and bread among the militiamen and the gun crews. Over the next thirty minutes, they rotated the militiamen who had eaten, from within the fort, with the men out guarding the road. By the time the feeding rotation had been completed, dawn was breaking on the eastern horizon and from their position on the eastern fort, they could see the masts and sails of *The Dragon* approaching. With the better light now available, the gun crews began making their final adjustments to the cannons as they prepared to fire them. Using a lantern in the fort, one of the gun crewman signaled to Captain Donovan that the eastern fort had been taken.

When the warning alarm at the western fort sounded at the approach of *The Dragon*, James saw the Dutch soldiers of the western fort and the main fort moving to the ramparts to ready their cannons. "Boom! Boom!" James knew the two cannons Mr. Richard's and his gun crews had aimed at the western fort had now announced their presence to the city and the other forts. From their positions they could see one cannon ball strike just below the top rampart, while the other tore through the bricks in front of one gun and into the gun crew behind it. Seconds later, two more cannons fired at what they knew must be the main fort, but from their positions they were unable to see the damage. The thump of the balls' impact was unmistakable, however. James watched as the gun crews worked feverishly to reload the 32 pounders.

Gallows Bay

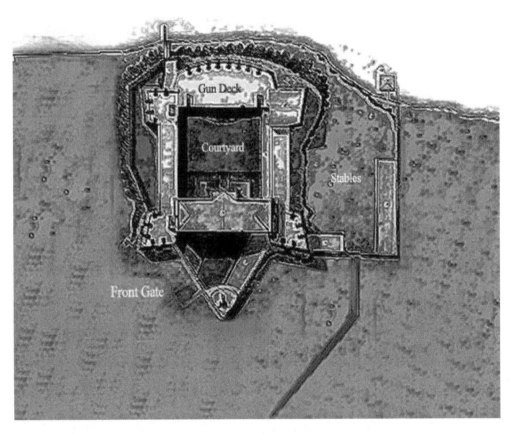

The captured cannons fired nine more volleys at each fort before one of the forward militia scouts came running back to where James and Bode's forces were positioned to announce that a force of forty Dutch soldiers was marching in formation down the road, with a draft horse pulling a field cannon. James was actually surprised and impressed that they were able to organize a force that quickly.

The instructions to the militia were to fire their long rifles and reload, to use their British muskets with bayonets only if the Dutch charged their positions, and even then only to fire them at point blank range first and then use the bayonets. From his hidden position, James could see Captain Hendriks was leading the Dutch soldiers. He smartly stopped his men just outside the range of the grapeshot-loaded cannons on the eastern fort. Unfortunately, and unknown to him, he was only 60 yards downhill from where the militia was hiding with aimed muskets. The Dutch captain quickly surveyed the situation in the growing light of morning and, seeing only the gun crews actively firing and reloading, he turned his attention to the surrounding area and to the low hill and tree line above him. James knew that they were seconds from discovery, and he had no intention of allowing the Dutch captain time to position his men. He gave him men the order to fire from their prone positions. In the brief moment from the time he issued the order until the militiamen discharged their guns into the Dutch soldiers below, he and the Dutch captain made eye contact. James saw the instant recognition by the Dutch captain, and saw his expression change to intense hatred.

The smoke from the forty muskets hung thick in the air before them, initially blocking their view of the enemy below and the results of their volley. The men immediately sprang to a standing position to begin reloading their muskets, most of them wisely taking a position behind whatever cover was available. When he turned back to the Dutch force before him, the ocean breeze had thinned the smoke enough to see that the Dutch soldiers were moving chaotically, trying to form battle lines. He could also see that the Dutch captain had survived the volley, but there were at least ten Dutch soldiers who had been wounded or killed lying on the ground before them. James continued to watch as the Captain briskly walked behind the Dutch soldiers, loudly barking orders to each group to encourage them to form a firing line. Four or five soldiers had initially turned to run from the fire, but his piercing voice and threats had brought them running back to join their comrades, taking their place in the now quickly forming firing line. James could see that his men would not be reloaded in time to fire again before the Dutch would. He stepped over to stand behind a group of small trees and waited for the Dutch muskets to take aim at them. He then yelled. "Down! Down!" Bode echoed his orders.

Just as they had trained on the plantation, at once their men either dropped to the ground or stepped behind cover. The roar of the Dutch muskets firing in unison from below was deafening and the snapping sound of the musket balls passing by or as they impacted the trees and bushes around them added to the chaos. A branch in front of James' face exploded from the impact of one of the lead balls, blinding him briefly and burying a wood sliver in his left cheek. He reached up and felt the short stick protruding from his face and tugged it out, casting it to the ground. He thanked God that it had not pierced his eye. His men were already on their feet and striving to finish loading their muskets.

James glanced down at the Dutch soldiers to see the captain yelling orders and giving the signal to charge the rise where the militia positions were located. James could see that several of the militia had reloaded and were preparing to fire.

"Fire at will men, then fire your British musket when they arrive!" he yelled. He raised his own musket and shot the lead Dutch soldier as he took his first step toward them. He thought about aiming for the Dutch captain, but he was behind the front ranks of soldiers. James set his long rifle down and picked up his British musket, pulling back the lever. Shots were beginning to be fired by the militia as their muskets were now reloaded. James saw one of the militia fire his long rifle and then start to reload it.

"No time, Jeb, grab your British musket!" The order brought the nervous soldier to recollection of the battle plan and he set down his long musket and picked up the shorter British weapon with the bayonet attached to the front of it. He took aim.

"Wait for them to get closer, Jeb. Make the shot count!" Jeb first lowered the British musket, then raised it again and waited. James looked back down to where the Dutch were charging up the hill and saw that the second shots from the militia, fired from a much closer range, were having a devastating effect on the Dutch soldiers charging up the hill. By the time they had all fired their second reload, another ten to fifteen Dutch soldiers were either down or had stopped their forward progression. As the remaining Dutch soldiers closed on the waiting militia, they were surprised to see them grabbing yet another loaded musket that had lain at their feet, now suddenly raised and aimed directly at them.

It was as if their heads understood the consequences that awaited them but their legs did not. When a *kill or be killed* moment comes in battle, most will choose to kill in spite of the display of courage or the sadness before you. The first twelve soldiers who tried to close with the militia were literally blown backwards from the point blank impact of the lead balls slamming into them. The last six, including their captain, recognized their deadly folly and stopped to determine their next course of action. The captain holding his cutlass and pistol looked down the barrel of James' musket aimed at his chest. James shook his head as he saw the captain consider his options.

"Don't," James said to him as the Captain and the remaining soldiers stood in silence and anticipation. "There is no need for further death. Put your weapons down and surrender." The remaining members of the militia who had not been forced to fire their British muskets, began walking closer to where the remaining Dutch soldiers stood, each aiming his weapon at the soldier closest to them. James knew the soldiers wanted no more of the fight, but he thought the Captain was going to charge forward anyway. To his relief, the apparent hopelessness of the situation overrode the anger and pride of the Dutch captain. He slid his cutlass back into its sheath, released the hammer on his pistol and placed it back in his belt. His men quickly followed his example and dropped their weapons. The militiamen moved forward and took control of the Dutch soldiers' weapons and then stepped back and waited for orders.

"Daniel, take some men and see to the wounded, ours and theirs," James gave a gentle order to the oldest man in the militia. Daniel had a dusting of gray hair and next to Elijah King he was the wisest and most gentle man he knew. He was assigned to be the lead medic for the militia because he took care of the animals at the plantation.

One of the militiamen approached the Dutch captain and pointed to his pistol. The Captain looked at the militiaman and upholstered it, but ignored the militiaman. He walked over to where James stood ten feet away and handed it to him, then withdrew his cutlass and formally presented it. James accepted them both and handed them to the original militiaman to hold.

"It appears my prophecy was incorrect, it was not to be you, but me in chains," the Dutch captain said coldly and then took a moment to look around at those of his men still standing and at those who were either dead or dying around him. "We should have blown you out of the water when we had the chance," he said. James nodded in agreement and then raised an eyebrow and shrugged. "Or you could have just sold us the supplies we needed and we could have avoided all this death," James said coldly. "Unfortunately, your arrogance was your undoing." The captain at first seemed to get angry at his words, but then he calmed his expression. The sound of the four 32 pounders firing in succession again suddenly echoed from the east fort. The Captain turned toward the sound and then back toward James and shook his head.

"We underestimated you and the members of your crew, Captain. I know I would never have guessed that you could go from anchored to under speed in less than 15 minutes."

"They're not my crew," James said softly and thought about his words.

"Pardon?" The Dutch captain asked.

"I said the ship's crew is not mine. We are just being transported by them," he clarified and then continued with a question. "So I was counting correctly and you opened fire earlier than the time you set had expired?" James queried. At first the Dutch captain seemed confused, but then understood his meaning and nodded.

"The commander's word, not mine," he said and smiled smugly, looking away. It was James' turn to be confused as he tried to grasp the officer's meaning. James suddenly felt his own anger flare.

"So you ordered the guns to open fire on us early?" James asked again. The Captain at first did not respond and then looked at James and nodded, but seemed embarrassed.

"When it was evident that you would escape our cannon fire well before the fifteen minute deadline, the Commander made it clear multiple times that he had given *his* word that *he* would not issue orders to fire early. I didn't understand at first, but finally got the hidden message and ordered the guns to fire early," he said as he looked away again and then back to James. "It seemed like the right thing to do in the heat of the moment. Based on our current situation, my hesitation proved wrong." James looked at the man for a moment before responding. "No. You should have kept your word and all this would have been avoided."

"Bull, take your squad and escort the prisoners to the fort and secure them there." James ordered the closest leader of five.

"Yes sir," he replied, and gathered the men and their own muskets and motioned the prisoners to start walking toward the east fort.

"The rest of you, reload both of your muskets. Bode, take two groups, gather the weapons and the cannon, and move it to the fort, then use the wagon to carry the wounded. We will move forward and form a new defensive line to make sure no one takes any shots at you. Have you and your men join us when you are finished." James looked across the field of battle and saw Daniel kneeling down over one of the Dutch soldiers.

"Daniel, give me an update on our casualties." James asked him as he reached down, picked up his long rifle, and walked toward him. He was trying to brace himself for the dreadful words that he knew would be coming. Daniel looked up and then around the field as if counting. "At least twenty dead and almost as many wounded," he replied. James was stunned and quickly looked around again at the various militiamen, who were either reloading or helping out where ordered, and then he realized that Daniel was not talking about the militia's casualties, but the Dutch casualties.

"No Daniel, our casualties," he clarified. Daniel seemed to misunderstand his question, then it dawned on him what James wanted. "None sir. Actually, you seem to have gotten the worst of it. I'll take a look at that left cheek in a moment," he said as he continued attending to the Dutch soldier lying in front of him. James was greatly stunned and relieved by this information and he thought about the incredible outcome. He thought back to the sight of all the bullets that had ripped through the trees where they were and not one man in the militia was hit. James looked around a moment and then closed his eyes and began a tearful prayer of thanks to God.

James was not sure exactly how long he had been praying when a gentle hand on his shoulder caused him to open his eyes. There was Daniel tipping his head back as he tried to look at the wound on James' cheek. He saw the tears running down James' face and at first thought they were tears of pain, then realized the real cause and stepped forward to put his arms around him.

"It's okay James, God is with us," he said and patted him on the back as they continued to embrace.

Chapter 10

When the full report finally came in, James learned that of the seventy-five men of his militia and merchant gunners, only three men were wounded, none critically. They had killed or captured sixty-two Dutch soldiers, sixty usable muskets, one pistol, one cutlass, one 9 pound wheeled cannon, and a wagon with shot and powder for the cannon. The fort itself was filled with four 32-pound cannons and two smaller 9 pounders currently aimed at the road approaching the fort. Their position was truly a miracle but, unfortunately, they still did not have the supplies they needed to survive in the open sea long enough to return home. Bode had returned with his men and was reinforcing the forward defensive positions. James asked Bode to take the leadership role with the forward position as he went back to evaluate their situation at the east fort and the progress with the other forts.

When he arrived, he saw the makeshift infirmary that had been set up outside the fort. It was on the protected side of the east fort in order to keep any direct return fire from reaching that area. As he entered the fort, he was surprised by the number of prisoners sitting on the floor with their hands tied behind their backs. There were only ten militiamen guarding over thirty prisoners in a tight area. James ordered the prisoners to their feet and outside the fort, where he directed them to sit in a very tight circle thirty yards from the front of the fort. He then ordered both the wall cannons with their loaded grapeshot aimed at the prisoners and positioned two of the merchant gunners to stand guard on the cannons and the prisoners. He asked Robbie and his men to wait for him.

"If even one of them tries to escape, fire on the whole group," James said loudly to the two men guarding the prisoners. He then turned to where the Dutch Captain was sitting and asked him to repeat his order in Dutch to the group and to tell them that the cannons aimed at them were loaded with grapeshot. He nodded and spoke a series of words that, although James could not understand, he saw the effect the information had on those listening; most turned to look at the guns and then back at James.

"Thank you, Captain. I do not wish to see any more of your men killed or wounded senselessly because one man wants to be a hero," James said. He headed up the path to the east fort's entrance. There was a strong concussion of three cannons firing from the ramparts so closely. He looked back to see the prisoners looking at the walls above him, grateful to know that the cannons were not firing at them. James entered the now empty lower section of the fort and went up the stairs to the gun ramparts. As he stepped onto the upper gun deck, he saw the masts of *The Dragon*, which was sitting just inside the entrance of the bay. Her sails were down, the anchor had been lowered and two longboats were paddling toward the shore in front of the east fort. Mr. Richards was instructing each gunner as to where he wanted the next shot to go, adjusting the cannons as needed. He turned and saw James standing behind him.

"Excellent work out there, James! This is going better than planned," he exclaimed with a smile and slapped him on the back.

"It sounds like things are also going well here," James replied and waited for the update as he watched three gun crews reload the three cannons aimed at the main fort. James could tell that Mr. Richards was truly the expert gunner that Captain Donovan touted him to be. Mr.

Richards pointed to the west fort and continued to speak too loudly. James smiled, knowing that he did not realize he was yelling at James even though there were no cannons or noise calling for it. That the ringing in his ears from the cannon blasts made him think he needed to yell over the noise.

"No one is showing himself at the west fort. We have knocked out two of the guns and decimated the crews that were trying to man them. We have the one gun dialed in on them should they come back out." James nodded as he looked over at the west fort and saw the damage caused from the 32-pound cannon balls pounding away at them. Mr. Richards then turned toward the main fort.

"The main fort is proving to be a more difficult target, not to hit it, but to do enough damage to the gun emplacements. We have their range down, but the walls are proving to be very thick. I've requested that *The Dragon* send over more powder and 32 pound shot; for we're running low on both and unfortunately we have a long way to go." James nodded as he listened to him yell. "From what I can see, they are also working very hard to reposition their 48 pounders to aim them at us. We're trying to keep their heads down, but it's only a matter of time before they can bring one or two of them to fire on us. When that happens, well these walls won't be a very safe place anymore." He smiled, but James could feel his urgency in the matter.

"Then we will march to the city early to prevent that from happening," James said and patted him on the shoulder, starting down the stairs at a quick pace. Outside, he joined Robbie, who was with the ten guards and the prisoners. He stopped and looked around the area a moment, making sure everything was secure. He noticed the draft horse and wagon near the infirmary, where it had been used to transport the wounded, and the 9-pounder artillery cannon sitting off to the side, where they had unhitched and left it.

"Lieutenant, have your men attach the cannon to the wagon and reload the shot and powder. Tell Mr. Richards we need one of his gun crew to join us," James ordered and retraced his steps into the fort. Robbie nodded and started giving directions to his men.

"You don't really believe you can take the fort do you?" the Dutch captain asked with a chuckle as James re-emerged from the fort. James looked at him and shook his head.

"I came to get the supplies that you wouldn't sell us. You can keep your fort." James replied and moved toward the wagon that now had the cannon reattached to it. One of the men was leading the horse to the front entrance of the fort. Robbie and five gunners came out the front door and started loading the wagon again. James figured that the Dutch must have plenty of shot for the cannon since it had not been fired during their encounter. He heard one of the gunners instruct the militiamen to also bring some of the grapeshot loads, as another cannon blast roared above their heads, causing his ears to ring. James wanted to get away from the noise of the cannons as quickly as possible.

Once loaded, the draft horse, wagon and cannon, followed closely by five gunners and ten militiamen moved at a quick trot toward the forward defense line, where Bode and the rest of the militia were waiting. Although James was happy with the results so far, he knew that things would get a lot more difficult as they moved onto the city.

They joined the rest of the militia and they began to cautiously move forward toward the eastern outskirts of the city, each man carrying his two muskets. They expected to be greeted with armed resistance when they saw the first building. Instead they saw a short Negro boy standing and staring at them as more and more of them came into view. Then without a sound he turned and ran down the street. Not seeing any defensive measures in place, James signaled for the men to follow the boy down the street. James was very impressed as he watched his dark clad men move like a wave down both sides of the street, Bode on one side and he on the other, with the wagon following. They came to a cross street and James could see people fleeing in the distance down them, but the vast majority were Negros, fleeing with their families. On one corner, an older woman stepped out slowly from behind the door to stare curiously at the men of the militia.

"Madam." One of the men nodded his head and smiled as he passed by her. She continued to stare in disbelief. With each building they passed, James saw more Negro citizens either staring out the windows or standing at their front doors, but no white citizens could be seen.

Glancing down the streets, James could see several horses attached to wagons sitting on the streets, some loaded and others empty as if they were getting ready to leave. It appeared that once word had spread that the militia was on the outskirts of town, the citizens had abandoned the wagons and fled. He ordered one group of five to set up defenses using the wagons as cover and to hold this cross street in case they were attacked from behind. James was unsure how many troops were here, or if an attack would come from someplace else.

As they advanced they came to another cross street and repeated the same process, using two more wagons for cover. James could tell that they were now only a few buildings away from the open field that led to the main fortress. He ordered his men to move forward more cautiously. Bode was on the protected side of the street and quickly moved down the line of buildings in order to reach the corner that would allow him to observe the fort. He glanced around the corner, then quickly moved his head back. He leaned his British musket against the wall next to him and quickly raised his long rifle musket, stepped out from around the corner and fired at someone who was beyond James' sight, and then quickly stepped back. Bode's men each took turns stepping out and firing as Bode had, while James and his men continued to move forward looking for a position where he could see what was happening. He finally reached an opening between two buildings. In front of the next building was a loaded wagon. The wagon was sitting on the street between the fort and the closest building and offered not only an excellent view of what was happening, but also great cover. James ran, keeping low, to the wagon.

James looked at the open field, now in total chaos as people; mostly citizens ran toward the fort. There were many wagons lined up near the fort entrance, with draft horses still attached. James could see that the gunfire was causing many of the draft horses to dance nervously with each shot. Soldiers and citizens were hastily unloading the wagons' contents, carrying them into the fort. Meanwhile a protective line of about twenty Dutch soldiers had taken up positions between the fort and the city boundary in order to buy the workers more time to unload the contents of the wagons. James could see that three of the Dutch soldiers had already fallen as the rest were trying to maintain their skirmish line. James leaned his

British musket against the wagon, then raised and rested his musket on the wagon railing. Taking careful aim, he fired at one of the soldiers in the center of the line. The smoke and recoil of the blast blocked his view of the immediate result, but he could see, once it cleared, that there was an opening in the line where he had fired. He immediately began to reload as five more of his men took up positions with him behind the wagon.

"They have cannons on the wall, probably grapeshot, so don't stand in the open!" he yelled across the street where Bode and his men were firing and reloading. Bode nodded and passed the warning to the men in his area. Once the firing started, the citizens who had not reached the fortress walls had dropped whatever they were carrying and were now running as fast as they could toward the entrance of the fort. Soldiers and citizens continued to unload the wagons near the front gate. As he finished reloading his musket, James heard muskets fire behind him and turned to see four of his men aiming west down the street that ran parallel to the closest wall of the city. Two citizens, still clutching their muskets, were crumpled over, while three other armed citizens were now fleeing in panic. James did not like the idea of having to engage the civilians in battle, but there was no choice if they entered the battle.

Turning his attention back to the fort, James raised his musket to fire again and saw that there were five more Dutch soldiers down and several more were stumbling back toward the front gate of the fort. As he was aiming, the top of the back wall exploded as one of the balls from the 32 pounders at the east fort slammed into it, sending a shower of brick and debris out into the open field. Instead of firing again, he took a moment to observe the fort as a whole from his vantage point and saw, that there was a great deal of damage to the buildings surrounding the main fort caused by the east fort's cannons during their bombardment, as shots had passed over and behind the front walls. A great deal of smoke and dust arose from inside the fort. There were only a few Dutch soldiers manning the corner tower guns facing them. He watched a soldier fall and then another, as the militia's long rifle muskets with their greater range and accuracy took their toll on the now all-but-abandoned skirmish line.

He sensed that panic was starting to run through the Dutch ranks and moments later the line broke and the few remaining soldiers withdrew at a run toward the protective walls of the fort. The soldiers who were offloading the wagons saw the soldiers running towards them and ran with whatever was in their hands through the gate. There were a few parting shots from the militia, and then momentary silence that was briefly broken by a thud as the heavy metal bound door of the main gate was shut. A moment later the fort suddenly shook and the sound of exploding brick echoed up the street where James stood, followed immediately by the sound of a cannon being fired in the distance.

James, Bode and the men stood in silence for a moment waiting for some immediate response or attack to come from the fort, but none came. James ordered the men to pull back from the vulnerable firing positions and move behind the protection of the buildings along the street. Once everyone was safely behind the buildings, James asked Bode to establish a defensible perimeter that would allow them to secure the major buildings in the city. James, with a squad of five men, began to go from building to building searching for the needed supplies that they needed.

The first building that they entered was some sort of government office; however, the second building they searched was immediately recognizable as the main warehouse of the

Dutch East India Company. They carefully moved through the offices of the building to the open warehouse area. As they stepped inside, they saw that the main double doors that faced the harbor entrance and fort were open. He saw bags and bags of sugar and crates filled with bottles and barrels of rum, but as James and his men searched through the stacks and piles, they found very little in the was of essential food supplies. He knew the crew would be happy with the rum, but what they really needed was food and lots of it. James stepped to the edge of the open door and looked at the fort and all the wagons that were lined up in front of it. His heart sank as he realized that the most essential items must have been moved along with the townspeople inside the protective walls of the fort. All the people in the fort had to do was to wait out any siege until help came. James' plan had failed and although they had rum and sugar, it would not be what they needed to get them home.

A cursory search of the nearby buildings and homes within the city provided some basic foodstuffs, but it was nowhere near what they had hoped to secure. In spite of the shortfall, they began loading the wagons the men had used as cover with the supplies they had found. James assigned an escort of militia to drive the wagons back to the east fort. Once there, the supplies were to be transferred onto the longboats and rowed to *The Dragon*. James knew that Captain Donovan would be as disappointed as he was with the sparse supplies, but it was the best they could do at present. He stood and looked out the second story window of one of the official buildings toward the main fort in front of them, watching the steady bombardment raining down on it from the east fort.

The unfamiliar sound of a nearby heavy gun jarred him from his thoughts. He knew immediately that the Dutch in the main fort had finally brought one of the 48 pounders to bear on the east fort. He had been hoping to avoid a direct assault on the main fort, but now it seemed that he had no other option if he were going to protect the men at the east fort. He turned and ran down the stairs and onto the side street. James had previously given orders to the gun crew to have the cannon loaded with solid shot, primed, and to be ready to fire on the main fort's front gate, should the east fort come under fire. The plan was to force as many Dutch soldiers and gun crews as possible to shift from the east facing wall to the front gate in order to defend against a direct attack.

With the help of six militiamen, the gun crew from *The Dragon* quickly positioned the already loaded and primed cannon on the street next to the warehouse and aimed it at the fortress's front gate. The cannon's first shot went a little to the right, slamming into the stone wall, but James was sure that it let those on the back side of the fortress know that they were under attack from a nearby cannon. They were able to load the second shot without interference while Dutch crews on the walls tried to grasp where the fire had come from. When they fired the second shot, James was frustrated to see it hit low in front of the door, but it still managed to bounce up to strike the door with a crashing sound. Although the door held, some of the wood below the lower iron band splintered and James knew that it was vulnerable. The commander inside must have realized the same and began firing his wall cannons facing in the direction of the militia. It was not with the intent to hit anyone, but to clear the grapeshot with which they were loaded so they could reload the longer-range balls needed to reach the distant and exposed cannon and crew firing at them from the city.

With no fear of the grapeshot raining down on them from afar, James ordered the militia to fire their muskets at the ramparts in hopes of slowing their reloading of the wall cannons.

The race to reload first was won by the militia gun crew, as the cannon erupted again and sent a 9 pound lead ball directly into the hanging front door, tearing it off its hinges and opening the way into the front courtyard of the fortress. James knew there was another metal door inside the fort that they would have to get past to take the fort, but they had achieved their initial goal. He quickly ordered the cannon and crew to withdraw behind the cover of the buildings, but not before the Dutch wall guns sent several balls toward the gun crew, one striking the warehouse and another passing over the heads of the cannon crew and down the street, tearing through a building with a crash.

Climbing back to the second story of the warehouse, James surveyed the bay: *The Dragon* anchored in the entrance, the west fort with two small merchant vessels anchored in the harbor near the wharf, the east fort, and the main fort before him. The 48 pounder roared again. It had been many minutes since its previous firing, which meant the crews were either hard pressed, or they were having difficulty keeping it secured from the recoil when the cannon was fired. One of the longboats from *The Dragon* was rowing toward the west fort with a full compliment of men on it. James tried to imagine how he might be able to help them, but decided that they were on their own in the attack on the west fort. The single cannon on the east fort that was aimed at the west fort started firing on it again, and James hoped that it would buy them enough time to avoid any cannon fire from the west fort and allow them to reach the shoreline in time. The longboat beached soon thereafter and a short time later, James burst forth with a "Yes!" when he saw the Union Jack being raised above the ramparts of the west fort. The Dutch soldiers had apparently surrendered the fort without much resistance. James knew the men now in control of the west fort would be working diligently to bring those guns to bear on the main fort. The remaining gun on the east fort was also now free to fire on the main fort. Elated as James was, he knew that even with the west fort in hand, the main fort would prove to be a very difficult if not impossible objective. If the Dutch were to get additional 48 pounders in action against the two forts, the smaller forts would quickly be destroyed. He knew that they did not have the time to wait it out, nor did they have the supplies they needed to leave the area. As another 32 pounder slammed into the interior of the main fort, James suddenly had an idea.

Five minutes later, James and two men stood by one of the trees that lined the walkways between the city and the fortress; one of the men with him was holding a white flag and waving it back and forth for the fort to see. He saw the activity he was hoping for from the men on the walls. Bode was not a big fan of the plan, but they were running out of options. He made it clear to everyone that Bode would be in charge if this did not go well. It took awhile, but eventually a flag was waved back and two Dutch soldiers armed with muskets stepped through the broken front door to await their approach. James knew that at least two of the 9 pounders sitting above the ramparts would be loaded with grapeshot, as they slowly began marching toward the main fort's front gate and the awaiting soldiers.

As they stopped in front of the two Dutch soldiers who stood in front of the broken door, he saw one of the men near a cannon step back from the wall. The Commander suddenly appeared in the man's place, looking down at James. James could see the anger and hatred in his eyes as the officer looked down at him, recognizing who it was standing before him. A 32 pounder slammed into the fort causing everyone to flinch, including the Commander. The Commander suddenly withdrew from the rampart without a word, leaving James and his two men standing in front of the two Dutch soldiers. A minute later, the

Commander stepped through the destroyed front doorway along with five men, glaring at James as he approached.

"Have you come to surrender, Captain?" James was not surprised that in spite of the pounding of the 32 pounders and repeated defeats, the arrogance of the commander remained intact.

"I have come to offer you and your men terms." James replied coldly. "Your main guns cannot reach our positions. We have already killed or captured over eighty of your men. In spite of your hostile treatment of us, I do not wish to see you or any more of your men or citizens killed in your hopeless defense of this fort."

The commander seemed to be gathering his thoughts while at the same time controlling his anger before replying. "My young Captain, that small fort does not have enough shot or powder to accomplish the job you intend. In fact, I'm guessing you're almost out or you would not be coming to me. Contrary to your presumptuous notions of victory, this fortress remains fully armed and able to defend itself." He smiled as he removed his gloves to hand them to one of his men. "So I suggest you take your little band of men and run back to your ship while you still can, for there are forces heading your way that you are ill-equipped to handle."

It was difficult for the James to be disrespectful to an older man, but he felt he must cross the line in this situation. "May we speak privately Commander?" The Commander looked about and smiled, giving the signal to his men to wait, as he and James stepped to the side of the rest of the group. With cold steel in his eyes and a seriousness that belied his youth, James spoke sternly and directly to the commander.

"Sir, your actions have been less than honorable from the beginning of our prior meeting. Let me be clear one last time so that you can avoid a very unfortunate end for you, your men and the citizens of this town. The ship that sits outside your gun range is loaded with powder and 32 and 48 pound shot that was destined for a British fortress not far from here. Much of it is being shuttled to the east fort as we speak. We have also positioned cannons from the ship to the heights behind the city that will allow us to place deadly shot directly into the fortress. The result will be death for everyone inside. As I'm sure you are aware, we now control the western fort and those guns will be added to the bombardment of the main fort. I assure you that we have more than enough to turn this fortress of yours into a sand pit. You also betrayed your word and fired prior to your 15-minute deadline." James paused for effect. "You gave me and my men a 15-minute chance, so you will be given the same amount of time to decide whether or not to surrender. If you refuse this opportunity now, please understand that every man in this fortress will be shot whether it is now or later, and then we will burn this city to the ground. So, the question to you is: Are you so foolish and arrogant as to dismiss me, or do you want to listen to my terms?" The Commander responded with an arrogant smile, and then looked with distain at the two black soldiers that had accompanied James. He seemed about to reply with one answer, then stopped and changed his demeanor.

"I will listen to your terms." He said softly.

"The terms are simple, your men (including your wounded), would be allowed safe passage to board one of the small Dutch merchant ships currently anchored in the west harbor. You and your officers will remain our guests until we depart, at which time you will be free to return to your fort, homes and businesses. The troops on the merchant vessel will be provided with enough supplies to reach the closest Dutch port. All weapons and cannon are to be left. If any of the cannon or facilities on the forts are sabotaged or destroyed prior to their leaving, one man will be shot for each gun or facility sabotaged, starting with you at the top and working our way down the chain of command." James stopped to let the commander think a moment. The Commander smiled as James finished and looked him in the eyes as if to intimidate him.

"Captain, here are my terms, you will…" The commander started, but James cut him off.

"Commander, I will not entertain any counter terms; you have the only ones I am willing to extend to you. You have fifteen minutes to decide, and unlike you, I will give you the full fifteen minutes, but not a moment longer. If you agree, then you will run up the flag of surrender from your ramparts, if not, we will begin the burning of the town and the full bombardment will begin and no prisoners will be taken." James bowed to the commander and started back to his men, then stopped and turned back to the commander. "I will begin the count now." James and his men headed back to the warehouse just as another series of cannon shot slammed into the fortress.

James put his men to work in plain site of the fortress, each with a torch in his hand as if waiting for the orders. As the count wound down, James stepped out in front of the wharf and warehouse and raised his hand as if to signal to his men. He could see the Commander on the ramparts of the fortress watching him and his men. Just as James was preparing to give the signal, the Dutch colors began to descend, replaced a short while later by a white flag. The guns from the east fort immediately fell silent. The bluff had worked. James exhaled, relieved that he did not have to burn down the city. James saw Bode grinning at him and shaking his head. It was an amazing victory; the crew of a single merchant vessel, along with fifty unique men from North Carolina, had taken the Dutch port of Christiansted with only a handful of casualties, or had they?

James saw movement from the front door of the fort and ordered his men to prepare to defend their positions. Slowly, sixty plus Dutch soldiers filed out from the fortress and took up positions in front of the wall. They were still armed with muskets and fixed bayonets and their Commander and several lesser officers were behind them. James waited for additional orders to be given to them, but none came. James stepped forward with the original two men and approached the Commander.

"I request that my men be allowed to leave with the honor of their weapons," the Commander spoke from behind the line of men. James was relieved to see that there was no one still on the wall cannons. He thought about it, but was not willing to give in to any of his terms.

"You understood the terms before the surrender, have them lay down their arms or the offer is rescinded," James responded coldly.

"You realize that I could shoot you down right now and your rabble would flee." The Commander threatened. James realized that he was vulnerable, but he knew his men would hold strong. With a cold smile, James replied, "I'm the only person holding this 'rabble' back from tearing you and this town to pieces. Shoot me down and you will have a bloodbath of your creation that will never be forgotten." The silence between the two men was deafening as they stared at each other. Finally James nodded and said, "So be it." He turned and raised his hand as if to give the signal and the sixty-plus Dutch soldiers began raising their rifles for battle.

"Wait!" the Commander yelled, breaking his composure. "Stand down!" the Commander yelled the order to his men. "Sir, the fort is yours." James turned to face the Commander again while keeping his hand in the air.

"Have your men step forward and place their weapons on the ground and then withdraw to the edge of the wharf for further instructions." The Commander gave the orders and his men came forward to do as commanded. Finally the Commander stepped forward.

"Captain, I hope you are a man of your word," he said as he stepped forward and surrendered his pistol and sword to James.

"We shall see if my word holds more weight and honor than yours," he replied as he took the Commander's weapons and pointed toward the wharf area where the rest of his surrendered troops now waited.

"There are wounded in the fort who need attention. My surgeon is still with them," The Commander informed James, who nodded his understanding as he turned and signaled for his men to come out from behind the walls and doors of the city. A wave of dark clad men came from behind the walls and out the doors of the buildings and marched across the field, taking up guard stations around the Dutch soldiers. James stationed thirty men of the militia in a half circle around the Dutch prisoners. Each had his two muskets, and each man was given an additional captured and loaded Dutch musket to have close at hand. The captured men were ordered to sit on the ground, facing the harbor.

James gave Captain Donovan an 'all clear' wave of his hat, and Captain Donovan fired a single cannon shot acknowledging the signal. Leaving Robbie in charge of the prisoners, Bode and James, accompanied by the remaining twenty soldiers, began walking toward the main fort. They stopped briefly to survey the supplies that were still in some of the wagons and what had been dropped in haste as they had withdrawn into the fort. James assigned five men to guard the wagons and the walls in case anyone should try to steal from them. They moved through the broken door of the fort and into the front courtyard. With weapons at the ready, they moved across the debris and scanned the area. The inner door was closed as they approached it. James tapped the butt of his rifle against the metal reinforced door and waited. A few seconds later the latch was thrown and the door was pushed out toward them.

An older gentleman, not the one he had seen several days ago, peered out the doorway with an expression that conveyed he feared the worse. James addressed the man sternly. "What is your name sir?" he asked the man, who looked over his shoulder as if listening to someone else. Then he turned back and spoke very softly.

"Linden, Henry Linden," he said in broken English. James nodded and smiled.

"We will be coming in to examine the fort and its contents. We do not wish any additional injury or harm to come to the citizens of Christiansted, so please notify the other citizens. If there are any weapons in anyone's possession, they must put them in the center of the inner courtyard prior to our entering. If weapons are found on anyone after we enter, he will be shot." James spoke very slowly and clearly to the man, who nodded and then turned and spoke loudly in Dutch to those inside. A few moments later, he pushed the door the rest of the way open and stepped back into the shaded area behind the door.

James handed his musket to one of his men next to him, then took a deep breath and walked through the door with his hand resting on the pistol tucked securely into his belt. As his eyes adjusted to the darker area, he could see a very large crowd of people standing inside the covered structure and even more outside in the inner courtyard. Many of them had been injured, from shrapnel and falling debris caused by the shelling. They had makeshift bandages or slings covering their injuries. In the center of the courtyard, he saw ten or more muskets, several pistols, a few knives, a sword, and several clubs in a pile. He walked up to the pile and spent a few moments looking down at the sword, then reached down and picked it up, turning it in his hands. "Who does this sword belong to?" he asked the people standing in the courtyard. At first there was a nervous silence, and then a slight commotion as an older woman tried to stop an older gentleman from stepping forward. James watched as the man calmed the woman with a smile and a few gently spoken words, stepped away from the rest of the group and walked toward James.

"It is mine, Captain," the man replied in proper English. James looked at the man, who was almost entirely gray, yet thin and healthy. He guessed him to be in his early sixties and his eyes reflected an inner confidence and trust. He was without fear as he spoke. James knew he must be a retired soldier, perhaps British.

"It's a very good sword." James stated in appreciation.

"It is yours to keep, Captain," he replied humbly and motioned with his hand toward it. James shook his head. "No. It is a sword of earned leadership. It belongs to the man who earned it and should not be a spoil of war," James replied and handed it back to the man. The man seemed to glow and returned the smile. "Thank you. You are very kind," he replied.

"What is your name and what rank did you attain before retiring?" James asked the man.

"Stephen Massman. I attained the rank of Colonel in his majesty's service, Captain," he replied proudly. James thought a moment before continuing.

"I need someone to assist me in communicating with the citizens and directing them as needed to avoid any confusion or further injuries. Would you be so kind as to handle that role for me Colonel Massman?" The man thought a moment, nodded and saluted.

"I would be happy to, Captain." James returned the salute, enjoying the man's obvious pleasure in being selected for service.

James and Bode began looking around the courtyard and the shaded areas at the people who had sought the protective walls of the fort, only to be disappointed. Some held bags in their hands, some cases, some just held their children. Some seemed to be standing guard over the items directly behind them. Each person seemed to have fled in haste, with their most loved or valuable item. James remembered his mother when it appeared that their house was in danger of burning. After making sure all the children were safe, she grabbed the portrait of her parents and family. In looking at these people, James tried to think what he would have grabbed had the situation been reversed. Then he noticed something very shocking as he walked around the courtyard, stopping now and then to examine the various items of value scattered around the area. As he held open a bag of silver utensils that was at the feet of a middle-aged man and wife, he looked around at the several hundred citizens within the wall. There were only three Negro women and two Negro children in the whole fort. Two of the women were standing in front of several young white children and the two Negro children, as if protecting them. The other was holding a white woman's hand, as if for mutual strength. James searched the area one more time and felt an inner sadness at the realization that the attitude was no different here from back in the colonies. The vast majority of them were more concerned about protecting their material items than their workers, servants or slaves. Had the servants been turned away at the door, or had they just not cared about them enough to even try to protect them? He thought briefly about taking everything they owned away from them, but knew it would be the wrong thing to do. He handed the bag of silver utensils back to the owners and turned to the retired English Colonel. He did not know how to handle this situation, but he also wanted to put the citizens at ease.

"Colonel, please notify the citizens that there will be no harm that will befall them as long as they cooperate as needed. The men will not pillage their personal possessions, homes, or harm their women or children…" James hesitated and then continued. "Nor will their servants or slaves be harmed, which they do not seem concerned about." He walked away back toward the middle of the courtyard as the Colonel repeated James' words to the people, and a sense of relief seemed to come over them. Then James continued.

"Everyone is to remain inside the fort until further notified. While here, we will load the supplies we initially came to purchase peacefully and be on our way. Once we are finished, they are free to leave the fort and remain in their homes until we depart." James paused before continuing to let the Colonel repeat his message to the citizens.

"Colonel, there were several citizens that bravely, but unwisely engaged our forces when we arrived. I'm sorry to report that they were gravely wounded or killed and will need the attention of their families and friends."

James looked around again and then asked the colonel to organize a group of men to carry the food supplies that had been stacked chaotically around the inside of the fort, to the wagons and then returned to the inside of the fort to await further orders. The Colonel turned and within moments the men were gathering the supplies and heading out the front gate with them. Slowly, the rest of the citizens settled down and moved to the shady areas to wait.

James felt more overwhelmed with the needs at hand now, than he had trying to figure out how to secure the supplies by force. He shook his head and Bode seemed to read his friend's mind.

"Don't worry James, it'll all work out," Bode said quietly. "Captain Donovan will be here soon and he will know what to do and how best to do it. I'll work with him on organizing the men and materials so you won't have to. You have enough on your plate." Bode smiled and patted him on the back. "Besides, we all know you can't even run a plantation, let alone organize supplies," he said and smiled. James was always the big vision man, while Bode was the one who always put the pieces together to make it all work. They had the same working and friendship relationship as their fathers.

James and Bode walked up the stairs to the main gun rampart facing the bay. There were seven bodies laying to the west of the rampart, and blood covered the rampart in various areas next to two of the big guns. There was rock debris from where the 32 pounders had smashed into the walls of the ramparts, blasting through or breaking chunks off. They saw where the Dutch defenders had blown away a top section of the wall so that they could position one of the 48 pounders to face the east fort. It appeared that they were working on two others, but had yet to properly secure them. They could see that one of the guns to the west was in the beginning process of being repositioned. James looked at the size of the 48 pounder cannons and the balls next to them and knew why they were so deadly. He knew that they were very fortunate to have been able to secure the fort before the Dutch had brought all these guns to bear.

From the top of the rampart facing the bay, James looked back toward the fort and the city. He was surprised at the amount of damage their 32 pounders had caused to the upper interior of the fort. The roof of the east tower had been completely destroyed, and most of the roof on the south center tower that overlooked the initial courtyard was smashed to pieces. There was rubble all over the place. He tried to imagine what it must have been like for the citizens below, and the soldiers above, during the bombardment. The ongoing fear and chaos created by the shells striking the fort and the debris flying everywhere and the sight of the dead, and the screaming of the injured and the dying. It probably added to the pressure on the Commander and his decision to surrender the fort to James. James wondered if there had been only troops within the walls of the fort would they have stayed calm, positioned the 48 pounders and eventually won the day? He glanced back at the big guns and turned to one of the soldiers below him. "Joel!" The young man looked up toward James. "Go and bring the gun crew that came with us here right away. We need to get these guns repositioned to face the mouth of the harbor."

"Yes sir," Joel replied and weaved his way through the various citizens, who were either sitting in the shaded area or were loading the supplies in the wagons.

James looked out at the bay and saw that *The Dragon* had sailed in and anchored behind the west fort and next to the two smaller merchant vessels in the protected inner harbor. James could see the size difference between *The Dragon* and the other two small merchant ships. Both of the other vessels could almost fit inside the hull of *The Dragon*. He could see the men on the west fort scurrying around the ramparts and positioning the cannons that were there. He looked over to the east fort and saw two big holes knocked out of the side of the fort; the few shots that the 48 pounder had fired had left their mark. The gaping holes in the walls said a lot about the bravery of the men manning the east fort, who had continued to fire, fully knowing that one well placed shot would have decimated them all.

James and Bode walked to the eastern wall and looked over it; to their surprise they saw a walled stable and storage area that was about the same size as the main fort. The north side was open to the bay, while the east and south sides were walled and the south side that faced the city had a heavy gate. He could tell the walls were not as thick or as high, but they still made for a secure area to station troops and supplies. He made a mental note to examine that area more closely later if time allowed.

James and Bode walked back down the steps just as the gun crew of the 9 pounder was heading up the stairs.

"What a bloody mess they made of these guns…" James heard one of them say as they walked across the courtyard. They took a brief tour of the rest of the fort and saw that each corner tower had another floor below ground and a pathway to each corner. The troop quarters were located along the western wall and the ground floor southwest tower had been converted to a temporary infirmary. James stopped to introduce himself to the surgeon and to tell him that once their crew was ashore, he would send additional help. The man nodded his appreciation and offered his assistance with their wounded. James did not share that they had very few injuries or needs; he just thanked him and let him know that everyone was being taken care of and that he would send help at his earliest opportunity. He walked down some steps to the lower section of the Southwest tower and saw that it was a prison holding area, with several former Dutch prisoners currently in custody.

Underneath the main gun battery was the shot and powder room. There were plenty of 48, 32 and 9 pound shot available, and along with it, plenty of powder. The Northwest tower had a privy that poured out from the wall and dumped into the sea. "Clever." James said to Bode, and they both took a moment to relieve themselves and then poured some water from the nearby bucket to wash down the path. They chuckled at the results and efficiency of it and moved on.

On the ground floor of the eastern wall, they came upon the various offices and quarters of the officers. He walked toward what he knew was the commander's office. He thought about his interaction with the Commander, and then about the gentleman and son that he had met. He did not remember seeing the man among the citizens when they entered the fort. As he stepped into the office, he glanced at the various items lying about. Pen and ink, paper, boxes, wax and stamps sat about the desk or in the drawers. Bookshelves lined two of the walls, each holding other items of interest and value. There were basic maps lying about that caught his attention, but he knew that anything of importance or secret was a part of the pile of ashes in front of the office, burned prior to the surrender of the fort. The room was filled with books and several oil lanterns sat on the desk or hung from the wall. A portrait of the Commander in full military uniform hung on the wall to the right of the door. James could see there was a small room just off the office area that had a cot, table and full closet on the wall. He was surprised at how cool it was in the room compared to outside. There were three more offices with quarters along the eastern wall, similar to the one he left.

The kitchen and dining area were on the main floor of the southern interior wall, the one shaded area they had walked through when entering the main fort. To avoid the hot sun, this is where most of the citizens had tried to reside. He could see that the chimney from the fire pit and oven had been severely damaged by the 32 pounders, but the roof overhead and floor of the upper room was still solid and secure. James knew that it would require a lot of work to return the fort to its former shape.

James and Bode were stepping through the damaged doorway on their way out when he saw Captain Donovan, followed by about twenty of his men moving toward the fort. He could see some of the other sailors from *The Dragon* laughing and embracing the various militiamen that they encountered as they walked around the area. The wagons were being loaded as directed, several had even been escorted to the wharf area and were being unloaded and their contents transferred into the waiting longboats. The retired colonel was doing an outstanding job and James nodded and smiled to the man. The supplies that had not yet been loaded onto the wagon were being stacked alongside the wall of the fort. James and Bode continued to wait by the door as Captain Donovan, wearing a huge smile on his face, had closed the distance. As he got close he started shaking his head and laughing.

"I thought you just wanted to get the supplies from the city?" He spoke so loudly that everyone nearby could easily hear. James shrugged and looked at Bode.

"They moved them into the fort and left us no choice," he replied and returned the smile just as Captain Donovan got within reach and clasped hands and then embraced each of them. Then he stepped back and looked at the two men before him.

"Do you realize what you have accomplished here today, Captain?" he asked.

"We," James replied

"Sorry?" The merchant captain said in confusion.

"I said 'we' what *we* accomplished captain you, your men, and my men. 'We.'"

"Okay, 'we', but no matter how you look at it, this is a legendary feat, my friend, and I'm just glad I was able to play a part in it." He laughed again as he looked around and then exhaled sharply. "The British have been trying to secure a key base in the Caribbean for decades, sending vast amounts of ships and soldiers and you..." he started and then corrected himself, "We... come in here with a merchant ship and a handful of militiamen and capture one with hardly a loss to be felt. This is historic! Absolutely unbelievable!" He laughed again and then put his hands on his head and looked around again. James and Bode nodded, feeling almost embarrassed by the attention.

"Desperate times sometimes require taking desperate measures," Bode commented and the Captain nodded.

"We were definitely in a desperate situation, but this." The Captain spread his arms again as he waved them around in all directions, "This is..." He seemed to have trouble finding the right word.

"An answered prayer," James supplied with what he felt were the right words. The Captain at first just stared at him, then started nodding.

"Indeed it is," he said, and then added quietly as he looked around, "With God, all things are possible." Both James and Bode nodded and smiled, surprised by his Bible knowledge.

To James and Bode, the idea of "impossible" did not enter their minds. It was simply the only choice they had left to them if they were to survive and get back home. James tried to wrap his mind around the victory, but apparently did not grasp its importance beyond the immediate needs of the men.

"I hope when the story is told, they tell of the brave men in the black and gray uniforms," James said knowing better than to hope for it.

"I promise you that I will tell it accurately... What a day!" Captain Donovan laughed out loud again and slapped the two of them on their backs one more time as he walked past them toward the fort. "Much to do-much to do," he mumbled as he headed toward the fort entrance.

James followed him and related what he had told the citizens inside and that he was unsure of what they should do next. He wanted Bode to work with the Captain to make sure they were working together on things. Captain Donovan seemed confused for a moment, and then smiled.

"Not to worry James. Bode and I will take care of everything." Bode smiled and winked as he and Captain Donovan stepped through the damaged doorway and into the fortress.

James stood at the entrance and looked back toward the city and the wharf area. There were close to a hundred or more servants and slaves either sitting on the steps of the buildings or in the grass area in front of them. Most of the slaves seemed to be calmly watching everything, while some were speaking with the men of the militia. James knew it would be as strange for these slaves to see Negro soldiers as it was for the slaves in the colonies. He could see smiles and even laughter being exchanged between them as both sides tried their best to communicate with the other.

James' attention was directed to movement from the city as the thirty Dutch prisoners captured at the east fort and from the aftermath of the initial defense of it were marched down the main road toward the wharf. Each prisoner, with hands bound, was tied to the one in front of him. The prisoners were escorted to the wharf by the men from *The Dragon*, who each carried two muskets. James could see Captain Hendriks in the middle of the group of prisoners. He sensed that he was being watched and he looked toward the fort and James, who was standing at the doorway. The man seemed to be trying to comprehend the situation laid out before him as he glanced at the row of Dutch prisoners sitting on the wharf area, and then looked back at the main fort; then finally at James. Their eyes met briefly before the Captain turned away.

James tried to imagine what the situation would have been like if things had been reversed. How would he and his men have been treated if *The Dragon* had not escaped yesterday, but instead been destroyed. Would those that had survived and swam to shore have been shot or put in prison? He was grateful to God that he had all his friends still with him after such a dangerous series of events. God had definitely protected them and guided them at every turn.

Bode stepped out of the fort and offered James a chunk of bread and a cup filled with some sort of stew. "Captain Donovan told me to pass this along to you." Bode smiled and took a bite of his own piece of bread that he had dipped in the cup of stew. As James held the two items, he suddenly realized how hungry he was. He saw four other men exit the fort and walk past him and down the hill toward the militia below, one carrying two large baskets of bread, two others with a big kettle of stew between them, and the fourth with a box of cups. He walked over and sat down next to the fort's wall facing the city.

As he sat there holding his stew and bread, he felt the stress of the day still clutching him and he knew that he was exhausted down to his core. He leaned his head back against the cool stone of the fort wall and closed his eyes. He realized that he had not taken the time to thank God for the victory that was given to them. As he slowly began to work through the various aspects of the day, he could see how God had worked to protect them and he thanked Him for each blessing. Although he was grateful for the victory, he was more grateful that he had lost none of his friends. As he opened his eyes, he looked down and dipped the bread in the stew and brought it to his mouth. The food smelled and tasted incredibly good.

As he chewed and savored the stew soaked bread, he glanced up to see the retired colonel looking at him. James wondered how much of his expression of hunger was written on his face with those first bites that he had taken. Should he even be concerned? After all, it was clear that he and his men were hungry, weakened and desperate for food.

"I'm sorry we laughed," he said to James from where he stood directing the work crew as they continued loading the wagons. James stopped chewing as he tried to understand what he meant. He seemed to read James' confusion. "When you and your men were forced to run to your ship," he said and James swallowed hard at the memory. "It was cruel of the people to do so, although I do not believe they understood at the time the deadly consequences you faced," the Colonel explained. James thought a moment and nodded as he looked away. It probably did look humorous seeing him and his men running and paddling at top speed, thinking they were just being scared off, or whatever the situation appeared to be to them. He looked back at the man after he had swallowed his most recent bite.

"I have trouble believing you were one of those laughing," he replied. The man looked away, gave an order to one of the men loading the wagons, and then back at him.

"No, but I did not try to stop it either. I have learned that in life there are no innocent bystanders," he said humbly. James nodded and took another bite. He really liked the man and wondered if in different circumstances they would have been good friends. He knew his father would have liked him.

"Thank you. Apology accepted and forgiveness granted," James replied and smiled as he took another bite. The man seemed to smirk and then shake his head. "You are a unique man Captain Thornton. Does not anger, hatred or revenge burn inside of you?" he asked James. James thought a moment before responding.

"When I let those guide my actions, I do stupid or horrible things that I feel embarrassed or regret later. I have learned, and have been taught by my father, that staying calm and thinking clearly always works much better." He started to take another bite and then stopped. "Don't get me wrong, all three of those feelings were screaming for me to take action." He smiled. The man smiled and nodded back and returned to his work of directing the loading of the supplies on the wagons.

Chapter 11

Within the hour, Captain Donovan and Bode had a variety of tasks in motion, with the ship's crew and the militia as well as the local citizens actively working on them. The first task was to remove all the supplies, money, and the small 9 pounder cannons, four on each vessel, along with any shot from the two small merchant vessels in the harbor. Once those items were removed, the prisoners, minus the officers, were moved to the below-deck areas for temporary holding until they could figure out what to do with them. Captain Donovan was very concerned that they would try to organize an escape attempt, so the Dutch commander, the captain and two lieutenants were placed in the prison section of the southwest tower of the fortress. James smiled as he watched Captain Donovan repeatedly issue orders in front of the prisoners regarding various "ghost" troops that were supposedly stationed at different places on the outskirts of the town and in positions on the hills further out. He also purposely inflated the number of troops that were stationed at the east, west and main forts. He did this consistently, first while the prisoners were sitting on the wharf, then when they were transferred to the longboats, and then even when they were unloaded on the newly converted prison ships. Once the Dutch soldiers were secured, they focused on dealing with the citizens in the fort.

Captain Donovan stationed Bode and five militiamen, along with the two Dutch translators, to interview and search each person leaving the fort. He wanted to know their names, career and position in the city, and what they were carrying with them and why. James and Captain Donovan had a disagreement initially as they discussed what they citizens could keep and what they could take with them. Captain Donovan wanted to keep all moneys, items or documents, and James wanted to allow them to keep their things since he felt they did not come to loot the citizens. Captain Donovan felt strongly that there were people in authority that should have certain items confiscated. They settled on something in between and agreed to document and hold all money taken from the citizens, with the plan that it would be returned at a later date, based on their cooperation or their relationship with the Dutch East India Company, the fort, or with the officers or soldiers.

That final decision proved wise, as Captain Donovan had each individual separately escorted from the inner main courtyard to the front gate courtyard, where they were interviewed and searched. Several "citizens" were found to be carrying a great deal of gold and silver coins in hidden places. They learned, upon threat of severe flogging, that officials of the Dutch East India Company were secretly distributing small amounts of their precious coin through the people with the understanding that they would return it back to the company once they were all out, with a reward waiting for them. When Bode informed Captain Donovan of the scheme, he followed up on the interrogation of the citizens and discovered who the trading company officials were that were organizing the covert activity. He shared with James and Bode what his plan was to address the situation. After both hesitantly agreed, he then marched into the inner courtyard with ten of his men and ordered the two officials that were behind the activity to be taken captive, whereupon they were tied and held in the middle of the courtyard. He then turned and addressed the citizens.

"It has come to our attention that these men have approached several of you and asked you to conceal and covertly carry money for the Dutch East India Trading Company on your person, and return it at a later time for reward once you leave the fortress. Such activity has greatly violated our trust in you and as a result, there will now be unfortunate consequences." Captain Donovan waited as the retired Colonel translated his words to the citizens, then he nodded his head and the soldiers marched the two men out the front gate. Looks of concern and whispers and murmuring raced among the group at these words, while additional soldiers took up positions within the inner courtyard.

James watched as the citizens became increasingly agitated and began asking the retired colonel for assistance, who then turned to approach James. James held up his hand to stop the Colonel, who nodded and withdrew from approaching him. Suddenly a shout and the sound of pleading could be heard from outside, before being muffled. The citizens went silent as they tried to imagine what was unfolding outside. Then, from the west wall just outside, the sound of the orders "Ready-Aim…" was heard. The Colonel looked straight at James in disbelief at what was happening and James looked away from him. When the order "Fire!" came, James estimated that four muskets were fired. There was sudden wailing from those who must have been the wives and children of the two men and there was stunned disbelief from the remaining citizens. Shortly afterwards, Captain Donovan marched back into the inner courtyard and addressed the citizens.

"As a final courtesy, I would strongly recommend to those remaining that have been approached by company officers, that you refuse to comply, or report your involvement immediately to avoid similar punishment for you or your family." He then turned to where Bode, who was standing by the inner door watching.

"Lieutenant King, please continue with your interviews," Captain Donovan said calmly and walked past him. Bode followed him to the front gate again as the next citizen was escorted to the exit. He looked back over his shoulder, his eyes pleading for help or some sort of guidance from the other Dutch citizens. James watched discreetly as various citizens started removing items from their bags, purses, hats, and shoes dropping them on the ground and then walking away from where they dropped them. *'Very effective'* he thought to himself as he stepped through the inner door and then out of the fort. He saw the two men, hands tied, gags still firmly in place, one with his pants soiled, both sitting next to the walls. The younger of the two had tears running down his face, while the older man just stared at the sky. One soldier stood guard over them. Captain Donovan stepped next to James and shook his head in disgust as he looked at the two men.

"Neither of them was willing to risk carrying any money on themselves or their families, but both were more than willing to put their neighbors at risk," Captain Donovan whispered to James.

"For the love of money is the root of all evil: which while some coveted after, they have erred from the faith, and pierced themselves through with many sorrows." James quoted 1 Timothy 6:10 and the Captain nodded his head in agreement.

James turned to see the first citizen to clear the check-point look curiously over to where the two bound and gagged men sat. Expecting to see something very different, he seemed at first to be shocked at the sight, and then relieved.

What remained of the day was spent processing the citizens, feeding the troops, and positioning the various cannons to point back to the bay entrance. More and more food was transferred to *The Dragon* and placed in her hold. There was a skeleton crew left on *The Dragon*, which put nearly 100 of her crew on shore, each working diligently on whatever task the Captain had set them.

Once processed, most of the citizens had chosen to flee the city and shelter in the surrounding hills, waiting to see what would happen. Just before nightfall, they fed the men an even larger meal from the provisions they had captured as well as a ration of rum as promised. The guard was doubled on the now secured prison ships; the guard was also doubled in the three forts. Captain Donovan retired to *The Dragon*, while James, Bode and roughly 100 men took up residence in the main fortress. Robbie, with twenty men of 2nd Group and a gun crew, stayed in the east fort while petty Officer Sanders, of *The Dragon*, and a similarly sized group of men stayed in the west fort. After organizing guard duty and rotations they retired for the night. With the help of the food, the day's hard work, and the small ration of rum, rest came easily to all of them.

Before the sun even rose above the waterline, Captain Donovan was already giving specific direction to his men. As James walked the edge of the wharf with two of his men, he saw that Captain Donovan's crew was transferring supplies to one of the smaller merchant vessels. James climbed onto one of the longboats and rode out with them to the vessel. Once aboard, Captain Donovan, who was still shouting orders, came over to where James was standing, away from listening ears. "James, with regard to allowing the prisoners to sail away on one of the merchant vessels, I would not have offered them the terms you did, nor give them a valuable vessel." He hesitated a moment before continuing. "But because you gave your word to them, I will honor it. Just so you know, I'm only giving them a skeleton crew of captured sailors to sail it. In addition, they will have a limited set of sails to use, which will allow them to sail freely, but will greatly reduce their speed. Lastly, I'm only giving them enough supplies to get to one of the nearby ports to the south of here with very clear and specific orders to only sail south. Should I see the ship depart from its southern direction, or return to these waters, we will chase them down and sink them with all hands," he said coldly.

James nodded and asked, "Where do you think they will go?"

"I expect the Dutch Antilles, since it is the closest Dutch port from here, but they may call my bluff and double back in the night to Frederiksted on the west end of this island. That would mean we'd probably end up fighting them again in the near future, something I was hoping to avoid," the Captain said and smiled, but James frowned.

"We would need to be here to fight them." James replied. There was a long silence and the Captain seemed to be looking for the right words.

"James, I'm not sure that leaving is the right thing to do. If we have managed to capture this valuable port for the Crown, and then turn around and hand it back to the enemy, I don't think that would go well with the King," he said quietly but firmly. "It might even be labeled as treason and I don't think you want that image to be attached to yourself or your men."

The news hit James like a punch to the stomach. He was silent and grim-faced as he thought through the ramification of the Captain's last words. He had hoped that they would be loading *The Dragon* with supplies and going home to North Carolina at the earliest opportunity, but now he was being asked to somehow hold the fort and city with 50 trained troops and 100 sailors? He turned and walked to the railing of the vessel and looked back toward the city where his men were resting and recovering from the prior day.

The last thing he wanted was to tarnish their amazing accomplishments by making them the "Idiots of the Caribbean," by giving a strategic city and its fort back into the hands of the enemy. He could already imagine the degrading stories and the laughter that would ensue. He hated the fact that, no matter what they accomplished, it would never be enough, or the credit would somehow go to someone else. As he stared out over the bay toward the city and the fort, he could not think of any solution that would allow them to leave without being ridiculed. It seemed that only their deaths defending the fort would be a satisfactory solution. The idea of dying was not one he wanted to embrace, but at least they would not have to hear about it the rest of their lives. He turned back toward the merchant Captain.

"I'll tell the men. We'll begin preparations to defend the city and fort for as long as needed." The Captain seemed to be trying to read James' face as he spoke.

"James, I know that this is nothing close to what we signed up for, but live or die, we'll do it together," the Captain declared and James nodded.

"I'm guessing the latter seems more likely," he replied and the Captain smirked.

"Then let's make them pay dearly, if it is to be such an ending," the Captain whispered intently and patted James on the shoulder. James could see that the Captain was earnest and James decided that if this were their only option, then he would approach it with every ounce of determination that he could muster. He nodded and headed back to the railing where the longboat was tied.

"Let's have breakfast at the fort, for we have a lot of planning and work to do before we die," James said and smiled as he stepped over the rail and down the ladder.

"Breakfast it is!" Captain Donovan replied and then started calling out orders to his men and to the captured crew that would be sailing the vessel out of the harbor. As they rowed back to the wharf, James guessed that the Captain hated to see the merchant vessel set free, but Captain Donovan was an honorable man and would honor the conditions of the surrender that James had presented.

When he arrived back at the main fort, James pulled Bode and Robbie aside and explained the points Captain Donavan had made. Although they also wanted to return home at the earliest opportunity, they agreed that they could not hand the fort back to the enemy until British replacements arrived. James and Bode and a small group of men took a wagon to the east fort to inform Robbie and the men stationed there of their plans to remain. They then went to the main fort and called the men together, apprising them of the situation and their decision. There was disappointment and concern from the men, but they agreed that staying and defending the fort was the best course of action. He was very proud of his men and those who were leading them.

Climbing the steps to the main rampart, as he seemed to do every hour, he saw that the small merchant ship with the Dutch prisoners packed onboard was slowly sailing out of the harbor. He agreed, as Captain Donovan suggested might happen, that he and his men would have to fight them again in the future. Even as the ship sailed east out of the harbor and eventually turned south, the men were already busy with the work at hand. With no prisoners to guard, they left the two remaining ships in the protected harbor with a minimal crew to guard them. Captain Donovan gave the remaining crewman of the captured merchant ships two options: either to join them, or be placed in prison. To the man, they joined with his men in whatever assignment was given them.

During breakfast, Captain Donovan, James, Bode, Mr. Richards, Mr. Sanders, and Robbie had a lot to consider. They laid out all the maps that they had found or captured from the fort, the East India Company offices, and the other official buildings of the town. There were various maps of the surrounding islands of the Caribbean, St. Croix, and maps of Frederiksted, and one twenty-year-old map of Christiansted with roads and hills included. They pushed all the maps aside except the one of Christiansted.

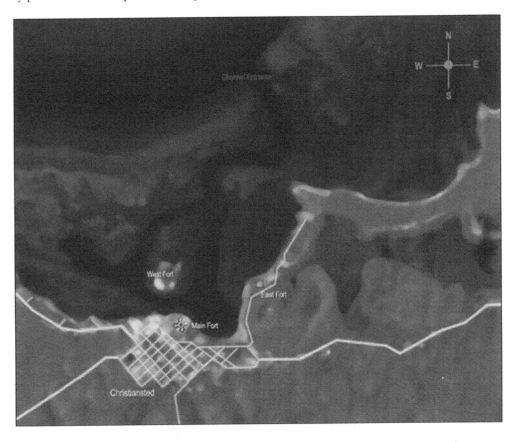

"No sense in worrying about anywhere except where we currently are." Captain Donovan said. "Not much we can do about the rest of the area or cities at this time," he finished and they nodded in agreement.

James was surprised at the size of the city laid out before them and the number of streets and roads shown on the map. The road from which they had entered the city during the attack on the main fort, the wharf and the buildings of the eastern side of the city, were actually only about a fifth of the city's overall size. They surveyed the surrounding areas outside the city and realized that there were several sizeable plantations nearby.

"Should they be considered a threat?" Bode asked the group. The Captain looked up from the map toward Bode.

"Son, you will not find any armed or military trained 'workers' on any plantations you encounter here. They are terrified of an uprising. What you will find is an armed family and their hired workers, perhaps ten to twenty at the most, but they will not be trained." Bode nodded and then replied, "But if three, four or perhaps more of the plantations came together, we could potentially be facing fifty or more armed men in battle, perhaps a hundred should more plantations unite." James nodded in agreement as he thought about the neighboring plantation back home that was attacked by a group of local citizens who banded together.

"Unless their fear of us is too great, or we win their hearts, it's only a matter of time until they either get the courage or are organized by outside leadership to take action." James opined. The Captain seemed to understand the concern.

"What do you suggest?" The Captain asked James and Bode.

"I don't see us winning their hearts any time soon, so we need to be ready to defend the city and the fort as best we can," Bode replied as he tapped the city area on the map.

"Let's only defend what we can defend effectively without our lines and resources being stretched too thin. Let's start with the forts and the bay and slowly expand from there," James suggested and the Captain agreed.

They spent the next hour discussing how best to do just that. Since the gun crews of *The Dragon* were spread out between the ship and the three forts, they determined that they would begin training the militia on how to use the big guns. To avoid losing their guns and supplies from sabotage by leaving them on *The Dragon*, they would transfer all the shot, the powder, the muskets, and the four British 9 pounder wheeled artillery pieces from *The Dragon's* hold to the main fort and distribute supplies as needed to the other lesser forts. The spare muskets were to be moved to the main fortress and locked in the gun storage room. The inventory list, not counting the long rifles and weapons already with the militia or the fixed cannons and the crew's weapons on *The Dragon*, listed over 150 captured Dutch muskets, 100 spare British muskets, and five 9 pounder wheeled cannons. The east fort had four 32 pounders and three short-barreled 9 pounders manning the walls. The west fort had the same number, whereas the main fort had eight 48 pounders, and twenty 9 pounders, five on each tower. Captain Richards noted that they had taken four 9 pounders from each of the two smaller merchant vessels, but Captain Donovan was planning on putting four of them back on the other remaining vessel in case they needed to use it later for transportation or as a fighting platform to block the harbor.

They discussed the coin that was at their disposal from what was captured at the fort, secured from the East India Company, or "on loan" from the citizens, who departed once they left the city.

"Gentlemen, we have the following currently in our treasury: 340 copper duits, 210 silver two stuivers, 85 silver ten stuivers, 31 silver one guilders, 23 silver three guilders, 65 gold one ducats, 28 gold two ducats and a large number of bank notes detailing monies owed by several of the plantation owners to the East India Company." He looked up and smiled at the men. Mr. Richards and Mr. Sanders seemed to understand the value of the notes before them, but James, Bode and Robbie did not.

"One silver guilder is equal to twenty silver stuivers and one gold ducat is equal to ten silver guilders," Captain Donovan explained and James nodded, but James did not try to sort through the various conversions, deciding to leave that aspect to the Captain. But he did have one question. "How much of that belongs to the citizens?" James asked. The captain looked down at the numbers before him. "Less than one tenth of it," he replied.

"So how does having this money benefit us in defending the fort or city?" James asked the Captain.

"It gives us the ability to spend it should we need to buy anything from the plantation owners," he said.

"Why would they sell us anything after we've taken their city and fort?" Bode asked, but James seemed to see an opportunity. "They have goods to sell and generally there is not an issue with who the buyer is as long as he is willing to pay a fair price for the goods. In fact, they need to sell those goods if they are to have the money to buy the supplies they need to survive," James explained.

"So we need to get them to participate in the commerce here on the island," Captain Donovan said. "And exactly how do you propose to do that?" James thought a moment. "We offer to buy their goods at a fair price. Their rum, sugar, cotton, corn- whatever they are selling, we buy it," James replied in a "matter of fact" way. The Captain blinked and sat in silence a moment before speaking.

"We don't need cotton, or sugar. Perhaps some corn and okay, yes, we could buy some rum. But the rest would just be a waste of money."

"It would get them to re-engage in the town's marketplace and we would show them that we are here to stay and fill the role of a commerce outlet for them. The only difference to them is that we are British instead of Dutch. I would guess that they don't care anymore about who they are at war with, other than how it will affect their ability to sell their goods and produce," James added. "We just need to show them that we are not here to raid and pillage their plantations." They all sat in silence. The Captain finally spoke up.

"So, how do you plan on doing that?"

"We take a few of the wagons, an escort of troops, and a bag of coin and visit them and offer to buy their goods. We can also take with us a small amount of basic product that can be sold or traded," which Bode and Mr. Sanders nodded in agreement.

"You can also offer to cancel their bank notes. If that doesn't peak their interest, nothing will," Mr. Richards said with a devious smile.

"Then it's agreed. James, you're in charge of reaching out to the local plantation owners," the Captain said with a smile and they all agreed with the decision except James and quickly move on to the next key topic. James thought about arguing the point, but he knew that he was the best person for the assignment and knew that he would not succeed even if he tried.

The next discussion turned to the defense of the forts. It was decided that it was a high priority to finish removing the angle barriers on the two right and left main 48 pounder cannons that proved so dangerous for the Dutch, allowing the ponderous cannons to be rotated enough to fire at either of the smaller forts should they ever be captured. The group adjourned their breakfast meeting with the understanding that the list of "to do" items they discussed was more than enough for the men to try to accomplish that today. They would have another meeting during the evening to evaluate their progress and to make plans for the following day.

Preparing and repairing the forts took much longer than they anticipated. They spent the next few weeks repairing the forts' brickwork, doors, and structures. The gun crews of *The Dragon* worked with the men selected from the militia, training them in the use of the heavy cannons. Once they had done all they could with the city and the forts, James began to focus on reaching out to the Dutch citizens to encourage them to come back to the city to operate their stores and shops. James had made sure that no one, including the merchant captains' men, looted or destroyed personal possessions or goods from stores or homes within the city and had posted a rotation of four two-man patrols that guarded the city at night. They had secured some food stuffs and tools from a merchant store on the wharf, but had left a note in the coin box detailing what they had acquired, promising compensation from the fort coffers upon the shop keeper's return. The officers understood that they would have a difficult time swaying the opinions of the citizens after what just transpired here, not to mention the skin color of the militia, so they made every effort to represent themselves better than any other army the citizens had ever witnessed.

James started by speaking with the Dutch citizens who had stayed in the city, and let them know that they would be converting the port to a British port for trade and that the moneys on hold at the fort would be returned to those who began their business operations again. The retired British Colonel was one of the citizens who had stayed in town and James enlisted him to act as his interpreter for the citizens as he walked around the area. As a show of force and demonstration of the courtesy and professionalism of his men, James always brought five soldiers with him wherever he went.

James also posted signs in Dutch inside and well outside the city limits, on the major crossroads leading to and from the city. The notice stated that the citizens had two weeks to return to their homes and businesses within the city or they would be considered abandoned and the goods and moneys would be confiscated or turned over to other citizens as the military saw fit. He knew that many of those who were still on the outskirts of the city would be hungry, as most had left in a hurry, either in sheer terror with little more than the clothes on their backs as the militia had entered the city or fled once they were released from the fort. He truly hoped they would return and get things moving and the city functioning again.

The Dutch citizens (about 350 of them) of Christiansted began slowly to come back to the city. Extremely untrusting of the offer mentioned on the posted notice, a few men came in first without their families to survey the opportunity. When they found their city in good order and their homes and businesses as they left them, they sent for their families. By the end of the second week of the offer, 90 percent of the citizens had returned and Christiansted began to operate once again as a city. James and his men personally went to visit each place of work and family (with translator in tow) to ensure their safety and livelihood and to explain the conditions of their occupation. He also made it clear that any resistance or sabotage of the fort, city, or soldiers would be met with force and punishment, and would result in the loss of their business or home. All weapons were to be turned over to the fort for holding. The occupiers would purchase or trade for all goods and services offered by the citizens for which they had need, and they would not withhold goods and supplies that the citizens needed unless urgently required for the defense of the fort and the city.

Chapter 12

Early in the morning on July 16th, seventeen days after the capture of Christiansted, James, Colonel Massman and five soldiers, were in town speaking with one of the families when the alarm bell suddenly could be heard ringing from the main fort. He excused himself and along with his men, charged down the street. When they reached the fort he was directed to the top ramparts where James could see Captain Donovan and Bode looking out to sea.

He ran up the steps and still breathing hard, looked out on the northeast horizon where he saw the sails of three large ships in formation coming from the northeast toward the island. Captain Donovan noted out loud that one was a Dutch ship of the line, third rate at least, and the other two were large merchant vessels. Still breathing heavily from the run, James looked around to see men scurrying about and taking up the defensive positions they had been assigned should this situation arise.

"Troop ships?" Bode asked without looking at anyone. Captain Donovan continued to stare through his telescope at the ships and then shook his head. "Could be, but I don't think so. It's too early to organize and supply a small army to reclaim their fort. As they stared in silence, James recalled some of the interactions he had had with the citizens the past week. "In my discussions with the citizens, several mentioned that the scheduled supply ships from their home country are late, which is why their key supplies are so low. Perhaps this is the fleet they've been waiting for?" he speculated. Captain Donovan looked over to James, back to the city, and then back to the ships out at sea.

James looked up at the fort's flagpole above them and saw the small Union Jack they had borrowed from *The Dragon* gently blowing to the south. He guessed that the three vessels with their square rigged sails would have a difficult time holding the tight angle needed to catch the wind, which was why they were coming in so far to the north of the port instead of sailing down the edge of the island. He wondered how many guns were on a third rate ship, how many troops were in the hold of the three vessels. How many of his men would die trying to hold this fort for the Crown? He prayed a silent prayer asking for God's protection of his men.

The three continued to watch as the three ships sailed east toward them. The captain continued to relay orders to his men as he watched the vessels come almost directly north of them.

"They will tack any moment and then sail with the wind directly at us. It could not be a better wind position for them and a worse one for us," the Captain said and then signaled to one of his men in the courtyard below, who immediately headed toward the fort's front door. "With that favorable wind, the ship of the line will be able to sail directly and quickly into the harbor without needing to tack one time. We will be lucky if we get two, maybe three shots off before they deliver a 26-gun broadside from their port side guns at the east fort, then turn slightly to deliver a 26-gun broadside from their starboard side guns to the west fort as they pass by each one. Then it will be a cannon fight between our eight guns and their twenty-six guns. That is assuming their plan is to come right down the middle to retake the port." He ended the lesson and smiled.

"Any way to counter it?" Bode asked. The Captain looked back at the harbor as if calculating time and distance.

"We could have used one of the merchant vessels to temporarily block the harbor entrance, but there's not enough time nor do we have enough men available to get them to the ship, raise the anchor and sail it to the harbor entrance before they arrive," he replied as they continued to watch the three ships.

Just as the Captain had predicted, the eastern most merchant ship suddenly turned to the south and headed directly toward the harbor. They watched and waited for the other two vessels to also turn. After several minutes of anticipation, they were stunned to see the third rate warship and the other merchant ship continue sailing east, while the lone merchant ship kept sailing toward them.

"Escort." Captain Donovan mumbled. "It seems we are blessed once again. It appears that the ship of the line was escorting the two merchant ships; one was to be delivered to Christiansted, the other twenty-five miles west of us to Frederiksted. They have no idea that the fort and port now belong to the British, so they have assumed that they have safely escorted the inbound ship to the port entrance, and are now continuing on to Frederiksted." He seemed to breathe easier as he watched the merchant ship closing the distance to port.

"Now what?" Bode asked the Captain, who seemed to be thinking as he watched the remaining two ships continuing east.

"When the merchant ship sees the Union Jack flying over the fort, they will turn away and head east." He said and pounded his hand on the top of the ramparts. "This will give us more time to prepare, perhaps try to blockade the entrance now that we know the warship is in the area." He banged his hand on the nearby cannon in frustration. "If I'd have known this, we could have used *The Dragon* to chase her down and capture her. No time now." James thought about the captain's words and knew that there was no way any of them could have known this would happen, but appreciated how Captain Donavon was always looking for ways to capitalize on any opportunity before him.

They watched as the merchant vessel, with the wind pushing it perfectly and beautifully toward them, closed the distance. Captain Donavon could tell that the captain of the vessel had visited this port many times before, for even at their great distance he was already lining up his ship to miss all the dangerous corral heads while still taking full advantage of the wind. The Captain noted that it was a beautiful merchant ship, although not as fast as *The Dragon*. It had good lines and it appeared to have a good crew.

"Any moment now we will get to see them wet their pants and then turn away and head back out to sea." He laughed and James and Bode smiled as they watched the ship close the distance. As the ship continued toward them, James watched the posture of the Captain change as time passed. Then he leaned forward and placed both hands on the rampart in front of him as if anticipating something incredible.

"Keep coming, keep coming." He started mumbling under his breath and James and Bode suddenly realized what he was seeing.

"They are not turning away." Bode said softly as the vessel continued on toward the port entrance, approaching the coral heads on each side of the dangerous and narrow port entrance.

"Lt. King, he appears to be more interested in navigating the waters than looking to see who the new owners of the fort might be," he replied, never taking his eyes off the vessel. The ship continued forward, passing the most dangerous and narrow part of the entrance to the port and then it began its turn toward the protected bay and the waiting guns of the three forts. James could even see that some of the crewman on board the merchant ship were waving from the rigging and decks at those manning the guns on the three forts. James smiled when he saw the gun crews from the eastern fort wave back.

James saw, that for the most part, the crew of the merchant ship were quickly pulling up sails and tying them off to the yards as they coasted into the bay area with only a few of their sails still up and loosely billowing in the light breeze. James looked up to see the Union Jack was now barely moving on the flagpole, hanging straight down. The Dutch ship's crew had missed it, or had just assumed the fort was still in Dutch hands and sailed right into the harbor. It was a very costly mistake for them, but an immense blessing for those in the fort. The Captain ordered the guns to maintain and reposition as needed to fire at the vessel should it try to leave.

"The wind is not favorable for an exit by sail without great difficulty," the Captain said to no one in particular. "So they are now our guests." He shook his head in disbelief. "We are a group of very blessed men." There was a sudden change in activity on the merchant ship and James could see the Captain step forward and stare at the main fort and the men looking down at him from it. It was as if everyone on the vessel suddenly froze in place and began staring at the various forts and cannons that were now aiming at them. He seemed completely taken aback by the situation and was trying to struggle to find a solution to it, but there was none available unless they were to open fire with their six 24 pounder cannons that were not even loaded or run out yet.

"If they move to put up sail, or run out their guns, open fire, Mr. Richards, until they cease to do so," the Captain ordered and turned to James.

"James, shall we pay the captain a visit? Lieutenant King, would you be so kind as to take charge of the fort," he said with a smile and started down the steps with James following behind.

James looked at Captain Donovan, wearing his full British uniform, standing in the bow of the longboat as six of his sailors rowed them out to meet the captain of the merchant vessel. As they approached, James could see twenty or more Dutch soldiers, armed with muskets, lining the deck of the vessel, along with a large contingent of the merchant crew behind them. They pulled alongside the ship and waited.

"We request permission to come aboard to discuss the terms of your surrender," Captain Donovan stated as the longboat floated nearby the massive vessel. There was a long silence as a lieutenant in the Dutch army stared down at them from the railing.

"You vill spreak from wheret you are," the lieutenant snarled down at them in broken English. Captain Donovan took a deep breath and then nodded.

"When you sailed into this harbor uninvited, you and your men became our prisoners and your vessel became our property Lieutenant. It is only with respect and restraint that orders were not given to destroy your vessel. So, I will ask one last time before rowing back to the shore and watching how well you might fare under our guns," the Captain said coldly and clearly to the man above him.

"Maybe ve take you prisoner and exchange us fer you?" he replied smugly to the Captain. Captain Donovan looked at James and his men and back to the Lieutenant above him.

"As you can see Lieutenant, we were sent out here because we are expendable. Sadly for all of us, taking us hostage as you cleverly suggest will not save this vessel, you would only be forfeiting our lives, the lives of your men, the crew of this vessel, and yourself in doing so. I can promise you that such actions will not elicit mercy from the commander of this British fort." The captain looked over his shoulder toward the fort and then back to the lieutenant as a muffled discussion could be heard above. "So what will it be, Lieutenant? You hold our very lives in your hand and I'm sure we are all dying to know what your response is going to be," Captain Donovan continued with his bluff.

The Dutch Lieutenant seemed to survey the longboat crew, the militia, and the captain below him. There was silence from his own crew as he looked toward the main fort and the guns that stared down at him from there, as well as the 32 pounders from the other forts.

"Stand down, Lieutenant." A voice could be heard from above as the captain of the vessel stepped to the railing and looked down. "My arrogance and complacency put us in this situation and I will not have you throw away your lives or the lives of my crew," he said in clear English as he looked down at Captain Donovan below. "You have permission to board-" The man hesitated before continuing, "-your vessel, Captain." He then stepped back from the railing as the ladder was lowered into place and room for them to board was opened. Captain Donavon was the first to climb the ladder and James could see him return a salute from the captain of the merchant vessel as he made it to the top of the ladder and stepped onto its main deck.

"May I present to you the *Eenhorn*, Captain Ruyter at your service," he heard the man say as his men continued up the ladder and onto the deck. Captain Ruyter began the introductions of his officers and crew, who nodded or saluted nervously. As the five militiamen boarded the vessel, the atmosphere changed noticeably and the crew and soldiers on the Dutch merchant ship stared at the men.

"Captain Ruyter, may I introduce Captain James Thornton of the North Carolina Militia." The Captain saluted and James returned the salute. There was an awkward silence as the three Captains stared at each other with their men looking on.

"It was foolish of me to sail into the harbor without first looking to see who occupied it," the Dutch Captain remarked apologetically and Captain Donovan nodded.

"It was very surprising to us as well, Captain. I'm just glad that no lives were lost in the process," Captain Donovan replied. "Let's continue with the unpleasant discussion before us," he proposed, and the Dutch Captain nodded. "We will begin by offloading the Dutch soldiers and your crew. I imagine that you have already ordered the destruction of your confidential papers and charts..." Captain Donovan left the question hanging until the Dutch captain nodded. "...I would have done the same." Captain Donovan smiled sympathetically. "Please understand Captain, that the destruction of the papers and charts will be forgiven, but should there be any further destruction or sabotage of this vessel or any of its cargo or weapons, you and your men will be punished and the offender executed. If we are clear on this point, I would like you to convey this now to the men under your charge." He looked over at the Dutch lieutenant and back to the captain, who nodded and began repeating Captain Donavon's words to his crew and the soldiers. When he had finished, he turned back toward Captain Donovan for further instructions.

"Captain, please let your troops know that we do not wish any harm or injury to come to them and that they will be treated with respect as long as they cooperate." The captain nodded and repeated the words in Dutch to the crew. Meanwhile Captain Donovan walked back to the railing and looked down at his men below and issued an order.

"Please inform Mr. Sanders that we will begin transferring the men from this vessel to the facilities we use for the officers and the crew. Ask him also, to send additional longboats and crew to facilitate this process." Captain Donovan turned back to the Dutch captain. "I would like to begin with the Dutch soldiers and officers. Captain Thornton, please secure the weapons of the Lieutenant and his men prior to departing the vessel." James nodded and stepped toward the lieutenant, who did not move, but only glowered at James. James was fed up with the arrogance toward him and his men that were continually displayed by every Dutch officer they had encountered. The Dutch lieutenant practically dared James to take his weapons by force. James took a breath, then reached down and withdrew his pistol in a single motion and placed the barrel of it against the man's forehead, and cocked it. They man's eyes went wide with fear and his arrogance drained from his face as he stood there motionless. Several of his men raised their muskets and aimed them at James. The silence of the moment was deafening and everyone seemed frozen as they waited for the next action.

"You can either surrender your arms to me, or I will take them off of your dead body," James said coldly to the man. The Dutch Lieutenant understood enough to reach into his belt and withdraw his pistol and carefully hand it to James, who passed it to one of his militiamen. The Lieutenant then unclasped the cutlass that hung from his belt and handed it to James. James lowered his pistol, released the hammer, and returned it to his belt. The color returned to the face of the Dutch officer and his expression changed to one of embarrassment.

"Thank you," James said curtly and turned and walked toward the remaining Dutch soldiers standing around them, all of whom had quickly lowered their muskets once the Lieutenant began handing his weapons over to James. James looked each of them squarely in the eyes as he slowly walked around. "The next time any of you choose to raise a weapon against me or any of my men, you will be shot," he said, stopping in front of one of the men who had raised a musket a moment ago. The man lowered his eyes and handed James the gun. James turned to one of his own men, who stepped forward and collected the musket. The silent order seemed to be understood and the rest of the Dutch soldiers came forward and handed their muskets and any other weapons that they carried to James' men, who began leaning them against the railing. As James walked back toward Captain Donovan and the Dutch Captain, Captain Donovan gave him a strange blink and look of surprise. "Thank you, Captain," was all he said and then turned back toward the Dutch captain and began speaking with the familiarity of a man sitting around a table speaking with an old friend.

For the next hour, James and his men stood guard on the vessel as more and more of the Dutch troops and crew were unloaded into the longboats. With the exception of the officers, they were all ferried to the smaller merchant vessel, which they had once again converted to a temporary prison ship. At the same time, a small contingent of Captain Donovan's crew was transferred onto the vessel to finish securing it. As the men were leaving the vessel, Captain Donovan took great care in asking each member of the Dutch crew where they were from and how they came to be Dutch sailors. Those who were captured British sailors, or sailors from nations not at war with England, were given the opportunity to join them. Of the 142 captured soldiers and crew, 18 chose to avoid prison and join Captain Donovan.

During the debriefing of the Dutch sailors, they learned that the other two vessels were heading for Frederiksted. The merchant vessel carried supplies and twenty soldiers to reinforce the garrison there as the city and its needs had grown. The ship of the line was there to escort the vessels to the harbors, load the supplies, and escort them south to the Antilles where they would rejoin the rest of the fleet and return to Antwerp. The three ships were part of a much larger fleet of 12 vessels, 4 ships of the line and 8 merchant vessels. When they had sighted the Virgin Islands to the north as planned, the main fleet continued south, while their three ships departed for the two harbors of St. Croix. None of the vessels were carrying an invasion force, only enough troops to either replace or reinforce their current ports of call.

Once the crew had been removed and the officers sent to the main fort to be added to the new prison quarters, James and Captain Donovan began to tour the ship.

"I expect the Dutch ship of the line will return to these waters after docking at Frederiksted and learning that the fort and city of Christiansted is no longer the property of the Dutch. If we're lucky, it will be tomorrow and we will have more time to prepare, if not, well, we'll see," Captain Donovan shared his thoughts with James now that they were finally alone. James nodded as he looked toward the northwest as if expecting to see the enemy sails coming toward them.

"James, is everything okay? I mean you were uncharacteristically aggressive back there. I bloody well almost handed you my own weapons and I'm on your side." He chuckled and waited for James to respond. James looked down and shook his head.

"I'm sorry; I suppose I just lost my patience with their continual arrogance and disrespect for me and my men," he finally replied. Captain Donovan patted him on the shoulder.

"It's okay son, sometimes we have to step a little harder to get our point across. Just don't lose yourself in the anger," he said calmly and with deep concern. James nodded.

They walked down into the captain's quarters and stared at the accommodations. They were very impressive and extravagant compared to Captain Donavon's own quarters on *The*

Dragon. His men had already searched and had placed the ships manifest and other important items that they had discovered on the room's meeting table for Captain Donovan's review. As he and James perused the manifest, they came across a list detailing the many specific items that had been purchased by the local citizens and nearby landowners. Plow blades and equipment, cookery items, giant kettles, wheels, lumber and tools, and desks and bolts of cloth. There was also a great deal of cannon shot, musket shot, and powder for the fort. On the table was also a box filled with personal letters to be delivered to the citizens in the surrounding area.

The items listed in the ship's manifest and the letters presented James with a great way to either establish communication and perhaps strengthen the ties and trust he was trying to build with the citizens and landowners of the area. He shared his idea with the Captain, who was at first unwilling to let go of any of the items they had captured, but came to see the potential of delivering the items the citizens had already paid for.

There was another box that sat on the table, this one reinforced with metal bands. At the request of Captain Donavan, the heavy metal padlock had been hammered and pried against until the latch that held it had given way and now hung from the side of the box. The broken padlock was still attached. As they opened the battered lid of the box, they could see that it was the ship's coffer. Inside were two compartments filled with coins, it appeared that one compartment was for the military, and the other for the East India Company. All combined, the ships coffer carried over 500 silver one-guilders and 25 gold one-ducats, plus a variety of one, two and six-silver stuivers mixed in. The general purchase orders on the East India Company side gave instructions for the purchase of as much rum, cotton, sugar and other raw produce and materials as possible from the islanders. These goods were to then be loaded on the ship and brought to Copenhagen for sale to their European market. Payroll instructions for the officials who worked for the company were also found among the documents. The military side of the chest contained payroll documents for the soldiers formerly stationed at the fort, listed by rank.

Once they had secured the guns, searched the cannons and ship for signs of sabotage, and verified that no traps were waiting on the vessel, Captain Donovan's crew sailed the vessel behind the west fort and anchored it next to *The Dragon* with both ships' portside guns facing the only area that a large deep-keeled vessel could approach. Once the ships were in position, they moved the smaller prison vessel and anchored it securely just inside the entrance of the bay near the coral reef to the north and within range of the forts' guns. They then ran several long anchor ropes across the southern entrance and tied them to several coral heads to the south. This would make it very difficult for a deep-keeled vessel to enter the harbor without running into the lines and hampering the ship's ability to turn until the lines were cut or removed. They could remove them easily enough, but the encumbrance would slow them down long enough to gain time for the crew to fire a few additional cannon shots. They kept the two top deck guns on the port side in place, aimed toward the entrance of the port, not to sink a vessel, but to thwart or warn off any boarding party entering the bay by oared longboats or small sailing vessels.

With the sun beginning to sink in the western sky, it had definitely been a busy day. They had hoped for more time, but everything changed again at the sight of the Dutch ship of the line rounding the western edge of the island and heading toward them. The wind would favor them again should they turn toward the port, but not as they sailed east. Captain Donovan felt confident that the visit from the Dutch vessel would be only an intelligence gathering one in order to make plans to reclaim the fort and the vessels anchored safely in the harbor.

"Unless they are foolish, they won't try to run the entrance and engage the fort at this time. They just want to ascertain the fate of the merchant ship and its crew and why they did not sail to Frederiksted once they saw the fort was in British hands," the Captain theorized. "The question is, what can we do in the interim to gain more time to prepare our defenses?"

The big warship sailed directly at the port entrance, as if the Dutch were going to try to run the gauntlet before them, but then turned away and into the wind just short of the entrance and dropped anchor. It was clear that no one was going to sail out of the harbor while that vessel rested offshore. The bigger concern on their minds was whether or not an army was marching from Frederiksted while it waited.

James had an idea, but was not sure it was worth expressing. The captain always seemed able to read James better than James would have liked. "James?" He questioned. James started to speak, then stopped. Then took another breath and began again.

"This idea depends a great deal on how honorable the Captain of that ship is," James said.

"Not a proven characteristic from what I have seen," Bode immediately scoffed. James nodded and replied.

"The character of each man is different. You never know until you look them in the eyes," The Captain replied. "Even then you cannot be sure until their actions honor their words," James conceded as he recalled the former Dutch commander of the fort and his poor character.

"It is not in our best interest to expend the resources guarding and feeding all these prisoners. It seems like it would only be a matter of time before they tire of their situation and try to break free or do something potentially harming our men in the process," James stated and the two men seemed to agree, but were waiting for James to continue his line of thought. "So why don't we offer to give them, or better yet, trade this captain and the prisoners for something in return?" They both stared back at James.

"Like what?" Bode asked.

"Their word." James replied. The Captain sat in silence waiting for more and then raised an eyebrow in question, so James continued. "Their word that if the Dutch officers and soldiers that we are holding are released, they will all be sent back to Europe and not used in any military capacity against the fort." Bode just stared at James, while Captain Donovan smiled. "You have a lot of faith in a man's word, especially a man that is your enemy," Captain Donovan replied and James nodded. "Either way, it will show them our character. I don't know about you, but I don't want those prisoners in the harbor, or their officers locked in our fort under my care. I know that I would not want to be kept prisoner if given the choice,"

James concluded. Captain Donovan considered James' comments several moments and then replied.

"The careers of most of these officers are over. One group lost a fort to a merchant ship's crew, the other group sailed their vessel into an enemy's harbor," he seemed to mumble to no one as Bode interjected his thoughts.

"If the captain fails to keep his word, they will have more officers and a considerably larger force and they will also have first-hand information of our defenses and strength from our prisoners." Bode interjected and they all nodded in agreement. They sat a few moments longer as they contemplated their predicament.

"I'm pretty sure that they have someone on the inside, perhaps one of the citizens, who is reporting everything to Frederiksted anyway," James added and Captain Donovan finally nodded and shrugged. "Shall we ask the Commander to join us to discuss the idea?" James and Bode nodded in agreement.

The initially arrogant demeanor of the Commander quickly changed when the idea of him and his officers' being set free was presented. They discussed the various options at great length before he finally agreed to the terms. The challenge that was now before them was how to inform the Dutch warship without being blown out of the water.

Chapter 13

After a long discussion, they finally agreed that sending two of their three officers to the Dutch Warship, as they had with the captured merchant vessel, was not the best plan, especially since they would not have the leverage of twenty cannons aiming at them from the forts' defenses. James argued that Captain Donovan had the experience needed to negotiate their offer, while Captain Donovan argued that his reputation as a privateer might cause concern and mistrust. He felt James, as a Colonial Captain, might be viewed as less of a threat to them. To James' great disappointment, the others, including Bode, decided that he was the best choice to visit the Dutch warship on their behalf. The Captain kept referring to James' luck as the main reason to send him, but James would correct him and explain his luck as simply God's grace and mercy. Deep within, James was nervous and he hoped that the mercy would not be withheld.

It was important that they act quickly, engaging in dialog before an attack was launched, or the ship withdrew; but not too quickly to seem desperate. They decided to wait to see and base their timing on what the morning brought. They doubled the guard duty, sent out several three-man scouting patrols, stationing them at different parts of the coastline to the west and east of the forts, and kept a guard detail on each vessel in the harbor to avoid any sabotage attempts. They were spread very thin, but they had no choice. The city patrols had reported that many of the Dutch citizens who had stayed in the city spent the evening celebrating. They were even so bold as to mock the troops in broken English as they passed by; addressing them directly with statements like:

"Ready to be my new slave?"

"Chains and beatings await you, for sure now!"

Although James was proud of his men for not responding to the taunts escalating the confrontations, he was more proud that they had not lost heart, or been fearful of those threats; instead they seemed more determined than ever. James felt more insecure than they did, but then again, most of his men were used to such treatment, and had experienced it on many occasions during their lives. James realized that such words were relatively new for him to hear personally. The more he thought about it, the more he was proud to be joined in with his men receiving his share of the derogatory abuse. He wondered if his fate would be far worse than that of his men should they fall into the hands of the enemy. The satisfaction of such thinking was brief and he cleared his mind of such thoughts and remembered the scripture in James 1:2 that his mother had taught them repeatedly during school about dealing with tough times and challenges.

"Count it all joy, my brothers, when you meet trials of various kinds, for you know that the testing of your faith produces steadfastness."

It was a long reach for him to joyfully embrace the idea of riding out in a longboat to meet with a massive ship of war loaded with very upset seamen. If his joy was based on the "troubles" before him, then he should be rolling on the floor in delight. He thought his faith was weak in spite of all the amazing victories God had given them. He prayed for a long time before he was finally able to fall asleep.

The next morning found the Dutch warship still sitting off the harbor entrance as if waiting for something. Was a ground attack forthcoming? It seemed far too early to organize all the logistics for such an attack, but perhaps the Dutch were that well trained. As Captain Donovan selected his longboat crew, James, Bode and Robbie shook hands and chatted about everything, but really nothing. James could read the concern on his friends' faces. Captain Hendriks, in full uniform, was led out of the fort prison and placed in the longboat. James asked the men who had escorted him to remove the shackles from his wrists.

"He is an officer. His word that he will not escape is stronger than those shackles," he said to the men and looked at the captain. The man's face was momentarily downcast, perhaps at the reminder of his breech of personal honor. He looked up resolutely, embracing the opportunity to regain some of his honor.

"I will not try to escape," he finally replied to James without looking away and then smiled. James nodded his head and climbed into the boat.

The Dutch Captain sat in the bow of the longboat with his back to the bow, while James sat in the middle facing forward. Although he never took his eyes off the waiting warship that they rowed toward, James could feel the Dutch Captain staring at him, seeming intent on trying to find something that was somehow hidden inside James. They rowed for several minutes before the Dutch Captain finally spoke. "You are a strange man, Captain Thornton," he said with a faint smile. James looked back and finally met his eyes. "How so, Captain Hendriks?" he asked as he once again surveyed the distance that remained between the longboat and the Dutch warship. "At every opportunity that arises to exact revenge, you choose mercy. Why?" the Dutch Captain asked sincerely. James did not meet his eyes, but looked back toward the fort as they passed the outer boundaries of the port entrance, then looked at the warship again and shrugged.

"You'll have to ask my father about that; it was just the way I was raised and what I was taught," he replied without too much thought. The Dutch Captain seemed to ponder the information, and then said "I hope I have that opportunity." James was confused.

"What opportunity?" he asked.

"To meet your father and ask him about you and how you were raised," he said with a smile. James looked the man in the eyes trying to determine if the smile was one of sincere interest.
"Perhaps God will grant that for both of us," he finally replied and smiled. They rowed a little longer before the man spoke again.

"You remind me of Mr. Hamilton," he said as he looked to the side and then back at James who obviously did not know a Mr. Hamilton. "Alexander was an English colonist who lived in Christiansted for a short while. He moved back to the colonies two years ago. He was a wild dreamer who believed in the impossible just like you." He chuckled. "The talks we had about the colonies and his dreams, it kept life interesting to say the least," he said with a smile. James just nodded as he watched the smile gradually fade from the Captain's face and then the man mumbled under his breath. "The dreams of youth are powerful, but rarely are they lived out," he said as he looked out over the water.

"There's always tomorrow, Captain," James replied, but the man only shook his head. James remembered a proverb that his father referred to when training the militia on tactics.

"Better a live dog than a dead lion," James replied quietly.

"You are more like Alexander than you realize," he said and his countenance brightened slightly.

With the white flag waving on the bow of the longboat, they continued to approach the warship, all the while waiting for the responding flag to be flown indicating that they were allowed to approach the ship. James said a "Nehemiah prayer" as his father called them, short and powerful prayers that asked God for strength and courage in urgent moments.

"Captain James Thornton of the North Carolina militia, with me is Captain Hendriks of the Dutch army. We are seeking to open a dialog for discussion of the exchange of prisoners," James announced to those along the railing. James could see the captain of the vessel looking down at them and then replied.

"Captain, we do not have any British or Black Dragon prisoners to exchange with you." James was caught off guard by the term *Black Dragon*, but not understanding; he shook his head and raised a hand.

"My apologies Captain, we are here to negotiate the return of your officers, soldiers and sailors. I was not assuming you had prisoners to exchange," James replied as he stared up at the man, who seemed more confused than before.

"What exactly do you intend for us to exchange for their release?" he finally asked James.

"Just your word," James answered and waited. The man stared a moment in confusion and blinked. "What is it that you require of me that would secure the release of these men?" he asked and James started to answer, but was interrupted by Captain Hendriks. "May I explain on your behalf Captain?" he asked James. James at first hesitated, then nodded and added.

"In English please."

The Dutch Captain smiled and replied, "Of course." He looked up at the Dutch Captain at the railing. "Sir, the Captain is willing to release all the officers, soldiers and sailors currently in his custody with their word and yours that they will be returned to Antwerp and will not be used in any effort to retake the fort or the city. The Commander and all officers have agreed to such terms, if it is acceptable to you." The Dutch Captain looked down at James, then to Captain Hendriks, then back to James.

"Do you understand that whether we agree to the terms or not, we will retake this fort by force from you and your Black Dragons?" he said confidently. James nodded, yet was still confused by the term Black Dragons. Then it dawned on him; the captain was referring to the men of the militia.

"Captain, we did not come here as invaders or enemies, we simply needed supplies. Once fired upon, we were forced to act accordingly to secure the supplies we needed for the survival of our men. We never wished ill will or harm to come to either your soldiers or the citizens of this town. Fate has it that we both now find ourselves in a difficult position, one that does not seem to have an ending that avoids death or injury to both of our forces," James explained and took a deep breath, watching as the Captain above nodded and considered his response. Captain Hendriks interjected. "He speaks the truth, Captain. Had we simply sold him the supplies they needed, or turned them away without trying to inflict harm, we would not be in the situation we are. He has proven to be an honorable man and a worthy adversary," he finished and looked toward James, who gave a nod in return, acknowledging his compliment and the uncharacteristically humble demeanor.

James looked up again at the Dutch sea captain. "I understand and respect your position and your duty to reclaim the fort and town that we now hold. I hope you understand mine and why, as your new enemy, we cannot simply return it to you. We are now bound to use all means at our disposal to prevent such efforts." James looked up at the Captain again as if waiting for his response to the offer.

"And if we refuse your offer?" the captain asked and James conveyed by his expression that the answer was already evident, but had somehow been missed by the Captain. He looked at Captain Hendriks and then back to the captain above.

"Then your opportunity to secure the safe release of your fellow officers and their men is gone," James said slowly, wondering if the Captain had failed to understand the offer since it was conveyed in English. The man stared down coldly at him. "Our terms are simple. You will release all prisoners, you will hand over the fort and city to our forces, and we will grant you your lives. You may leave in your original ship taking with you the supplies needed to return home. These are my terms," he stated arrogantly. James felt doubt creep into his heart. He had known better than to believe that his offer would be accepted, but he had somehow hoped it would. He started to reject the offer and return to the fort, but the laughter of Captain Hendriks interrupted him. The ship's Captain said scornfully.

"Captain Hendriks, perhaps you could share with the rest of us as to what you find to be so funny?" Captain Hendriks looked up and with the smile still on his face, replied. "I had hoped that you would have learned from our own repeated arrogance, but it appears not. The man next to me is not only a man of his word; he is also a very dangerous foe. An opponent that one should strive at all costs to avoid confronting. Do not be arrogant as I was, Captain; his offer is not only noble, you know it to be very one-sided in our favor, and will save many lives." When he had finished, James could see that the ship's captain was angered by his peer's words.

"When you say lives, you mean yours, I assume, Captain?" the ship's Captain snapped derisively. Captain Hendriks smiled and shook his head. "No, Captain, my life and my career are already forfeit; I speak of my men, the merchant crew, the city, and of you and the lives of your men." James was initially stunned by the captain's words as he waited for the response from the ship's Captain, who was considering the information.

"How do you know we will honor such an arrangement?" he responded smugly.

"Prior to a few moments ago, I had seen nothing to demonstrate that any Dutch officer's word was of any value or could be trusted. But I now see that there is still an opportunity to believe that you might," James replied. The Captain seemed about to be overcome with a fit of rage, but suddenly a man in full military dress of a navy Commodore put his hand on the Captain's shoulder and stepped to the railing and looking down at James.

"My apologies for not stepping in earlier Captain Thornton, but I hope it is not too late to rescue these negotiations." James could see that Captain Hendriks immediately recognized the man, but remained silent waiting for James to answer.

"Commodore, my father taught me that even when shots are fired in anger, although more difficult, there is still an opportunity for peace to win the day." James then extended his hand signaling for the commodore to continue.

"We accept your kind offer. In turn, and in appreciation, we will withdraw our vessel back to Frederiksted for a brief period so that, should you choose to do so, you and your men may return home to your families without hindrance," the commodore replied kindly. James nodded and tried to think through the offer and the opportunity to return home.

"That is very kind of you and much appreciated, I will convey the offer of free passage to my men and officers. Please know that your citizens are being treated respectfully and as long as they do not take up arms, they are in no danger from us while we hold the fort." The Commodore smiled and said, "Thank you and I have already had confirmation of that." James stared up a moment in silence and then realized what it was that seemed so familiar about the man and glanced over at the Captain standing next to him. He thought he would risk the assumption.

"We will begin by releasing Captain Hendriks to you and your family." James stated and he saw the confirmation as the Commodore looked over at Captain Hendriks and nodded. "Your ship's longboats can begin the retrieval of your men from the holding vessel anchored just inside the bay immediately," James concluded as he looked over at Captain Hendriks, who was now staring back at him and smiling. He could see preparations were already being made to lower the ship's longboats into the water.

"Did you know he was coming?" James asked Captain Hendriks softly. The Captain shook his head. "No. I had no idea and there was no reason for him to be here," he replied.

"I think he had every reason to be here and I'm glad he found that reason still alive when he came," James said quietly. "I mean, can you imagine how upset he would be with me if we had killed you?" James asked jokingly. They both laughed.

The longboat was moved to the side of the warship near a ladder that was now hanging down over the side. James motioned Captain Hendriks toward the ladder. As he moved to grasp the ladder while maintaining his balance in the gentle swells of the sea, he turned and extended his hand toward James. James reached for his hand and smiled as he grasped and shook it.

"Long life to you, James Thornton."

"And to you, Captain Hendriks," James replied with a smile and thought how strange life was that two people who had tried to kill each other only days earlier, were now parting as friends.

"Stephen," he said, offering his first name to James. James smiled and nodded as they stood in awkward silence a moment. Captain Hendriks stared back at the fort and city.

"I will miss this island and her people, but I also long for home," he said. James again smiled and thought *I miss my home and family too* He watched the Captain climb the ladder and step onto the deck, where he saluted the Commodore and shook hands.

Two of the warship's longboats followed James and his crew into the harbor entrance and alongside the prison ship anchored in the harbor. James gave orders to the men guarding the prisoners to release them gradually to the awaiting longboats. The rest of the morning was spent shuttling the prisoners to the warship.

He discussed the Commodores' offer with Captain Donovan and the other officers, who considered the options. All agreed that to have captured a fort, then relinquish it back to the enemy would be viewed very unfavorably by their British superiors. The last longboat, with Commander Kroeger and his officers aboard, departed the wharf, and some time later reached the awaiting Dutch warship. A silence fell over the fort, and indeed the whole city, as the big ship's sails were unfurled. As promised, she gradually sailed west toward Frederiksted. James watched the ship sail down the coast and it momentarily was blocked from view by the *The Dragon*, moored in the inner harbor. Then he realized where the name "Black Dragons" came from. James mumbled the name and Captain Donovan, Bode and Robbie who were standing closest to him looked puzzled.

"What about Black Dragons?" Captain Donovan asked and James smiled. "The Dutch called us the Black Dragons, because we came on *The Dragon* and we are black – well, most of us," James explained and then corrected himself on the last part. Bode and Robbie raised an eyebrow and then smiled as they nodded.

They all thought about the name, realizing it complimented not only the merchant crew, the vessel name and the soldiers carried by her, but also the men of the militia. Each man repeated the moniker to himself. Captain Donovan suddenly laughed out loud. "I like it! WE ARE THE BLACK DRAGONS!" He yelled the last part to all those within earshot. There was a strange silence as the men nearby took in the name. Then a slow rumble began to grow as the name was repeated louder and louder. "Black Dragons! Black Dragons!"

"Now all we need is a unit flag and we are all set," Robbie said and they laughed.

"I'll have one put together at the earliest opportunity!" Captain Donovan promised.

Captain Donovan listened as the name echoed across the fort and then he turned to James and those standing around them.

"Let history write that name in stone and tell of our courage and deeds!" He laughed proudly and then let his voice trail off, but he kept the smile. "You realize that all we might have done today is place over a hundred men back in the hands of our enemies," he said softly to the group of officers. They looked soberly at the captain a moment and nodded.

"On the other hand, we just freed up over 25 men from useless prisoner guard duty for use on the cannons or walls. By my calculation, one Black Dragon is worth 5-10 Dutch soldiers in battle, so I'd say we got the better end of the deal." Mr. Richard's stated proudly and smiled at his obvious exaggeration of odds and the others pretended to agree and smiled and nodded at the boast.

James watched over the walls as the men continued to talk about their new name. He then looked toward the city and saw the citizens standing rather disillusioned and disappointed at the sight of their heroic ship of war sailing away. In light of the verbal assault his men had received from them earlier, he derived a dark satisfaction from their sadness. He knew and understood the disappointment that they must feel, but he too clearly remembered the vitriol that they had spewed and the ill will wished on him and his men.

He guessed that the citizens of Christiansted would jump at the first opportunity to aid in the recapture of the fort by Dutch soldiers. "How many still have weapons hidden in a secret place, ready to be brought to bear against us?" he wondered. The anger and distain showed on their faces. Then something caught his eye as he continued to observe the crowd of people that was on the streets and lining the wharf area. For every Dutch citizen that was standing there with a scowl, there were at least two Negro slaves whose faces reflected the opposite of their owners'. There was an excitement and energy about them as they watched and listened as the Black Dragons celebrated the moment and their new name. James stood there for several moments and then turned back to Captain Donovan.

"How much time do you think we have before the Dutch organize an attack to reclaim the city and fort?" he asked and everyone nearby went silent as they waited for the response. Captain Donovan thought for a moment before answering. "They could march their existing forces overland and be here within a week," he said. "But from what information we have gathered on the strength of the garrison at Frederiksted, from the citizens, captured merchant marines and soldiers, they would have a difficult time putting together a substantial force. Of the 200 or 300 that they did muster perhaps less than 100 would be trained soldiers. They would be very hard pressed to succeed in taking this fort with so few men," he concluded. They all seemed to contemplate his words and calculate the defenses needed for such an encounter.

"Aye, they'd pay dearly for such an attack," Mr. Richards added.

"We have more than enough supplies and powder to withstand a lengthy land and water siege," Mr. Sanders replied, to which all agreed. James thought about the season and the discussions he had had with the citizens.

"It's harvest season," he mumbled and everyone except Bode seemed confused by his comment; he could see on their faces that they did not understand his meaning. "The next 30-60 days is harvest time and the hundreds of potential militia at the plantations cannot afford to leave their plantations to lay siege to a fort. They need to focus on the harvest," he finished and then looked at Captain Donovan again.

"Good point, James. That would greatly reduce the available number of troops they would be able to deploy against us in the near future," he replied, appearing to recalculate as he glanced out to sea again. The men around him remained silent as they waited. He suddenly nodded. "The majority of their fleet went south to their other ports and towns. I would guess that they would send the warship and remaining merchant ship to the south to notify the fleet of the situation. They will then wait for the rest of their merchant fleet to return from their various supply runs and reorganize their fleet and forces and then sail north to reclaim this fort on their way back to Europe," he theorized, then brighten a little. "I'd say we have anywhere from 3 to 5 months to prepare our defenses. We can hope that reinforcements will arrive before then." Bode could see that James was excited by Captain Donovan's calculation.

"What's on your mind James?" he asked and James looked back toward the city and pointed.

"There are over 300 Dutch citizens living around us, but more importantly, there are probably over 600 slaves who work for them. Of those, I would guess there are nearly 200 able bodied men who could be trained to be soldiers, Black Dragons," James answered and he saw Bode smile at the idea.

"They will never let you use their workers," Robbie said, but James smiled as he listened to Robbie and Bode interjected.

"I don't think James is planning on asking them for permission." Bode's smile grew bigger as he saw James acknowledge Bode's opinion. Captain Donovan suddenly laughed out loud.

"You aiming to stir up some trouble in this town, Captain Thornton?" the captain interjected, already knowing the answer, and James nodded.

"Do you really think they would join up?" Mr. Richards asked, knowing he meant the slaves, and James simply looked at Bode and Robbie standing next to him for the answer. They both nodded and Bode answered.

"If they have the choice, many will, but they need to believe that they will also be protected," Bode replied.

"They also need to know the consequences of such actions," James added, and Bode and Robbie went quiet for a moment and then nodded.

"I still think that many will choose to become Black Dragons," Robbie replied and Bode nodded in agreement.

"So how do we protect them?" Captain Donovan asked.

"You first give them a choice: to be freed or to remain slaves. Then you invite those who choose freedom to become Black Dragons," James replied. "They need to know that choosing to become a Black Dragon would very likely mean their deaths, but they also need to know that should we decide to withdraw from the fort, they and their families will be allowed to come with us, lest they be punished after our departure." As James finished speaking, he stared directly at Captain Donovan and waited for his confirmation.

The captain thought carefully before answering. "With two ships, we would have the space and supplies needed for transporting them, but that would require dividing our sailing crews and endangering everyone. Perhaps we could train some of the new men to be sailors instead of soldiers?" he proposed. James shrugged his shoulders and nodded.

"It would be their choice; perhaps some of the younger men who are more agile in their climbing abilities?" Bode suggested. They all stood and looked at each other as if waiting for someone to oppose the idea or give the order.

"So when do we start this madness?" Captain Donovan asked. James looked at Bode and Robbie, then at the sun that was heading toward the western horizon.

"Let's work out the details this evening, and implement our plans first thing in the morning." James suggested. Nods of agreement came from all present.

Bode broke the silence. "Now that we have twenty-five more men available, I'd like to add a few more guard posts around the city and perhaps strengthen the current ones in place," he proposed true to his nature of paying more attention to the details of a plan than focusing on the big-picture ideas.

When they came back together for dinner later that evening, there was a buzz in the air about the idea of expanding the number of Black Dragons by including and training the soon-to-be freed local Negro slaves. Bode had pulled together all the inventory counts on available supplies and weapons for the group to review. Combining the British muskets they had carried with the captured muskets from the Dutch soldiers and sailors from the fort and merchant vessel, they had nearly 382 extra muskets available. Retaining the practice that each Black Dragon soldiers would always carry two weapons, one long rifle and one British musket, that left 330 muskets to arm the 110 sailors from *The Dragon* and the 18 sailors who chose to join them from the captured Dutch merchant vessel. That still left over 200 muskets for arming additional Black Dragon soldiers and sailors.

They discussed what they felt were realistic assessments of the time available to train the soldiers based on past experience and the expectations of those trained under such conditions. They decided that the Black Dragon Militia would be able to train as many as a 100 soldiers, with each man being responsible for teaching and training two workers. Mr. Richards would train up to seventy to assist on the cannon and wall defenses and Mr. Sanders would train twenty to thirty recruits in the fundamentals of sailing. The real question now before them was how many workers would actually choose to join them?

The group of officers was keenly aware that the declaration of freedom for the slaves would create an uproar in the city, but not only was such an action within their power, it was an action that they felt strongly was the right thing to do. It was important that the city not be brought to its knees with the removal of their primary workforce, so they decided to implement a similar pay structure that James' father used at the plantation. They would strongly encourage the citizens to continue to house and feed the workers who chose to stay with them. Instead of employees of the plantation, the workers would become employees of the fort and they would collect their pay from the fort or exchange their pay for goods or services. In return, the authorities at the fort would use the local taxes levied on the Dutch citizens to pay the workers. Plantation owners and city merchants, who allowed their workers to train and retain residence on their plantations or workplaces, would be issued the tax credits to offset the loss of available labor during training. Captain Donovan was unanimously appointed the new acting mayor and commander of the fort by the officers; he accepted the position with pride.

"Mayor and Commander, Mother would be so proud of me," he said sarcastically and laughed.

"It just means your head will roll first should they retake the fort," Mr. Richards replied. After the ensuing laughter died down, Captain Donovan expressed the opinion that if the fort were to fall; few would be granted much grace. The truth of the comment sank in deeply and thus determination to prevent such an ending grew stronger.

They had no idea what to expect when they presented the plans to the people, but they were determined to move forward with everything first thing in the morning. James, Bode and Robbie prayed together that evening for wisdom and guidance as they looked out over the city and the bay.

Chapter 14

At first light, right after breakfast, they positioned additional troops in key locations around the city and then in the open grass area west of the fort. At 8am, they rang the town bell and sent troops to the various homes and buildings requesting all citizens and their servants to meet in the open grounds west of the fort. By nine in the morning, and after much complaining and resistance from various citizens, they had all gathered in the open terrain as requested. James then ordered the free citizens to the west side and all slaves and indentured servants to the east side, close to the fort walls. From his vantage point, atop the west wall of the fort, Bode and a few of his men tallied the two groups. He then sent the totals down to James. There were over 600 workers and almost 300 citizens.

Bode left the ramparts and joined Robbie who was seated at a table outside the fort wall near the main gate. They waited with paper and pen along with the retired British officer, who was on hand to translate. James then had the citizens come forward to give their own names and the names of their families, which Bode and Robbie wrote down in great detail. Then they were asked to have their slaves join them. They were questioned as to their names, age, gender, any close family relationships, and duties they performed for their owners, all of which was added to the entry for each white family. As each family completed the task, they and their slaves were allowed to return home, but with the understanding that everyone, with absolutely no exceptions, would meet back at the open area at six that evening for further instructions. It took until almost noon to complete the whole registration process; upon completion they returned to the fort and spent the next five hours evaluating the data they had gathered.

As they sat around the table, Bode and Robbie shared the numbers that they had gathered with the rest of the officers. Of the 627 slaves residing in the city, there were only 174 who were of appropriate age and health and deemed fit for soldier or sailor training. As expected, most of the family servants were women and older men, while the able-bodied men worked the plantation fields around the city. The good news was that of the 174 available, 127 worked for the East India Trading Company as dockhands, warehouse workers and supply wagon drivers. Since the Dragons, having taken the fort and city, had seized control of the assets of that company, they were now the slaves' new owners and soon-to-be employers. Transitioning the slaves to soldiers would be much easier and less antagonistic to the citizens. That still left forty-seven potential soldiers and the issue of their owners to be addressed.

Based on the number of workers and the type of work they performed, Bode had calculated the amount of pay that would be required to employ everyone and compared the current revenue to the tax revenue that was gathered in the past based on old records. Then they compared it to what would be gathered at the reduced tax rate and found that with their estimated rate of tax income and the coin they had captured and had available to draw upon, they could operate for about nine months. They needed to generate more revenue if they were to continue with the project.

Mr. Sanders pointed out that, if they were still here after 9 months that by itself would be a miracle, while Mr. Richards expressed a strong desire for the British to show up and take over the whole operation and sp that the financial burden would fall on them. They just needed to focus on making it through the next several months; the rest of the issues could be addressed later. They knew that the 6:00 pm meeting was almost upon them, so they hastily ate and redeployed the troops as before.

The citizens and their workers had assembled again in the open grass area, this time many had brought chairs to sit on and something to drink. Their servants stood behind them. The whole scene only deepened James' conviction that what they were doing was the right thing. Once again, he asked the servants to move to the grassy area near the fort, while the citizens were asked to move to the western end of the open area. Once the citizens had repositioned their blankets, James stepped forward and with the help of the retired British officer translating he addressed the two groups.

"I'm sure you are disappointed that the Dutch warship from yesterday, decided not to reclaim the fort by force," James started but was interrupted.

"They will be back!" a citizen called out from within the crowd of citizens. James hesitated and then nodded.

"Yes they will," he replied as he stepped closer to the area that the voice came from. "Which is why things will be changing drastically around here." He finished and continued moving forward as he waited for the translation and stopped in front of the man that he was certain was the source of the comment and stared at him. "As of this moment, all slaves within the city of Christiansted are hereby proclaimed free," he finished and let the words being translated soak in. There were immediate looks of shock followed by outburst of anger from most citizens. Even the retired British officer translating seemed taken aback.

"You cannot do that!" the man in front of James who had spoken first, blurted, barely containing the rage evident in his eyes.

"How can we run our businesses and farms without our slaves?" another citizen protested in English. This was followed by an onslaught of comments spoken and yelled in Dutch that he did not understand. The volume and the agitation of the crowd grew in intensity. It dawned on James that he recognized who the man glaring so defiantly before him was; he had worked with the East India Company and was one of the men who had tried to get the citizens to smuggle out the company money from the fort when it was captured. James finally held his hand up to silence the growing rumble of the crowd.

"Every former slave will now be employed by the fort as workers for hire. They will have the opportunity to choose to either stay under your direction, or offer their services to other employers whose treatment is more favorable or who offer better living conditions and work environments. The employers will continue to provide food and housing for the workers they employ and the wages paid to the worker will be deducted from the taxes due to the fort by each business." James let the translator catch up before continuing; he could see their faces try to grasp the meaning and impact of it all.

"We will also be employing and training a portion of the workforce as militia, which will require employers to allocate additional hours beyond a normal work day for such training." As the translation was completed, the man opposite stood up to confront James.

"You are going to give them weapons?" he blurted as he stabbed his finger toward the area where the workers were now gathered. "They will kill us the first chance they get!" he ended with his face growing more red and his voice louder.

"Only if they have been treated badly in the past by their prior owners," James replied and then pretended to suddenly grasp the man's concern. "But I'm sure that's not something most of you will have to worry about," James said sarcastically, and then coldly smiled at the man. "If there is concern for such retribution from past workers, you will have the opportunity, just like they do, to decline service from any workers formerly in your service. If your reputation is poor with the workers, then you might find hiring them a little difficult." James looked up at the rest of the citizens. "For the rest of you, you will find this to be a great opportunity to acquire enthusiastic workers and, as workers may now choose their vocation, new talents may be discovered in this reallocation of labor." The translation continued as James watched the faces of the citizens. He could almost tell which citizens were worried about the new workforce arrangement and which ones saw it as a great opportunity. More Dutch citizens were asking questions in Dutch of the British officer who was trying his best to listen to them, until finally overwhelmed, he held up his hands for them to stop. He then turned to James.

"They want to know how much extra tax they will have to pay?" he asked on their behalf and James shook his head before answering.

"Nothing extra; in fact we intend to actually reduce taxes. It will remain the citizens' responsibility to feed and house the workers they hire," he replied and waited for his words to be translated. He watched as the citizens listened and then asked more questions through the translator.

"They do not understand exactly how it is any different from before?" Mr. Massman said, doing his best to compress their various questions into a short sentence. James nodded in agreement.

"It might appear to be the same, but there are several very clear differences," James started and then held up a finger as he counted off the differences. "One, the Negro workers are no longer your property to do with as you please. They are now free men and women just as you are, who can either choose to continue to work for you, or to explore other opportunities should they desire. Should the environment you provide prove to no longer be desirable, they are free to seek other employment and living arrangements. Two, we are the judge and juror of such working arrangements and should complaints be reported by either the worker or the employer, we will hear both sides and make a fair ruling on the matter. Finally, the workers are now free citizens and they will be accountable to and protected by the same laws as you are. Should you choose to break such laws from here forward, you will be punished accordingly; just as they will be should they do so." As James finished and his words were translated, he could see the last statement seemed to stun the crowd. Again, the questions began pouring out.

"What will keep them from just going to someone else each day?" the officer asked on their behalf.

"There are only so many jobs available and so many workers. How you treat them will determine if they will stay with you or not. If your workers are not putting in a fair day's work, you ask us to find a replacement worker. It is a mutually fair structure that will eventually balance itself out," James replied and waited while the translation was completed. Then he held his hand up to quiet the new round of questions.

"That is all I will be saying at this time. Understand that we will strive to work through all complications as they arise and to explain and educate in greater detail as time progresses. I now need to address the workers and explain the new structure to them. Please return to your homes and await further instructions." Then he walked toward the workers who were waiting near the fort wall. Mr. Massman finished translating and then ran to catch up with James.

"Well, I'm sure no one saw that coming," he chuckled as they walked toward the waiting workers. "This next discussion should be very interesting, to say the least." he commented as James stopped before the workers. They all seemed keenly interested, many having overheard the discussion with the Dutch citizens.

"Thank you for waiting so patiently," James began and waited for the translation before continuing. The workers smiled and nodded at his words. "As the new owners of this fort, the city and areas surrounding it, we are happy to announce that you are no longer slaves of the Dutch. You are free men and women and are free to choose to make your own decisions on your life and employment," James informed them as he paused for the translation to finish.

He watched the various expressions on the faces of the workers. Some were of joy, others of fear, and others were even of scorn or mistrust. "I know you must feel confused as to what the word *free* means and what impact that meaning has on you. In the simplest of terms, it means you are able to make your own choices of where you work, where you live, and who you choose to marry." He paused and watched the eyes of the workers widen and then look back and forth at each other as the information was translated. Many placed their hands over their mouths and then shook their heads as if they were almost afraid to embrace the idea. James smiled and then continued.

"Although this is a great moment, it is not going to be an easy transition for you. You also need to know that it could be short lived should the fort fall back into the hands of the Dutch, something we are determined not to allow to happen." He paused a moment before continuing.

"You need to understand what this means and how this freedom works. It does not mean you do not need to work, or that you will receive free food and housing for no effort. It means that you are not forced to work for your past owner if your treatment was harsh. They understand that they cannot treat you in such a way and expect you to stay with them, but they also expect you to provide them with a fair day's labor in order to receive your food and housing." He paused and waited for Mr. Massman to complete the translation.

"In addition to your food and housing provided by your employer, you will receive a small weekly payment from the fort in order to purchase or trade for goods and services that you desire." He waited and then continued. "You receive this additional payment because we will require the use of your time and skill in the defense of the fort and the city."

"Is that why we are being set free?" an older worker asked in perfect English. James looked at the man and understood his question.

"Yes and no," he replied. "As many of you already know, all of the men in our militia are free men and work for a plantation in the Colonies, but we also choose to be part of this militia, the Black Dragons, because it gives us the strength to protect each other and to guard the freedom we so dearly cherish. In the same way, we are seeking to train a number of you to be members of the Black Dragon militia, not only to help defend this fort, but to defend the freedom of all of us," he stated clearly to the man who asked the questions and then waited patiently for it to be translated to the others. The man held his eyes and then nodded his head.

"I believe you," the man said, "but make sure that the rest of the men and women understand that any who choose to take up arms against the Dutch as freed slaves, will be put to death if you fail to hold this city," James nodded.

"I'd like you to help me make sure they are aware of such choices, as those were the same choices with the same consequences that we have already made in deciding to hold this city," James replied. "They also need to understand that it is their choice to become part of the Black Dragon militia. No one will be forced or coerced to join. If they choose to, it will require extra work and time to learn to shoot a musket, fire a cannon, march in formation, or even how to trim a sail. It will not be an easy task, but it will be one that they can be proud of," James finished and he nodded for the translation to begin, giving a motion with his hand as if to say "please proceed" and the man turned and began speaking to the rest of the workers.

James watched the responses and reactions of the workers as the man explained the dangers of choosing such a course, standing up against the Dutch as a member of the militia. He saw in some fear, in others pride, but in most uncertainty. There were many questions that were asked of the man, who seemed to respond to each one carefully and kindly. James could tell the man was well respected within the community of workers. Eventually, the questions subsided and the man turned back toward James. "They are now very aware of the consequences of such choices," he informed James. The former British officer nodded to James, verifying that his words and the concerns had been translated correctly. He then turned toward the female workers and addressed them.

"For those who may not wish to return to their former owners, we are in need of cooks and seamstresses at the fort. Although we are able to meet our basic meal needs, we are greatly lacking in the quality of our meals," he said with a smile and watched the smiles and listened to the laughter from the workers as his words were translated. He then put a very serious look on his face before continuing.

"I want you to know that you will not be at personal risk or subject to physical assault from my men or from the sailors. You will be protected and respected while under our care." He saw the differing expressions from both the men and the women workers as his words were translated. He could see that some doubted while others seemed relieved by his words. "Even outside our employ, you will be treated as free men and women and will be subject to and protected by the same laws and moral values which we impose on the white citizens.

Should your employer break such laws, they will be punished just as you will be punished should you break them. We do not show favoritism nor will we allow revenge. We cannot respond to offenses that occurred prior to today, but I promise that we will not allow such crimes against your persons. Your first step is to decide whether to stay with your current employer, the person or business that was previously your owner. If they are dangerous to work for, you are free to leave. You must understand that wherever you choose to work, you must work with all your energies. Those who choose not to work, or who are not employable because of a bad attitude or poor work product will not be paid or fed by the fort or an employer. You are free to leave the city to find work elsewhere, but you will no longer be under the protection of the fort, nor will your freedom be acknowledged by the Dutch." James could see that they were already thinking through all the various angles and choices before them. He allowed the workers a little time to discuss everything between them before continuing.

"We have a list of names of men whom we would like to invite to join the Black Dragon militia. When your name is called, please step to the open ground where Lieutenant King is standing. From there we will answer any questions. Then you are free to choose to be trained as Black Dragon militia, return to your former employment, or ask to be considered for other opportunities." James nodded to Bode, who pulled out his list and began reading names, waiting after each name to see if the man had stepped out and moved to the open ground next to him. James saw the faces on many of the selected workers light up in pride, but he could tell that some feared the idea and the selection.

While the names were being read and the workers responded, James decided to walk over to the older gentleman who spoke on his behalf earlier and for whom the workers seemed to have a great deal of respect.

"My name is Captain James Thornton. Thank you for your assistance and frankness," James said with a smile and extended his hand to the man. Although hesitating a moment in surprise at James' kindly approach, he reached for the offered hand and shook it.

"William Booker. I am already a free man, Captain, but I thank you for granting such an honor to my fellow workers." He smiled and looked into James' eyes as if trying to read his reaction.

"If you are free, then why did you go with the workers when they were separated?" James asked.

"I was concerned for them and wanted to make sure they were taken care of," he replied. James nodded and shook his hand with even more confidence and saw that the man was older than he first thought, maybe sixty or older.

"What is your trade Mr. Booker?" James asked.

"I have been entrusted with the spiritual guidance and teaching of the workers and any others who the Lord may call. I'm a missionary by choice, a baker by trade, Captain," he said proudly and James smiled.

"Those are both noble pursuits, Mr. Booker. I would be honored to discuss your beliefs and visit your congregation if the invitation is open." The man seemed to light up at his words.

"Invitation extended and I would be honored to have you and your men visit us," he replied.

"Perhaps you can join my officers for dinner two days from now?" James asked. The man seemed stunned.

"I will make sure of it. I will also bring some of my best bread to add to the meal," he said proudly and smiled. James returned the smile, adding, "I will look forward to it."

The men whose names were called moved cautiously or proudly to the waiting area near Bode. Over the course of an hour Bode spoke in detail to the group of workers as the British officer translated for him. Bode seemed to have a better reaction from the workers than James had had as he explained the duties, responsibility and training requirements to the men. He then listened to the translated questions of the men and took great care in answering each one of them. Of the 174 men whose names were called, 39 of the men chose not to take part in the training and when given the opportunity, they politely excused themselves and went to stand with the other workers. That left 135 Black Dragon recruits, most of which were the former workers of the Dutch East India Company. It was at that time that Bode announced that the pay that the new soldiers would be receiving was to be five times the standard worker's wage. James had instructed Bode to wait until after the men had made their decision to enlist to announce the higher wage; his experience had taught him that an army of men who fought for a cause was much more valuable than one that fought for pay. He and his men would be putting their trust, and perhaps their lives, in the hands of these men. In the heat of battle the allure of money soon looses its luster. James was confident that they had the men that they desperately needed with the hearts required to be Black Dragons.

They closed the evening by selecting five of the female workers and two of the men to be the cooks assigned to the Black Dragons at the fort. They also drew up a contract with Mr. Booker for him to provide the fort with bread on a daily basis. He went from a part-time baker and preacher, to one running one of the busiest bakeries literally overnight. They also hired, on a part-time basis, three seamstresses to begin the work on new uniforms for the men. Everyone hired was to meet in the open field in front of the fort first thing in the morning, where they would work out the various housing and work assignments. James ordered that, once again, the guard and patrols around the city be doubled, not only to be prepared should an attack come, but also to keep the citizens from fleeing with their former slaves.

As the sun was setting in the west, Bode, Captain Donovan and James looked out over the entrance of the bay. They agreed that it was a good day, but they wondered if they would have enough time to see their plans to fruition before the Dutch fleet and troops arrived. They smiled at each other and headed for their rooms for a good night's sleep.

The following morning they began the process of organizing and cataloging the requests of the new workers, and their decisions to either stay with their current employers or their desire to be available to work for new employers. There was definitely a buzz about the city as the workers approached the table and began submitting their decisions. Many of the citizens had walked their workers to the table and explained what they wanted them to say. In an effort to avoid any undue influence or fear on the part of the workers, Bode asked the Dutch citizens to return to their homes while the workers remained.

After the citizens were gone, Bode then asked additional questions to determine what the workers' true desires were, reassuring the workers that they were free to make their choices based on what they wanted to do, not what the citizens' desires were or any pressure that was placed upon them the night before. Although most were simple decisions, Bode discovered cases in which some had been threatened with harm should they chose not to return to their former masters. Bode reported these cases to James who intended to visit those individuals personally. He assured the workers that the men of the fort would protect them from any retribution from their former masters and again assured them that they were free to leave and offer their services elsewhere.

After the lists were completed, James, along with five soldiers, visited the establishments and prior slave owners within the city and the nearby areas. At each stop, he presented the decision of the worker or workers. If the workers had chosen to stay with their former employer, then he would determine if the former owners desired to offer the workers employment, including food and housing. If there were conditions, such as the former slaves having children who were previously sold or traded being returned to live with them, increasing the cost of food and housing, then the employer would have to decide if that was acceptable. If the employer did not want the worker back, then they would have the option of choosing other available workers. James soon realized how much the various Dutch citizens knew about the talents and abilities of other citizens' former slaves and some were very interested in gaining those workers as employees, whether or not there were hard feelings generated among the citizens by it.

There were three prominent families that had their various workers removed and were not allowed to hire additional workers due to their harsh treatment, threats and attempts to manipulate their former slaves. It was their great loss, for their workers were the best trained and most talented, which made them sought after by the other citizens. Cooks, nursemaids, stablemen, plantation workers, laborers, seamstresses, and more, James loved that the worker was able to choose who they wished to work for, as it seemed the new workers also knew which of the former slave owners were the kindest and most appreciative. It was a strange twist of fate that those who were the harshest and wealthiest owners lost their best workers to those who were the kindest yet much less affluent. He could not help but smile at the twist in fate.

By the end of the fourth day after the freeing of the slaves, James had met briefly with every former owner and had negotiated on behalf of the employer and the workers so that everyone was relatively happy, or as happy as could be, considering the profound changes that had been made. Bode had also managed to progress quickly with the initial training of the new Black Dragons. The new militia had already chosen a name for themselves; they wanted to be called the *Black Lizards* until they were truly trained. The name came from the heckling by their prior owners and other citizens who jeered at the trainees attempting to humiliate and discourage them. The jeering actually seemed to galvanize the trainees, who embraced the name so that the name calling had the opposite effect from that intended. Bode had loved the idea and welcomed the new name, initiating use of it immediately.

Captain Donovan, Bode and James all agreed that the most important aspect of their initial training was how to assist the existing Dragons and sailors. Each man was assigned a section of the wall within the main fort as a gathering site should an alarm be sounded. Once their stations were understood, training began in loading and use of muskets. Just like the early days on the Thornton's plantation, the new recruits were more than eager to learn and were actually very adept and capable, proving to be fast learners in every aspect. The recruits worked extremely hard, taking on the urgency that they sensed the Dragons felt about training them. Those who just could not seem to get the process of loading the muskets were transferred from the infantry squads. Some were to be trained as sailors by Mr. Sanders, others to man the cannons by Mr. Richards.

The dinner and discussion with Mr. Booker proved to be not only enjoyable, but also very educational, for he knew the various stories and background of the families in the city. He did not share it as gossip, but more as "here is what you need to be concerned about when dealing with this family". This information was common knowledge for those who had lived in the city these past 40 years, which he had. They learned that he had gone to school in London at an early age, sent there by his devout Christian owner, who was very wealthy and well connected, and upon his graduation he was given his freedom. His benefactor then sent him funds to preach to the Negro and slave population in London in the evenings and on weekends, all the while working as a baker during the days. Sadly, upon his employer's death, the wealth and connections that had allowed him such opportunities ended. The ministry was quickly ended by the authorities and his stipend was terminated by the heirs of the man's estate. He had been granted a sizable financial gift from the man, with the understanding that he should make the most of it for God. Mr. Booker had heard of the Caribbean and the peoples and opportunities that were there, and of the growing Negro population. The first island he came to was St. Croix, so he got off the boat, established a small bakery with what funds he had left and had been here ever since. For the price of a "donation" to the former fort commander, he had been allowed to build a small church in which the slaves could meet and worship. It had been a hard journey working with owners, convincing them to allow their slaves to attend worship on Sunday, but in spite of the difficulties, his flock had grown to over a one hundred members, including several Dutch citizens. James asked if he would lead service this Sunday in the open area in front of the fort for him and his men and any Dutch citizen and worker who might wish to attend. The man's face was a smile from ear to ear at the suggestion and said he would begin preparing the lesson right away. He commented that it was a dream come true and an answered prayer.

By the end of the first week, James and Bode felt the new *Lizards* could at least load a musket at an acceptable speed and fire with basic accuracy. They would not be able to pick off a lone soldier at a hundred yards, but they would be able to fire into a line of advancing soldiers from the top of the fort walls. Mr. Richards was also pleased with the progress that his Lizard artillerymen were making. By taking on the support work of carrying shot and powder to the guns freed up his men to be able to man additional guns across the various forts should a multi-pronged attack, such as from the sea and two sides of the fort by land, ensue. With the Lizards able to participate in the various support roles, the Black Dragons were able to incorporate more and more of them on the watch or patrol shifts, thereby reducing the workload.

They had decided to start the paying wages on a weekly basis to allow the workers to experience the joy of receiving payment for their work and to apply their pay toward necessities. Bode had the workers report to the fort to pick up their pay. Each was given the ability to either put the pay in their pockets to use later, to leave it at the fort to use later, or to purchase items available from the fort. As each arrived, every worker had a different response: some just held the money and stared at it, some immediately tried to understand what they could buy with it. Others seemed to think long-term and wanted to watch it grow or to leave it on account with the fort where it was protected.

There were discussions between the workers and those in charge of the distribution about how each decision and process worked. It was necessary to assure the newly freed men that once purchased; an item was theirs to keep. Anyone taking it from them would be arrested. Most preferred to trade for items, food or clothing, rather than hold the money or keep it on account. With life so uncertain, perhaps they placed greater value on having something in their hands now. James totally understood their choice and probably would have done the same until there was stability in place and the risk was less. Either way, it was a special moment watching them respond to the new choices in their lives.

Bode always took the time to personally introduce James to his "Lizards" and the able-bodied workers that had been employed by the fort. He talked about how strong, smart and capable they were and how well they had been doing in their training or position. James knew that the most challenging part of the training would be overcoming their lack of confidence and building courage to stand up against their white Dutch adversaries. These former slaves had been trained their entire lives to submit and surrender to the wishes of others. It was his job to make them understand that this was no longer the case. They now lived in a new world and he hoped that the Dragons' support would allow them to grow into it.

As he expected, the Dutch citizens proved difficult and would continually request or demand that James come to their establishment or home to discuss the challenges that the new working relationship had caused, mostly on how difficult and unproductive the newly freed workers had become. They felt it was somehow demeaning to have to speak with Bode or any of the other key Black Dragon leaders. James was determined to convince them that they would need to get used to the changes if their livelihood were to survive. He knew they were not happy about any of the changes and that they would work hard to see them fail, but he was determined to stand firm in his decisions.

James decided to require complaints and requests to be formally submitted in writing to Bode at his office in the main fort. Once filed, complaints or requests would be discussed with both parties either separately or together as needed. They initially found that some of the citizens, as if to punish the workers for being free, had either reduced their workers' food allocation or housing conditions. This caused the workers to diminish their full effort in response, which only exasperated the employers and increased their dissatisfaction. If it seemed that there were no solution, Bode would offer to remove the worker to allow the employer to hire another worker, in turn allowing the worker to offer his services to another employer. There was often a shortage of workers willing to work for the disgruntled employer, and this would almost always bring the discussion to an end in favor of the worker. Faced with the prospect of having no worker at all, the employer would concede and be open to new negotiations as to how to keep the worker employed through the offering of better food or better housing.

In the end, things began to balance out and return to a relatively normal arrangement as the populace learned to work together instead of against each other. Unfortunately, it was not the case in every situation. Either the pride of certain Dutch citizens did not allow them to adjust, or the deep rebellion and even hatred that the employer had created within the worker would not allow them to work together, no matter what arrangements were made. Several of the difficult Dutch families who had very poor reputations with the workers choose to pack up and leave the city because there were no workers who were willing to work for them. James was more than happy to see these people go, despite wealth or the skills that they might have. His father had always taught him to watch out for such men and women and deal with them quickly, or like a little yeast working through a batch of dough, the bitterness and resentment of people would work through a whole community and cause all sorts of rebellion and trouble.

The second week since the freeing of the slaves closed, finding the skills and unity of the Lizards developing quickly as less time was being diverted to civil matters, and more attention was being given to the actual training of the militia. In contrast to the early training on the Thornton plantation, these workers no longer had the time encumbrance of daily farm work and most of the trainees were able to dedicate themselves full-time to training. Robbie, who was in charge of the training, took full advantage of each hour of the day, working men diligently. Over the course of the next few weeks, an additional twenty-four workers had a change of heart after watching the newly formed Lizards train and speaking with them during their off hours. These men were assigned to the gun crew or sailor training groups. Their addition brought the total number for the defense of the city and fort to almost 300 armed men.

James watched from the fort walls as the order to assemble was given and noted how quickly and professionally the newly formed Black Lizards lined up into their respective groups of twenty-five. Bode had already assigned a Black Dragon sub leader for each group of five Lizards, and a Black Dragon leader for the group of twenty-five. With six Black Dragons now assigned to leadership, it left 1st Group somewhat depleted. The Black Dragons who remained were now responsible for increased duty on patrol or watch. James and the men knew they were spread thin and tired, but they also understood that they had no choice if they were to get these men trained quickly enough to make a difference should battle come.

James remembered that trying to make soldiers out of the trainees appeared hopeless that first week and he recalled the citizens' ridicule of their efforts. Still, Bode had continued with the drills until now there was no more laughter or ridicule coming from the citizens. Not only could they form a line and march together, they could shoot and were beginning to shoot with proficiency.

First, the basics of proper cleaning and care of the muskets were taught, soon followed by the procedures of how to load, aim and fire the muskets. Every day, they spent the afternoon training to load and fire the muskets. As they had done at the plantation, each group of five men formed a line and with the careful instruction of the Black Dragon leader the men would fire the muskets from a distance of thirty feet into upright logs that were cut to the height of a man and leaned against a brick wall. Although at first they had been scared by the blasts, the trainees became accustomed to the sounds and even began to cheer as the occasional lead ball found its mark. Robbie had the groups fire at random times so that the men would get use to keeping a cool head amidst the sound of muskets firing around them. The Lizards initially fared very poorly, but by the end of the second week, they could hit the logs one out of three times. Robbie reported to Bode that group there were several men among the group who had some natural talent with the musket. Bode took special note of these men and slated them for additional instruction.

From the second week on they always trained with their muskets. When the fortress bell was rung, the men would come running to form up outside the wall, while the cannon crews and sailors would dash to their respective areas. They were very proud of their accomplishments and it showed in their attitude. James had assigned the seamstresses to make special vests and pants for the new militia. The vests were dark gray and the pants were black and matched the main Dragon uniforms as closely as material on hand would allow. At the end of the fourth week, they were given the uniforms as a public acknowledgement that the trainees were officially members of the Black Lizard militia. The uniforms were only to be worn during their training or if the bell sounded for emergencies. When the men assembled for duty in their new uniforms, they exuded pride and confidence.

James followed through on his commitment to deliver the supplies and personal letters that they had captured from the merchant ship that were destined for the plantation owners. Although they knew of several large plantations near the city, prior to the training of the Lizards they had too few men to be able to spare them to make contact with them. Now that the Lizards could take on some of the duties, James felt it was important for them to reach a little further out from the city to not only deliver the supplies he knew they needed, but also to ensure nothing ominous was developing under their very noses. The closest major plantation was roughly three miles west of Christiansted; they had passed near it the evening they took the fort. James detailed ten Dragons and ten Lizards to accompany him and asked Mr. Massman to join them as translator. As the men marched, they escorted two wagons loaded with the plantation owner's purchased items and personal letters that were found on the captured merchant ship. In addition, they carried foodstuffs that were not available on the island which were intended for sale to the planters.

The men were keenly aware of the danger of venturing away from the security of the fort in order to perform such a service, but they also needed to sway the nearby plantation owners to participate in their new marketplace if they were to develop a sustainable economy for the city.

When they arrived outside of the closest plantation's boundary, the field slaves stood and looked at the armed Dragons carrying their muskets behind the two wagonloads of supplies. It was as if the world had been turned upside down for them. All the soldiers suddenly assumed military stance and walked more proudly. A young Dutch field hand broke from his trance and ran toward the main manor; his yells could be heard across the fields. James, along with Mr. Massman and the five Dragons marched toward the main manor while the remaining fifteen took up guard positions near the wagons to await further orders.

As they approached the manor, five men armed with muskets stepped out to greet them. A well-dressed man with a pistol in his belt moved to stand in front of the five. James immediately recognized him as the man with whom he had spoken at the fort while waiting for the Dutch commander on their initial meeting. Mr. Massman raised his hand in greetings and called out in Dutch to the man out front, who returned the greeting and walked down toward them. Speaking Dutch to Mr. Massman, the man kept glancing over at James as the two of them conversed for several minutes. Even though James knew the man spoke English, he waited patiently until finally the man stepped in front of him and in perfect English, said. "It seems that God gave you the speed you needed Captain." He smiled at James and James was relieved that the man recognized him.

"God can be very gracious at times and looked with favor upon our efforts to leave the fort and harbor faster than some would have preferred," James replied and the man chuckled.

"So much so, that he even allowed you to take the whole fort and city with just a few men and a merchant ship!" he remarked and laughed heartily and then the smile faded as he continued. "It serves the commander right for the arrogant manner in which he treated you, despite the fact that it turned out rather poorly for the rest of us," he finished.

"I hope to remedy that problem with our visit. We have not been properly introduced. My name is Captain James Thornton and we are here to deliver the long overdue supplies that you and your family purchased and I assume are in need of." James looked over his shoulder at the wagons where his men waited and then pulled a sheet of paper out and handed it to the man to read. "I show the following items were ordered and are available to be unloaded at your request," James informed him as the man looked at the paper and the list of items written on it. He glanced up at James as if confused or cautious.

"And what cost shall I bear for such a delivery?" he asked. James just shook his head.

"No cost. We are just here to deliver what is rightfully yours. We also came to offer you the ability to trade with the city, without concern for the safety of your family or goods. If you ask the citizens, they will confirm that…" The man cut him off. "I know all about your honorable actions at the city, Captain. I personally think you are a fool to have stayed; any other man would have plundered and burned the city to the ground for the way you were treated by the Commander and sailed off." He seemed to try to look into James' very heart with the statement, as if trying to detect any hidden anger or embarrassment. "I was there, so I know that it was very humiliating and very unprofessional of the Commander to treat you that way." James held his gaze for several seconds trying to read whether the man was joking or meant what he said. He finally decided that it did not matter and responded, "We did not return to exact revenge. We needed supplies and taking the fort and then the city was the only option available to us. His actions forced us to resort to violence. It should have been avoided."

"Yes it should have," the man responded. "And I don't believe you did come back for revenge. So who are you and what do you want exactly by staying on this island?" he asked James rather sternly.

"Duty sir. My men and I are from a plantation in Virginia, conscripted into the British army to assist them with a military matter elsewhere. Circumstances, led us here and, since the Dutch had declared war on the British and denied us our needed supplies, we were obligated to this course of action. To be honest, we're not sure how to untangle ourselves from the situation. We hope to make the best of it for everyone until the answer becomes clearer with time." He smiled. James liked the man he spoke with, as he reminded him of his father's frankness.

"So you did not come to take the city or the fort, but now you're trying to figure out how to hold it long enough until help comes?" the man said and then chuckled. "You are an honest man, I must give you that. My apologies, my name is Thomas Edlund." he said and cautiously shook James' hand. "So how can I assist you and your men?" he asked.

"As I said earlier, we are here to let you know that you are welcome to buy any supplies you require from the town and to sell the sugar, cotton or rum you produce at a fair price. We will see that it is distributed through the correct channels for a profit." He turned and signaled to the wagon, which began to move forward up the road toward the manor. "Please accept the delivery of your items as an example of our good will and commitment to you," James ended and then realized something. "Oh, and we have several personal letters that were taken from the ship that we wanted to make sure were delivered," James said, removing the letters from his jacket and handing them to Mr. Edlund. Mr. Edlund looked at the names on the envelopes, where they were from, and then nodded and smiled.

Mr. Edlund watched as the wagons rolled closer and closer with the militia walking with it and then spoke up. "If you think this will buy my support and allow you to acquire my slaves for your militia, then you are wasting your time, Captain." James was stunned by his remark, as it had not crossed his mind.

"I have no immediate desire to acquire or train your workers for the militia; this is truly just a gift to help you in a time of need." He then thought about the impression Mr. Edlund had, so he tried to address that. "Conscripting your men had not crossed my mind until just now, but know that should the time ever come for such a decision, I would prefer that offering the use of your slaves were by your choice, not by our force. That will be left to you to decide at that time and I will give you the respect of advance notice to keep your family safe." He concluded as the wagons pulled alongside the men.

James turned and looked at the Dutch men standing behind the leader. "Perhaps your men could assist my men in unloading the wagons, as we need to be heading back right away." There was a moment of hesitation from Mr. Edlund, then he gave a nod and his men behind him leaned their muskets against the nearby wall and began helping to unload the supplies.

The two of them seemed to be sizing each other up during the unloading, and then James asked Mr. Edlund, "How is it that you speak English so well?"

"I was not always Dutch, Captain. I was once a British citizen just like you, but I tired of their desire to control and direct my family's beliefs and work, so we left and came west on a Dutch merchant vessel that stopped here 18 years ago. This has been our home ever since." James nodded.

"How large is your family?" he asked without taking his eyes off the men unloading.

There seemed to be a hesitation, then he responded, "I would have thought you would have asked that question before you came here, Captain."

"True, but it's always good to hear it confirmed by the family head. Please understand that I did not come to verify your numbers, only to deliver your purchased supplies and offer any additional supplies you may need that are not commonly available," he replied.

"This is very kind of you, Captain. We are in need. I have three sons and two daughters. There are also three other families from Christiansted, along with their slaves, who are living with us at this time," Mr. Edlund replied. James had not expected such honesty.

"That was very kind of you to take them in. It's unfortunate that they did not take advantage of the offer to return when it was made. I cannot guarantee that their homes or businesses are still available, but they are welcome to visit and I will do what I can to assist them. I imagine the burden on your family would be lightened considerably if they were to return," James said. The man just stared at James.

"I think they are concerned about losing their slaves should they return," Mr. Edlund said with a smile as if baiting James.

"That would happen only if they were unkind to them and the workers chose not to work for them, otherwise it…" James was suddenly interrupted by Mr. Edlund.

"I know the structure you have in place Captain, we are still in touch with those in the city," he said and paused as if trying to read James' reaction before continuing. "Are your men of the same disposition as you, Captain?" he asked and James thought about it a moment before responding.

"They are, for the most part, Christian in their beliefs and all are men of character and courage. I'm honored to be able to lead them. Most of us have grown up together on my father's plantation. We trust and depend on one another. We are trying to instill the same character and trust in the men we are training in the city. It is a little more difficult without a common history and the difficulty of the language challenges, but we hope, with God's grace, to succeed."

"So I see," he said as they watch the militia and Dutch boys working together to unload the last supplies from the wagons.

Once they had finished unloading the wagons, Mr. Edlund took the time to introduce the men around him to the captain and he identified which ones were his sons. The oldest son was Edward, who James estimated to be in his early twenties, then Thomas, who was in his late teens, and finally Samuel, who was perhaps ten. He turned to the youngest of the boys and said, "Go ask your mother and sisters to come out here to meet the Captain."

"Yes sir," the young man replied, with the same courtesy that James would have given to his father. Moments later three women stepped out onto the porch and walked toward them. The older woman took Mr. Edlund's hand, and he turned to James.

"Captain, this is my amazing wife Gweneth." James bowed slightly and smiled at the introduction. A young auburn-haired woman came forward. James estimated her age at about 20. "My oldest daughter Rebecca," Mr. Edlund stated and waited as James turned to greet her, but his words failed as his heart jumped at the sight of her. She was absolutely stunning, yet simple in dress and adornment. He smiled as he recovered and bowed his head to her. The other young woman, blonde and small, who looked to be about 16, stepped up. "And my youngest daughter Allison," Mr. Edlund finished and James repeated his slight bow and smile before replying to all of them.

"Hello," they said in unison, and Rebecca added "Captain." The word was like music to his ears and he was having difficulty holding his concentration as he took a deep breath.

"It is a pleasure to meet all of you. I'm sorry for any inconvenience that may have been caused by our presence, but please know that my men and I are at your service," he said and tried to avoid looking at the taller and older daughter across from him, who seemed to have picked up on his anxiety and even seemed to relish it.

Although James had demonstrated that he could stand toe to toe to a line of muskets or cannon aimed at him, he felt like retreating from the older daughter out of fear that what was happening inside would be revealed. He felt extremely vulnerable.

"Perhaps it would be best for my men and me-I, to head back to the fort and allow you and your family to return to your duties," he stammered as he turned back toward Mr. Edlund. "Please accept my offer to openly resume trade in the markets. It has been a pleasure meeting you and your family." He offered his hand to Mr. Edlund's in a friendly gesture, who grasped it in his own firmly and smiled.

"I believe we will take you up on that offer. Thank you for your kindness."

He dared one more glance at Rebecca as he headed down the hill with the wagon and his men. He thought he saw a smile, but did not dare to return it. The march back to the city was short and he felt annoyed, for he could not keep his mind on his surroundings, but instead his thoughts continually returned to Mr. Edlund and his family, especially one daughter with auburn hair. *Rebecca.* He repeated the name in his head several times and it sounded like music. He hoped that they would soon visit the city, but at the same time he somehow feared the very thought of it.

Over the next week, James visited four more plantations, delivering their imported items, personal letters, and offering the same arrangement that he had offered Mr. Edlund and his family. Although grateful, they were not as friendly as Mr. Edlund had been and expressed little interest in trading with the city.

The following week word was delivered to James that some of the members of a plantation family they had visited had arrived with several wagonloads of sugar, cotton, rum, fruit and vegetables. They had asked for Captain Thornton personally and were waiting on the outskirts of the city. Bode at first voiced his concern that it might be a potential ambush, but James, after discovering that there were women along, assumed that it was Mr. Edlund and from what he knew about the man and his family, thought it unlikely. Taking Bode's advice, he brought five Dragons along just in case. When he arrived to greet them, he saw eight loaded wagons driven by Mr. Edlund, two of his oldest sons Edward and Thomas, three citizens and fifteen workers. More importantly to James, Mr. Edlund's daughter, Rebecca, was sitting next to her father on the lead wagon. His heart skipped again. He learned during the introductions that the three Dutch citizens were from the other families staying with the Edlunds, and came to revisit the idea of returning to their former homes and establishments.

"We have come to do a little trading and purchase some tools and kitchen items that you may have for sale." Mr. Edlund's sounded more like a request than a statement. James smiled at the various workers and men who sat on the wagons.

"You are welcome to drop your goods at the warehouse where Commander Donovan will give you a fair price in either credit or coin. Although not needed here, I will travel with you to ensure your safe passage," James said with a smile and Mr. Edlund translated to Dutch for those in the other wagons. As the translation proceeded, James tried to identify who each returning citizen by not only their looks, but what was in the back of their wagon. Once the translation was completed, James turned toward the men from the other families. Addressing a man with big muscular arms he said. "The smithy is still as you left it, for we do not have anyone else with your expertise to work it. You are free to bring your family back and continue your profession here." The man seemed stunned and said, "I have three skilled-" He hesitated, "...workers that I would like to have remain with me, as they are much needed." James nodded.

"That will be up to you and the three workers to decide, but I will do my best to encourage them to remain with you, as I understand your need." Turning to the other two, he said to the man with the blond hair of whom he had heard other Dutch citizens speak often the last few weeks. "If I am correct in assuming that you are the doctor, your house and office has been occupied by our ship's medic while you were absent. If your desire is to return, and your skill is as good as it is reported, I will ensure that it is returned to you with the understanding that you will help to further train our medical staff in your profession." The man agreed and thanked him.

James then glanced at the other man. "My apologies, but I'm unable to guess your profession or who you are. Perhaps you can enlighten me with more information and I will see what I can do." There seemed to be nervousness from the man as he sat in the wagon and looked down at James. Mr. Edlund broke the awkwardness of the moment.

"Mr. Vos is from Fredricksted on the other end of the island. He was visiting the town when you arrived and came to stay with us, but he has no family with him," Mr. Edlund stated and then translated both James' and his own words in Dutch to the man. As the words were translated by Mr. Edlund, an obvious fear went through the man as he glanced first at Mr. Edlund, then back at James to see what his response would be. James was unclear as to why the man had not returned to Fredricksted but instead remained near Christiansted.

Warning flags were waving inside of James' mind as he continued to stare at the nervous man on the wagon. Had Mr. Edlund purposely exposed this man's hidden secret to him? Is that why he waited on the outskirts of the city instead of coming in? James turned to one of his militia and asked for his canteen and some basic rations, who gave it to him without a thought.

"Your presence is not welcome in this city and my better judgment says I should go as far as to lock you up. I will give you this option, but only once. Go back to your city and let them know that if they start any trouble here they will leave us with no choice but to march upon Fredricksted and burn it and the fort to the ground." He handed the water and food to the man on the wagon. "Now go, and know that if you are seen here again, you will be put in chains."

As the man stepped down from the wagon, he glared at Mr. Edlund and said something under his breath. Mr. Edlund responded calmly but coolly in Dutch to the man. The man then jogged off down the road in a western direction toward Fredricksted. Once the man was out of earshot, James turned to face Mr. Edlund.

"Thank you. I appreciate your action of protecting the security of the city. I imagine that choice has generated some animosity between you and Mr. Vos. What he would have discovered has more than likely already been leaked in messages sent from other citizens," James commented.

"He is well aware of what is going on in the city, but I was protecting the long-term relationship of our family with you. If we were discovered helping someone intending to betray you for his personal benefit, it would be more costly to me than I am willing to pay. You see, Captain, based on what I have seen and heard so far, I do not see you leaving anytime soon, so cultivating a working relationship with you is simply our best alternative at this time." He smiled and James was not sure if he should feel happy or hurt by the assertions. At least the man was direct.

"Well, I appreciate your honesty and your confident evaluation of our presence." He returned the smile. "Shall we continue into the city?" Mr. Edlund tapped the reins onto the oxen urging them forward, beginning their entrance into the center of the city. The beautiful young woman at her father's side seemed to watch every step that James took.

James spent the rest of the day personally escorting Mr. Edlund and his family around the city, introducing them to those in charge that were new, and making sure that they were able to sell their goods and to use the money to purchase whatever additional items they needed. In the process, he learned a great deal about the family and their life over the past eighteen years since arriving in St. Croix. He also was able to see more of Rebecca who seemed to be always watching and listening to each conversation that he had with her father and those around. There finally came a moment when just he and Rebecca were standing on the walkway outside the warehouse while her father and brothers were negotiating with Captain Donovan on the purchase and sale of goods. They stood quietly for a moment and then James finally broke the silence.

"I'm glad you were able to make the journey Miss Edlund. Is there a particular store or item you had in mind that I can help you locate?" he asked, and she smiled at his offer.

"I'm not sure 'item' is the word I would use to describe the reason I came," she said and laughed sweetly, but James did not seem to grasp what she meant. He did know that he now also loved how she laughed, her voice and even how she pronounced each word with a slight accent. He was happy that she spoke English as well as Dutch.

"If not an item, what might I be able to help you with?" he asked, giving up on trying to figure out the meaning of her words. She seemed to be trying to read his face for some sign of joke or hidden meaning and then finally she turned away and looked out at the ocean a moment as if gathering her courage.

"I came to meet and learn more about you Captain James Thornton," she said confidently. She stood watching his expression as her assertion sunk in. James at first missed it, then realized what she was saying, or he hoped he understood her meaning correctly. He made as if to answer, stopped, tried again, and then took a deep breath.

"I-I feel honored beyond words," he finally mumbled, but then suddenly second-guessed the situation and wondered if he had misunderstood her meaning. "You mean to understand what I do, or more about the Black Dragons, or…" She suddenly laughed at his stumbling over his words as his mouth tried to articulate his thoughts. James felt embarrassed that he had misinterpreted her meaning.

"I came to learn more about who you are, not what you are or what you do," she said very seriously, while keeping that gentle smile on her face. "I have spent the past few years being pursued by, and fending off, the son's of local plantation owners and visiting soldiers. All of which I had no interest in being courted by." She chuckled.

"How were you so sure?" James asked and she looked at James a moment before answering.

"To the chagrin of many, my father's own character has set a very high standard by which I measure the character and humor of other men. Unfortunately, there are few men that I have met that even come close to him," she said and James nodded.

"Your father is a good man. I can see how it would be difficult to find a man of such character. But sometimes it takes time to reveal the character of a man, or woman." James replied nervously, hoping to delay her judegment of him.

"Sometimes, but from what I have seen and heard about you Captain Thornton, you may be one of the few. If you are such a man, I felt the need to know quickly," she said as she looked in his eyes.

James just stood there in silence as he realized that in one short sentence she had removed months of agonizing courtship rituals, routines, and second-guessing of her interest in him. All he could think to do was exhale in relief the breath he had been holding as she spoke. She suddenly seemed embarrassed or uncomfortable at his lack of response, which encouraged him to express his thoughts.

"You have removed some very awkward and tedious social mountains which I am ill equipped to handle. I'm so grateful for your directness. I too have strongly desired to visit your family again in order to have another opportunity to know you better, for I have not met a woman that has captured my heart so quickly and completely as you have," he said with all sincerity as they stood looking at each other and she gave him a dazzling smile. He suddenly remembered the last of her words. "But why the need for urgency Miss Edlund?" he asked her curiously. She smiled and looked away and then back at him with deep concern.

"Because I know, Captain Thornton, that war is coming to the fort and if you are the man I hope you are, I will know what to pray for," she replied.

"And what would that be?" he asked.

"For the British to arrive and strengthen the defenses of the fort so that there will be no attack; and if that is not possible, then for your success and safety should an attack come," she said softly. He thought about her words and the reality behind them. He grimaced a moment and then smiled.

"To pray for our victory over your countrymen's is very inspiring Miss Edlund." He hesitated a moment as he considered her words. "This is definitely not the best moment in time for two people to be courting, especially an officer of the enemy," he said and she smiled and nodded.

"Thirty days ago our countries were friends, Captain. By the stroke of the pen are we now to be enemies? I choose to follow my heart, not my country's politics when it comes to the matters of courting."

"Who's courting?" the voice of her father suddenly asked from the doorway of the warehouse, interrupting their heartfelt discussion. James was immediately expecting wrath from her father, but Rebecca coolly turned toward him to answer.

"Captain Thornton and I were just discussing the challenges and dislikes we have had with prior courtships," she said sweetly and far more calmly than he felt. He glanced at the two of them and then at his two sons standing behind him, who had stepped outside to join him.

"Seems a strange subject to be discussing, my dear, anything I can add to help in the discussion?" he asked and then smiled.

"Perhaps during another discussion, but I think we have found the answers we were both looking for," she replied and then turned toward James and smiled. Mr. Edlund watched his daughter's expression and James knew that he was well aware of what they were discussing. Perhaps he even brought her with him for this very matter.

After a few more stops for some specialty items for his wife, Mr. Edlund motioned for his family and his workers to board the wagons.

"It has been a pleasure, Captain, and my thanks to you for your assistance. I will soon be transporting additional goods to sell and to have added to your warehouses for future trade. I do hope that additional freedom of trade will open for you," he said sincerely.

"Thank you, Mr. Edlund. Please be careful and know that we are here to assist should you need us," James replied, and then turned toward Rebecca. "I'm very grateful that your father allowed you to join him on this visit. I look forward to seeing you and your family even more in the future and the opportunity to continue our discussions," he said and nodded at Thomas and Edward.

"Our prayers will be with you and your men, Captain, and I will look forward to your next visit," she said coyly as she looked into his eyes.

With the urging of the reins on their backs, the oxen pulled the wagons forward and down the street heading to the east and their home. James' eyes followed Rebecca until the wagon turned a corner and was finally out of sight. He tried to come up with a reason to visit them within the next day, even week, but could not think of any.

"Umm, you may have forgotten, but we are trying to prepare to fend off a potentially large force that is intent on killing us," Bode said from behind James, watching him stare down the empty street. James at first was embarrassed that his friend caught him in the moment, but then smiled.

"We? I thought that was your job?" he replied and turned away from the street to face his friend.

"Well, it always has been, but I like to try to include you so you can get a little credit now and then," Bode answered dryly and James nodded as if agreeing. They both started walking back to the fort, neither saying anything for the first few minutes.

"Is she the one?" Bode suddenly asked. James remembered the many conversations that they had over the subject of courtship. He at first did not answer, but then suddenly stopped walking and turned toward his waiting friend.

"I think so," was all James could say. Bode took a deep breath as if exhausted and then exhaled slowly.

"You have some terrible timing," Bode joked as they entered the fort and took in the bustle of the building repairs and troop movement going on around them.

"You think?" James replied and, although he smiled at his friend's words, he knew there was a great deal of truth in them. He wondered why God would bring this woman into his life during such challenging times. Was it a blessing because he knew that his time was short? Was there something bigger going on around him? Would he and his men even survive this whole unwanted ordeal to enjoy their lives? He walked to the kitchen area to get a bite to eat before heading to the end-of-the-day meeting that the officers had each night.

The following week two more loads of sugar, cotton, corn and rum arrived from the Edlund Plantation and, to the surprise of everyone, five other plantations also began bringing their goods to be sold to the city, although not in such large quantities. The second delivery from Mr. Edlund's plantation saw the return of Rebecca and her father. James went out to great them and Mr. Edlund stepped down from the wagon and then helped Rebecca down. He turned to James with a serious expression.

"Captain Thornton, it has come to my attention that there is a mutual interest between you and my daughter." James simply nodded as his throat constricted and he waited for the wrath of the father to come, as it had in so many other similar situations. Mr. Edlund appeared angry and his tone was deadly serious.

"Well, let me be very clear, Captain Thornton; my daughter Allison has no interest in a courtship with you," he said sternly. James blinked at the name and tried to quickly clarify the misunderstanding.

"Mr. Edlund, I'm not interested in…" James started to say just as Rebecca cut him off "Father!" she said indignantly and slapped her father on the upper arm with the back of her gloved hand.
"Ouch…" He pretended to be hurt by her blow and then continued, "But it appears that my older daughter, Rebecca, has an interest in you." He smiled and stepped aside to let Rebecca join them.

"You are truly the meanest man I have ever met and I have no idea what mother sees in you," Rebecca interjected with a forced face of anger. James decided to act upon the opportunity presenting itself since he had not been able to formerly request permission to court her.

"With Rebecca's consent, I would like to formally request your permission to court your daughter Mr. Edlund," James stated and waited for the response. Mr. Edlund took another long look at his daughter before replying. Rebecca nodded to him and smiled.

"Well, I have not seen her quite this happy in some time, so it would be cruel of me to deny her," he replied. "It might prove to be the shortest courtship on record, so I guess I don't have too much to lose by giving you my approval," he said sardonically, and smiled as he then offering his hand to James. James raised an eyebrow and nodded as shook his hand.

"There is truth and merit in your words, but I hope you will not withdraw your permission should they be proved wrong," he replied dryly and smiled.

"No. If you can manage to get to the other side of this situation alive, I will not stand in your way. In fact, I would say I would be fighting against God if I did," he replied as he let go of James' hand.

"In that case, I look forward to seeing Captain Thornton frustrate your plans," Rebecca said coyly as she stepped forward and slid her hand onto James' elbow and faced her father. "Could James and I have lunch together while you conduct your business with the commander?" she asked her father, who smiled and nodded.

"I do not have an escort to provide for you, so I will agree only if you have your lunch in the open area in front of the fort," he stated and James nodded.

"I will see that food and drink from the fort is…" he started to offer before Rebecca interrupted him. "I have already packed a lunch just for such an occasion," she said and smiled at her father, who seemed bothered by the forethought of his daughter.

"She is an overly confident young woman, Mr. Thornton, run now or you will never escape her wiles." He laughed and kissed her on the forehead as she removed the basket from the back of the wagon and headed back toward James.

"I'm afraid, Mr. Edlund, your warning has arrived too late," he replied as she placed her hand back on his arm and they turned and walked toward the open area in front of the fort.

Although they were on display in front of every man, woman and soldier in the city and fort, James would not have traded the moment with Rebecca for anything. He could see the soldiers looking over the walls at them and the citizens staring out their windows and from the walkways at them. He knew he had responsibilities to attend to, but he saw that Bode had either addressed the needs personally or had assigned someone else to handle them. He knew that Bode was looking out for him and allowing him to enjoy the moment.

The lunch was the most enjoyable time that he could remember. They ate and laughed and told stories of their childhood, their dreams, and asked each other very deep questions about life and religion. They talked about his friendship with Bode and all that they had been through together. The more they talked, the more he realized how much they had in common, but how different they were. His strengths were her weaknesses; her strengths were his weaknesses. The way they complimented each other was very much like the nature of his mother's and father's relationship. Their differences made them both stronger as a couple than they were as individuals. Too soon for James', their time was at an end and her father motioned to her that it was time to return to the plantation. They both walked slowly back to the wagons, savoring the last moments together. James thanked Mr. Edlund for the opportunity to spend time with Rebecca and then helped her onto the wagon.

"I will try to visit you soon," he said to her.

"James, although I would love to see you every day, I would prefer that your efforts are spent in preparing your men and this fort to be safe and strong. Having the shortest courtship in history certainly will not do." She finally let go of the hand that had helped her onto the wagon.

"Be safe Captain Thornton," Mr. Edlund said, as the wagons slowly began to move down the street and James nodded and smiled.

"Please give my regards to your wife and family… and the daughter that has no interest in me." Mr. Edlund just shook his head and smiled, as did Rebecca.

This time it was Rebecca who did not turn away from watching him as the wagon moved down the street and finally around the corner. His heart was strangely heavy as he turned and started walking back toward the fort. As he got close, he glanced up to see Bode and Captain Donovan standing by the entrance, both with their arms crossed as if they were ready to give a strong scolding to him when he arrived. He stopped, and then pretended that he forgot something and turned away from the fort. Moments later he could hear the noise of their feet and rattle of their gear catching up with him.

"Not so fast, Mr. Wonderful- give us an update." Captain Donovan demanded as he caught up with James on his right.

"After all, you basically rubbed our noses in it as you flaunted it in front of all of us over lunch," Bode added as he slid next to him on his left. James just shook his head and smiled, knowing that they would not let him off the hook until he told them everything, yet he wondered what he could negotiate out of them first.

"You two are either too young or too old to understand," he started and they immediately went into a verbal attack mode, which he expected and wanted them to do. The three of them wandered off toward the wharf, heckling each other as they went.

Chapter 15

August 26, 1776

Six weeks had passed since the onset of the training of the new militia and fifty-six days since the capture of the fort and James took stock of their current position. They had progressed nicely in all aspects of the defenses. They had repaired the fort's damaged walls, bastions and ramparts, rebuilt the kitchen, added additional guns from the three captured merchant ships to the wall defenses of the three forts. They had trained 158 workers to be Black Lizards; 100 as infantry soldiers, 35 as cannon support crew, and 24 as journeyman sailors. They even had a waiting list of another 22 men who desired to be trained, and another list of the various skills and services offered by a large percentage of the remaining worker population. They had installed a port entrance barrier consisting of a heavy chain attached to several thick hemp ropes on each end, drawn taught across the inner entrance of the bay. The chain could not be cut and the hope was that it would prevent or considerably slow the progress of an invading fleet from sailing directly into the port in force. James reasoned that this would buy more time for the defense before such a fleet could position their vessels and guns to overwhelm the fort's own guns. They knew that the barrier would eventually be circumvented, but they hoped it would prove costly should someone try, since it was placed within range of all their guns.

Extra attention was given to the defenses of the east fort, as it was more exposed and they did not want to see the same tactic that they had used to take the main fort to be used on them. James had ordered a firing platform to be built for one of the longer-range field cannons. It would be used on any forces attacking from the land; the 9 pounder wall cannons were ideally suited for short range grapeshot or close cannon shot, but did not have the range of a field cannon with their longer-range shot. This strategy gave them the ability to engage long range enemy cannons with one of their own. Although it was only one gun, they hoped that the protected walls and elevation would allow them to use it more effectively. All in all, they were as prepared as they could be for an attack that they knew would come at any time.

James was awakened by urgent knocking on the door of his sleeping quarters. He was informed that there was some sort of trouble and that a young man was waiting to speak with him in the inner courtyard. James quickly dressed and raced to the courtyard. James immediately recognized Thomas Edlund, who was covered in sweat, out of breath, and bruised from having fallen several times during his journey. James saw that he had already been given water and one of the soldiers was attempting to clean and dress his various scratches, but he wanted nothing of it until he saw James.

"Captain Thornton! They have attacked our family's plantation and taken everything and they have taken most of our family. Father sent me to let you know," he shouted between breaths. James' mind was racing with all the questions he wanted to ask, but he knew he needed to keep calm.

"Thomas, when did this happen?" he asked calmly.

"This morning, just before dawn," he replied.

"Who attacked you and how many were there?" James asked and looked up to see that Bode and Captain Donovan had now stepped into the room to join them.

"Vos... It was Mr. Vos and some men from Frederiksted," he exhaled. James remembered Vos as the man on the wagon that he had sent back to Frederiksted for spying. He had stayed with Mr. Edlund and his family and he was furious that he had been exposed by Mr. Edlund. He apparently went back to exact revenge.

"How many men, Thomas, how many soldiers?" he asked, trying to stay calm, but feeling the urgency rising at the same time.

"Twenty, maybe thirty men. They were not soldiers, but armed free plantation men." Thomas answered. "They came with a lot of wagons, maybe twenty or more. They took our crops, ransacked our house, and took our slaves... I mean our workers." He said the last part nervously as he remembered Bode and the men around him. "They were still stealing and loading when I managed to escape. I ran the whole way here." His voice raised in pitch slightly as he relived the memory. James patted him on the shoulder.

"You did well in coming here so quickly Thomas, really courageous," James said and turned to his friends standing around him, seeking their input.

"Who is Vos?" Captain Donovan asked.

"He was the citizen from Frederiksted that was trying to sneak in with Mr. Edlund and his family, but Mr. Edlund exposed his deception at the city entrance. He was not pleased, to say the least."

"It could be a planned diversion to get us out in the open or to pull some troops out of the fort prior to an attack," Captain Donovan commented, James turned to Bode, who shook his head.

"It could be, but it might be just as it looks: revenge and a message to the rest of the plantation owners not to sell to Christiansted, or else," Bode replied and James nodded.

"We don't have much time. I'd like to take whatever men we can spare and intercept them if possible," James asserted, and the others agreed.

"If they are traveling by wagon and the boy ran all the way, we should still be able to get in front of them," Bode commented.

"Or if they are attacking with an army, you will run into the main force just outside the city. Either way, we need to go and find out," Captain Donovan added and both James and Bode nodded. James looked at his friends and then focused on Robbie.

"Sound the alarm and have Sergeant Willie's 3rd Lizards and the five Dragon leaders armed and ready to travel with full rations and shot in ten minutes or less," he ordered and Robbie turned and ran toward the barracks. James then turned back to Bode and Captain Donovan. "If we run into a larger force on our way there, we will forego any rescue attempt and return immediately to defend the city and fort," he stated and turned to gather his uniform and gear.

"I'm going with you!" Bode declared and followed him toward their rooms. James let him get close and then stopped.

"If it's a trap, then you need to be here to defend this fort and lead these men. No one can do a better job of it than you." Bode tried to find a rebuttal, but he knew James was right.

"No heroics James! Just stay alert and recognize when you're out-matched." James smiled and then gave Bode that look that always worried him, then ran toward his room to change and prepare. He had not asked Thomas if Rebecca was captured and taken with her family, he somehow knew instinctively that she had been. He prayed that God would keep her and her family and all of the workers safe.

The fort was coming alive as more and more men were manning the walls and loading their muskets. James returned to the inner courtyard where Thomas was somewhat recovered. The thirty men of the Dragon Lizards 3rd Group were gathering, dressed and ready. Once the men of the 3rd had assembled, an additional musket with the bayonet mounted on the tip was handed to each of them. Robbie had ordered half the men on watch to load the muskets while the 3rd Group dressed. Robbie and Bode and the Dragon leaders of the Lizard 3rd Group were giving directions to each man, refreshing the steps of their training and, explaining when to use the spare musket. Other Dragons were checking to make sure each man had powder, shot, water and rations. Captain Donovan returned with a map and showed James a spot where the roads would intersect, and noted that he would be able to tell if the wagons were ahead of them or behind them by the ruts left in the roads at the junction. James could see both the fear and the excitement in the eyes of the Black Lizards; he could even see the same in the Black Dragons leading them. He wondered if his own fear also showed. He stood before the men and spoke briefly.

"Men, we will need to move quickly if we are to be successful. A nearby plantation friendly to our endeavor, and thus under our protection, was raided this morning and the workers and the family were captured and are currently being taken to Frederiksted. We all could choose to find a personal reason to fight in this situation, but I want us to fight because it is the right thing to do and not let our emotions sway us from our training." He looked at his men, now fully dressed and ready, paying close attention to his words being translated by one of the fellow soldiers who spoke both English and Dutch. "Stay close, watch and listen to your patrol leader, and be strong and courageous. That is the mark of a Lizard and future Dragon," he said and nodded to Bode, Robbie and Captain Donovan. They opened the outer door of the fort and the men filed out and began a brisk jog toward the western side of the town and down the main road leading to Frederiksted.

James carried his long rifle and his pistol, with the spare musket slung over his shoulder. He had left his sword to lighten his load because it would be awkward and noisy running with it. Although it was relatively cool as they started out in the early hours, the humidity and activity of running began to turn his dry shirt into a sweaty sticky mass. Even the Lizard soldiers, who were acclimated to this weather, had sweat pouring down their faces. James was looking intently, far ahead of him, to the sides of him, and at the road for signs of traffic as they ran. He half expected to see someone jump out and fire, or to have one side of the road explode with musket shot as they ran into a trap, but none came. They stopped briefly about one mile from the city to make sure everyone was staying with them. He could see pain on one mans face, as if he was battling a side ache or worse, but when James asked if he wanted to return to town, he immediately shook his head and said in broken English, "No, me learn to fight today." and then stood as if ready to go. James directed the men to take another drink and then they started down the road again toward their target crossroad several miles ahead of them.

James had been down this road on horseback several times, scouting and visiting plantation owners, and he knew that a sharp bend in the road was only a few hundred yards ahead. That was where they would make their ambush he decided. He held up his hand and signaled for silence and each man stepped to the side of the road and into the cover of the deep foliage. After several moments of silently listening and resting, James signaled for the six Dragon leaders to come to him, where he told them his plan. When they understood the plan they moved back with their squads of five men and repeated the directions. They were to move quietly westward several hundred yards through the foliage and then turn south to intersect the main road, remain in the foliage and await further orders.

Although it was hard going, the moist air helped to suppress the noise as they pushed their way through the cover. James crawled forward to the edge of the foliage bordering the road and looked at the ground. He saw wagon wheel tracks, horse tracks, and footprints, but they were all heading east. His heart leapt at the realization that the raiders had not passed by them yet on their return to Frederiksted. He tried to think of the best defensive positions for maximum safety of his men. He also had to take into consideration the family and workers that could be with the raiding party. He knew that the Lizards were not expert marksman, let alone good shots even at 50 yards, so he struggled as he worked to come up with a plan that would be effective and safe.

"The closer the better," Willie said and the other Dragons agreed as they huddled together to discuss the situation.

"Twenty wagons, even tightly lined up are going to cover a great deal of distance. Our men will be spread out pretty far. If they were all Dragons, it might work, but these are freshly trained men that have never seen a fight or fired at a person before," James pointed out. James ordered one Dragon and one Lizard to head down the road as sentries to alert him as soon as the wagon train was seen or heard. He seriously thought about letting the wagon train pass by them to avoid taking any chances of harming someone innocent in the exchange, but he knew this would be his last chance to free Mr. Edlund and his family. He figured that once they arrived in Frederiksted he would probably be punished or executed for treason for working with the British, if he had not been shot already.

By the time they had decided what to do, the men were well rested from the run and ready for battle. The initial plan was to let part of the wagon train pass by them and then strike hard in the middle with four groups of five, plus the squad Dragon leader, cutting their forces in half and perhaps causing enough panic that the two ends would scatter. The 5th squad would lay logs across the road and be out front to stop any wagons from bolting. They would then return to the main group in the middle, staying on the side of the road shooting across it as they worked their way back. He pulled the leaders together quickly again to explain the plan to them.

"This will be a difficult fight and there will be many innocent workers and family members mixed in with the soldiers, so making sure your aim is true is of vital importance," James said, thinking about Rebecca. "Once you fire your initial shot, pick up your other musket with the bayonet and move forward to engage the enemy. Stay together to protect each other's flanks, and yell your battle cries as loud as you can. Remember, your spare rifle will have another shot available. So if anyone comes toward you, fire it at close range, and then engage the rest with your bayonet." He stopped and let the translators catch up as he smiled. He could tell they were very nervous at the idea of shooting or killing someone, especially a white man. "When those that run return to their towns, we want them to fear the Dragons and the Lizards so much that they never return." He growled at them and they laughed softly at first, then louder when the words were translated.

He sent Willie and his five Lizards to hold the front. "Remember, three per side of the road as you come back toward us so you can use the cover- and don't shoot any of us in the process." James smiled and sent Willie and his men on their way. He then positioned the other four squads, equally distanced apart, with about fifteen yards between each squad and about five deep into the foliage for cover. James would join the squad furthest down the line so that he could see what was coming and make changes as needed. He took a moment to pray and ask God to protect the workers and the families, and his men.

Twenty minutes later, the two sentries came running along the edge of the road toward them. They were not in a panic, but they moved with speed. As they got closer, James stepped out of his cover, motioned the two men to where he was sitting, and listened to the report.

"We went up on a hillside to be able to see further down the road, Sila's idea, since he knew the area." He smiled and nodded at the man next to him who just grinned back at them. "We saw fifteen armed men out in front of the wagons followed by the workers, who are tied together by rope around their necks, then the wagons. It looked like there were a few armed men guarding the wagons in the middle where the family was riding, and then the majority of the rest of the armed men were in the back, maybe twenty or thirty. It was hard to count at that distance." James was very impressed at the amount of information they had gathered and realized his plan had missed a key element. The raiders were prepared for an encounter at the front of the wagons, whereas James' plan had them expecting one to come only from behind. James decided to send another squad up to the front to re-enforce Willie's squad who would engage the lead group of fifteen men. He warned them that they needed to quickly press forward, defeat the advanced group, and rejoin the other three squads. The three central squads led by James would engage the middle of the wagon train and secure the release of the families, taking up defensive positions against the force that will surely be charging forward from the back of the wagon train. The middle groups would not engage until the front group engaged. Surprise was crucial for them if they were to succeed quickly. The adjustment to the plan spread to the rest of the men quickly and everyone moved back into their hiding places to wait for the two squads at the front to engage.

It was almost ten minutes later that the creak and rattles of the wagons could be heard in the distance, which meant that the armed men and workers in front were very near. Then the sound of marching could be heard, and then a few low voices speaking in Dutch. Looking through the stocks at the base of the ferns that they were hiding under, James could see the feet and legs of the armed men passing by, then the bare and dark skinned legs of the workers as they walked closely together on both sides of the road. As the workers legs ended, he saw the feet of the horses pulling the lead wagon, followed soon by the wheels. Knowing how far his men were positioned in front, he knew that the sound of musket fire would be heard any moment, but he hoped that more wagons would pass before it occurred. The fifth wagon had just passed when the rumble of the muskets firing was heard. He immediately jumped to his feet with one musket hanging by its strap over his shoulder and the other in his hands. When he had moved forward enough to be able to reach the edge of the opening, he began searching for his first target.

Three muskets went off rapidly to his right. The wagon in front of him was loaded with supplies and there was only a single old man sitting on the buckboard trying desperately to calm the horses that were pulling his wagon. His eyes went wide at the sight of James' musket aimed at him.

"Kore!" (Run) James yelled in Dutch at the driver of the fifth wagon. The man seemed to understand in spite of his horrible pronunciation and dropped the reins of the horses. He was jumping off the wagon as James turned and moved toward the back of the wagon train. The driver of the next wagon was also struggling to calm his horses. As he saw James moving down the line toward him with his musket aimed at him, he quickly dropped the reins and put his hands in the air. "Kore!" James yelled at the man, who responded as the prior driver had, and James moved toward the end the seventh wagon in the line. A sudden banging noise nearby, followed closely by the sound of an explosion further away, caused James to jump to the side. He realized that a musket ball had struck the wagon in front of him, just to his right. He raised his musket, aiming left then right, searching for the source of the shot. As he looked past the sixth wagon, he saw two men, one sitting on the buckboard and the other standing with a smoking musket still aimed at James. James aimed his musket at him and the man stepped back as if trying to get away from him, but only managed to fall backwards into the loaded bed of the wagon. As the man fell, James was able to look past where the man had been and could see the eighth wagon and those who were in it. Sitting in an open wagon, just behind the driver, he could see Mrs. Edlund, Allison and Rebecca, along with two armed men. With the wagon now stopped, the two men were standing up in the back of it looking forward. They saw James moving toward them at the same time. The man closest to the front raised his musket as the other tried to move to his side for a clear shot. James moved to use the wagon as cover and began to take aim at the man closest to him. James' move to the wagon allowed the man closest to fire first and James could hear the sound of the musket ball snap through the air as it passed only a foot above his left shoulder. The other man had moved into position and was starting to aim his musket at James. James shifted his aim to that man and fired. James watched as the man was blown backwards from the impact of the musket ball, catching his legs on the back tailgate and tumbling out the back of the wagon.

James instinctively ran toward the wagon, seeing that the man who had fired at him was desperately trying to pull the rod out of its holder in order to reload his musket. Rebecca had watched the man tumble out the back of the wagon and then looked toward the area where the shot had come from. She saw James for the first time as he ran toward the wagon and she looked around frantically trying to find a way to help. James dropped his long rifle and reached across his chest, pulling the other musket over his head and quickly moving toward the wagon. He saw another man, who was standing behind the ninth wagon raise his musket so James angled to his right as he ran and put the horse and driver between him and the wagon as he continued moving toward the right side of the wagon. The man in the wagon was busy reloading and had not moved from his standing position, so as James came around the right side of the wagon, using both hands he thrust the deadly tip of the bayonet upwards underneath the man's ribs and into his chest. He knew that it was a killing wound and just as quickly he withdrew the point and moved toward the back of the wagon. He stopped, raised the musket to fire and waited. Almost on cue, the man who had tried to fire at him moments earlier suddenly stepped around the back of that wagon and into James' aim. The man went down instantly as the ball smashed into him.

"James!" He could hear Rebecca's voice as he stepped around the back of the wagon.

"All of you stay low and run toward the front of the train, my men are there and they will protect you!" he yelled as he looked down on the ground and saw the man whom he had shot and who tumbled out of the back of the wagon. He thought about pulling his pistol, but the man was dead. James saw the dead man's unfired musket lying next to him. He leaned his musket with the bayonet against the wagon, then picked up the musket and checked to make sure the primer was ready. The musket had an awkward feel to it, but the thought left his mind when he saw more armed men several wagons back moving toward him. He moved forward toward the next wagon hoping to stop their advance long enough to allow Rebecca and her family to get safely away.

The driver of that wagon had already leapt off the side and was running as fast as he could away from James and toward the back of the wagon train. Keeping that man between him and the approaching armed men, James followed the man until he reached the end of that wagon where the last man he had shot laid. James saw three men running toward him down the right side, so he raised the awkward musket and fired, missing the man he was aiming at, but hitting the man behind him in the thigh. James quickly dropped the now useless musket, bent down to pick up the one lying next to the dead man at his feet, and aimed it at the remaining two men charging toward him.

The lead man had enough sense to stop at the sight of the musket aimed at him and turned and ran, while the other just pushed by him. James fired at the new target and watched as the impact of the ball spun the man clear around striking him in the left shoulder. He thought about continuing with the plan of using other people's muskets and going for that man's weapon, but he saw more men coming. He had pushed his luck far enough, so he turned and ran back toward the front of the wagon train. He hesitated briefly to retrieve his bayoneted musket leaning against the back of the wagon tossing the used captured musket into the brush to the side of the road. He stooped down as he ran and grabbed his long rifle that was lying on the ground near the buckboard. He saw the man that he had run through with the bayonet crumpled and unmoving on the buckboard of the wagon, but glanced away quickly.

He could see Rebecca, her mother and sister just one wagon in front of him, moving toward the front of the wagon train. He also saw his militia moving toward him. James grabbed the halter on one of the horses hitched to the wagon he was next to and pulled and yanked them furiously to the side of the road into the foliage, leaving the wagon more or less sideways on the road.

"Form up behind the wagon!" he yelled, pulling the hand brake back setting the stopping block firmly against the rear wheel. James glanced to make sure that Rebecca and her family were still moving safely away from the area and then turned and began reloading his long rifle as he called orders to his men.

"They are moving forward, so form a firing line behind the wagon and reload there! We will hold them here," he yelled over the musket fire coming from both his men and the armed men two wagons down. As musket balls whizzed by or slammed into the wagon more and more of the militia joined him, moving into the area behind the wagon. He counted fourteen Lizards and three Dragons, which left eleven Lizards and three Dragons still coming; at least he hoped they were still coming. He glanced back over the top of the wagon and saw that the armed men were gathering in numbers. James finished loading his long rifle, leaning it against the wagon while he began loading his spare musket.

"Load both muskets while we have the time men. If you do not have cover, move into the foliage and get behind something," he said. As the men followed his example, James finished loading his spare musket. He saw Willie and his men coming down the line of wagons toward him. James counted seven Lizards and two Dragons, his heart sank at the thought of losing five of his men.

James signaled Willie to take one group into the foliage to the left and move forward and to send the other group into the foliage to the right and move forward. They quickly followed the orders. James leaned his now loaded bayonet musket against the wagon, picked up his long rifle and took aim. There were several targets available; most were in the process of reloading. At first James selected one man who was bringing up his musket to fire, but then he saw Mr. Vos yelling orders to the armed men in front of him. James could tell Mr. Vos had military experience and the men seemed to be following his orders. James decided to ignore the other man and took careful aim at him. Although Mr. Vos was obscured by the ensuing smoke, at such short distance James knew that he had not missed. As James tried to visually confirm his shot, he suddenly felt a strong tug on his left side and glanced down to see a hole where a musket ball had passed through his open jacket, barely missing his side. He glanced to his left and saw that he was exposed to fire from the left side of the road and moved in a little tighter behind the wagon. As he reloaded, he could hear that the fire coming from the armed men was slowing, so in between each reloading step, James looked around. He saw that several of his men had been wounded, one in the leg, one in the arm, one was bleeding over the eye, another was bleeding profusely from a deep gash on top of his head.

"Would you be so kind as to see to the wounded for me, Sergeant Gibbs?" He asked calmly and nodded toward the severely bleeding man. The sergeant pulled out a handkerchief and fumbled around as he tried to figure out how to apply pressure and bandage the man's head at the same time. He finally rolled it up, placed the center of it on the wound, pulling the two sides past both ears and tied it underneath his chin. Although effective, the man now looked like a grown man wearing a baby's hat. James looked away, but one of the Lizards nearby said something in Dutch to the man, which caused the rest of the group to start chuckling. The wounded man turned toward the rest of the men and shrugged, smiled and made a baby's pouting face. What started as a low chuckle, suddenly turned into a loud roar as the laughter became infectious. Soon even the man with the baby's hat was holding his belly and his head in pain while laughing loudly with the rest of them.

Looking at the sight, James could not control himself either and started laughing along with the men, not sure if it was really that humorous, or if it was just nervous energy looking for a way to escape. Either way, it broke the tension and greatly improved the spirits of the men as they waited for what was to come next. James knew that such exchanges of fire would be bloody, exacting a toll from both sides, but James needed to keep them pinned down until his troops were all together. They were trained to work as a group, and stood a better chance if they worked as a unit.

The firefight that James expected to happen did not and what actually happened was far different. James was not sure if it was the laughter, or the tenacity of the Dragons and Lizards, but the armed men that had been massing at the end of the wagon train, suddenly disappeared into the foliage. Disbelieving, his men shifted their defenses, waiting for an attack from the foliage on the side of the road. When that failed to happen, he then became concerned that the raiders were moving to the front of the wagon train where the unprotected workers and family members were waiting.

James, taking advantage of the lull, ordered men to move several more wagons into a ring creating strong defensive position from both the front and back of the wagon train. James announced that he would move forward with one squad to gather their wounded, the freed workers and family members. Willie seemed confused, by James' order and plan.

"I'm sorry, Captain, I sent them to the city," he said as James was preparing to head toward the front with the five men. James tried to understand the words correctly.

"Who did you send to the city? The workers?" he asked? But Willie at first shook his head and then nodded.

"All of them. The workers, the family, and two prisoners. I thought it would be best to get them out of the battle area as quickly as possible." James was stunned by the news, and then became deeply concerned at the thought of the armed men pursuing and catching them.

"They're unprotected!" he said as he motioned for the squad of five to follow.

"No, sir, I sent four Lizards and Bo to escort them. Mr. Edlund and his family also had picked up muskets. They were going to head straight to the beach and then east to the city." James looked around again. He was happy to hear that Mr. Edlund had also been freed, but he quickly did a count based on the new information.

"No casualties? Were any of the family members hurt?" James asked anxiously. Willie hesitated as if thinking and then shook his head.

"No, not that I know of," he finally replied. "Our initial volley brought down five or six of the forward party and wounded several others; they returned fire recklessly into the woods where we were laying. We took advantage of their empty muskets and charged them as you instructed. The majority of those that remained either ran or fell to our attack, and two surrendered." He took a breath and continued. "We untied the workers, then moved forward and secured the lead wagons and the family members that were on them." James listened as Willie described the engagement. "We heard the gunfire down here on the line so I ordered Bo to take four Dragons and escort them to the city and out of harm's way. Miss Rebecca and the other ladies joined them as they were leaving." James' expelled his held breath and relaxed.

"You did well, Willie. Very well." James turned to the rest of the men who were still staying low and behind their defensive positions. "You all were outstanding soldiers. I'm very proud of you, of your courage, your toughness- and your humor." He paused and they all started laughing again as they pointed to the Lizard with the head injury. "I must say, I have never been in a battle where men were laughing as musket balls were flying by them. That had to be very unnerving for the enemy," he commented and started laughing along with the men as the words were translated. Watching the men, he loved how they laughed with all of their hearts and cared deeply for each other. They were Dragons; James could feel it in his heart.

After an hour of waiting and probing the nearby foliage with several small forays, James took a small group and moved forward to the enemy's last defensive positions by the wagons. They saw that the enemy had literally moved en masse to the south and into the hills of the island. As they moved forward, they found nine dead enemies, including Mr. Vos. They tracked the remaining group for a short distance and did not discover where any tracks had turned west in an attempt to get behind their defenses. By all indications, it appeared that the enemy had fled the battle in haste.

When he and the patrol had returned, James began directing the men to turn the wagons around one by one and line them up. They then gathered the dead and wounded of the enemy, as well as their muskets, and loaded them on various wagons. They stopped briefly to put two horses down that had been struck by random musket fire and were wounded beyond recovery. Within thirty minutes they were ready to start the wagon train of supplies moving back toward the east. They assigned a Lizard driver for each wagon and placed their loaded muskets within reach in the back of the wagons. James knew it was their turn to try to guard the slow moving wagons as they were driven to Christiansted. Having little other choice, James employed a similar strategy of five men in front and six at the back of the train for extra protection. When they reached the crossroad several hundred yards up the road, they turned left toward the city where, not only did the road improve, but also their speed.

Less than an hour later, they could see the taller buildings of the city in the distance. Shortly afterward, they were met by one of the advance patrols, obviously having pushed out a lot further than they were supposed to. James moved to the front to greet them.

"How are the men?" The lead Dragon asked. James recognized Duchy as he stepped forward to shake hands.

"They are all with us; some are a little beat up, but all present. Did the workers and family make it back?" James asked, and Duchy nodded and looked surprised by James' question.

"Yeah, they said it was a pretty wild and bloody battle raging as they left. They were worried because they thought they heard laughter?" James was at first confused by the statement. But then smiled as he remembered the moment, *we must have been louder than we thought.*

"They did. That was us. It's kind of an odd but funny story that I promise to share with you later tonight," he said with a smile and then stepped to the side as the first wagon passed them on the way into the city. "The men fought bravely, all of them. You and the other Dragons have done a fantastic job. I'm very proud of all of you." Duchy beamed with pride as they watched the wagons roll by. The Lizards sat straight and proud as they either drove or walked past, waving and smiling at their friends. The Lizard with the head wound had replaced the funny scarf with a hat that he had picked up from one of the dead enemies. James smiled as the man drove the wagon by him.

"Nice hat," he said and pointed to his own hat. The man smiled and nodded.

James waited for the wagons to pass and then joined the six men at the end of the train as they entered the city. They had pulled the wagons off the road and were in the process of unhitching the horses as James and the last of the men came around the corner. As other Dragons and Lizards were either shaking their hands, patting them on the shoulders, or speaking words of encouragement to them, James did his best to seem appreciative, but he was busy searching for one person in particular in the crowd of hundreds of people gathered in the open area. He saw the workers and spotted one of Rebecca's older brothers standing in the group, but there was no sign of her. His heart was beating fast and his mind racing in concern as he stepped onto the raised front porch of one of the buildings that faced the open area for a clearer look.

"She's in with the doctor." James turned to see Bode standing on the same deck walking toward him. He started and looked questioningly at Bode. "She's all right, just a cut and bruise from a fall," Bode said. James relaxed as he grasped Bode's hand and they both smiled. Bode stepped back, had James turn around in front of him, and then held his hands up as if confused.

"You usually get the worst of it, what did you do, hide in the woods this time?" Bode joked, knowing better. James smiled and opened his jacket.

"They shot my good jacket!" he said as he pointed to the hole. Bode knew all too well that had that shot been over a few inches to the right, that it would have been deadly one, and just shook his head.

"I thought you were not going to be a hero?" Bode said.

"The men did all the work, I just gave orders," he replied and smiled.

"Rebecca said you were a fool and that you tried to get yourself killed again. She was worried sick about you, so was I," Bode observed sternly and James knew by Bode's expression that a joke would not be wise at this moment.

"I did not feel as if I had a choice. I got separated from the men and it was the only thing I could think of doing at the time," he retorted and held Bode's concerned gaze.

"We can't do this without you, James. If you get killed the rest of these men will be at the mercy of the British officers when they finally arrive. Captain Donovan will do his best, but the men trust you. And I'm not really interested in losing my best friend," he added and James nodded as he thought about his words. There was a long uncomfortable silence as they both looked away and around the area.

"We're best friends?" James finally joked and Bode just looked down, shook his head, and sighed. "I don't know, it looks like Miss Rebecca has acquired that honor, so now that I think about it, maybe your life really doesn't matter," Bode replied, feigning coldness.

"Wow! How shallow is your friendship?" James responded sarcastically and then smiled. "I must admit she is definitely a whole lot prettier than you are."

"Yeah, but can she shoot and spit?" Bode asked dryly and James thought about it.

"She might not be able to out-spit you... but uhhh. Well we all know your weaknesses." He slapped Bode on the back and headed for the doctor's office. Bode just frowned and shook his head as he followed James into the office.

As he entered the open door of the doctor's house, he could see the men lying, sitting or standing around in various states of triage.

"James!" He looked over and saw Rebecca smiling with her knee wrapped and elevated. He saw that her dress was dirty and ripped and there was a bruise on her left cheek. As he walked toward her with a smile, her face suddenly changed. "Don't you ever do that again! You could have been killed or captured!" she called out across the room and he hesitated a moment before moving to her side.

"I was kind of hoping for a 'thank you', or 'you're my hero' speech," he replied sarcastically and smiled as he took her hand in his and sat down next to her. She blushed.

"Thank you and you are my hero; I just can't imagine ever, well, loosing you," she said softly and squeezed his hand. James looked at her wrapped leg.

"Are you all right?" he asked, and she looked down and seemed embarrassed by the question.

"In my rush to leave the wagon, my dress caught on one of the side panels when we jumped down. I went face first into the dirt," she said and pointed to her eye and lifted an area of her torn dress. "Then as we were running through the underbrush at top speed, I tripped and hit my knee on a rock." She pointed to her wrapped knee. "They had to take turns carrying me all the way back to the city." She ended the story by rolling her eyes in embarrassment. "I'll be all right, but there will be a nasty scar where the cut is."

"It sounds like I need to be more worried about your getting hurt than you me." He said with a smile and she raised an eyebrow.

"Funny! Next time, you try fighting in a full dress and see how you do." she declared and he cringed at the idea, which made her laugh. She reached up and put her arms around his neck and pulled him close to her. "Thank you. You are my knight in shining armor," she whispered in his ear and then hugged him close one more time, which he returned, before letting him go. She suddenly moved her hand away from his as she looked over his shoulder. James turned to see her father looking at them. He smiled and walked toward James.

"My family and I wish to extend our deepest thanks to you and your men," he said to James and extended his hand, which James shook.

"It's what friends do for each other," he replied and Mr. Edlund just smiled and continued shaking his hand for a while.

"Yes. Yes it is," he finally replied. "Lieutenant King has offered to send twenty men to accompany my sons and workers, along with the wagons, back to our plantation to make sure they have not returned to cause additional harm. Would you be so kind as to watch over my wife and two daughters during our absence?" he asked James, who nodded.

"Of course. From what we saw, the attackers have fled toward Frederiksted, so I do not think any additional dangers are in store for awhile," he replied and then added, "And Mr. Vos will no longer be an issue to your family." James ended and Mr. Edlund understood the meaning.

"So I was told, but I greatly appreciate the armed support, none the less," he said to James then to Rebecca, "Help your mother until we return," her directed as he turned to leave.

"Mr. Edlund, have Mr. King supply you with ten of the captured muskets," James offered as Mr. Edlund reached the door. He hesitated, then nodded and smiled as he walked out.

Rebecca and James spent the next several hours telling each other what had happened from the time the armed bandits came to the point that they met in the fort. It was fun to see and hear her tell her events, but James left out a great deal of what had happened and what he had done. He felt saddened that she had to witness him impale the man in the wagon with the bayonet. It must have been horrible watching the man writhe in his final death throws right in front of her. She never mentioned it when she told her side of the story, but he knew by the way she avoided it, that it had bothered her.

Chapter 16

Following the rescue of Mr. Edlund, his family and workers, the confidence of the Black Lizards soared. Their desire to learn more weapons use, formations and tactics was evident by the constant questioning of James and the other officers. James and Bode knew that although efficient training was essential, battle experience provided the best test of its effectiveness. Excluding the twenty-five Lizards that participated in the rescue mission, the rest had yet to prove themselves. James felt confident that they would and could perform courageously in battle. Still, the recent battle had been a huge boon for the entire militia. The battle had unified the Dragons and the Lizards and had served to bolster the courage of the trainees who had not fought and the confidence of those who had. In addition, the fort's arsenal had increased with the addition of twenty-three muskets and two pistols captured from the plantation raiders. Ten of these muskets were currently on loan to Mr. Edlund.

On the morning of the 3rd day after the attack, a message arrived from Mr. Edlund requesting that Rebecca and her mother return to their home. To say that James and Rebecca made the most of the three days together would be an understatement. Although never without an escort, they spent a great deal of time together and James cherished every minute of it. James and fifteen Lizards escorted Rebecca and Mrs. Edlund home to the Edlund plantation. James could see that Mr. Edlund had managed to restore the look and feel of the plantation and their home to its original condition, but some things were beyond repair.

Food and water was offered to James and his men upon their arrival and they reconnected with the ten men that who had escorted Mr. Edlund's party back to the plantation and remained with them. During the three days, with the help of the other workers and with the permission of Mr. Edlund, they had built several elevated watchtowers that overlooked the plantation fields and the approaches to the main house. Although crude in design, they were strategically positioned and provided good protection for anyone watching or firing from them.

As Mr. Edlund was showing James the work completed by the men and workers, he pulled James to the side to speak in confidence. James could tell that the subject he wanted to discuss weighed heavily on Mr. Edlund.

"Captain, I have unwillingly been forced to pick a side in the war that you are in. In selling my goods to your city, I have brought the wrath of Frederiksted down on my family and my workers," he said and James nodded in agreement.

"It does appear so, although Mr. Vos will not be returning; and he seemed to be the ringleader of the attack," James replied and Mr. Edlund acknowledged the point.

"I cannot risk that one evening while we are sleeping; another group might come and burn our home and crops in revenge, or worse, harm my family and my workers."

"You and your family's safety is also a concern for me," James replied and tried to understand where Mr. Edlund was heading.

"I saw what you have accomplished with your new militia. I have also seen what you and your men are capable of in battle. Now that you have over 300 trained men at the fort, I do not feel as concerned about your success and survival as I did before. In fact, I believe with a little more help from the nearby plantations, the city would be able to not only survive, but to prosper," he said and waited for James' reaction.

"What are you proposing?" James asked.

"I have at least fifty men on my plantation that could be trained as militia for the city and the fort," he said. "My plantation cannot survive with them stationed at the fort, but if they were trained and armed, we are close enough that they could be sent to the fort to help defend it in time of battle." James was stunned by the offer, but quickly began to think through the challenges and advantages such an opportunity presented as Mr. Edlund continued. "I have had several of the other owners stop by to offer their support and condolences. In speaking with them I found that four of the other plantations that have traded with you expressed an interest in exploring such a militia training option." He waited for James to reply.

James thought about the idea of adding 100 more militia to their forces, and realized the difficulty of defending the plantations with the number of militia currently available. Training them to defend themselves and come to the aid the fort and city should it come under attack, sounded very promising. James knew that they had over 200 unused muskets stored at the fort that could be supplied to the plantation owners for such a force. The two biggest questions he faced were whom they would be training, slaves or free workers, and how to train them?

"Mr. Edlund, I think it is an excellent idea," he declared and tried to think of how best to address his concerns. "The challenge we face with such a course of action lies in the fact that we do not train slaves. Only free men can become Dragon soldiers and even then training is the individual's sole choice, never a choice made by force or order. The other Dragons will trust them with their lives and only a life freely given can be counted on in the heat of battle," he watched for Mr. Edlund's reaction. The man took a deep breath as he thought over James' statement.

"If I free my workers, they may leave," he finally said and James nodded.

"Some might, but based on what we have seen with the freed city workers, most stayed with their former employer, as long as they had been treated well. It is clear that they need you for food and shelter to survive as much as you need them, but there are no guarantees," James asserted and then continued. "From what I have also seen, your workers respect and appreciate you and your family. I do not see them leaving once their freedom is granted; instead, they might even become more loyal to you and your family, but again, there are no guarantees." James ended and Mr. Edlund stared out over the plantation. He finally nodded.

"If I do nothing, I fear my family and the future of this plantation are in danger. If I do something then at least there is hope. I will choose hope. I will free any worker who chooses to risk his life to be trained and I will provide food, shelter and in addition pay a fair wage." He turned to James for advice on how to proceed.

James would have preferred to see all the slaves freed, but this was a beginning and he conceded the point. He nodded.

"I will send five Dragons to begin the training of your fifty workers and your sons. The workers will be trained in twenty-five man shifts. The Dragons will bring an additional twenty-five muskets, powder and shot for the training and defense of your plantation. They will require at least two to three hours a day with each group if they are to get them trained quickly. I would like to have them visit the fort several times to train there with the militia and to learn the role they would be playing in defense of the fort or supporting the other troops in battle." James outlined the training schedule. Mr. Edlund considered the plan and agreed.

James spoke privately with several of the escort detail that had stayed on the plantation to guard the Edlunds. From what he was told, they had already planted the seeds of hope for their own freedom within the workers, and even some of the workers expressed their desire to become Black Dragons too. James ordered ten Lizards to remain at the plantation informing them that five Dragons would join them within the next two to three days to begin the training of those workers who wanted to be trained.

James spent the rest of the afternoon with Rebecca and her family talking to her brothers about the qualities necessary in positions of leadership in a militia and that those qualities also had to be trained and developed. He spoke of the importance of believing in the men, and the need to keep them well trained and ready. Finally, there came a moment when the rest of the family had left and it was just Rebecca and him at the table. She smiled at him and reached her hand out, which he took in his. "I'm afraid your and your men's arrival have turned this island upside down, Mr. Thornton." she said.

"Perhaps, but I think the true reason God brought me here was to meet you," he said softly. "And I pray that He will keep all of us safe and grant us a long life together." She smiled and nodded. "He will." She said confidently and James nodded. Her faith was one of the character traits that he loved most about her.

Later that day, James and the fifteen Lizards who had come with him said their goodbyes. Because the other ten Lizard militia had already built strong relationships with the other plantation workers, they decided to have them remain at the plantation until the five Dragons arrived to begin the initial training. James discussed with them what was going to be taking place in the next few days. Specifically, how they could help encourage and clarify for the workers what the transition from slave to freeman would mean and how it would work for them. They seemed confident and very supportive of the decision for them to remain at the plantation.

Within two days of returning, they had selected, prepared, equipped and sent out the five Black Dragons that would be training the plantation militia. By the end of the week, James had also visited the four additional plantation owners who had met with Mr. Edlund and discussed the idea of training their workers. Two of them accepted the conditions of freedom for the militia and the obligation to participate in the defense of the fort should an attack come. The other two plantation owners could not agree to such terms, mainly the freeing of their slaves. Of the two that accepted, one had about the same number of workers as Mr. Edlund's plantation, while the other was smaller. They estimated the larger could train a force of fifty fighting men, while the smaller would be able to train thirty. It required the fort to send ten additional Dragons, five to each location, to train the workers. The short-term loss of Dragons at the fort was initially of concern to James, Bode and Captain Donovan, but they ultimately agreed that gaining 130 trained militia was worth the short-term risk and investment. They also felt that after the defeat of the armed men from Frederiksted, that the Dutch military might be a little more concerned about retaliation from the Black Dragons than how to reclaim the fort. They hoped that their confidence might have been shaken from the defeat.

Over the next six weeks Bode continued to work with and train the fort-based Lizards on tactics, defenses, and skirmishing, while James visited the various plantations to evaluate the training progress with the plantation militia. They also began to send out patrols of thirty men (five Dragons and twenty-five Lizards) to various areas across the island, even to the west of the city of Christiansted. This helped to unify the groups and to further train the Lizards on how to work together. They would visit the various plantations to ask if they needed any security assistance or if there were any problems, and would always invite them to trade their goods with Christiansted.

On many occasions they encountered loaded wagon trains heading clear across the island to Frederiksted to sell their goods, and they would always offer their assistance, even escorting them to their destination, never requesting payment or threatening them. They would only warn them against taking up arms against the Dragons, offering to allow them to sell their goods at Christiansted should Frederiksted prove to be too far to travel. James wanted the plantation owners in their area to believe that the militia was not there to harm them but would protect them. Their actions were, for the most part, tolerated by the plantation owners but not appreciated. They wanted to demonstrate to the plantation owners and to the Dutch at Frederiksted that they were more than capable of extending the reach of their military capabilities but were currently refraining from doing so.

On one occasion, a patrol that Bode was leading west of the city spotted a small detachment of fifteen Dutch soldiers marching east toward the center of the island, but still west of Christiansted. It was late in the evening, so they followed at a distance until the Dutch soldiers had setup camp. They visited the troops very early in the morning, and while they slept Bode and his men crept into their camp. With muskets pointed at the ready they woke up the Dutch. Bode took the time to ask questions of the officer and each man through an interpreter and was happy to discover that none of the men were from Christiansted, nor did the Lizards recognize any of them. Bode thought about capturing the men in case of need for future prisoner exchange, but felt it would only be draining to the fort. Instead, they cooked breakfast for themselves and the Dutch soldiers, then wished them well, and sent them on their way. They did confiscate their muskets, powder and shot after explaining that since their countries were still officially at war, and they could not allow them to keep their weapons. They were so happy and relieved to be released and not killed or brutalized as they had heard would be the fate of any prisoners captured, that they did not object to the confiscation. Even as they marched back toward Frederiksted, they still acted as if the Black Dragons would change their mind and kill them. The Dragons added fifteen muskets and another pistol to their arsenal when they returned later that day.

It had been almost four months since the capture of the fort and Captain Donovan had made it clear that if the Dutch fleet was coming back to retake the fort, it would come soon, as the trade winds were changing and the hurricane season was almost upon them. He was actually surprised that they had not yet experienced any storms. The rain fell more frequently and heavily, which only increased the humidity of the area. They had stationed, rotated and supplied a secret three-man lookout from Captain Donovan's crew on the highest mountain, just a mile south of the city. They put them there so that they could watch the south for sails and keep an eye on any merchant activity around the island. Earlier in the week, they had seen three large, three-masted vessels sail in from the south and then on toward Frederiksted. It appeared to be the same Dutch man-of-war that had anchored off the port following their capture of the merchant ship and two large merchant vessels. They assumed it carried either all or part of the invasion force that would be used to retake the fort. They recalled 100 of the 130 men forming the plantation militia to the fort, leaving ten soldiers at each of the plantations to protect them and to escort the families should they need to withdraw. They agreed that it would be safer and easier to remain outside the fort during an attack.

They discussed the development that night over dinner. Captain Donovan estimated that the three ships could carry, at most, 250 to 300 soldiers. From what they knew of the fort at Frederiksted, they estimated another 100 troops could have been stationed there. They could probably acquire another 100-200 armed civilians to supplement the trained militia. That would be an army of 500 or 600 men. They had 50 Dragons, 110 armed Dragon sailors, 34 armed Lizard sailors, 100 well-trained Lizards soldiers, and another 100 partially trained plantation militia. That created a force of nearly 400 muskets available to defend the city and the fort. They examined the various strategies that could be used against them one more time.

"They would need to leave some soldiers to defend the city, so that would reduce the number of soldiers slightly, maybe by fifty," Captain Donovan estimated and then turned to Bode and James. "Would you attack a fortified position with less than overwhelming odds?" he asked and Bode raised an eyebrow and tilted his head toward James. Captain Donovan understood the gesture and realized that was exactly what James had done and corrected himself. "I mean if you had half a brain in your head." Then he laughed, as did the rest of the men sitting at the table. Once the laughter faded, the responses came out.

"If I was desperate enough and it was my only option, then yes, but otherwise, no," James replied.

"What if you were given an order by a superior to take it, even though he did not have all the information?" Bode asked James.

"If that were the case, I might feel I had no choice in the matter and at least make an attempt," James replied.

"They know the British have not shown up to reinforce us, and we can assume they know exactly how many men we have, so they might feel that it is a now-or-never situation," Mr. Richards mused.

"Well we have enough food and water in each fort to survive for at least two months, but unless the 48 pounders on the main fort are silenced before we vacate them, we would be pounded to dust within a few days," Mr. Richards warned.

"The main fort can really only hold from 200 to 250 men at maximum, leaving 150 to 210 either hold up in the other two forts or have them sitting on the ships," James added.

"We'd never make it out into the open seas if that man of war is sitting off our shore during an attack." Mr. Sanders commented. Bode started to say something, and then he hesitated.

"An idea?" James asked him and Bode nodded.

"As Mr. Richards suggested several weeks ago, we could use the two main merchant ships as cannon platforms to support the forts during ground attacks. We sail them as close to shore as possible near where the attack is unfolding and fire on their flanks from protected waters." They nodded as they remembered the earlier suggestion. "But we could keep a mobile force of 50 or 100 men away from the city to either attack their flanks, or…" He hesitated a moment. "If they lay siege, we march them on Frederiksted. They would have to choose whether to let us take it, or to withdraw to protect it." Bode finished.

"Do you think you could take Frederiksted?" Captain Donovan asked Bode, who smiled.

"We don't have to. We just have to make them think we're trying to. Someone will send word to warn them, they will either break camp and march back or send a contingent back to defend the city." Bode replied and James smiled.

"They will just run you away, reinforce it and then march back," Mr. Sanders speculated.

"Exactly. Either way, they will be weaker at the fort and we will have an opportunity to harass them either on the way to Frederiksted or on the way back to Christiansted. Our challenge right now is that we do not know when they will be coming to attack or how many will be attacking us, but once they are at Christiansted, we'll know where they are and have a much better idea of how many there are." They sat in silence for several minutes, as each man weighed the idea and calculated the impact it would have on the defense.

"We have the patrols out on the major roads, so we should have enough warning, night or day, to know when their army is marching toward us, allowing us enough time to get the mobile force out of the city before they lay siege and bottle us up," Robbie pointed out; he had been in charge of the patrols. More silence followed before Captain Donovan finally spoke up.

"Agreed. Bode, can you put a mobile force together that will be ready to march immediately if needed?" Bode nodded.

"I would suggest 100 men, or four groups, maybe one Black Dragon group, and three Black Lizard groups?" James added, wanting to make sure that Bode had enough men to do the job at hand. "We can keep things pretty busy around the city with troop movement to hide their departure. There are certain to be eyes watching. I want them to think we have all of our men, including the plantation militia, behind the walls of the three forts." James concluded their meeting with his remarks and the rest of the group agreed. They knew tomorrow would prove to be a very busy day.

As James headed off to bed, he could not help but think about what would happen to Rebecca and her family should war come to the city. They and the other two plantation owners were now committed to their allegiance to the English and the success of the city's defenses. James wished he could have convinced more of the plantation owners to train a militia, but he also knew they were very fortunate to have trained the extra men that did join them. Mr. Edlund, his family, and his non-militia workers were to flee into the hills or to live secretly with other plantation owners until the battle was over; this was also the same plan the other two plantation owners had.

As he lay in his bed, he thought about all the trained workers and the ramifications toward them if they should fail to hold the fort. He knew full well his and his men's destiny should they fail, but depending upon the reaction and mercy of the Dutch, the workers who took up arms could also have a very harsh punishment awaiting them. He felt it was important to offer them another chance to avoid such an ending.

When James shared his thoughts about addressing the men and offering a choice to flee now, Bode was unfazed and not even concerned by the suggestion, but Captain Donovan and Mr. Richards felt strongly that it was a bad idea. However, they agreed to go along with James' desire plan anyway.

The men not on patrol or on duty in the forts were called to assembly in the courtyard of the main fort, while James and the other officers stood on the main gun deck that looked down into it. Mr. Massman stood next to James ready to translate.

"Black Dragons!" he yelled and the cry came back to him in a roar that was three hundred fold. He smiled at the men and their passion.

"My brothers, we are fast approaching a moment in time that will test our training and define for history what we are truly made of as men. Three Dutch ships have been sighted on their way to Frederiksted. We are presuming that the Dutch have brought with them an army with the intent to reclaim this fort and this city and to punish us for taking the city from them, and those who have risen up in support of us against them." He waited and watched their faces for a change in expression as the words were translated, but did not see any.

"You have risked a great deal in choosing to be trained to carry and fire a musket, to be Black Dragons, to be free men!" He waited for the translation, and then a proud rumble came from the men. "But there are times when decisions made during emotional moments can lead to regret later, once difficult times present themselves, times like what we will surely face here, should the Dutch decide to attack this fort." He waited until his speech was translated before continuing, but one man raised his hand.

"Why do you ask us this? We already made our decisions when we agreed to be trained," he said.

"Yeah, Preacher Booker pounded that into us hard," another said and they all chuckled at his words.

"We just want to make sure that there are no regrets with your decisions and that everyone has an opportunity to change his mind if there were regrets," James responded and waited for additional questions. The men seemed to look around for those that may have such feelings.

"If anyone wishes to talk about this, speak with any one of the officers." James ended the discussion, and then turned to Bode, who stepped forward and addressed the men.

"We have a lot of work to do to prepare our defenses; I will be pulling aside my Black Dragon group and three Black Lizard groups for specialized combat. The rest of you, especially you Lizards and Plantation Lizards, make sure you are clear about your assignments and keep your muskets clean and ready for battle," Bode barked at the men, who then gave a deep grunt, the new response that acknowledged the order. Bode had instituted the guttural response from the men several weeks prior; he felt it gave him a good way to judge the resistance, apathy or understanding of the orders that were given; the louder they responded, the more he knew they were clear and on board with them.

James confided in Bode that he needed to do something important before the attack. It had become a burning desire and was consuming all his thoughts. Bode understood where this was going, and agreed that James should make a quick visit to the Edlund plantation. James dashed into town to visit a shop that was located in the inner part of the city. He then ordered six horses to be saddled and took five men along with him to the Edlund plantation to visit Rebecca and to check on the status of their efforts. Upon arriving, he was met by Mr. Edlund's sons, who ran out to meet with James even as he was sliding off his horse.

"James! Father needs to see you right away," they stammered and James felt a jolt of anxiety.

"Is everyone all right?" he asked as one of the boys took his horse's reins and they headed toward the house.

"Yes, but we just heard some news that you need to know about." So they both jogged toward the house. Even before he reached the house, Rebecca had stepped through the door and met him on the porch with a distant smile and then she embraced him.

"I've missed you, James," she said as she stepped back from the embrace and looked into his eyes and smiled.

"I've missed you also, I'm also very worried about your and your family's safety," he said as they both moved toward the front door. He stepped through the door that was now being held open by the brother who met him. As they stepped into the main room, he could see Mr. and Mrs. Edlund standing by the fireplace. The contents of the house were in various stages of being packed in boxes, crates and bags. James could see that they were preparing to leave. Mr. Edlund embraced Mrs. Edlund and she smiled as she looked over her husband's shoulder at James.

"Hello James, may I get you some water or tea?" she asked.

"Water would be greatly appreciated, thank you," he replied and Mrs. Edlund tilted her head to Rebecca and motioned to the kitchen. Mr. Edlund stepped forward and shook James' hand.

"I'm glad you're here James; I just got word from a friend of a friend who had just returned from Frederiksted. He said that an army is forming there, hundreds strong. He estimated 400 or more soldiers, not counting the militia. They also have wheeled cannon. It sounds as if they intend to march within the week." He watched for James' response to the news.

"Those numbers are fairly near to what we expected. We saw the ships sail into Frederiksted and estimated their numbers to be in excess of 500. That is good news," James replied. Mr. Edlund seemed stunned and then shook his head.

"I tell you that 500 or more men are marching to attack, and you say it's good news?" he asked James, who smiled.

"What I should have said was that it was better news than I expected. Those numbers are manageable. If there were 600 or 700, then I'd be more worried," he replied as if trying to reassure the man that he was not crazy. "How is the family? You appear prepared to leave."

"Yes, yes- we're ready if it appears there is a need to leave." He hesitated. "We can make do without the ten militia; you need them more." But James shook his head.

"No, you might need them to make sure you and your family is able to move safely eastward. But should the time come that would require you to fight any Dutch soldiers, it would go better for you and the men to lay down your muskets and tell them that you were forced to go along with the fort," he said quietly so that only Mr. Edlund could herar. Mr. Edlund just smiled and nodded.

"We'll see what God has planned," he replied to James.

James quickly finished his water, when Rebecca and Mrs. Edlund returned to join them at the table. They spoke briefly about the town, the men, and their plans.

"May we speak in private about the defenses you have in place here?" James asked Mr. Edlund, who seemed taken aback, but agreed and they excused themselves and stood up, walking outside. James headed for one of the sentry towers the militia had built, but asked a question as they walked.

"The safety of your family is very important to me and it's why I came to visit, but I have another reason for visiting you," James said and paused. "I would like to ask for your daughter's hand in marriage," he said and waited, watching for the older man's reaction, but when none came, he continued. "I know that this is not the best time to be asking such a question, but I need her to know that, no matter what happens, I love her with all my heart," he finished and decided to wait, however long it took, for Mr. Edlund to respond.

"The timing is rather poor on your part, but I can't fault you for asking it. She does seem to have a slight interest in you," he said wryly. "Only under one circumstance will I give my blessing to such a marriage. You must survive this coming battle," he said and smiled. James' heart leapt in his chest in relief.

"Those are pretty steep terms, but I accept," James replied, returning the smile and shaking Mr. Edlund's hand.

"You will break all of our hearts if you fail, Mr. Thornton. You've managed to even get my dog to like you," he said as he looked down to see their dog at James' side.

On October 17, 1776, James asked Rebecca, along with her brother as a chaperone, to take a walk with him. As they walked, they talked and shared memories of their youth and dreams they have about life and the last few months. James found what he felt was the perfect spot to stop and rest, so they sat in a field that overlooked the blue waters of the Caribbean. With the warm sun low in the sky to the west and the waters of the Caribbean sparkling before him, James suddenly dropped down on one knee, opened the palm of his left hand to show a beautiful gold ring sitting in it. He looked up at Rebecca standing above him and taking her left hand into his he asked her to marry him. She smiled nervously.

"Yes James, I will marry you." He slid the small ring onto her finger and then stood and embraced her and she him. Her brother came running over as if to break up a situation, but she interrupted his charge and held out her hand.

"James asked me to marry him!" she declared happily and her brother glanced at the ring and then at James and beamed as he walked over and shook James' hand. Rebecca hugged James again and asked if they could return to the house so she could tell the rest of her family the news. Rebecca almost floated back to the house, while James felt lost in reflection. A new page had turned in his book of life and everything seemed suddenly new.

Chapter 17

It was three days later when word came that the Dutch were marching toward Christiansted. The advancing army made no effort to hide its advance; on the contrary, they made their presence very clear by setting up camp just two miles southwest of the city where they prepared to mount their attack. Bode had slowly slipped his 100 men out of the fort throughout the day. The men had left in groups of five spaced out every 15 minutes. Reggie had his Lizards also marching in and out of the fort in groups of five throughout the day so that anyone watching saw groups of five constantly leaving and entering the fort, making it very difficult for anyone watching the fort to know that any groups had slipped away. That evening, as planned, Bode and his men set up in a small depression in the hills west and above the city. From their vantage point, they could see the ocean, the harbor, the city and the surrounding country. They would remain out of sight, just west of the city until the Dutch began their siege, then they would move on Frederiksted and lay siege to it. Captain Donovan found it interesting that they did not blockade the port entrance with the warship, but left it open. He could only read into it that they wanted to give them a final opportunity to leave the city and the fort on the three vessels that were anchored in their harbor.

The following morning, a Dutch Colonel and small contingent of men approached the city with a flag of truce. Word was sent to James and Captain Donovan, and both men, along with five Black Lizards, approached the Dutch contingent. Captain Donovan spoke first.

"What brings you and your army to our city Colonel?" They both saw the insignia on the man's shoulders. The man smiled. "I've come to inform you that your stay in *our* city has ended and that you and your men have two days to vacate. You may take any non-citizen that you wish to accompany you as you leave, as long as it is their desire. During these two days, we will refrain from blockading the harbor so that you will be free to sail back to your country unmolested. The Commodore also wished me to encourage you to take as many supplies as you feel are needed to assist in your journey home." He seemed to smile wryly at this and James saw the humor hidden within it.

"Please tell the Commodore that we appreciate the offer that has been extended and that we will take it into consideration." Captain Donovan responded. The Dutch officer took several steps forward and looked at James and then at the Black Dragon Lizards standing crisply at attention behind him.

"So, I presume you are Captain Thornton of the Black Dragons?" he questioned James.

"Yes Colonel," he replied.

"The Commodore wished me to express his appreciation to you and your men for being such hospitable invaders and for your kind treatment of our citizens across the island. It is because of your actions that he is granting you this generous offer. I strongly suggest that you take the offer, Captain, as I would hate to carry the burden and tarnish my reputation by having to put an end to the legend of you and your men." He ended and smiled. James nodded and returned the smile.

"Colonel, please tell the Commodore that he is most welcome and that we have never desired to harm the Dutch citizens nor the soldiers of this beautiful island." James replied. "As far as your reputation goes, I would hate to have to put such a burden on your shoulders Colonel, but I do not think you need to worry about that legacy, for history has shown that legends live on in victory or defeat," James stated. The man just stared at James as if trying to understand something that he could not grasp. Then he smiled and shook his head.

"You are definitely shorter and less stout than the rumors speak of," he said with a smile and James raised an eyebrow. "And no doubt a whole lot less handsome." James replied and returned the smile and the man suddenly laughed. When the laughter came to an end, there was this moment of uncomfortable silence.

"I wish you fair sailing, Captain," the Dutch officer finally said to James.

"I wish you wet powder and poor aim, Colonel," James replied. The man seemed saddened by James' words, but gave a smile and a nod of his head; then he and his men turned and marched westward down the road to their waiting army. James, Captain Donovan and the five Dragon Lizards walked back toward the city center and the troops waiting at the fort.

"Legends? How come I'm not a legend, we were named after *my* ship," Captain Donovan said pretending he was angry as they walked.

"To become a legend, you have to be either really handsome and brave, or very ugly and scary." James suddenly stopped and looked at Captain Donovan as he finished the last part of his sentence. "Wow, you're right, you have all the makings of a legend." Captain Donovan just shook his head.

"I walked right into that one didn't I?" the Captain declared and James nodded.

Once they had arrived at the fort, they explained the Dutch offer to the other officers. James wished Bode were there to weigh in with his thoughts, but he felt that he already knew what his response would be. Simply sailing away was not an option: such an action would create a stigma of cowardice that would live on and overshadow their achievements thus far. They knew they could not only give a good showing in the ensuing battle, but they felt strongly that they could actually win the battle and hold the fort. The main cannons on the fort could reach further than the smaller wagon-pulled field cannons, and they had built additional tiers that would allow them to rotate and fire two of the cannons inland. The challenge would be found in their ability to withstand a direct ground assault on the western fort while fending off a ship of the line sailing into the harbor.

The next day James visited the Dutch citizens who had remained in the city to inform them of the impending attack. He suggested strongly that they leave the city to avoid cannon and musket fire from both sides when the battle ensues. He asked them to withdraw to the east to avoid any accidental fire from the nervous Dutch soldiers. James knew that some would go west to tell the Dutch army, but he also wanted them to know of his concern for the safety of the people and that he would not use them as hostages. James was hoping they would in turn show his men mercy should things not go well and the city and fortress fall.

That evening James was pleasantly surprised to see Pastor Booker making his rounds, speaking with the men inside the main fort. The pastor, who had taken on the role of the Militia's spiritual leader, stopped by James' room and shared a few passages of encouragement with him. He talked about how proud he was of the men and that, if even for a short time, they had experienced the freedom that he had enjoyed, maybe even more freedom than he had known. He thanked James and they prayed together for each other and for the men. James shared with him that he had asked Rebecca to marry him and that they hoped that he would preside over the ceremony. Pastor Booker said he was honored and would be happy to do so.

The next day a quiet settled over the city that was very strange to James: no longer were there citizens scurrying around, no aromas of meals being cooked coming from it, no sounds of happy or busy voices, instead there was just an eerie silence, only broken by the occasional group of soldiers moving about the streets. Once the citizens had left, the soldiers moved all the wagons to the eastern storage area of the fort. Anything that could be used as a fixed defensive position by the enemy was removed from the area surrounding the main fort. With all the buildings and homes that either faced the fort or were near it, they carefully and securely boarded up the doors of each home and either secured the storm shutters with nails, or used planks across the windows to make it difficult for the Dutch soldiers to enter the homes and use them for defensive cover while firing. Although he knew they would eventually break into the homes and buildings, James wanted to keep the enemy out in the open for as long as possible.

In the early afternoon, a Lizard came running up to James as he was helping secure some storm shutters.

"Captain Donovan requests your presence on the main gun deck of the fort. He said that it was very urgent!" he stammered between breaths. James patted him on the shoulder and handed his hammer and nails to another soldier. He jogged back toward the fort with the young man, and as he entered the fort, he saw to his surprise, an almost peaceful look on the faces of the men as they stood their posts. He entered the inner courtyard and saw Captain Donovan on the gun deck with his telescope aiming toward the east. As he climbed the stairs and slowly approached his side, he glanced toward the east to try to discover what he was looking at. At first all James could see were low clouds scattered across the eastern horizon, but then he saw them, first one and then another white sail in the distance.

"James, you are by far the luckiest man I have ever known," he said without lowering the telescope. James could not believe it. "British ships?" he exclaimed and then tried to calm his voice. The Captain finally lowered the telescope. "Yes, I can make out at least nine of them at this point," he said and smiled, but James suddenly frowned.

"How do you know they are British?" he asked. The Captain feigned that he was hurt by the question and then smiled.

"The sail configuration on the larger vessels; four are ships of the line, one of which is a second rate vessel. The other five are large merchant ships," he replied. "They will be here by the end of the day, assuming we are their destination." Instead of rejoicing, James became very concerned.

"We need to have the men on full alert. If the Dutch see them coming, they might try to take the city before they arrive," James commented to the other officers, who seemed to grasp the concept, but it took a moment for them to react.

"They would be hard pressed to get their men organized and marched to the fort in time, but it is possible. Besides, I'd hate to get caught with our pants down and lose the fort with reinforcements so close at hand," Captain Donovan retorted and nodded. The officers began sending out orders and the men at the defenses jumped to action.

The level of excitement grew as the British ships came closer and closer to the fort and the chance of an attack from the Dutch faded. They were beautiful to look at as they bore down on the port; their destination was clearly Christiansted. James felt the pent-up anxiety and urgency recede from his body as the nine massive vessels sailed closer and closer toward them. He wondered if the Dutch colonel was sorely regretting his decision to give the militia those two days to vacate the fort and avoid a battle. James then thought how terrible it would have been for them to have accepted the offer and to have left; not knowing that their long awaited hope for help was less than a day away. Some might say fate was taking a hand, but James saw the hand of God at work. Deep down, he somehow knew that God was going to send help and that everything was going to be fine. He knew that God's ways are so much bigger than man's ways or plans. He felt joyful, almost giddy, as he and his friends watched the ships reduce sail as they approached the outskirts of the harbor. It was going to be a great day and his men would finally receive the honor and praise that they had worked so hard for these last four months.

Captain Donovan ordered that the harbor chain protecting the entrance of the port be lowered so that the massive ships could enter the harbor. They watched as the several heavy ropes connected to a huge shackle on the end of the chain were untied and slowly let out from the small merchant vessel. The chain quickly disappeared below the water, the weight of the heavy chains dragging it towards the bottom of the channel. The small merchant ship was then moved and anchored further to the north to allow the ships easy entrance into the harbor. One by one, the five merchant ships began to drop anchor outside the port entrance, with three of the four bigger ships of the line forming a protective ring, anchored around them. The fourth ship, which was a fast frigate, continued sailing westward. Through the telescope, they watched as the crews scurried about.

"Why didn't they anchor in the harbor?" Robbie asked as he took his turn looking through the telescope.

"They don't know for sure that it is still a British fort," Mr. Richards replied. "Something I'm sure the Dutch merchant captain wished he had made sure of," Mr. Richards said and everyone chuckled, except Captain Donovan who had taken over the telescope again and was surveying the ships.

"They have more eyes looking at us, than we do at them," Captain Donovan finally replied.

"They definitely want to make sure that we are friendly before they pay us a visit."

"I'd like to send a small patrol to let Bode know that the British are here," James said to Robbie and Captain Donovan.

"If he can't see them sitting in the harbor from where he and the men are located, I'd be worried. Besides, we might still need him to keep the Dutch occupied should they get desperate," Captain Donovan added. James thought about it and then agreed; he just wanted to have his best friend and his lead officer here when the British arrived at the fort.

It was almost an hour later when a longboat from the second rate warship began rowing toward the port entrance. James turned toward Robbie. "Can you call together one of the groups to join Captain Donovan and me at the wharf to greet our guests?" he asked Robbie, who nodded and immediately began to give orders. Men began to withdraw from the walls and assemble in the inner courtyard. James turned to Captain Donovan and smiled. "Shall we go meet our guests?" Captain Donovan suggested before James could ask him the same; James smiled and nodded his head as they headed down the steps.

Thirty members of the Dragon militia had assembled crisply and professionally in formation at the edge of the landing near the wharf, where James and Captain Donovan awaited the arrival of the British longboat. They watched as it worked its way through the channel, cheers could be heard and waving hats could be seen from upper ramparts of the eastern fort as the longboat passed by. The longboat paused briefly near the small merchant vessel, whose crew cheered as they passed. James and Captain Donovan smiled at each other as each fort came to life with joy and celebrated as the longboat passed them. It moved deeper into the harbor and closer to the wharf. They both tried to put on a professional look as the longboat glided against the wharf. Two of the soldiers took the lines and secured the longboat to the wharf. They stepped back from the edge to allow the British soldiers and three British officers to disembark. The men saluted, as did James and Captain Donovan once the officers were standing on the wharf. As they held their salute, James saw that the three officers, who now surveyed James and Captain Donovan, and then his men, bore the insignia of two captains and one colonel. They remained stone-faced and expressionless as they finally approached. Captain Donovan was the first to speak. "Sir, Captain Donovan of *The Dragon* and Captain James Thornton of the North Carolina Black Dragons welcome you to Christiansted." The Colonel gave a brief smile and then returned the salute.

"So the stories are true of the capture of the city and fort of Christiansted," he said and looked around at the men standing at attention behind them and then at the fort in the distance.

"Quite an accomplishment for a group of militia, Captains. The fact that you have been able to hold it until our arrival is another worthy achievement," he added.

"Sir, you need to be aware that there is a Dutch army of more than 600 soldiers camped less than three miles southwest of the fort waiting to attempt to reclaim it. Your arrival was very opportune," Captain Donovan replied. James watched, as a brief moment of panic crossed the faces of several of the British soldiers and one of the Captains. The Colonel contemplated the news a moment before responding.

"The need to turn the fort over to us and the offloading of our troops to secure it seems even more urgent, wouldn't you say Captain?" he said. "I'm sure you and your men are ready to relinquish your duties and avoid conflict," he ended. James thought his comments odd, under the circumstances.

"Sir, we are not seeking to avoid conflict. We are able and willing to hold this fort against our enemies. Your assistance in the matter would greatly enhance our chance of success," James replied and it was the Colonel's turn to be confused.

"Are you threatening me, Captain?" The British officer asked and stepped closer to James, staring into his eyes in an attempt to intimidate him. James was trying to understand what he had said that had incurred the Colonel's wrath toward him. Captain Donovan tried to soften the situation.

"Sir, I think you misunderstood. We are willing and wanting to help defend the fort." The Colonel cut him off.

"Against whom?" he barked and now the look of confusion was on Captain Donovan's face.

"Against the Dutch army that has assembled outside this city. What other enemy is there?" he replied slowly and carefully. The Colonel stood and stared back and forth at the two men, then turned toward his officers and chuckled, who also joined in. He finally composed himself and turned back toward James and Captain Donovan.

"You have no idea?" he asked and both men glanced at each other a moment.

"About what, sir?" James finally responded. The officer hesitated a moment, then answered.

"The British colonies have declared their independence from England, Mr. Thornton. Since July, we have been at war." James' heart sank and he tried to think through all the ramifications and what they meant for him and his men. He had a force of 600 Dutch soldiers at his back, and now a large fleet and a force of British soldiers anchored offshore. The situation seemed hopeless, as both he and Captain Donovan remained silent. If the Colonies were at war with England, and knowing how his father felt about the abuse of British rule, that meant his father and the militia back home were also now at war with the British. James could feel the news reverberating through the men standing behind him. The British Colonel took advantage of the moment and proceeded forward with his terms.

"Mr. Thornton and Mr. Donovan, you and your men will immediately lay down your arms and surrender the fort, the port, the city, and all of its contents. You and your men will then become prisoners of war until the colonies are brought back under full British control, which I estimate will only be for a few months, perhaps a year." He stood and stared at James and Captain Donovan waiting for their surrender.

James tried to imagine what the prisons and conditions would be like for his men while under British rule and knew that it would be harsh and very likely few would survive, if so, they would be stripped of their freedom and become indentured servants or deck crews. All that he had promised his men and the newly trained militia would be lost. He tried to imagine what was happening back home; had the plantation been destroyed by the British? Were his family and the plantation workers safe?

"Mr. Thornton, it is in your best interest to accept these terms to avoid the annihilation of you and your men," the Colonel declared and appeared ready to continue but James interrupted him.

"Captain," was all James said abruptly, as the Colonel halted, mouth open in mid speech.

"Excuse me?" he asked coldly, James turned his head and looked straight at the Colonel.

"It is *Captain* Thornton and *Captain* Donovan," he stated clearly and coldly. "We have fought bravely and honorably *for England* and have worked diligently to hold and retain this fort and city *for England*, and now without any appreciation or demonstration of gratitude, you arrogantly step forward and demand that we surrender and become your prisoners of war and be tossed in your prisons?" James stated angrily and waited for the Colonel's response. He could see the man was taken aback by his strong his strong response and his failed attempt at intimidating James. James could see the blood rushing to the man's face and the angry expression building, but then the man seemed to calm down and his expression softened.

"You're efforts are appreciated… *Captain*, but the politics and arrogance of the leaders of the colonies has changed our appreciation into concern and left us no choice but to secure this fort and we will do so either by your choice or by force," the Colonel said and emphasized the last word as he tried to reclaim control of the conversation.

James looked over at Captain Donovan who seemed caught in the moment of indecision. James finally shook his head.

"Colonel, you and your men will return to your ship and we will discuss the news you have brought us and how we will choose to respond to your request of surrender. If we agree with your current terms, we will fire one cannon from the fort. If we do not, we will fire two cannons and you are welcome to return to offer or discuss other conditions," James asserted. The Colonel lost his composure at James' refusal to be cowed.

"There will be no other discussions or conditions. This offer is accepted now, or we will destroy you and your men. Do you understand?" he almost yelled at James as he continued to try to stare him down. Captain Donovan stepped forward and leaned in close to the Colonel's face.

"Get off of my wharf!" he growled at the man through clenched teeth. The Colonel was stunned by the words coming from the merchant Captain, as was James. The Colonel seemed on the verge of pulling his sword or pistol as he fought to control his rage and embarrassment. The ten British soldiers and two officers standing behind him were becoming anxious. Robbie seemed to read the moment and barked a brief order. All the men suddenly brought their muskets up to their chests and pulled back the hammers on the muskets. Robbie remained standing with his arm in the air preparing to give an order. The Colonel looked past James and

Captain Donovan at the thirty men who were poised for battle and at his men as they scrambled to form a line.

"Stand down," the Colonel yelled and time seemed to stand still as each side tried to determine what should happen next. James broke the silence.

"I think I now understand more clearly why the colonies have chosen to rebel against you. Twenty minutes ago our men would have been willing to fight and die together in battle against the Dutch, but now instead they will die at each other's hands because of your arrogance. You have our answer Colonel." James motioned his hand toward the longboat that had brought them to the wharf. The Colonel tried to maintain a smile as he turned and walked toward the boat.

"You're a fool and have condemned yourself and your men to death," he said as he turned to look at James one more time before climbing into the boat.

"Colonel, we have faced the idea of death on England's behalf ever since we left our homes in North Carolina. To do so now, for our own reasons and country, I can assure you is much more attractive," James replied and the man seemed to search for a response, but finding none he turned and stepped back into the boat and the rest of the men followed. Once they were seated, they began to row the long journey back to their vessels anchored outside the port entrance.

Captain Donovan was the first to shake off the moment and began issuing orders to several of his sailors.

"Take a crew out to get that harbor chain back in place and to anchor the smaller ship directly in the entrance. Then pull the crew off of the vessel. I want *The Dragon* and the *Unicorn* positioned with guns loaded for a broadside facing where the harbor chain is positioned. They will have to sail straight in, so the ships should be safe from an enemy broadside initially. Hopefully they'll be more interested in trying to silence the larger shore guns than the smaller guns on the ships." He turned toward James. "Captain, I will send word to the two forts to prepare for both land and sea attacks from the British; that they are not friendly, and intend to inflict great harm on us." James nodded and yelled a few orders out to his men. He also sent two groups of runners to Bode, with the information and the order to return as soon as possible to the fort, for they would need every man. James was very impressed as he watched Robbie execute orders and take control of the responsibilities that were assigned to him. Captain Donovan was moving toward the city, barking orders right and left to men that were running toward them from the fort. They appeared to have already received word from the earlier runners warning them to get prepared.

James looked out to see that the longboat had only now passed by the small merchant ship sitting at the harbor entrance; the crew assigned to secure the harbor chain had not even loaded into a longboat yet. He knew the British had a long way to go. Even after they reached their ship, it would take time to prepare an attack, but he hoped they would take their time. At that very moment, he saw one of the officers on the British longboat begin signaling with flags to their ships outside the harbor. He knew his wish for more time had been dashed and that the attack would come very soon. Bode would not make it back to the fort in time.

Once James reached the fort, he began answering questions and explaining what was happening. He also took a moment to explain what defeat at the hands of the British would look like for them. James knew that they could not fight both the Dutch and the British at the same time, so they decided to focus on the most urgent threat of the moment, the British. Although the wall guns remained ready and loaded to repel a land attack by the Dutch, they decided that focusing the soldiers on the supply and support of the main harbor guns should be the priority. Orders were being sent out and questions were returning from the outlying forts and the ships every ten to fifteen minutes, which Captain Donovan and James handled quickly and decisively.

James could feel the normal zeal and energy of the men fading and that a sense of hopelessness was creeping into the ranks. In spite of encouraging words from James and the other officers, the feeling did not seem to dissipate and James did not have a solution to remove the darkness.

As the men were preparing, James saw Captain Donovan on the upper gun deck looking through his telescope at the ships beyond the harbor. He realized that they had not really spoken since the encounter with the British Colonel, so he ran up the steps and walked up beside him and looked out at the fleet of eight ships, now enemy ships.

"James, if they came for battle as it appears, they could easily have over a thousand foot soldiers on those eight ships," he said, somehow knowing who stood behind him. James' heart quickened as he tried to think of how they could win against such numbers. Why had God allowed this to happen? Why would he have blessed them all along the way, only to now destroy them? He tried to understand, but it was beyond him. He surrendered that it was not for him to know God's ways or reasons.

"What tactics can we expect?" James replied with a question, as Captain Donovan lowered his telescope and then nodded toward the ships.

"I expect they will begin unloading their army to either our west or our east, perhaps both, and then march on the city, lay siege to the fort and wait us out," he said. "If they are more concerned about the Dutch taking the fort first, they may try a rapid and overwhelming two-pronged attack from sea and land. It will be more dangerous and costly for them in the numbers of men, but it will force the conflict to a head." He raised the telescope again.

"Get off my wharf?" James suddenly mimicked. "It's not the most memorable heroic quote you'd want shared around the dinner table," James said sarcastically. Captain Donovan remained silent a moment and then James could see the smile growing on his face.

"I was a little upset and was not thinking clearly. I'm sure the history books will change it to sound better," he replied and James nodded, but then considered that their story might not ever be told if things turn out badly for them. Captain Donovan turned back toward James and raised an eyebrow.

"Maybe I should have stuck a pistol in his face when I said it? It seemed to work for you." James shrugged.

"Then I'd have gotten credit for saying it." He smiled and Captain Donovan shook his head and nodded.

"Probably." He looked back out to sea.

After a few more minutes and several new requests and orders, Captain Donovan shook his head. "They are taking the urgent route," he said and James looked out toward the ships and could see longboats being lowered into the water from all of the ships.

"Based on the wind, they won't try to row against it, so that means they are going to make a landing to our west," Captain Donovan said as he looked up at the flag waving above them, then had a realization and turned to a group of men nearby and pointed. "Black Dragons! Get that flag off of that pole and replace it with our Black Dragon banner!" The men immediately began untying the lanyards and lowering the British Union Jack that had flown above the fort since they had taken it. As the Black Dragon banner was raised, a gray flag with a Black Dragon embroidered in the middle of it, a roar went up from the men in the fort. James smiled and saw that shortly afterwards, the other two forts also lowered their smaller Union Jack flags. They did not have a Black Dragon banner to fly, but the point was made. James felt it was just what the men needed to change the darkening spirits of the moment.

They watched as eight soldier-laden longboats from the five large British merchant ships began rowing toward the shore line several miles west of the fort. Captain Donovan tried to do a head count on the number of soldiers that were on this first wave of longboats, hoping to estimate the total number of troops being put ashore and ultimately what they would be facing. He counted fifteen troops per longboat, so over a 120 soldiers would be landing on the first wave. James watched as the longboats encountered the shore waves, and then observed as first one, then another, and soon all eight of the longboats managed to navigate through the waves, past the shore reef and into the shallow and calmer waters beyond it. As the lead three boats approached the shoreline, James could see even without the telescope that they seemed to be having difficulties and were scrambling around on the boats, but he could not grasp what the problem was.

"Bode! Bode and the Dragons are engaging the British on the shoreline!" Captain Donovan yelled and everyone ran to the top ramparts to watch the battle unfold several miles away. James realized that the messengers had reached Bode in time and he must have seen the British unloading and preparing to land troops on the shore. A cheer went up from the men on the wall as the battle unfolded in front of them.

As James watched and prayed, he could see the musket smoke blowing westward from the tree line where the Black Dragons had been waiting. The crews on the other five longboats were trying to urgently row toward the shore, while those on the front three boats were trying to reorganize after the initial volley from the Black Dragons. James realized that the stumbling was actually men falling from the volley. Some were trying to stand and fire, others were climbing over the side and into the water, and others seemed to be trying to stay low. As the next two closest longboats passed by the three that were recovering in the water, another volley came from the shore and into them. Based on the timing, James knew that Bode had used a staggered firing line from two groups of fifty men. The first group was now reloading while the second would engage, and so forth. James could see that the second two boats were now in the same chaotic state as the first three, the surviving crew trying to now row and steer as the dead and wounded were tumbling onto them.

The surviving soldiers from the first five boats had given up trying to row their boats and instead had jumped into the waist deep water and were wading toward the shore. Meanwhile the last three boats rowed past them toward the shoreline. James was counting in his head and knew that the first Dragon line would not be reloaded for another 10-15 seconds, so as the three boats slid into the sandy shore, the officer unloading with the rest of the men began to have them form a firing line. Everything in James was wishing and urging the Dragons to load and fire before the British line could be formed, but knew that it would be close. He saw a massive amount of smoke suddenly erupt from the tree line thirty yards from the British line of forty-five soldiers and slam into it, wreaking havoc on the line of men. James was saddened but thankful that the volley had decimated the British line. James remembered that they carried an additional musket, so Bode must have had them use their second musket in an attempt to thwart their volley. Nonetheless, the remaining British troops, disciplined and trained as they were, even then managed to return a volley toward the tree line and James felt a deep pain in his chest knowing that his friends were on the receiving end of that volley. He was glad he could not see the results.

It was as if time stopped as they watched the British soldiers begin reloading their muskets as they stood on the beach. The surviving soldiers from the other five boats had waded through the water and were forming up with the other troops and filling the huge openings in the line caused from their fallen comrades. James knew that Bode would have his men using the cover of the trees, but even that would not be much. The three longboats that had dropped off their men on the shoreline were already rowing back toward the breakers, while the other five were still struggling to make headway.

Based on his count, James knew the first group of Dragons that had fired should be ready well before the British and waited anxiously. It came moments later as the tree line erupted again with smoke and the line of British soldiers crumbled or staggered back. James saw that the British officer had not survived the volley, which made James cringe at the thought that Bode may not have survived the prior British volley. He wished he could somehow be there with Bode and the men. To everyone's surprise, the Black Dragons suddenly charged from the tree line toward the much smaller number of remaining British soldiers. A cheer went up from the walls of the fort as the dark gray and black uniforms swarmed around the red-coated soldiers and into the water toward the longboats. James was proud of his men and their leader, knowing that the charge would not have happened without Bode having led it.

"James," Captain Donovan said as he tapped him on the shoulder with the telescope. James could see concern on his face as he nodded toward the fleet and away from the battle on the shoreline. James stepped away from the men and walked toward the wall with Captain Donovan.

"The warships are putting on sail; I expect they are planning on a direct run at the fort by sea. We need to get the men's attention on preparing for it," he said and James looked over

Captain Donovan's shoulder at the sails on the warships being lowered and filling with wind. James nodded and turned toward the men on the walls.

"Black Dragons! Our brothers on the beach are buying us time and inflicting grievous wounds on the enemy, but now is not the time to watch their battle, for our enemy is now sailing toward our position with their mightiest ships of the line. It is now our turn to demonstrate our courage and determination to repel them. Man your posts and cannon. They all turned toward the ships offshore. Then, to a man, they moved toward their posts and duties, stealing a glance now and then at the battle on the distant shoreline.

Captain Donovan stood on the wall facing the bay and turned toward the men in the fort.

"The harbor chain is up and the smaller ship is securely anchored and blocking most of the entrance to the north, so they will have to sail south around her where a ship will run not only into the chains to get past her, but also into our guns. We may only gain a brief advantage, so make sure we inflict as much damage as possible. Aim true and wait for my order to fire, but then reload and fire at will. Make them never forget the day they fought against the Black Dragons," he roared and the men cheered back at him.

As the big warships began moving toward the entrance to the bay, James took a moment to glance back at the battle on the shoreline. He borrowed Captain Donovan's telescope and saw that the remaining British soldiers were now surrounded by men clad in the gray and black uniforms of the Black Dragons and that five of the eight longboats had been pulled onto the shoreline. The remaining three longboats had almost reached the merchant ships again. Would they try to take on more troops and attempt another landing? James did not think that they would row into such a trap again, so that left the only way for them to quickly secure the fort was by sea.

Captain Donovan addressed the men again as the ships drew closer to the entrance. "The only faces I want looking over the defensive wall are the gunners and the spotters. Anyone else is just looking to die, so don't let your curiosity get you killed. You will get your turn to see the enemy soon enough should they land troops. Stay out of the high places and close to the main walls and you should be safe from the shelling. We need you to stay alive so you can do your jobs later." The unnecessary men on the walls quickly moved to the ground floor. James saw that the guns had been aimed to the furthest right to take advantage of the earliest opportunity for a shot at the first vessel coming through the gap. James knew that the channel leading into the bay would require the British ships to enter northeast of the fort, exposing them to the eastern fort's guns. From there, the channel angled back to the southwest, toward the main bay area and into range of the guns stationed on the main fort and the western fort that was built on the small island in the middle of Gallows bay.

After watching the warships for awhile, it became apparent that the smallest of the three, the fourth rate, was not moving with the other two ships, but instead remained behind to protect the five anchored merchant ships and their soldiers. Of the other two ships of the line sailing toward the entrance, the lead one was a third rate with two gun decks carrying over seventy guns, while the other was a second rate with three gun decks and ninety guns. Each side of the third rate had fifteen 32 pounders on the lower deck and fourteen 18 pounders on the upper deck, and a crew of over 500 men. The second rate carried fourteen 32 pounders on each side of the lowest main gun deck, fourteen 18 pounders on each side of the middle deck, twelve 12 pounders on each side of the upper deck, and a crew of over 700 men.

"Why is the third rate coming in first?" James asked Captain Donovan as they watched Mr. Richards checking the aim on each cannon.

"Because the Colonel is on the second rate and he knows the third rate is going to take the majority of the damage and casualties," Captain Donovan replied and smiled.

"Wow, a brave man and a true leader," James replied sarcastically.

"We'll make sure we save plenty of shot for his pretty vessel too," Mr. Richards said as he overheard their conversation and he smiled his mischievous smile.

"Mr. Richards, you may give the order to fire as you best see fit," Captain Donovan stated so that the crews would know who to listen to during the battle. He then turned toward James. "I'm afraid our men at the eastern fort are going to bear the brunt of the initial return fire as those ships round the entrance corner and turn toward the bay. We'll make them pay later, but they will be hard pressed initially," Captain Donovan stated solemnly. James tried to imagine a broadside of thirty cannons blasting away at you, followed by another forty bigger cannons shortly afterwards. He knew the walls were thick and could withstand the poundings for a short time, but anyone exposed on top behind the thinner rampart walls would be at risk. Captain Donovan seemed never to take his eyes off the ships as they sailed closer and closer to the entrance.

"James, each vessel is towing two longboats behind it. They are riding low in the water, which tells me they are not empty. I'm guessing they have troops just out of sight to peel off from the ships as they make the turn into the bay and head to the shore. You may need to send a group to assist the eastern fort, or they could be overwhelmed." James started to turn, but Captain Donovan touched his arm. "I need you here to run the defenses of this fort," Captain Donovan said. Robbie picked up on the moment.

"I'll lead two groups to reinforce them," he offered and James hesitated before finally agreeing.

"Don't engage them directly. They are too well trained and better shots than our Lizards are at this point. Wait until they set up to attack and hit them from behind, then pull back. Do it again if needed. Take the remaining spare muskets and use them only..." James started, but Robbie interrupted.

"I know James," he said and smiled. James realized he was being overly protective and that Robbie was the one that had been training the men these past few months.

"Be safe." Was all James said and then watched as Robbie ran down the steps and called out orders for the 6th and 7th groups to form up. The men of the 6th and 7th seemed to come out of the woodwork of the fort to gather around Robbie. Moments later they were gathering their weapons and supplies and heading out the gate and east of the fort. James prayed for their safety and then turned back toward the bay to see how close the warships were.

James saw the massive two-deck ship sailing on a south easterly heading, enter the narrow mouth of the channel leading into the protected bay and only several hundred yards behind was the even more massive, three-deck warship. James could see hundreds of men scrambling, crawling, climbing and standing all over the two ships. He had watched the militia gun crews during training these past few months as they practiced firing the big 42 pounders and knew their range was just inside that entrance, while the 32 pounders' range was about 700 yards closer. He could see by the angle of the cannons that Mr. Richards was very intent on making sure they would have the experience of getting to know those cannons the moment they came into range.

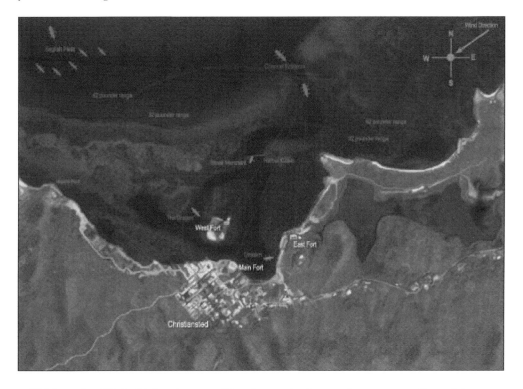

"Wait, wait…" Mr. Richards was yelling down the line at the men standing with a burning stick near the back of the massive guns. As the big shipped suddenly turned slightly right and began its southern angle down the channel of the entrance, Mr. Richards gave the order.

"FIRE!" he yelled and the men responded by touching their smoking sticks of embers to the top of the cannons where the gunpowder fuse leading to the massive charge inside the cannon waited. Seven of the eight cannons erupted immediately with a thunderous "BOOM!" belching noise, flames and smoke from their barrels, while the eighth seemed to take a moment longer before it also belched noise, flame and smoke. There was a sudden ringing in James' ears as he watched the warship over the walls as it moved gracefully toward them. The crews did not wait or even glance at the results; they immediately began swarming over their guns to prepare them for another shot. James on the other hand, could not take his eyes off the ship as he waited for the results. For a moment James thought the cannons had either missed or they had forgot to put the cannon shot in the barrel, as several seconds passed without effect, but then came the terrifying sight of the eight massive balls tearing through the decks and sides of the ship, seven of them simultaneously. The ship almost stopped in the water as the massive balls passed through it, leaving carnage and death at each contact point. Although the sails fluttered from the impact, the wind did not feel the pain of the ship, nor hesitate as it continued to push the immense vessel forward.

James remembered watching the French 32 and 18 pounder cannon ball broadside tear through the *HMS Ames* during that fateful encounter. Although similar, he realized that the ship before him with its thicker sides would have fared far better that the *Ames* in that ship-to-ship barrage. Now, however, against the 42 pounders, it was as if the massive shot was passing through paper.

James was very impressed as he watched each of the eight crews clear, clean and load the cannons. Even with their fast pace, James felt the desire to speed them up as he watched the ship being pushed down the channel toward the bay. The three-deck warship had now entered the channel and was moving southeast down it toward the right hand turn. As with the first ship, the wind coming from the east was not strong or favorable for them at this point, but once they turned south and then eventually to the west to follow the channel, it would aid them greatly. As part of the crew was loading, the other part was repositioning the cannon for its next shot. Mr. Richards was walking down the line of cannons and directing his expert cannon crew who he had transferred from *The Dragon* to operate the bigger guns of the fort. The lead ship was fast approaching the starboard turn that would take it due west past the inner bay reef and toward the last southern turn that would lead them to the waiting merchant vessel and harbor chain. Captain Donovan was right, as the two longboats being towed behind the vessel suddenly came alive with one man at the tiller and another, who had untied the tow rope from its bow, at the stern. Both boats suddenly angled to the east and away from the massive vessel and men began running out oars on both sides.

The 42 pounder crews had almost completed their reloading when the four 32 pounders from the eastern fort belched their smoke and fire as the lead warship completed its starboard turn west and into their range. The four balls found their marks in various places on the ship and the delayed sound of wood being smashed and men screaming could be heard coming across the water. The massive vessel suddenly belched smoke from the port side of the lower deck where the 32 pounders were facing the eastern fort, with the sound of the cannons following moments later. James knew that the 32 pounders on the warship did not have the same range as the longer barreled shore guns, but he saw that they were still able to reach the fort as dust was suddenly rising from the walls and the surrounding area around the eastern fort from their impact.

As James was watching the results of the broadside, suddenly the massive 42 pounders fired again and James, recovering from his start, shifted his eyes to watch the results. Again, the massive projectiles tore through the vessel at different points of entrance. Even with the ringing in his ears, James could hear the screams of the wounded and the dying coming from the ship and from the carnage they left. He knew that although the entry holes that the shot made were small, the damage they generated as they continued on through the ship's walls and bulkheads, and the splinters and shrapnel generated from their impact were wreaking havoc on the inside of the ship. Moments later it was the western fort's turn to fire their four 32 pounders at the ship that had just came into range of their guns. While it appeared that most struck into the lower decks, James saw one of the shots tear through the upper deck area, plowing through a gun crew, shattering the cannon, and continuing on as it cleared a path from there forward of anyone or anything that was in its way.

James knew that the orders of fire for all forts were to focus on the lead vessel, which they had done an excellent job of following so far. The lead ship was gaining speed as it was being carried forward by the wind that was now blowing directly from behind them. It was preparing to make the final port side turn to the south toward the small merchant ship that was waiting, void of crew, with one end of the harbor chain tied to it and the other end tied to a coral head to the east of it. The eastern fort fired another volley at the lead vessel, this group slamming mostly into the raised stern of the vessel. James could see that the next vessel, the massive second-rate ship, had almost completed its starboard turn to the west, which meant that the eastern fort would be receiving a larger broadside from this new warship. Not a moment had past since the thought entered his mind, when fire and smoke roared from the ship and the loud rumble followed moments later. The eastern fort was suddenly encased in a cloud of dust as the broadside of forty guns impacted all around the stone fort. His heart sank at the thought of the men enduring such a barrage of shot, even though he knew the stone walls were built to withstand such attacks, at least for a little while. The wind blew the dust toward the bay, gradually thinning the cloud of dust as it passed over the water.

This time James heard Mr. Richard's signal to prepare to fire and he reached up and covered his ears with his hands. The captain of the vessel was aware of the position of the fort and had turned as late as possible, keeping the small merchant ship between him and the main fort guns. Mr. Richards continued to order the men to hold their fire until it came into view to the east of the smaller vessel. As the British vessel turned east, its starboard side guns belched at the bow of the smaller and defenseless vessel. The bow of the smaller vessel seemed to jump upwards at the impact from the broadside, and then settled back down into the water into the enveloping cloud of smoke. Although he could not see it from the smoke, James knew that it was mortally wounded. Mr. Richards had the 42 pounders waiting for it to sail into view and gave the order to fire. The eight massive cannonballs slammed into various locations of the front starboard side of the bow, just above the waterline. The resulting damage had literally caved in the starboard side of the big vessel's bow, yet the wind in the undamaged sails above continued to carry it forward.

James and Captain Donovan watched with anticipation as it sailed into the harbor chain that they knew was just below the waterline of the vessel. The first sign that it had run into the chain was the sudden movement of the smaller merchant vessel as it was pushed backwards in the water. Then they could see the chain and rope suddenly jumping out of the water to the side of the massive vessel as the pressure drew them taunt. You could hear the creaking sound as the big vessel strained to push against it, but by God's grace it held and the ship came to a sudden dead stop in the water. Then the damaged ship slowly moved backwards from the pressure of the chain against it. James could see men scrambling about on the deck and in the masts and, carried by the wind, he could hear the yelling of orders, somehow even drowning out the cries of the wounded. With the bow of the ship tight against the harbor chain, the wind in the sails was starting to push the stern of the ship around toward the bow of the merchant ship to its west. With the smoke mostly cleared, James could see that the bow of the merchant ship was nearly gone and the front of the vessel was already beginning to sink into the water. It had served its purpose well.

The west fort suddenly released another volley toward the now motionless ship, tearing into it above the waterline. Suddenly *The Dragon*, anchored to the northwest of western fort, released a broadside at the exposed British ship; then moments later the *Unicorn* also released a broadside scoring a direct hit, all of which added to the carnage and destruction.

James could see that the huge second-rate ship was beginning to make a port turn to the south and into the two ships that were now blocking the entrance. They watched as sail on the bigger vessel was quickly dropped, leaving no choice but to make the turn or crash into the reef in front of it. Although sail was dropping rapidly, the momentum of the huge vessel continued to carry it forward toward the now affixed vessel in its path. The helmsman of the incoming vessel tried to sail it to the port side of the third rate ship, but his choices were limited to running into the shallow reef to the east, or into the frozen vessel. He chose the vessel.

They watched from the walls as the two ships came together, their rigging and crossmasts tearing through each other, followed by the crunching sound of wood on wood. The men cheered at the sight of their enemy's situation. To add to the moment of chaos, the eastern fort, recovering from the earlier broadside, sent another volley into the two ships. The British crews began trying and clear their rigging and masts, but the wind from the northeast was pushing and holding the two ships together. James could see that crewmen from the lead ship were boarding the quickly sinking merchant ship as they strived to release the harbor chain. The lead ship continued to fire the free starboard guns that were not blocked by the hull of the merchant ship in front of it, most being aimed at the west fort that faced its starboard side. The bow guns did their best to maintain some fire into the east fort.

The next ten minutes prolonged the sickening visage as the three forts and *The Dragon* and the *Unicorn* continued to fire volley after volley into the two British warships that sat dead in the water, doing their best to return fire from their available guns. By the end of that time, the lead British ship was a mangled mess that James and Captain Donovan knew would not be leaving the harbor under its own sail, if ever. Any guns that could have been fired had been rendered silent by the constant barrage and its stern was now jammed on top of the merchant vessel, which had sunk below the waterline and rested against the shallow reef to the west. They had cut away most of the rigging on the lead vessel in an effort to free the bigger ship, but with the wind direction coming from the northeast, they were unable to sail their vessel around the lead vessel.

James felt sick by it, but conceded to Captain Donovan's strong urging that they continue firing at the huge second-rate warship until they stopped returning fire, struck their colors or signaled for a ceasefire. He felt the best way to get an arrogant British officer to negotiate was to inflict as much damage as possible to his vessel. Although they could not target the hull of the second rate due to the lead ship's hull protecting it, they did focus their fire into the upper structure of the deck, masts and rigging of the second rate warship. Eventually, several longboats from the merchant ships and the smaller warship began approaching the two vessels, crossing the shallow reefs to the north. James talked Captain Donovan out of firing on them since the longboats only had enough crew to row the boats. They continued to fire into the ships, with more and more effect and accuracy. At one point two of the longboats suddenly appeared at the bow of the huge second rate ship, attempting to tow the massive vessel out of the harbor. Mr. Richards adjusted and aimed two of his 42 pounders at the two vessels. The first shot struck so close that it capsized one of the longboats, while the other struck just behind the other longboat. The point was made as the remaining longboat rowed back to the protected side of the second rate and no further attempts were made at towing the vessel from the harbor. Over the next hour, they continued to rain down cannon on the two ships and first one, and then a second mast on the second rate ship was struck by a cannon ball and fell to the side of the vessel. It was no longer capable of sailing out of the harbor on its own. Finally, a white flag was raised from the deck of the second rate warship and with an order from Mr. Richards, the guns of the forts fell silent. Moments later a longboat began rowing toward the main fort. Captain Donovan and James, along with their original contingent of men marched out to meet the officer at the wharf. Once the boat had arrived, an officer climbed up the ladder and onto the wooden dock. James could see that the officer was not the same man that had arrogantly threatened them earlier in the day. His hands were shaking and he continually whipped his brow.

"How can we help you, Captain?" Captain Donovan asked. The officer seemed to be struggling with how to proceed.

"I request a ceasefire to allow my men and ships to withdraw." Captain Donovan turned toward James as if confused, and then back to the Captain.

"I believe it was you who attacked us, so the idea of just letting you, your men and your ships leave without consequences does not work for us. Perhaps you can come up with a better plan?" he asked. The man was nervous, but also seemed to be holding back a fit of rage.

"We have a large number of wounded; I request a little compassion to allow the wounded to be rowed to our ships for treatment," he said, more humbly than before.

"So you are not surrendering, just asking for compassion?" Captain Donovan asked and the man hesitated and then nodded. Captain Donovan turned toward James. "What do you think Captain Thornton?" Captain Donovan asked James.

"I do not recall the colonel extending such grace or mercy to us during our earlier discussion. I believe his words were that he would *destroy us* if we did not submit to his demands," James replied.

"He did seem very determined to do just that," Captain Donovan agreed. James stepped forward and approached the English captain.

"In spite of your undeserved aggression, we have no desire to continue pounding you and your men into submission. But we have also seen your determination to take this fort by land or by sea, so to simply let you and your men return to your vessels does not seem wise." James stopped long enough to look over the officer's shoulder at his disabled vessel. "Here is the only offer that we will extend to you, with no other conditions. We will send four longboats to escort you back to your vessel, once there; ten of my men will oversee the removal and loading of the ships muskets and pistols into those two longboats. You will escort my men through your two ships to verify that all weapons are accounted for. They will then row them back to the wharf. Once they have returned safely, you may proceed to start unloading all of your men onto your longboats, and rowing them back to your vessels outside our harbor. You may take as many trips as needed to accomplish this. If we see any muskets accompanying you or your men as they load into the longboats, we will open fire," James stated and waited for the officer to respond. He thought through the situation and the offer.

"How do I know that if we surrender our muskets that you would not just attack us?" he replied.

"You don't. But I hope you understand that we could sink your vessels, killing the crews of both if you refuse. The troops that line the banks of the channel can pick off any survivors that swim for the shore. I'm protecting you from any foolish action that would encourage you to continue in your folly," James declared and waited for the officer to respond, but nothing came. James turned away from the man and walked back over to where Captain Donovan stood.

"Good day, Captain. I'm sorry we were not able to reach an agreement that would have spared you and your men." James turned back toward the English Captain. The man slowly moved toward the ladder leading down into his longboat, then stopped and turned back.

"Agreed," he finally said. "But I will not surrender my vessel to you." Captain Donovan was the one who responded. "We never assumed that you would. When your men are safely off the ship, you may sink it where it stands. However, if you try to first move it to further block the channel, we will be forced to fire upon you and your men. Please understand that if we are attacked by any of your forces on land or sea during this reprieve, we will be forced to resume and step up our bombardment. Should any of my soldiers who board your vessel be met with hostility, I will see to it that you all die today," Captain Donovan asserted coldly. The officer's eyes widened slightly and he moved away from the Captain.

"It will take a moment for us to organize our four longboats to escort you back. Thank you for your patience," Captain Donovan informed him without waiting for the Captains approval.

Within fifteen minutes, they had pulled together the rowing and boarding crew for the four longboats. Captain Donovan wanted to make sure that his sailors were the ones who boarded the vessel and supervised the unloading of weapons. Mr. Sanders had volunteered to lead the four longboats and the ten boarding crews, and personally take the tour with the captain.

The sun was setting as the four heavily laden longboats returned to wharf, where their contents were quickly unloaded onto the docks, then transferred into several wagons and driven to the entrance of the fort, where they were carried by hand into the lower storage areas. They did not even try to get a count on the ordnance as it was loaded and unloaded. They estimated that there were at least 300-400 muskets or pistols that were captured. James once again was looking over the fort's ramparts as they watched the British loading their men into the longboats and rowing them out to sea past the shallow reef. Just before sunset, the

British fast frigate that had sailed west when the fleet arrived returned and joined the remaining warship and merchant ships offshore.

Robbie returned and reported that the British troops that had landed on the northern beach, had withdrawn once they had seen their two vessels thwarted at the mouth of the bay. They had returned to their longboats and rowed out toward the other vessels anchored offshore and away from their two stricken ships. They had never attacked or even approached the eastern fort.

Later that evening, Bode and his men returned to the fort with 28 captured British soldiers, and over 100 "liberated" British muskets. They had allowed the British soldiers one longboat to carry their wounded back to the merchant ships and sank the other four before leaving the shoreline. Bode's men sustained four casualties in the encounter, and four Lizard militia had died. Eight Lizards and two Dragons had been seriously wounded. While securing the British prisoners and longboats, they had seen the massive ships sailing into the bay, and Bode pulled the troops back from the shoreline and marched them and the prisoners to the fort to provide reinforcements.

Despite an incredible victory that could have lead to the deaths of his entire force, James felt stunned and saddened by the idea of any of his men being killed or wounded. Four of them had died and the reality of war was clear to him. Although he felt selfish for the thought, he was grateful that Bode had not been one of the dead or wounded.

That night they tried to come up with a strategy that would best ensure survival against a land attack that they anticipated coming the next day. They felt the chance of a direct attack on the bay from the sea would not be a concern with the elimination of the two warships. They also figured that the colonel would be looking for a chance to repay them for the loss of his ship and the embarrassment of his failure. The only way to salvage his lost honor was to take the fort. They decided that the best approach was to keep the main soldier Dragons outside the fort in order to engage the British before they laid siege to the fort or burned the city in anger. James and Bode decided to go to bed early to get enough rest so they could rise early and be ready.

It was past midnight when one of the men woke James to let him know that the British ships in the bay were burning. Instead of the usual darkness in the inner courtyard for this time of night, there was a strange glow coming from the bay that created shadows on the inner walls. The fire must have been spectacular, but James had seen enough destruction for one day. He closed his eyes again and struggled to get back to sleep as the thoughts of the dead and wounded marched inexorably across his mind.

Chapter 18

The sun was still waiting to rise in the east and the dark shroud of night still lay over the land like a blanket. James and Bode along with 200 militiamen from both the Dragons and Lizards began marching cautiously westward using the blackness as a cover. In stark contrast to the darkness, they could see the glow of orange in the air and reflecting off the water, surrounding the black mass in the middle of the channel that was the smoldering remains of the three ships, small fires still burning in the timbers. They could smell the smoke drifting toward them as they marched west. A soft orange glow grew on the horizon as they passed by Hogan's Point. Once they reached the edge of the thick undergrowth of the inner island they would have an unobstructed view of the British fleet anchored offshore. They kept the men hidden just inside the tree line, and waited for the rising sun to reveal the state of their enemy. To their surprise there was no British fleet to be seen. James stepped out further onto the sand to look up the west coast, but there was nothing. His first thought was that they had sailed east to make a landing, but the wind had stayed steady from the northeast, so sailing in that direction would have taken a great deal of time and they would still be visible on the horizon. That meant either they had decided to sail north abandoning the invasion or they had decided to sail west.

They could only think of two reasons for sailing west. Either the British were planning to unload their troops in safety further away and then march back toward the fort, or they were planning an attempt on Frederiksted. James reminded them that they had informed the British colonel that a Dutch army was camped just outside the city. Perhaps they felt that they could sail west landing well behind the Dutch army and capture Frederiksted.

For twenty minutes, Bode and James debated the ideas of wether to stay close to their city in case of a Dutch attack, or to move west in order to verify where the British army had landed and to learn where it might be heading. They agreed that, once the sun had came up and the Dutch could see that there was no longer a British fleet in sight, they would head back toward Frederiksted to protect their only remaining city on the island. They did decide that they should verify that the Dutch had indeed left before they tried to determine the whereabouts of the British. They informed the men of the decision, then they headed due south to the Dutch encampment. James sent small patrols forward to probe and locate any Dutch patrols or sentries. He wanted to avoid having their whole group come upon the Dutch army or walk into a trap. One patrol that had approached the camp on higher ground sent a man back to report that the camp was hastily being vacated. Some forces were already marching west, while the rest were tearing down, loading the wagons, and preparing to move the more cumbersome cannons.

Once again, Bode and James debated the options before them. They could attack the supply trains and gather a great deal of goods, powder and artillery cannon, thereby weakening the Dutch army; or they could just allow the Dutch and the British to fight it out, weakening both sides. The real question before them was: which enemy did they want to fight in the future? Both enemies wanted Christiansted, and both had the ability to take it with enough time and resources. If the British army, numbering roughly one thousand strong, had landed their well-trained men and was marching toward Frederiksted, then the smaller Dutch army would not fare well against them. Part of the Dutch forces might be behind the walls of their fort, but the British would be equally capable of handling either a siege of the fort or a field engagement with the Dutch army.

If the British succeeded in capturing Frederiksted, they would have the fort and port, a strong base to which they could transport enough soldiers, supplies and equipment to march on Christiansted. If the Dutch succeeded in staving off the British, then the Dutch would similarly regroup, resupply and march upon Christiansted. Neither option had a favorable outcome for the small outpost of continental soldiers stranded in the middle of the Caribbean. *Continental soldier* - James thought about the name and what it now meant for them. The rest of the Continental Army did not even know they existed, yet here they were fighting for their very lives and the new country that they represented. The bigger question that they faced was what this section of the Continental Army should do next. They sat and looked at each other as if hoping the other person had the answer.

"What does your heart tell you James?" Bode finally asked his friend. James sat and tried to decipher what was happening and how to address it.

"I know what British rule looks and feels like. My father left the British army as a result of it and felt strongly about it, so much so that I know he is now fighting alongside the American Colonies against the British." He paused as he thought a moment. "We have both witnessed the arrogance of the Dutch, so there are no delusions there." He sat silently again. "If the British defeat the Dutch at Frederiksted, we would have more of an opportunity to organize and lead the Dutch population against the British. But I fear that the British would be a very powerful foe and would eventually overwhelm us should they secure Frederiksted and establish a physical presence here on St. Croix."

Bode commented, "After fighting them on the beach, I fear that if we wait for a battle between the British and the Dutch, even if the British defeat the Dutch army and take heavy losses, we will never drive the British from the island or have the equipment and cannon to lay siege to them should they take Frederiksted. They are too well trained and disciplined and we simply do not have the numbers." James nodded. He suddenly looked up at Bode as if he were struggling with something, but then looked away and shook his head.

"What is it?" Bode asked, trying to get his friend to share his thoughts.

"For now, we and the Dutch have a common enemy, the British. Instead of waiting to see who wins, perhaps the best plan would be to support the Dutch and attack the stronger British?" Bode thought through the idea before replying.

"Do we line up alongside them or fight independently?" Bode asked and it was James' turn to think through the options before answering.

"I don't think an additional 200 men in the Dutch line would be as effective as a second force of 200 men attacking the enemy's flank," James finally answered.

"Although I'm sure it would encourage the Dutch, I'd hate to have our men get into a musket for musket slugging match with the British and end up trapped at Frederiksted. If things go badly, I want the freedom to be able to withdraw back to Christiansted." James nodded in agreement.

They sent a runner back to Christiansted to provide Captain Donovan with updates on the movements of both the Dutch and the British forces. He also let Captain Donovan know that they intended to make contact with and offer to support the Dutch. James and Bode gathered the men together to explain their objectives and the role that the militia might play before they started their march west. As the men circled around, James could not get over how proud he was of these men. Although the two wounded Dragons were recovering at the fort, the remaining 48 Black Dragons assumed their leadership roles within the eight groups of twenty-five men. The Lizards looked to the Dragons much like a younger brother looks up to his older brother. Yet there was no arrogance among them; perhaps they saw an earlier version of themselves in the men they now oversaw. For every Dragon he could see there were three Lizards standing proudly near them at attention. Each man carried two muskets, one in his hand and the other slung over his shoulder.

James explained their situation, the officers' thoughts on the decision they had come to, and that the march would be a long one and they would more than likely be engaging the British at the end of the march, if not earlier. They would march with one group in the lead, and the rest would follow closely behind providing support and reducing the chance of being completely separated. They were going to follow one of the less-used roads and some paths that skirted the southern edge of the low range of hills that were northwest of Christiansted. They hoped to avoid encountering the Dutch army that would more than likely be traveling on the main roads leading across southern flat plains of the island. It would be more difficult traveling, but they wanted to remain hidden if possible. If they encountered any Dutch or British troops, the plan was to either overwhelm them, or slip around them and avoid detection. If they ran into the main force of either army, they were not to engage, but to withdraw immediately. James pointed out that since they only had three days of rations and the journey would take at least two days, the men were to forage, taking whatever food they found as they marched.

As they marched westward, Bode and James would alternate leading the advanced group. They would rotate groups to keep them fresh and rested as the lead group was often required to clear paths and be in a constant readiness for battle. Often the second group would encounter a cluster of freshly cut bananas or breadfruit along the path and they were to distribute the fruit to those who needed to eat or could carry additional weight in their packs.

The militia was only twelve miles from Frederiksted as the crow flies, but with the route they had chosen they would be hard pressed to cover eight of those miles in a day. They initially stayed near the coast so they could keep an eye on the ocean should the fleet return, but then cut inland as they passed just south of Salt River Bay and followed the Salt River upstream until it ended. They rested and ate quietly near the head of the river. The sound of cannon fire in the distance interrupted the repast. It seemed to be coming from the southwest, so Bode and James looked at their map of the island to determine what direction they should follow.

They decided to continue on due west along the mountains, as initially planned, to avoid the battle that was taking place in the open plains to their southwest. It was about four miles further, just after passing south of Bloe Mountain, that they found two separate signs of recent troop movement. The initial set of tracks they came across on a back trail, was a force they estimated at close to a hundred men moving quickly. They were not marching as regular British soldiers would, but moving quickly in a southeast direction. The second set of tracks they found on the main road. These were deep and numerous and were accompanied by deep wheel tracks cut into the road by the heavy artillery that the British had brought with them. James and Bode quickly concluded that the British must have attacked and taken the docks at Cane Bay late last night. They must have rapidly unloaded their army and cannon there, and then marched south via the main supply road using captured wagons and horse teams from the nearby plantations. His father had always told him that the British army was well practiced in securing needed supplies from unwilling locals. They decided to continue southwest, staying north of the cannon fire and avoiding the main road.

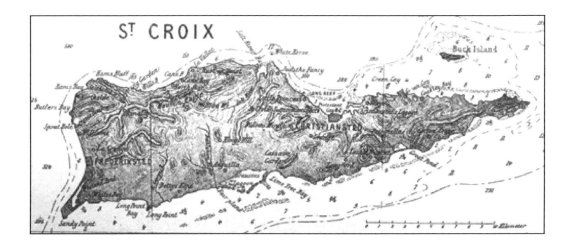

By late afternoon they had crossed the mountain ridge just north of the St. George River. From their vantage point they could see down into the flatlands below them and observe what was unfolding between the two armies. The British had arrived and positioned themselves in the flatlands before the Dutch army had reached the area; the result forced the Dutch to take up a defensive position on the small hill north of Betty's Hope. The British then moved, taking up positions in an attempt to encircle them from three sides, thereby holding and crushing the Dutch army between them. Their main force was west of the hill, while two smaller forces were encamped to the northeast and southeast of the ridge. That the Dutch had allowed themselves to become trapped in this way was beyond James' and Bode's understanding. They both knew that panic was a cause of many bad decisions, but the Dutch force, although in a good defensive position for a smaller force, was not in a spot that they could hold for a very long period nor could they easily retreat from it. They could see that the British were moving more of their artillery behind their main force, positioned to the west of the Dutch force, to bombard their defenses. They estimated at least ten artillery pieces were currently in place and being fired by the British.

As James and Bode looked around at their men, they could see that they were exhausted from the long and hard-pressed march to get here. They could see nothing that they could do this evening that would support the Dutch, so they decided to pull back a little further and set up defensive positions, watches and patrols and get what ever rest they might, recovering their energy while discussing a plan for the following day.

During the night, the British cannons continued a steady but light bombardment of the Dutch positions. James knew from what his father had taught them that they would keep up a steady bombardment through the night to keep the enemy from getting rest and to chisel away at their enemy's morale. Late into the evening, it sounded as if the Dutch had tried to withdraw from the hill but had encountered British defenders, as an exchange of musket fire could be heard for a brief period.

The plan of action was to march the militia down the west side of the St. George River while it was still dark and then cross over behind the main British force. They hoped to be able to make a quick surprise attack against the artillery crews, focusing on disabling the cannons and destroying their powder supplies, and then to withdraw back across the river.

Several hours before dawn, while it was still very dark, James and Bode assembled their men and outlined the plan they had put together, the options the men should be ready for, and the locations where they were to regroup should things go poorly. The first fallback plan was to regroup on the western side of the river where they had crossed. If that proved impossible, and the men were scattered, they were to work their way back to the hill on which they were camped and set up defensive positions until everyone who was able could make it back to that location. If all else failed, they were to make their way back to Christiansted to the east and rejoin the defenses at the fort. They all understood and moved south as a group until they encountered the head of the St. George River. They followed the tributary southeast until it once again turned south. They eventually came to a main road with a bridge that spanned the river, but they continued cross-country following the bank. The sun was pushing its way into the darkness, and they were able to move somewhat faster. The sound of the slow and steady firing of the British cannons made it easier for them to know how far south to travel before crossing the river. They did not plan on waiting near the river, but intended to attack immediately upon their arrival to avoid random detection. Concealing 200 men, even in a forest, was not an easy task.

The eight groups of twenty-five men moved forward in a line, picking up speed as they got closer to the cannons. Once they were as close as they could approach unseen, James halted the group and then crawled forward to take a quick survey of the forces before them. From his position, he could see that the British had set up their cannons in an open field about 200 yards behind their front lines. There were twelve cannons and, at this early hour, there were only four crews operating them. Fifteen yards behind the cannons were about a dozen wagons, loaded with shot and powder. There was a small group of tents fifty yards to the north of the guns and another small group to the south. There were open fields in front of the cannons that stretched all the way up to the hill where the Dutch were dug in. The main body of British regulars was positioned 200 yards west of the hill, well beyond the range of the Dutch muskets.

On his crawl back to the waiting men, James put together a plan that he hoped would be effective. He quickly presented it to Bode and the other group leaders. He assigned two groups to attack the British in the northern tents and two groups to attack those in the southern tents. The remaining four groups would initially attack the cannon crews, and then three groups were to move forward either to destroy the carriages and wheels of the cannons, or at least tip them over. They had only been able to form a few metal spikes from personal items to drive into the firing holes of the cannon, but knew that they could be removed with time and effort. Once the cannons had been spiked or taken out of action, they were to form a firing line and hold until the wagons were ready or a signal to retreat was given. The other group was to stay with the wagons and do whatever was necessary to destroy the supplies and powder in them. James warned them to make sure everyone was clear of the other wagons before setting fire to any of them.

The leaders signaled their men to follow them to their positions in the attack line and to check their loads and powder one more time. They rotated to their rifles with fixed bayonets and slung their spare over their shoulders. James was going to join the two groups attacking the northern tents; Robbie would lead the group against the southern tents, while Bode would direct the main group against the cannon crews and wagons. Once in place, they paused briefly and James looked across the line of men crouched low in the deep brush and waited for Bode to give the signal. Bode turned toward James after seeing Robbie's signal, his hand going up and pointing forward.

Almost on cue, one of the British cannons roared as it sent its projectile toward the Dutch lines and the Dragons moved forward in the gray half-light of the coming dawn. With as much silence as 200 men could manage, the militia pressed forward through the sparse brush border between the forest and the open grass area as they slowly made their way to the wagons and cannons.

They had covered half the distance when a British cannon crewmember, who was retrieving a barrel of powder from one of the wagons, looked up and saw the dark-skinned men, clad in gray, looking like wraiths hovering in the mist that made a thin layer over the grass. He seemed to freeze in place for a moment, then let out a yell as he turned and ran back toward the cannon crew. That was the signal for the Dragons to charge at full speed. James surged forward toward the tents and motioned for the men to follow. The men matched his speed. He could hear the sound of air rushing in and out as he breathed rapidly. He heard the sound of his and his men's feet impacting the ground, the rattle and shaking of each man's second musket, the slapping of belt pouches and backpacks as they ran. More warning cries came from the nearby cannon crews causing James to run harder to close the distance. The openings to the tents were facing east toward the Dutch lines. James saw the red, triangle-shaped hat of a soldier who was standing guard at the entrance of a larger tent who suddenly stepped to its edge and peered around it. The soldier's eyes went wide at the sight of James and his men bearing down on them and he turned back toward the front of the tent and disappeared. A musket shot rang out from James' right, then another. Now, a flurry of shots followed each single shot and James guessed that Bode and his men were now engaging any cannon crewmember who had chosen to stand and fight.

As he closed within fifteen yards of the center tent in which the soldier had disappeared into, James, wishing that it would not happen but seeing what he expected, saw the soldier exit the tent and move toward its side in order to get a clear shot. James debated whether to stop and fire or keep closing the distance to engage, but he kept charging, gaining speed, closing the distance faster. The soldier raised his rifle and took aim, but found that in his urgency or panic, he had not pulled the hammer back on his rifle. The moment that he took to lower the barrel and reach for the hammer was all the time James needed. He cleared the corner of the tent and impaled the soldier on the tip of his bayonet, the tip exiting out the man's back as he continued to push him backwards and onto the ground. James struggled to free his blade from the fallen man as another British soldier charged toward him from a tent to his left. He pulled one more time and the blade came free, but he was going to be to slow to raise the tip in time to stop the man. A second later the man's body convulsed as a musket shot, coming from behind James slammed into the British soldier, sending him to the ground in a crumpled heap. As his men dashed by him and around him, half dressed British soldiers stumbled out of their tents or struggled to stand up where they had lain sleeping during the night.

The flap on the tent the soldier had been guarding suddenly snapped open. The man who had opened the flap took a quick look at the surroundings and then locked eyes with James, who was standing in front of him. Although the man did not have his full uniform on, James recognized him instantly as the arrogant officer who had come ashore on the longboat when the British first arrived. Judging from the narrowing of his eyes and the way his upper lip curled up in a sneer, the British colonel also knew exactly who was standing in front of him. In a flash, James saw that he held a pistol in one hand and a cutlass in the other; James held his musket with both hands. The man glanced down at the weapon James held and then with a thin smile, started to raise his pistol toward James. James thought about trying to talk to him, but instead raised the tip of the musket and fired point blank at the man. In the moment of the aiming, James saw the dread in the man's eyes at the sudden realization that James' musket had not been fired. As his musket belched its fire and smoke and lead ball, the pistol also erupted sending the ball grazing past James' left arm at the shoulder. As the man tumbled back into the tent, James could feel the burning that the hot ball left on his upper arm. He glanced down briefly to see that it had torn away the light shoulder pad that had extended over his arms and left the wound exposed to the open air.

There was musket fire all around him now as his men engaged the British regulars. James realized that in his attempt to stay hidden, he had not seen or anticipated that the British soldiers who were not on the front line were sleeping on the ground in front of the tents. The number of soldiers they had attacked near the tents was a far larger group than they expected. He moved forward and caught up with his men who were now past the tents and pushing into the British troops that were trying desperately to organize a defensive line. The line held briefly, but then faltered and the men fled eastward toward their front lines facing the Dutch.

"Stand and reload!" James yelled as he took the same moment to reload his used musket. Reloading was something that he could almost do with his eyes closed, so the low light of the morning did not impede his speed. As he loaded, he watched his men fall back to the line he had formed and begin reloading their weapons. He saw two Lizards lying still on the ground in the grassy area in front of him. There appeared to be at least forty to fifty British soldiers lying next to them and all around, and James tried to convince himself that their surprise had been costly to the British, even though he could not take his eyes off the two Lizards laying on the ground in front of him. There were also British muskets laying on the ground everywhere, most leaning against each other where they had been placed the previous evening.

He glanced across the field to where the retreating soldiers were running and saw that the British soldiers who were facing the Dutch lines, several hundred yards away, were now standing and turning toward them. James finished loading his musket and swapped it with his long rifle musket, sending pain down his arm as the strap dragged across his wound. James could hear musket fire coming from their right, mostly further down where Robbie and his men were. He wondered if they had encountered the same mass of sleeping soldiers as James' group had, and if so, how well they were faring against them. James glanced to his far right and saw that Bode and his men had cleared or run off the cannon crews and was doing their best to dispose of the cannons as quickly as they could. He could see the men with the wagons were also busy doing whatever plan they had in mind to destroy the wagons and supplies.

James' ears caught a strange sound. At first it seemed like the sound of the wind, but then it grew in volume and finally, it became clear what the sound was. It was cheering and it was coming from the Dutch soldiers on the low hill to the east of them. James could see the front lines of Dutch waving hats and raising their muskets above their heads. He glanced down at the growing number of British soldiers who were forming into firing lines before them. James knew that they were too far away to fire an effective volley, but he also knew that the same was true for them and he was willing to wait as long as they were. Although breathing heavily, his men had formed in a line and were waiting for orders.

"Black Dragons!" he yelled and they yelled the name back. He yelled it again and it was returned not only from them, but also from the men with Bode and further down the line with Robbie. He even thought he also heard the name being shouted from the Dutch lines.

As the minutes passed without an attack from the British, James sent men forward to check on the two Lizards that were lying in the field in front of them. As the men returned, they confirmed that they were both dead. The sound of the wounded and dying British soldiers began to work its way into his James' consciousness. He sent five men forward to do what they could to help the wounded British, either to stop the bleeding or make them more comfortable in their passing. As they helped the men, James continued to watch the soldiers lining up across the open field between them. He counted at least 300 British soldiers across from them. They were waiting for the Black Dragons to attack, but there was no way he was going to lead his men into that deadly wall of musket fire. So they just stared at each other without moving or firing.

Glancing again to his right, James saw that the wheels on the cannons had been removed, or the spokes broken, and the cannons tossed onto the ground and filled with dirt. All the support tools and rods had also been destroyed. The wagons and barrels of powder and shot were now exposed and men were waiting nearby for orders to set fire to them. They had accomplished their goals for the day, but they were not sure what to do next. He knew if enough time passed the other British forces to the north and south would be able to circle around to flank them, or reinforce the forces in front of them.

The officer leading the Dutch troops must have come to the same conclusion as James saw the Dutch soldiers leaving their positions and forming up in lines preparing to attack. The British also realized what was happening behind them and the lead officer ordered half of their forces to turn to face the Dutch. James could see additional Dutch soldiers coming in from the other sides of the hill where they had been positioned to join the ranks of troops facing the British soldiers now caught between their two forces. Moments later the Dutch began marching at first slowly down the hillside toward the British line. In response, James, Bode and Robbie moved their men forward toward the British, keeping the full compliment of the

British muskets divided between the two approaching armies. As the Dutch forces came within musket range, they suddenly charged toward the British line. James immediately ordered the Dragons to fire their muskets into the British line before the Dutch arrived. In firing early, he hoped to not only inflict casualties with the British, but to avoid causing any Dutch casualties.

The men of the militia took aim and fired. Simultaneously the one 150 British soldiers facing east fired into the Dutch soldiers charging down the hillside. The smoke from their own muskets was slowly carried by the wind back toward the militia, blocking the soldier's ability to see the results of their volley. James was waiting for the horrible sounds of the British musket balls passing by, or worse, the feeling of one smashing into his body, but none came. As the smoke cleared, James could see the British that had been facing them had been ordered to turn to repel the Dutch charge from the east. The smoke from the British muskets hung in the air all around their men, but he could see that their volley, even at this distance, had done some damage to the British line and also created some chaos. Moments later the sound of men yelling and muskets being fired could be heard just beyond the British line of fading smoke.

The charging line of Dutch soldiers fired their muskets as they slammed into the waiting line of British soldiers and James could see and hear the impact of the charge. The British line held at first as the second line of soldiers, who had been facing the Dragons moments earlier, released their volley into the Dutch. James did not intend to see any of his men struck by British fire, let alone from friendly fire or a Dutch bayonet, so he ordered them to hold back and reload. He did lead them in a cheer of "Black Dragons!" It was only moments later that the larger number of Dutch soldiers began pushing the British line back in sections and working their way behind the remaining British soldiers. Then the British line collapsed and the men began fleeing north and south away from the Dutch and avoiding the Black Dragons behind them.

The Dutch soldiers at first began to pursue the fleeing British, but orders were given and men began to pull back and reform in the field in front of the destroyed cannons. James, Bode and Robbie had their men maintain their line as the Dutch gathered their wounded and formed up in front of them. A Dutch officer, bleeding from a wound in his thigh, stepped through the Dutch line to observe the line of Black Dragons. He limped forward with two other Dutch soldiers and seeing James, he veered off toward him. As the officer got closer, James recognized him as the Dutch colonel who had given them two days to leave Christiansted and the fort. He remembered the man as being honorable and gracious, not arrogant or overbearing, during the discussion. As he limped up to where James stood, he smiled briefly, started to speak, hesitated, and then continued.

"I'm trying to make sense of this moment and the right words to use," he said to James. "Our situation was desperate and your arrival was, well, unexpected." He took a moment before continuing. "But very much appreciated - coming from an enemy that is," he concluded and smiled.

"Is that what we still are?" James asked with a faint smile.

"I should hope not, Captain," he replied and waited for some sign from James. James smiled and shook his head as he looked to his left and right.

"Colonel, I feel we have opened the door only briefly for you and your men to get to Frederiksted, so I would suggest moving quickly to stay in front of the British before they have a chance to reform their ranks, or the other two groups join them. I'm not sure how much more assistance we can offer, but we will try to delay them or at least harass them along the way should they choose to follow you," James offered. The colonel seemed to disbelieve James' offer as James continued. "They will have a difficult time laying siege to the city without cannons to use, so that should even the odds considerably." James then turned toward the wagons. "If your men are low on powder or shot, I would suggest taking what you need from the wagons before we burn them."

"I am grateful for your generous offer," the Colonel replied and spoke briefly to one of the men next to him, who turned and headed back toward their line calling out orders. The Dutch forces seemed to move as one forward toward the line of Black Dragons and the wagons, while James sent a runner to Bode to instruct him to dole out the powder to the Dutch at their direction.

As the Dutch passed by the line of Black Dragons, there were smiles, nods, and many a "thank you" expressed to them. James watched as more and more Dutch soldiers were coming down the hillside to join their comrades marching westward, many carrying their wounded and spare British muskets. The Dutch colonel at first stood silently beside James as his men and wounded passed by, but then broke the silence.

"I received word that the British have an additional force of 300 laying siege to the city, though they have limited cannon at this point and I do not see them bringing any more up soon. We also have a second smaller force of 200 men to the east guarding our cannons and supplies. When we were surprised by the British troops, I sent orders for them not to follow or come to our aid, but instead to take up defensive positions on Kings Hill. I did not want those cannons to fall into the British hands," the Colonel concluded and James once again just nodded, not sure how best to handle this new relationship with a former enemy who was being very open with their military information.

"You've had a great deal more time to evaluate and estimate the strength of the British forces here; what have you learned?" James asked and the colonel responded without hesitating this time. "I believe they had close to 450 soldiers, counting the cannon crews positioned here. They have another force of 200 or so to the northeast and a similar sized force to the southeast of the hill," the Colonel replied. "In our haste to get back to Frederiksted, I carelessly marched our lead group right into their trap. In chaos, we withdrew to the hill to regroup and they quickly encircled us."

"Then based on their casualties, those three combined groups have around 500 or more remaining soldiers," James calculated as he was thinking and the Colonel nodded. "So what's your plan, Colonel?" James asked. The Colonel hesitated again as he considered the situation and then exhaled as if he were resolved.

"Our forces at Frederiksted are thin, as we marched the majority to Christiansted, so we will need to return to engage and drive off the 300 British there. Then our plan is to reinforce the city and wait," he responded. James nodded and tried to read his face, as one of the words he used stood out.

"Wait? So you have help coming?" James asked the uncomfortable question. The man at first seemed to resist the question, but then nodded.

"The remainder of the trade fleet will be passing through here in less than two weeks on their way back home. We were to have secured Christiansted and all the island harvest and production by the time they arrived. We obviously did not count on the British arriving."

"Nor did we, or I should say, as an enemy looking to put my men and I in chains. The American colonies have declared independence of England and they- we are now at war." James said, his frustration evident. "So the trade fleet will be bringing more troops to reinforce you?" James asked, knowing that the response would have more than just repercussions for the British. The colonel again hesitated.

"No, Captain, but with those two British warships burning in your harbor, they will have enough warships to drive off the British fleet anchored to our north." James nodded and then raised an eyebrow.

"My harbor?" he replied. The colonel seemed to have missed the word he had used in the exchange and smiled.

"Well, for now." He grinned. "We'll talk more on it once the British are gone."

"Talk is good," James replied and returned the grin. They shook hands and wished each other the best in the coming days looking forward to their next meeting.

James visited the tent of the British Colonel. Stepping over his body, he saw a disheveled cot, a small desk, a footlocker, and a uniform hanging from a peg on one of the tent posts. He walked to the desk and saw various papers and orders and a small map of the island. He gathered the various items and papers and placed them in a leather carrying case that was hanging from the desk. He placed it over his right shoulder, avoiding the wound on his left. As he was leaving the tent, he saw a leather cylinder peeking out from under a blanket on the cot. He stopped and pulled back the blanket to reveal a long leather tube with a shoulder strap and a cap on one end. As he picked it up and opened the cap, he saw the glass circle of the end of a bronze telescope. He smiled and put the cap back on the tube and swung it over his shoulder. Turning toward the exit, he hesitated briefly as he reached down and picked up the recently fired pistol lying next to the man's right hand. It was an incredibly crafted pistol, with beautiful engravings, silver plating and mahogany wood handle and stock. As he picked it up, he felt the fine balance of the weapon and slid it into his belt.

"Spoils of war," he mumbled as he stepped back over the body of the man and left the tent. As he stepped through the tent flap and into the sunlight, he thought about taking a moment to either bury or cover the man's body, but he decided it was best to leave things as they were.

As the Dutch forces marched past, James knew that Bode was calculating troop strengths and assumed the Dutch colonel was doing the same. James took a moment to evaluate their condition as a fighting force. James had lost two men and several wounded who could travel. Bode had only three wounded as the majority of the cannon crews had run the moment the Dragons charged toward them. Robbie had experienced the same miscalculation as James and had to engage a larger group of British soldiers than expected. They had put up a heavier resistance. Robbie had lost five men and had eleven wounded, five of whom could not travel on their own. Robbie was one of the walking wounded and had sustained a bayonet wound to his upper right shoulder. He could not use his arm or fire a musket, but he said he could still use a pistol in his left hand. James' heart ached at the thought of five more men being killed during the attack.

They carried the seven dead Dragon soldiers to the edge of the woods where they concealed their bodies under the brush as best they could, with the plan to return at a later date to bury them. The Dragons, carrying their five wounded who could not walk, followed the rear guard of the Dutch army as it headed into the low brush and woods to their west, hesitating only briefly to light the line of black powder leading back to the waiting wagons and then running as fast as they could away from it. The sound of the powder in the wagons exploding was deafening and James felt the concussion of each one as one by one they exploded.

They followed the Dutch until they crossed the St. George River, then turned right and headed back toward their original position on the hill that overlooked the flatlands below. They rested, treated their wounded, including James' shoulder. From their concealed vantage point, James and Bode took turns looking through the captured telescope and watching the British forces reforming in the flatlands below. They agreed that it was a better telescope than Captain Donovan's and they smiled at the idea of making sure Captain Donovan knew that fact at every opportunity once they got back.

They watched the British below whom, to their surprise, did not seem to be in any hurry to pursue the fleeing Dutch. Instead, they spent a great deal of time surveying the battlefield and the damaged cannons, and then setting up defensive positions. They gathered and buried their dead and set up a field hospital to treat their wounded. Had they lost their will to fight, James wondered or perhaps losing their leadership had brought them to a halt? They did not seem to have a plan, but the enlisted soldiers' excellent training enabled them to operate effectively in spite of an apparent lack of leadership. James' greatest concern was that there was another strategy unfolding that he could not figure out, perhaps one that involved the British turning east and heading toward Christiansted, with the knowledge that a large force of Black Dragons was no longer defending the city.

While Robbie rested, James and Body discussed their next course of action. They knew the Dutch were marching west with over 400 men to relieve the city, and had another 200 encamped on Kings Hill to the east. If the British forces withdrew from Frederiksted before the Dutch arrived, that would mean that the British could muster over 800 soldiers to use as needed against either force. It was the danger from the British cannons that worried both James and Bode the most. They knew the British would have more powder and shot on the ships, but how many more field cannons they held in reserve that had either not been unloaded, or were waiting on the captured docks to their north was a question that could tip the scales in an attack.

Assuming that the British did have more cannons in reserve, James and Bode knew they would eventually bring them down the main supply road to deliver them to their forces. They also guessed that if they were sent forward, they would be a heavily protected resource now that there were so few of them. As they waited and rested on the hill, they did their best to treat the wounded, but in spite of their best efforts, one of their more severely wounded men died from the musket wound he had received to his stomach. It was a hard thing for the men to see and hear and a quiet fell over them. Robbie took it very hard. They had now lost eight men. Seeing another of their men die, James felt the urgency of getting the remaining wounded back to the city for treatment pulling at him. However, he also remembered his father telling him moving the severely wounded could prove more dangerous to them. They debated marching the entire force back to the city, dropping off the wounded, regrouping and then coming back, but they knew they would then lose sight of the British and any chance of knowing where they might be heading next. It was Robbie, who had overheard James and Bode talking, who offered the idea that they ultimately chose.

They would march further back into the mountains from their current position and set up a small defensive base where they would leave one group of twenty-five, which would include the wounded, to guard the area. This would allow the wounded to rest and heal, while allowing James and Bode to utilize the remaining seven groups without being slowed by having to carry the wounded. James argued for leaving one or two additional groups to stay with the one base group, but Robbie felt that the main force should be as strong as possible. Robbie's view won out in the end, so they spent the next hour finding the most secure and easily defended position in the area, and then they moved the wounded there and helped set up the defenses for them. Robbie actually seemed happy not to be traveling, as it was clear that his shoulder wound was very painful.

Once they felt the position was as secure as possible, James and Bode mumbled a few words of encouragement and warnings to Robbie and then turned to leave. James suddenly stopped and looked at Robbie, at his right arm hanging in a sling. He reached into his belt and withdrew the British colonel's pistol and handed it to Robbie.

"Don't lose this; its loaded," he said as Robbie stared in disbelief at the pistol held out to him. "It's just for show, probably doesn't even fire," James commented as Robbie finally reached out and took the handle of the pistol. He felt the weight and balance and knew James was joking.

"Thanks James, I'll give it back to you later," he promised and James shook his head.

"No, you keep it. You've earned it," he replied and then smiled. "Be safe." He turned to leave with Bode. As they walked down the path toward their waiting men, Bode mumbled under his breath. "You're getting soft in your old age." James just nodded his head.

Chapter 19

They marched back to the secluded hill where they could observe the British forces that had camped in the flatlands below. In the distance, James could see a great deal of smoke coming from the south, but even with the telescope, they could not tell what was burning that was causing the thick smoke. In looking at their map and the captured British map, they knew that Betty's Hope, one of the largest plantations on the island, was located in that direction. They saw that not all of the smoke was coming from the south, but some was also blowing in from the east. As they checked their maps, they saw that another major plantation, Anguilla, was located four miles to the east of Betty's Hope. They continued to observe the clouds of smoke as they drifted westward.

"Would the British burn the plantations?" Bode asked as he looked through the telescope. James just shrugged his shoulders and shook his head as Bode lowered the telescope and glanced toward him for the answer.

"What would they gain by doing so?" was all James could think to say in response.

Two hours later, just after noon, they observed a small force of ten men, who appeared to be British soldiers, enter the British camp, followed a short time later by a larger force of soldiers. Neither group marched after the fashion of British regulars, but instead almost flowed into the camp like water, gathering off to the side of the camp. James immediately recognized the nationality of the smaller group, and thought that he could guess the nationality of the larger group of soldiers as well. The smaller group was North American Indians, scouts more than likely. The larger group, that flowed behind them with almost the same grace and showing the same confidence as the Indians were German Jaegers.

They were not the German Hessian troops that were of similar training as the British soldiers. James remembered his father telling him of a type of highly trained and deadly German soldier called Jaegers. They were ferocious, deadly soldiers who were excellent shots with a musket and traveled very quickly. The British would use Indian and Jaeger soldiers as scouts to go behind enemy lines to inflict terror on the populace. Where the British soldier was bound to give quarter and to remain above committing such atrocities in war, they gave free reign to their Indian and Jaeger allies. They were made up of woodsman and hunters from Germany who were trained and specialized in deadly hit and run tactics and instilling terror in the local population. To see that the two of them were working together made James' stomach knot up as he handed the telescope to Bode. It only took a moment for Bode to also grasp how dangerous this new enemy that they were watching was.

They spent the better part of an hour trying to count their numbers as they watched from their vantage point, but small groups of the new enemy were frequently coming and going making it difficult to get an accurate count. They eventually estimated their numbers to be from between 75-100 mercenaries. At the end of the hour, the mercenary force began moving west toward Frederiksted, disappearing into the tree line. James and Bode concluded that the British army's mercenary allies were raiding and burning the plantations in the area. James and Bode wondered if there were additional mercenary forces moving east toward Christiansted, burning and pillaging as they went.

They talked about strategies for protecting the plantations from this new, unpredictable and extremely dangerous threat. They knew they did not have enough men to protect every major plantation between here and Christiansted, nor did want to spread their men so thin that they could be easily overrun. They decided the best approach would be to travel as a group eastward and warn each plantation along the way, offering to escort the families and workers back to Christiansted. They would try to defend only the three plantations that had joined them prior to the battle, leaving two groups of twenty-five at each location. The British cannons would have to wait.

They informed the men of their new enemy and the sudden change in plans, and then headed back toward Robbie and the base camp. They had marched deep into the mountains and were very near to where the base camp was located when suddenly, one of the lead Dragons held up a fist and the Dragons froze mid-step. James moved forward. The troops took up defensive positions, peering into the trees around them. As James moved toward the front, he saw the look on the soldier's face and knew it meant trouble. The man was pointing worriedly down at the ground where the trail had headed toward the camp. There were many tracks heading up the hill toward the camp, tracks that were on top of their tracks left when they had headed down the hill earlier that day. They were not heavy British boots, but a lighter version that he knew was from the Jaegers. The Indian scouts had tracked them to their mountain positions and the Jaegers had followed close behind them, skirting around their main group and finding the tracks leading to the other camp. James turned toward Bode and gave him a signal that danger was present and close by.

With a few brief signals, the various groups quickly moved into full defensive positions, checking their powder and muskets to make sure it was dry and ready. Everything in him yelled to charge up the remaining half mile of the hill to where Robbie and the other men were positioned, but he knew that the mercenaries they faced were not only aware of them, but were probably watching them right now. Bode took two groups to the right side of the ridge; James motioned for William, one of the other group leaders to take his group and what had been Robbie's group to the left side of the ridge line. James and his three groups would hold the top of the ridge and support each side as needed. As the lower groups cautiously moved forward, James motioned his men forward.

They had covered about 300 yards when they heard the first musket shots being fired up the hill from where Robbie and the other men were. He wanted to run toward them, but knew he had to prevent his men from falling into a trap he knew was waiting for them. Remembering James' father's words of warning, James motioned for one of his three groups to face their rear area as they moved forward, telling them to watch for and prepare for attacks from behind.

They pushed forward a little faster in surges and stops, as the men would leap-frog past each other, moving quickly through the foliage. The amount of musket fire was increasing as they continued to move forward toward the sounds of battle. The first shot that was fired nearby came from the right side, down below the advancing men. The shot was quickly followed by the rumble of several more shots, emanating slightly to the front of Bode's group. The trap, that they had anticipated, had been sprung and the only thing left now was to determine how deadly it was and how far into it they had fallen.

Moments later a dozen or so muskets were also fired from the tree line in front of his group, striking several of the soldiers nearby and tumbling them backwards or spinning them around from the impact. The familiar "zipping" sound of musket balls flying past or ripping through branches and leaves forced James to duck behind a tree.

"Dragons... Charge!" he yelled as he stepped from behind the tree trunk and charged forward, weaving across the area between him and where the muskets had been fired from 40 yards away. He could hear and see on both sides other Dragons charging forward with their muskets out and bayonets pointed forward, yelling every step of the way. They had only covered half the ground when he saw the first of the mercenaries, who, it appeared, were not expecting the charge and were in the process of reloading. They suddenly turned and ran away from the mass of oncoming Black Dragons. James saw several more begin to retreat as the Dragons closed with them. James kept urging the men forward after the fleeing mercenaries.

James' mind was racing as he tried to keep up with the Jaeger mercenary in front of him; and he tried to take stock of their situation. If there were roughly 30 engaging them here, then that meant the majority of the mercenary force was attacking Robbie's group. He pushed himself to run faster but could not close the distance between him and the foe, who was staying ten yards in front of him. He was so focused on the mercenary in front of him and avoiding the branches whipping past him that he nearly missed seeing the mercenary step out and swing his long thin dirk at his throat; he managed to duck his head below the swing at the last moment. He stopped his forward momentum and tried to spin his long musket around in time but it caught in the thick brush. The enemy recovered his balance after missing the axe swing faster than James would have imagined possible. With the musket still caught, James' right hand found the handle of his pistol as the mercenary's own right arm, raised holding the long knife pointed down towards James. Suddenly the mercenary's eyes widened and he stumbled forward awkwardly, trying to reach behind him, but he could only fall forward as the momentum of the charging Black Dragon thrusting his bayonet into him from behind carried him forward and onto the ground in front of James. James nodded at the wild-eyed Dragon soldier, turned, and continued forward toward the base camp, where he knew Robbie's group was fighting.

James found, that after having to stop and engage the German mercenary who had attacked him, he was no longer leading the charge, but instead was in the middle of it as they came into the area just below where Robbie's group was defending. He could see that there were Jaeger soldiers all around and mixed within their group. Having discovered that they were now pressed between two groups on either side of the ridge and the groups from the rear driving up the center, the Jaegers turned and engaged the Dragon soldiers directly. What they did not expect and too late discovered was that their first encounter with a Dragon proved deadly. True to their training, the militia had not fired their volley and then charged, as was the common military practice, but refrained from firing and charged directly after the enemy had fired their first volley. As the mercenaries tried to close with the Dragon soldiers, most were hit by a .75 caliber musket ball, while still at this distance of ten feet away. As James ran past one Dragon who had fired into a charging warrior, he saw the man stop and begin to reload.

"No time, move forward, Dragon," he yelled over the din and the man checked his action and stepped in behind James as he weaved his way through the foliage. Fifteen feet in front of him, James saw three mercenary soldiers converging from several different directions on a Dragon who had just killed his opponent. James charged past the Dragon, firing his musket into the closest warrior, tumbling the man backwards from the impact of the musket ball. James then thrust his bayonet into the next closest mercenary, stopping his forward momentum as they came together. The shocked mercenary tried to swing his axe at James with one hand while holding onto the musket barrel that was attached to the bayonet that was lodged in his chest with his other hand. James responded by shoving the musket and the man impaled on the end of it forward, pushing the mercenary outside the reach of the dying mercenary's deadly weapon. James could see that the third mercenary had closed on the Dragon soldier and that the young man, who was scarcely more than a boy, was hard pressed to match the skills of the Jaeger mercenary. He awkwardly backed up trying to keep his bayonet between him and the mercenary. The boy's ankle caught on some brush and he fell backwards. James did not wait to see the inevitable outcome; he drew his pistol and shot the mercenary just as he leaped toward the boy. The mercenary tumbled to the side of the boy as the musket ball struck him in the center of his back. James tucked the pistol back in his belt and turned back toward the base camp, stopping only briefly to pull his bayonet tipped musket from the dead mercenary's chest. *"We take care of each other,"* he spoke softly as he smiled at the young man.

A loud cry arose from in front of him and James looked through the trees on the battleground and saw the Jaeger leader yelling and waving at his men. James stopped his movement, dropped his empty musket and slid his long rifle off his shoulder. As he cocked the hammer and raised it to fire, he could see that what remained of the Jaeger and Indian scouts were leaving the field of battle at a full run now that the three parts of the Dragon's main force had met in the middle. James' aim followed the Jaeger leader as he moved across the battleground through the trees. The man's speed and switching of directions made it impossible to acquire him as a target and James started to lower his musket. In his arrogance, the mercenary leader made one error in his retreat. As what remained of his men withdrew down the ridgeline, he stopped and turned to give a defiant battle cry back toward the Black Dragons. It was all the time and opportunity that James needed. The musket ball struck the Jaeger leader in his upper right chest, changing the battle cry into a loud grunt, sending him tumbling backwards down the ravine where the rest of his men had fled. James did not wait to see if the man got back up; he turned and ran toward the defensive positions where he knew Robbie and his men were.

James jumped and ran across the terrain, stepping over a small group of dead mercenary soldiers that lay along the path to the edge of the defenses. James leapt over the outer defenses and into the defensive area. He froze where he landed. His heart sank in his chest and he cried out loud.

"No! No, No," he mumbled and let the words fade as he moved from one body to the next, looking for signs of life from the men who had held these positions moments ago. He saw that, not only were the wounds they had received deadly, they were an abomination. The bodies appeared to have been purposely desecrated after they were dead. James had seen death before, but never like this, especially not to anyone who was so close to him. He looked down and saw the bloody hand that still held the recently fired pistol, the brass and mahogany wood was now covered with blood. James recognized the uniform and the insignia on the shoulder, but he could no longer recognize the face of his good friend. He reached down and touched Robbie's chest and found no heartbeat. Without any control or restraint, he leaned over and vomited as the tears flowed down his face.

It was not until several minutes later that he was able to control himself and even then it was only because Bode had arrived, and sat down and wept a moment with him, before eventually standing up.

"James, our grieving will need to wait. They will more than likely be bringing the British back with them, if they are not already marching this way." He waited for James to rise to his feet. James looked around at the men who seemed to all be in mourning over a friend and looking to James and Bode for guidance. James knew Bode was right, but it did not make the pain in his heart go away.

They gave the command to reload their weapons, and then he asked the group leaders to take a quick survey of their casualties and group's condition. As the groups were determining their condition, James and Bode walked through the area, trying to understand how the battle had unfolded for those at the base camp. Based on the dead of the enemy, their main force had come up the ridgeline, attempting to swarm the defenders. Robbie and the men had inflicted heavy casualties on the attackers; the dead mercenary soldiers were thickest in front of the ridge defenses. A smaller group of attackers had managed to climb the ridgeline and attack from behind. Once they had broken into the perimeter, and past their muskets, it would have turned into a hand-to-hand battle, where the Jaeger soldiers had the advantage. To a man, Robbie and his group had been killed, even the defenseless wounded. They had been too late to save them. Fortunately, they had arrived soon enough to prevent the mercenary forces from setting up defensive positions. James' decision to split the group and send forces along the right and left side of the ridgeline saved many lives. It had caused the smaller force of mercenary soldiers, sent to delay their group, to withdraw toward the base camp. Trapped between the two sides, they had tried to force their way through the middle, along the ridgeline, where James and his groups drove back their initial attack, forcing those mercenaries that survived to flee down the steep left ridgeline.

Counting the 25 men in Robbie's group, they now had 37 dead and 31 wounded or currently missing, 13 were unable to travel. James felt the pressure of the growing number of dead filling his mind and rattling his confidence. The fact that they had inflicted three times the casualties on their enemy did not take away the sting of the loss, although it did make him proud of his men.

Once they had moved the wounded into the defensive perimeter, James took a moment to survey the dead mercenary attackers. As he looked at the body of the first mercenary he came to, James reached down and picked up the dead soldiers musket. He then looked around at the other muskets that the mercenary soldiers had carried. They were long rifles. He sent the group that had taken up the rear position on the attack, to traverse back down the ridgeline and gather the dead and wounded, and any Dragon muskets, but he also gave instructions for them to bring back all of the mercenary muskets and search the bodies of the fallen for powder and shot.

James next ordered those nearby who were not tending to the wounded to gather all of the mercenary muskets within the perimeter and near the defense barricades and bring them and any shot and powder back to the base camp area. As the muskets, shot and powder were brought in and placed on the ground near him, James had the Dragons begin loading those muskets also. As they loaded them, they counted ninety-seven long rifle muskets, including the muskets carried by the dead Dragons. James determined that Robbie and his men accounted for the deaths of almost fifty of those mercenaries and the rest died at the hands of James' and Bode's men. James hoped that they had destroyed enough of the mercenary force that it would no longer pose a threat to the civilians.

James and Bode discussed various plans and ideas on how to best lead their men from their current location. If they left immediately, carrying their wounded, they could head down the eastern ridgeline toward Christiansted, but with Indian trackers working with the British army, they would very quickly identify the direction the Dragons were moving and would attempt to get in front of them, preventing them from reaching the fort. Even if the trackers were unable to pass them, chances were good that the British would catch up to them due to slower progress caused by carrying their wounded. They would be forced either to make a defensive stand in a place not of their choosing or to fight a slow retreating battle against a much larger force. Both options meant the deaths of many of their soldiers and they eventually would have to flee the battle, leaving their wounded behind, or be killed by overwhelming numbers while trying to defend them.

Remembering how they treated Robbie and his men when they overran their positions, he was deeply concerned that they would all face a similar fate if captured by the British. The militia had inflicted too much damage on the pride of the British, let alone casualties, to be shown mercy. That left them with one option, one that they both agreed, to stand and fight. The recent battle demonstrated how deadly it had been for the enemy to attack this position. A small force had exacted twice its number before being overrun. They would make their stand here where they could inflict the most damage on the British. Bode ordered three patrols to watch the ridgeline and the two sides leading up to where the base camp was, with orders to withdraw to the base camp once the enemy was sighted.

As James and Bode surveyed the field of fire around the base camp, they knew the greatest challenge they faced was the lack of protective cover for the men. As gruesome as it was, James ordered the bodies of the dead mercenary soldiers to be dragged to specific areas of the base camp and used either to strengthen the current natural defenses, or to create new defensive positions in key areas. Learning from the previous battle, they also positioned additional troops on the backside of the base camp.

The men completed the work on their defenses and James and Bode finished the placement of the men. A quiet came over the men. James picked up one of the long rifle muskets taken from the mercenaries, walked to the center of the area and stood on a stump.

"The enemies you just defeated are thought to be the most feared and best trained fighters in Europe and the New World," James shouted so all could hear. "But those thoughts have now been proven wrong. Now, the Black Dragons are the most feared and best-trained soldiers in Europe and the New World. And when we drive the remaining British from this island, they will carry fearful and terrible stories about us with them, striking fear into all future enemies who would consider raising arms against us." The men smiled and grunted. James held the musket up high for the men to see. "Because you have proven yourselves in battle and have defeated this fearful enemy, you are no longer Black Lizards, but Black Dragons, and you will now also carry the weapon of the Black Dragon!" James shouted. He had the Black Dragon soldiers present the long rifles to the men with them. A proud rumble went through the troops as they were presented with their new long rifle.

"You are all familiar with the long rifle and have watched your fellow Black Dragons carry and use such a weapon with deadly results. You know they shoot further and more accurately than the British or Dutch musket by thirty yards or more. When battle comes, they are to be used as your first and primary weapon, enabling you to inflict casualties on our enemy before you are within their range." They held their rifles and practiced aiming them. "When your enemy is at 130 yards, simply aim one foot higher above your mark than you would at 100 yards, a foot and a half for 150 yards, and two feet for 175 yards, which is the maximum effective range for this musket."

As they waited and rested, the men gathered the food and axes from the enemies' bodies and they did their best to remove their dead and place them away from the base camp. As they sat and waited, James sent two full groups out with the captured axes: one cleared the brush away from their field of fire in front of their positions, while the other group moved forward a 100 yards and took up positions with their long rifles in case the enemy cane into range. They knew the remaining Indian scouts and Jaegers could still be out there, but they wanted to keep them as far away as possible and make sure they did not have the opportunity to shoot any Dragons from concealed positions. They stacked the brush in front of their defensive positions, creating a tangled mess of sticks and branches that would be an effective barrier against attackers, while still keeping the Dragons field of fire open. Then they waited and James, slowly and purposefully, loaded a pistol, its silver and mahogany handle stained dark red with the dried blood of his friend.

A British soldier with all his gear was noisy enough, but when hundreds of them marched together, the sound was as if someone was banging pots together. The noise was so loud that advanced Dragon patrols pulled back long before they saw the British lines marching toward them along the ridgeline. The clearing crews and their protective guards were also pulled back to the camp, each new arrival taking up their positions. With their captured axes, they had been able to clear away most of the smaller underbrush along the ridgeline and remove the lower branches of the trees as high as they could reach. There were still areas that offered some concealment along the sides of the ridgeline, but there was now very little protective cover for the advancing soldiers in the hundred yards surrounding the perimeter.

They could see the red coats of the British soldiers pushing through the tree line along the ridge and an occasional Indian scout with their brown vests and muskets moving in front of them. The noise grew louder and louder as more and more troops filled in the blank spaces along the ridgeline and then filed in behind those already standing there. Gradually, the noise began to fade into a random rattle, cough or distant voice from the British lines. One thing was for sure: there were a large number of them. It appeared to James that they had brought all 500 soldiers who were in the flatlands with them.

As the two sides waited, James could hear the sound of troops moving and probing along the side of the ridgeline. He knew that the steep angle on the right side approach would prevent a direct attack from there, but the left side approach was vulnerable. Although it would be a steep climb, an attack from that side could be accomplished. The easiest and most direct approach, though, was along the ridgeline, but it was also the most deadly for an attacker.

The British seemed to be wrestling with the same dilemma, as they continued to probe the sides of the ridgeline, withdrawing as a Dragon long rifle would bring down an approaching British scout or patrol. James and Bode did their best to keep the men hidden from sight to avoid the enemies' determining the numbers at each defensive position. James was so glad that the British did not have any cannon to use against them. The small trail with its steep climb would have made it too difficult to bring a cannon, had they been able to repair one of the damaged ones. Keeping low and under the cover of the piles of brush, James and Bode moved back and forth between the groups of men evaluating their defenses again and again as the British awaited their orders. In addition to the long rifles they held pointed toward the British lines, they both made sure that most of the men had two additional muskets loaded and ready lying next to them. James had felt very concerned about having to stand and fight with no real chance for retreat. After the loss of Robbie and his men, he was determined to avoid leaving any men isolated again. Even though it had been Robbie's suggestion to split the men, James felt personally responsible for their deaths.

The standoff continued through the late afternoon as the British tried to determine how best to attack the base. The Indian scouts and Jaeger soldiers would continually cry out in a chilling high pitched scream from different locations around the base camp, trying to rattle the nerves of the men. As the sun sank lower in the sky, they discussed how to best defend against a night attack. They knew that, although it was not impossible, it would be a very difficult and noisy for the British to march across the ridgeline at night, let alone charge across the open area. A slow march meant plenty of opportunities to fire into their ranks, a fast charge meant soldiers tripping, falling and general chaos while trying to direct an army. The British came to the same conclusion and decided to split the difference.

Just after sunset, as the visibility was decreasing and the sky leaning more toward darkness than light, they heard orders being given by the British officers. They would make their charge while there was still enough light to see, but enough darkness to provide some cover. As the front ranks of British soldiers marched within range of the long rifle muskets, James and Bode signaled for the men to fire at will and to then continue to reload and fire as targets came into range.

The initial shots seemed to create more confusion in the British lines than casualties. Although men in their front lines fell, they seemed surprised that the sudden musket fire was able to reach them. Their rows of infantry continued forward and began to form up at about 110 yards out, with bayonets fixed and pointing forward waiting for the orders to charge. The Dragons had reloaded and were into their second round before the order was finally given for the British formations to move forward at a fast walk up the hill. The battle cries of 500 men were extremely intimidating, thought James. Bode seemed to have the same thought and began chanting "Dragons! Dragons! Dragons!" and the men quickly picked up the chant and yelled it back as they reloaded, pausing only briefly to aim and fire their weapons.

James and Bode were also aiming, firing and reloading their long rifles. As the British charged across the ridgeline, the dropping of the wounded and the dead in the front lines caused those following to stumble or hesitate as they stepped around the fallen. The closer the British got to their front lines, the more accurate and deadly the Dragons became. At forty yards, James ordered the men to fire their second muskets. The 120 Dragons facing the charging lines of British soldiers seemed to grab and fire their second loaded weapons within moments of each other. The British front line literally collapsed from the impact of the volley, while those following were forced to stumble their way across the dead in front of them. The charge halted briefly at the tangled mass of bodies. Many of the troops began to stop and fire toward the Dragons, but the British officers moved to the front and kept yelling orders for them to keep moving forward and attack. With the officers in front spurring them on, they once again began moving forward. The second wall of British soldiers was frightening to see so close, but it provided an incredible opportunity for the defenders.

"Short muskets!" James and Bode yelled at their men as they rotated to their bayonet tipped muskets and fired into the reformed ranks of the oncoming British soldiers. As James fired from his position, he heard the roar of the third set of muskets and watched the devastation they caused in the British ranks. James knew that without the two spare muskets, they would have never stood a chance against the British charge and they would have been overrun and quickly overwhelmed. Being able to fire an additional 240 muskets at close or point blank range would have caused devastation to any attacker. The charge faltered and then halted as the remaining British soldiers decided to regroup and stand their ground, exchanging fire instead of charging into the defenses of the waiting Dragons. James felt a moment of relief as he shifted from preparing to engage in hand to hand combat to reloading his musket.

James was once again impressed by the highly trained and disciplined British regulars. Any other force would have turned and fled after such destruction, but these men stood their ground and reloaded and fired as they were able to acquire targets. It was now a simple musket exchange between a smaller force with cover, against a larger force in the open. The sounds of musket balls passing through the air above and to the side of him, and slamming into the protective barrier in front of him was unnerving, but it was the sound of the wounded and dying of those he cared for deeply that kept him reloading and firing at his enemy. Although James' body was a blur of constant action, James felt a strong sensation of peace come over him as he came to realize that death could come upon him any moment, but he decided that he would not quit because his men would not quit. As he looked around while reloading, he saw a new look on the faces of the Dragons: not anger, not fear, not revenge, but a cold determination. Was it the look that Captain Donovan had told him about when they had first met, the look that made for a great soldier, or was it the look he had warned him about? He knew inside that he would not leave these men until either victory or death came and somehow knew they had that same determination.

As James was busy reloading, he saw one of the only remaining British officers standing in the midst of the roar of ongoing fire. He was trying to rally his men to get them to push forward the attack. He bravely stepped in front of the line of men and with his cutlass held high, motioned for them to follow him. The line of British soldiers behind him responded and gave up the task of reloading their weapons. Instead, they used their bayonet tipped rifles as spears and charged forward with him toward the defenses where Bode and the Dragons were waiting.

James watched the charge unfold as he continued reloading as fast as he could. As the officer leading the group came within ten yards of the defenders, he and the soldiers charging behind him were slowed by the brush and bramble that had been stacked there. He leaped in small jumps across the bramble as he fought to reach the line of Dragon soldiers who were either preparing to meet them with their own bayonet-tipped rifles, or who were busy reloading their muskets. James watched as Bode stepped forward to face the officer, exchanged words with him as the officer yelled at Bode and tried to climb over the short wall of bodies that was between them. James watched as Bode at first hesitated, then raised his pistol and fired at the officer. The brave officer fell at Bode's feet, finally having cleared the defenses. James knew that Bode would take no joy in the moment and watched as he reached down and picked up the cutlass and rallied the Dragons near him.

James would never forget the sight of his best friend facing the oncoming charge of British soldiers armed only with a cutlass and an empty pistol. As the nearest British soldiers cleared the brush and closed the distance, three Dragons stepped to Bode's side and fired at the three closest soldiers at point blank range as they charged at Bode. All three were mortally wounded as the musket balls tore through them. The Dragons then took their defensive stand with bayonets pointing out to protect Bode. There was a sudden burst of rapid fire that sounded like a drum roll on a marching snare as additional shots were fired into the charging soldiers from the left and right as the Dragons not at the front of the attack, James included, tried to support them. The rally was enough, and the majority of the charging soldiers were dropped short of the defenders. The attack faltered and the remaining men quickly withdrew to the line of soldiers now about fifty yards out.

The smoke was thick; the noise of muskets and wounded and dying men screaming was unnerving. All James could do was fire, reload, fire, and reload again as the volley exchange continued. James could hear the sound of war cries coming from Indian warriors somewhere behind him, but then the sound of muskets firing and the war cries soon halted. Shortly afterwards, twenty Dragons charged forward from the back defenses, carrying their spare muskets and taking up positions where others had fallen. The rapid double musket shots coming from the twenty new Dragons filling the defenses was enough to break the spirit of the British attackers. With no British officers remaining alive to organize a fighting retreat, what started as a gradual withdrawal became a full-fledged rout. The Dragons continued to fire their long rifles into the fleeing soldiers until they were out of range.

As the sound of musket fire ceased and the humming in James' ears subsided, the cries of the dying grew louder and louder. The smoke had drifted away from the area and James could see British soldiers moaning and moving in the jumbled mass of bodies. Some were trying to crawl away; one was repeatedly pulling back the hammer on his musket over and over and firing the unloaded rifle. Everywhere he looked horror met his gaze. Then he saw Bode and released a breath that he had been unaware that he was holding. He was standing with his men who began to slowly cheer "Dragons! Dragons!" Bode smiled as he looked across the circular area toward James, seeing that his friend had also survived. Their eyes met and they nodded at each other. Then there was a sense of overwhelming pride within James as he realized that it was Bode who had won the day with his bravery. He could not be more proud of his friend and the leader he had become in the eyes of the Black Dragons.

James could see Bode giving orders and then some of the men nearby began treating the wounded Dragons, while others were feverishly reloading their muskets as if they expected another attack from the British to come any moment. James had seen enough fighting to know that they would not be coming back any time soon.

As the initial relief of survival and the joy from the victory subsided, James took a moment to explore the various sources of pain across his body. His hand was burned from a powder flash; his right thigh had been torn open from a wound he did not remember receiving; his right shoulder was throbbing from the impact of a musket ball that had struck the stock of his rifle as he was aiming to fire it. Although it did not enter his arm, it did shatter the rifle and severely bruise his shoulder. He looked down to see that his left forearm was bleeding from a musket ball that had passed through his sleeve and across his arm while he was reloading. Blood was running down the right side of his head and as he reached up to find the source of the wound, and pulled out a small piece of wood that had embedded itself there from when the rifle stock was hit by the musket ball. James imagined that he probably looked far worse than he felt, even though seeing so much of his blood gave him a funny weak feeling in his knees. He glanced around the field of battle, trying to take in the moment and decide what he should do next.

Their decision to stand and fight here might have proved to be the best decision, inflicting the maximum casualties on the enemy, but it had also been very costly for them. As the sunlight faded and darkness fell heavy on them, they felt it was best to push their defensive lines out a little further. This would allow them to light a fire in order to better help the wounded and keep the enemy Indian and Jaeger marksman from using their long rifles to pick off soldiers standing near the lights of the fires. James posted sentries in a huge ring around the circle spaced roughly about 100 yards from the defense perimeter with twenty yards between each other. Once they had treated their own wounded, they slowly and cautiously picked their way through the mass of British casualties in the darkness and began treating their wounds as well, carrying them toward the light of the fire where they had more light to treat their wounds.

James and Bode quietly compared notes on their casualties and their situation. Since leaving Christiansted, 65 of their soldiers had been killed in battle and 76 were wounded, 28 of whom were not mobile. In two days and three battles, they had lost almost half of their men and in spite of the victory, the loss of so many friends was devastating to them. They could see that their men were exhausted physically and emotionally, as were they. As any good leader would do, Bode kept their minds off the losses and the cries from the wounded and kept them busy, occupying them with cleaning their weapons, checking their kits, and fortifying the brush wall. The sentries were rotated regularly and patrols were sent out at irregular intervals. The others took turns resting throughout the night.

When morning came, James could already smell the decay of flesh coming from the piles of British, Jaeger and Indian dead. The warm, humid air seemed to speed up the process and they knew that they would need to move soon or it would get worse. They spent the first part of the morning gathering British muskets and stacking them behind the base camp defenses. By noon, they had gathered over 350 British muskets, and the powder, shot, packs and supplies that had been on the soldiers. They did not have the tools to bury their own dead, let alone the enemy's dead, so they dragged the bodies of the enemy dead to the edge of the downwind side of the west ravine and slid them down the hill. It was a horrible job, but they knew that they could not leave the area until the wounds of several of their men improved. They had lost another one of their men during the night as well as a considerable number of British wounded.

They sent out small patrols, which were instructed to search the area for fruit and water to give to the wounded, who continually cried out for more. They began building stretchers for the wounded, using the belts and clothes pulled from the dead British soldiers.

Late in the afternoon, word was passed to the base camp that a contingent of Dutch soldiers was coming up the path to their positions. Despite the friendly last encounter that had experienced with the Dutch, they immediately went into defensive formation.

Would the Dutch be enemies this time, taking advantage of their weakened condition and attack or lay siege to their camp, or would they bring aid? They could hear them coming through the woods and up the ridgeline just as the British had. All went silent as a Dutch junior officer came into the cleared area with two soldiers by his side, one bearing a white flag hanging from the bayonet of his musket. James and two other men walked down from their defenses and through the thinly treed area to meet the young officer. The man smiled as he saw James.

"Our colonel will be happy to see you are well, Captain Thornton," the man commented in English, colored by a thick Dutch accent. James nodded.

"I appreciate his good wishes. How may I help you, Lieutenant?" he asked the young officer, who seemed a little off balance by the question.

"I have been sent by the colonel to offer our assistance to you, should you need it, Captain," he replied. "Yesterday our forces captured two British soldiers who had been running and were lost. They both told the same story of their battle and crushing defeat at the hands of the Black Dragons. The colonel organized this force and had the soldiers lead us back to where the battle supposedly had taken place," he said and looked around a minute. Seeing the lack of bodies, he continued. "They apparently exaggerated the situation."

"How many men do you have with you Lieutenant?" James interrupted him as he looked past the two men behind him.

"100 soldiers and 20 local militia who are acting as our guides," he replied. "We brought shovels to help bury any dead that you may have," he said softly and James felt moved by the young man's gesture. He took a deep breath.

"How much help are you willing to offer Lieutenant?" James asked sincerely and sternly. The man shrugged.

"The colonel said that I am to be at your disposal," he said nervously. James felt a wave of relief for the first time in days, knowing that he finally had enough help to carry the wounded, to defend their retreat if needed, and to get what remained of his men back home. James finally nodded toward the lieutenant and held out his hand for the man to shake.

"What is your name Lieutenant?" He asked.

"Lieutenant Jerald Hess." He replied and sent one of his men back to get the rest of the troops as they continued toward the base camp.

The young man's eyes went wide as he saw the huge pools of dried blood covering the ground leading up to the camp. James walked the lieutenant to the edge of the ridgeline and nodded his head down the hill to over 450 bloating bodies that had been piled up below them.

"We did not have the tools to bury the enemy's dead, so we dragged them downwind from us. There are over 350 British soldiers and 100 of their mercenary allies down there. I'm not sure how you would like to handle them." James stated and then asked at the end. The man was struck speechless as he surveyed the piles of dead below him.

"You also engaged the Indian and mercenary raiders?" He asked incredulously and James nodded.

"They hit us first and then lead the rest of the British army to our camp. We saw what the mercenaries did to our wounded when they attacked, so we did not want to leave our wounded behind again." James said distantly as he thought back on the events. The man just nodded humbled as he imagined the immensity of the battle that took place there. "Please accept my apology for my flippant remark and for the loss of your men," the young officer said to James.

As the Dutch troops came into the clearing and toward the camp, the Black Dragons remained at the ready, their former enemies making their way through the piles of brush carrying shovels in their hands, their muskets hung over their shoulders. Eventually the Dragons relaxed and joined the men who had started digging graves for their dead. From time to time different groups of Dutch soldiers would gather to the edge of the ravine and look down into the valley at the piles of dead soldiers below them. Every soldier who came away from the edge grave faced and seemed to have a change of heart and deeper respect toward the Black Dragons.

James learned that the Dutch army, led by the colonel, had driven off the 300 British soldiers stationed around the city of Frederiksted, and although the battle was short, it was a bloody encounter and costly for both sides. The officers at Frederiksted had received word that there were Indian and mercenary raiders attacking and burning the plantations to the south from runners sent from their forces that had been dug in on Kings Hill. It was a patrol from this force that had captured the two British soldiers who had reported the defeat at the hands of the Black Dragons. Believing that their route was now clear, they marched westward and arrived at Frederiksted without encountering the British. The arrival of the additional troops at Frederiksted bolstered the defense there and the colonel ordered the force that was with them now to march forward to see what assistance they could offer.

It took a great deal of time, but after burying the Black Dragon dead, the two, small, allied armies marched down the ridgeline and then east until darkness. James could not believe how humid it was getting and drank as often as he could get the chance. The Dutch and Black

Dragon soldiers took turns carrying the wounded, theirs and the British, and the stacks of muskets that they had bundled together and placed on the litters that they had fashioned by sliding two poles, each through the arm holes of a buttoned coat that one of the militia had devise. Their progress was slow and they did not make much distance, but they felt confident that they had the numbers to fend off an attack, so they kept to their steady pace. They camped at the base of Bloe Mountain and setup their defenses as if anticipating a full-scale attack. Neither James nor Bode wanted to have gone through all they had been through only to be caught unaware so close to home. James could not sleep, plagued by the thoughts and fears of being attacked again and the possibility of losing more of his friends. Runners were sent forward through the night to notify Christiansted and Captain Donovan of their impending return.

The Dutch and Black Dragon soldiers were initially cordial but cautious toward each other, keeping to their groups and carrying stretchers only with one of their own soldiers on the other end. By the end of the second day, however, there were now Dragon and Dutch soldiers on each end of a stretcher and they even spent a great deal of time discussing their battles and travels with each other as they marched. Captain Donovan had sent out two Dragon groups with fifteen wagons to meet them and help bear the wounded. Their gratitude was further increased when they learned that several were loaded with food and water, enough for the Dragon and Dutch soldiers alike. The men unloaded the bread, cheese and salted meat and they loaded the wounded and the captured muskets onto the empty wagons and drove them home.

James and Bode shook the young lieutenant's hand, thanked him and his men for their assistance, and asked him to convey his gratitude to the Colonel. The men of the two armies waved toward each other and smiled as they departed each toward their respective cities. The days did not seem as dark as they had following the battle on the ridgeline. In spite of their losses, there was a sense of hope with the prospect of peace instead more war and death. Despite the burden of the loss that every man felt, they had started laughing again. James looked around at the men. They were different; they were now "baptized with fire" Black Dragons. They carried their long rifles proudly, their heads high, and walked as free men, men who would never allow their freedom to be taken from them. He was so proud of them.

The city seemed the same as they marched into, although the harbor now included the hulls of three charred ships sitting on a reef just above the waterline. There were tears of joy at the sight of the returning Dragons and there were tears of sadness at the loss of friends and family. James felt different now, after bearing witness to so much death and carnage, he finally understood why his father acted as he did when he would return home from war. It always took time for his father's memories to soften, his nightmares to end, and his sadness to fade. Captain Donovan just shook his head as the two men had entered the fort and headed to their rooms, their faces long. He patted each one on the shoulder in congratulations as they went by, causing James to grimace as he touched his aching wound. Bode just nodded.

"Gentlemen." He stated, almost sounding like an order, and they stopped and turned toward him. "I know you might not grasp it or believe it now, but it was worth the cost." He said. The two men just starred blankly at him for a moment and then Bode nodded, but James still struggled with the senselessness and his powerlessness over the recent course of his life merely turned toward the officer's quarters again.

James' head was swimming as he held the silver-plated pistol that he had given to Robbie glancing at the unoccupied room where he should be standing with that huge smile and kind heart. As James stood by the door of Robbie's room, Bode came up behind him.

"I would give it to his dad the next time you see him." Bode said softly indicating the pistol and James nodded. *That would be a good idea* he thought, *but when would they ever be returning home*, he wondered? He felt completely exhausted, worn out to his very core, his legs feeling like two stone pillars as he stood there. His left shoulder ached from carrying the ten pound musket and the wound there throbbed. His thigh burned and the cut on his head sent sharp pains through his skull when he made certain expressions. It was as if he had been carrying the world on his shoulders as he led the Dragons back to the fort, fearing that something else terrible would happen before he could deliver them safely to it. At least that fear had kept his mind busy, but now that they were there, the fatigue and the sorrow threatened to overwhelm him.

"Were home now James. Time for all of us to rest and to let go." Bode said softly and James nodded. James thought that it was strange for Bode to use the word 'home' to describe Christiansted and the fort, but tried not to read too much into it. He was too tired to worry about it anyway.

As James rested in his bed, his thoughts lurched haphazardly, one moment thinking about Rebecca, the next a sorrow that grew to be so encompassing that it tasted like metal in his mouth and his head felt light as if he had taken too many deep breathes. He thought about Robbie, and about the men he had lost. Finally, the runaway wagon of his mind drifted into a black abyss of shame and guilt as thoughts of the families of the dead Dragons, there in town and those back home, those that he had known his whole life, accusing him of letting their boys die. Even the British soldiers that would never see their homes or families again rose up to blame him. He felt guilty for living through such an ordeal and being able to hold those he loved in his arms again knowing that those that had died would never share such an experience again. Instead of rejoicing that he was alive, he instead felt guilty for wanting to see Rebecca. He tried to close his eyes to sleep, but the images of the dead and wounded would fill his mind and he would have to open his eyes and light the nearby lamp to force them back into the recess of his mind. He wrestled with himself all through the night and when morning came he felt more tired than he had before. Upon seeing him at breakfast, Captain Donovan ordered him back to bed for more rest and recovery, clarifying that everything was safe and secure and there were no worries. James nodded and stumbled back to his room, barely making it to his bed before collapsing on it with a crash.

He tossed and turned as he fought back the nightmares that had plagued him over the past few days, yet his body would not allow him to sit up or even to open his eyes. He dreamed of burning fire, stabbing pain, and extreme thirst as he fought his way through the land somewhere between dreaming and waking. *Was he in hell for all the killing he had done?* he wondered as he prepared for the next dark attack of the dead British soldiers who were climbing out of the valley toward him. He killed them over and over again in his dreams, but they returned over and over again, with him somehow surviving only to have to fight them again.

It was during the darkest of these visions that a soothing light suddenly came into his mind, driving out the darkness and the screams of pain and suffering of the wounded. Then he dreamed of a gentle, soft caress on the top of his hand and warm water touching his wounded shoulder and cool water trickling into his mouth. A gentle stroking across his forehead and a soft, warm touch on his lips flowed through his whole body. However, it was the soft gentle whisper in his ear that had finally allowed him to release the grip on the ledge that he had desperately had clung onto. With muscles shaking with exhaustion, and his body trembling with fear of the depths, he let go and fell backwards, arms spread wide in the soft darkness.

"I love you." The words continued to echo in the welcome blackness that he had wrapped around himself like a blanket, no longer aware of the accusing faces and the horrors that had pursued him to the precipice. All seemed to fade away, he finally slept.

The distant melody of a beautiful song wove its way in and out of his dreams, no matter where they took him. He found himself chasing the source of this enchanting melody through his dreams and found himself running across the planted fields of North Carolina toward his home, but when he arrived, the source of it was not there. He then sailed across the blue seas of the Caribbean, and to where the sound became clearer and closer. He then found himself marching through the jungles of St. Croix and through the streets of a city that he recognized. The source of the music was near. He was close now. He entered through the gates of a yellow fortress and went from room to room searching as the music continued to grow louder and louder. Finally he stopped at a doorway; he could hear the music just beyond it. He reached and turned the handle and as the door swung open, he awoke. Annoyed that he had awaken so close to his goal, he closed his eyes and tried to will himself back to the doorway to continue his search for the source of the music, but he could not. His eyes fluttered and his fuzzy vision became clearer as he lay on his back and tried to focus on the ceiling above him, then he heard the familiar melody, ever so faintly, to his side. He turned his head toward the sound and saw her sitting there. She was the most angelic and beautiful thing he had ever seen. She smiled at him and reached over and took his hand in hers, then reached down and kissed him on the lips, then moved her lips to his ear and whispered.

"I love you James Thornton." He smiled at the memory of his dream and hoped that this one was real.

"I love you too Rebecca Edlund." He whispered scratchily in response and smiled. She placed her arms across his chest and pulled him close. James realized how weak he was and that he could not sit up or even lift his arms to return her embrace.

Rebecca raised his head and poured some juice into his mouth. His stomach groaned as the sweet juice flowed down his throat and into his stomach. He wanted more, but she would only give him small amounts. His face apparently showed his frustration.

"The doctor said to give it to you slowly or you would get sick." She said in a tone that reminded him of his mother and smiled at him. He tried to understand what was going on, and asked her how she had arrived so quickly to the city. She laughed softly and touched his hair again.

"You have been very sick the past ten days James Thornton and have worried us all to death." She chided him as he wrestled with the idea of having slept for ten days. "You did a horrible job of treating your shoulder wound and it got infected. Bode found you on the floor and called for the doctor." She said and he looked toward his shoulder and saw that it was wrapped with fresh bandages. She could read the concern in his face. "The doctor said you would be fine, but the scar is not going to be very pretty."

"It'll match the rest of you." A deeper voice said from the doorway and James looked to see Bode standing there with his smile. James searched for a witty reply, but could not find the energy to do so.

Bode spent the next half hour filling James in on all the events that had been happening during the past ten days since they had arrived back at the fort.

"The wounded men are recovering nicely, far better than you; The British fleet has departed and was last seen sailing north; Colonel Dekker of the Dutch army at Frederiksted sends his greetings and hopes for your quick recovery. Captain Donovan arranged and delivered the British prisoners and their wounded to be transferred to Frederiksted to deliver them to Europe to negotiate an exchange with the English. We sent out details of men to bury the dead and gather what equipment we could. The field cannons that we disabled have been recovered, although we had to negotiate with the Dutch to reclaim them. We settled on equal shares. It seems we are making headway with the locals as well; there have been seven additional major plantations and twenty or more smaller plantations from the center and eastern end of the island that have requested the permission to establish trade arrangements with Christiansted. They are also interested in discussing the idea of having their workers trained as militia." He said and let the words sink in a moment and James felt encouraged by the news. "Oh, and some lady has never left your side the whole time you have been slacking on your duties. I really have no idea what she sees in you." He finally ended. James and Rebecca both smiled as she squeezed his hand in hers.

Chapter 20

It was two more days before James had the energy and strength to get up and walk around the fort area. The men appeared happy even joyful, having moved past the grieving of their losses and embracing the gift of life again. Something that James knew he also needed to embrace. Rebecca had helped him understand that mindset while James regained his strength, as did her father during his visits to the fort to check on his daughter and his future son-in-law. They had purchased everything they could from the local farmers using the moneys that they had available. Captain Donovan had even sailed *The Dragon* out to anchor off the shores of the plantations, buying and loading their goods onto the vessel and sailing it back to Christiansted to unload. The warehouses were full and the people on the eastern end of St. Croix were happy to put another harvest year behind them.

At the end of the third week after the final battle with the British, the fort was brought to arms and the familiar tension returned to the soldiers of the city. Three days earlier, they had seen the Dutch trade fleet sail toward Frederiksted, they now were spotted coming from the west around the northern tip of the island. Captain Donovan initially guessed that the Dutch fleet was heading back toward home, but the ships suddenly turned south and anchored off the entrance, exactly where the British fleet had anchored prior to their attack. There were three ships of the line and eight heavy merchant vessels now anchored offshore. A short while later, a longboat rowed toward the harbor entrance and into the bay. Gradually the boat came within reach of their guns and continued toward the wharf where James, Bode and Captain Donovan awaited their arrival, a group of Black Dragons standing at attention behind them.

James recognized three men on the vessel. One was the Dutch colonel Dekker, another was Captain Hendriks, and the third was the Dutch captain's father, Commodore Hendriks. James and the rest of the men saluted as the men climbed onto the dock and took a moment to survey the officers and soldiers before them. Then the commodore returned the salute and smiled.

"I'm glad to see that you have recovered from your injuries Captain Thornton. You and your men have been in many peoples prayers." He stated as he looked past James, then at Bode, then at Captain Donovan, and finally the soldiers behind them.

"My men and I thank you sir." James replied. "May we ask what brings you to Christiansted?" James asked, getting to the point. The colonel smiled, as did the Dutch captain.

"You are a man who prefers to avoid wasting time with shallow conversations." The commodore said and then took a deep breath. "In the past five months since arriving here, you have managed to captured a Dutch fortress and the city that it protects, created a great deal of turmoil with the Dutch citizens by freeing their workers and training them to fight as soldiers, you captured a Dutch merchant vessel, and then refused to surrender to our army." He stopped briefly to take another breath and turned toward the other two Dutch officers. "Did I forget anything?" He asked them and smiled, who shrugged briefly and the Dutch colonel raised a hand.

"Just one or two minor items... But nothing of any significance." He replied and smiled back and the commodore pretended that he suddenly remember something.

"Oh right, I forgot... Let's see, you spared my son's life, defended the city against overwhelming land and naval forces, marched out from your safe defenses and attacked an enemy twice your size so that my army of trapped soldiers could escape. The same army that days earlier I had sent to destroy your army, so that they could rescue a Dutch city that I was trapped in. You then defeated a force of mercenary and Indian raiders who had been burning defenseless Dutch plantations, and then ended it by defeating the entire British force that had come to destroy my army and occupy the island of St. Croix." He said and turned back toward his men as if to see if he had forgotten anything, whom only shrugged and then smiled. James knew that they were jesting and he felt proud of their kind words, but knew they were wrong.

"I think you are greatly exaggerating." James hesitated, "Contrary to popular belief, I was not alone." James responded dryly with a serious expression that did not reveal that he was joking. Captain Donovan chuckled beside him, which caused Bode to look down at the dock. The commodore grasped the sarcasm and even appreciated it as he also started to laugh.

"Captain, you and your men have proven to be very dangerous adversaries, but more importantly, you have all demonstrated, as a whole, that you are a far better friend to the Dutch than an enemy." He said and hesitated a moment before continuing. "Because you are no longer allied with the British, we would like to end any hostilities between our nation and your new colonial nation." He ended and waited for the words to sink in. James turned toward Captain Donovan and Bode as if to get their thoughts. Both raised their eyebrows at the offer. James finally turned back toward the commodore.

"What demands or requirements are you requesting for such a relationship?" James asked and the man seemed to think long and hard before responding.

"Only that you continue to protect the citizens of this island, that you train as many Black Dragons as you are able, and that you allow us first rights to purchase the harvest from the plantations who chose to sell their goods in your city." James listened to the easy to accept 'requirements' and then smiled at the last two words. He leaned forward and looked toward the Dutch colonel and raised an eyebrow. The man smiled and nodded.

"Yes James, he said 'your' city." The Dutch colonel replied.

"From what I have seen and heard, I doubt that anyone could pry it out of you and your men's hands anyway." The commodore added and waited for his response. James again looked at his two friends, who both nodded, then extended his hand to the commodore. The man reached out and shook his hand firmly and confidently.

"I shall have papers drawn up for your signature." The commodore stated as they continued to shake hands.

"Captain Donovan can sign the papers, but you have our word that we will honor our end of the agreement." James replied and then stepped back and saluted the commodore. The man returned the salute.

"I do not know how full your holds are commodore, but we have a warehouse full of goods available for purchase." Captain Donovan added and the commodore nodded.

"I'll arrange for their purchase and with your permission, I will have our ships sail in to load the goods." The commodore replied, but Captain Donovan, Bode and James all seemed uncomfortable with the idea. The commodore suddenly grasped their concern. "I'll only have the merchant ships enter the harbor… and even then, only a few at a time." He said and smiled and they all seemed to relax as the words were shared.

Four days later, their warehouses were almost empty and their coffers were full from the exchange of plantation owner goods for Dutch silver and gold coins. Supplies and equipment orders were also taken by the fort and plantation owners and delivered to the Dutch merchant fleet allowing the locals to replenish their supplies when the trade fleet returned in the spring. The Dutch even offered to sell them powder and shot for the defense of the city and the training of the current and new militiamen, which they ordered and they agreed to a partial payment with the remainder due upon delivery. The show of faith went a long way with James, Captain Donovan and the other officers. Although they had enough powder and shot for the militia, they had expended a great deal of cannon shot during the exchange with the two British warships that had invaded their harbor and restocking their supplies would be important if they intended to fulfill their end of the agreement.

Captain Donovan and the commodore signed a peace & trade agreement that included a mutual defense clause that both cities garrisons would assist the other, or would work in union to protect the island and its inhabitants should an outside power try to invade the island again. As the ships departed for Europe and sailed off into the distance, there was a growing confidence and peace felt by the inhabitants of the city. Bode was the first to notice it, the lack of urgency and complacency that James' father talked about that often came after a victory. He felt that they should push forward quickly with the negotiations and training of additional Black Dragons with those plantation owners across the eastern end of the island that had expressed an interest while the memory of the recent danger was still fresh in their minds. He also felt they needed to keep the men busy and focused to keep them out of trouble.

Largely due to Bode's focus and determination, within two weeks they had finished the negotiations with the plantation owners and began the training of nearly 400 workers as militiamen at eleven different plantations on the eastern end of the island. Ten Dragons were stationed at each location and, within two weeks, muskets were delivered to each soldier that they were training. Lizard uniforms consisting of a shirt and vest and belts and packs salvaged from the British soldiers were provided to the recruits as they were completed by the seamstresses and leatherworkers at Christiansted.

From September until January they faced violent storms. They weathered a hurricane that barely caught the edge of the island yet caused considerable damage. The plantation owners were used to the effects of nature on the island and began to rebuild and replant as soon as they were able. The fort sent out the Black Dragons to assist those plantation owners who were hit harder than others were. By the end of January, militia training began for an additional 200 workers. The training took place on both large and small plantations. The Dutch had followed suit, taking a similar approach to training a local militia after sending officers to work alongside the Black Dragons as observers in order to learn how to train the workers. They initially had a difficult time recruiting, for they tried to train recruits without freeing them. Few wanted to participate and by spring, they adopted the practice of freeing the slaves, convincing the plantation owners of the need and value of such an approach using the testimonials of the eastern landowners that such decisions would prove worth the risk. They gradually began freeing their workers.

On April 12, 1777, James married Rebecca Edlund in a beautiful ceremony performed by Pastor Booker, in the open field just outside the walls of the fort. They were told that it was one of the largest attended weddings the island had every seen. Among those in attendance were his Black Dragons, the citizens of Christiansted, Dutch officers from Frederiksted and plantation owners from all parts of the island. Bode was James' best man, with Captain Donovan, and Rebecca's older brother Edward standing close by 'in case Bode caused any trouble' as James explained the need for their presence. After the wedding, they were rowed out to the *Unicorn* that was anchored at the western end of the harbor. Captain Donovan, his men, and some of the esthetically inclined women in the city had converted the Captain's quarters into an opulent honeymoon suite, seeming to spare no expense with regards to food, drink, linen, clothes, heating and surroundings. The ship was vacated, leaving them alone to walk the decks freely enjoying each other's company while aboard the large vessel. Every day for the next seven days, a longboat would arrive, announce their presence, then unload and carry to the captain's quarters a new feast of breads, fruits, meats, candies and drink for them to enjoy that day. They were spoiled beyond imagination.

On the evening of the seventh day, Captain Donovan rowed out to the vessel to jokingly announce that they had consumed all the food and drink supplies in the city and that no more could be provided; that rebellion was brewing across the island; that a British fleet was seen on the horizon, and that Bode had staged a *coup d'etat* and was demanding to be referred to as 'Emperor' from hence forth. Although they hated to leave, they both agreed that perhaps they should return to reality, if not to at least remove the threat of a Black Dragon Emperor. It had been a wonderful and deeply bonding week for them, one that they would never forget.

James and Captain Donovan had raised Bode's rank to Captain and ascribed to him the duties of acting commander of the Black Dragons. Captain Donovan was named Mayor of Christiansted. Repeated efforts were put in motion to name James as Governor of eastern St. Croix, but he refused, fearing that it would create animosity or concern with the leadership in Frederiksted. In the end, they all settled for the title of "Protector" of Eastern St. Croix.

After long and private discussions with Rebecca on what their future would hold, James' focus began to shift. He began to train others to take on his duties and tasks on the island and within the city. While Bode and Captain Donovan were thriving and growing in their joy and happiness, James, in contrast felt more and more restless as he purposely surrendered more and more of his duties to others. Bode could feel his friends gradual withdrawal from key duties and tried to replace them with other activities, even inventing plans or ideas with sole purpose of regaining James' passion, but James found that more and more of his free time was being spent at the Edlund plantation. While at the Edlund plantation, James felt a similar effort or pressure, Rebecca's father did his best to try to convince him to give up the life of a soldier and help Edward to run the family's plantation. But James did not want to infringe upon Edward's inheritance. Captain Donovan offered to put in his share of monies to buy a plantation on the island that James and Rebecca could oversee, but knowing that his family had his own plantation back home, the idea did not seem wise.

The summer returned and the plantations were in full operation. The arrival of summer also heralded the return of the Dutch trade fleet from Europe, bringing long awaited supplies and more news of the situation in the American colonies and their war for independence against the British. From what news they could gather, it seemed that the colonials' struggle for independence was much more difficult and costly than they first imagined. Despite this, the hearts and minds of the colonists were holding fast to their ideals. They learned that the French had pledged, at least in word, their support for the American Colonies and their war for independence from British rule. James wondered about his father, his family and what role he and the men of the North Carolina militia were playing in the war. Knowing his father, he felt strongly that they were involved; he just hoped they were safe.

Shortly after the Dutch trade fleet departed, the French fast frigate *Indiscrete* arrived, seeking safe haven and supplies after an encounter with a British fleet to the north. Seeing the British vessels behind it, they allowed the French vessel to enter the harbor and anchor inside the range of the forts' protective guns. In a strange twist of fate, the ship was the same French frigate that had pursued *The Dragon* across the Caribbean over a year ago. *'How strange is war'*, James thought as he watched the vessel, whose crew had tried to kill them just one year ago, sail into their harbor for protection. The British ships pursuing her blockaded the harbor, but after two weeks, must have decided that such efforts were a waste for one vessel and there was nothing that would force the Frigate from her safe harbor. During the two weeks the frigate was at anchor, James and the officers of the fort had gotten to know Captain de La Clocheterie and the crew of the French vessel quite well. Captain de La Clocheterie had standing orders to harass and attack and otherwise disrupt the trade of all British merchant ships along the eastern shore of the colonies and within the Caribbean waters in support of the American colonists.

Bode saw an opportunity for his friend and in spite of the pain it would cause him, he decided to approach James about pursuing it. That very day Bode had asked to ride along with James to the Edlund plantation. He even convinced James to take a longer, but more scenic route. During the first hour of the ride, they spent the time reliving their memories growing up, during training, with the militia, the time on the ship, the capture of Christiansted, the battles with the British, and even the loss of Robbie and those that they cared so deeply about. James finally asked the question he knew was waiting as they walked their horses along the beach.

"Bode, why did you really come with me?" James asked and Bode smiled.

"We're too good of friends to miss anything aren't we." Bode stated and James nodded. "I think its time to return home." Bode said and James' heart leapt in his chest in agreement as the desires of his heart were suddenly revealed.

"Bode, I think we've done all we can be expected to do and we have people in place that are trained to do our jobs." James replied excitedly, but then grew silent as he did not see the same excitement on Bode's face.

"I didn't mean we, James, I meant you. You and Rebecca." Bode said and then smiled. "You're right; you've done everything that needs to be done to transfer leadership of the fort to any number of capable men so that we all could leave. But I can't go with you." Bode said, took a deep breath, and looked around a moment. "For whatever reason, God has put it on my heart that this is my new home." Bode said, "For how long, I don't know. But I do know that the only thing that hurts more than the thought of leaving this place behind is the thought of you leaving and the two of us never seeing each other again." Bode said. "You're a part of me that I feel I cannot lose or live without, you've been there for almost every breath or step that I've taken. I'm not sure if I know how to do either without you. However, to see joy return to your eyes and your heart, I will learn to breathe and I will learn to take new steps again on my own. I would do anything for you James; give the heart from my chest if I could. That is how much I love you and how much I will miss you." He said as tears rolled down his face. "Captain de La Clocheterie and the *Indiscrete* will be leaving within a week. I have already spoken to him about trading supplies for transport for you and any others who desire to return or move to North America." James just stood there in shock at not the idea, but at the thought of Bode not returning home with him. He started to shake his head and speak, but Bode put his hand on his shoulder and interrupted him.

"No James, this is best for both of us and what's best for you and Rebecca." Bode said and smiled. James just stared at his friend and then nodded.

"There is no one that has taught me more about friendship, leadership, and loyalty than you, Bode. I can't imagine sailing away from that friendship, without you in my life to pick me up when I fall, believe in me when I doubt," James stated and Bode shook his head.

"That's Rebecca's role now. And in so many other ways, she provides that which completes you. James, it's time we grow up and turn a page in our lives." Bode said and then smiled, "before we start disliking each other," and they both laughed.

"It has been an amazing friendship, one that I will treasure my entire life."

"Yes it has, James. I too treasure it, more than you can ever imagine." Bode replied and they walked in silence for a while before Bode stopped and mounted his horse. "James, I'm going to ride back to the city. You have a lot of planning and packing to do, assuming you can get Rebecca to join you." He said and smiled.

"Thanks Bode." James said and Bode nodded and turned his horse and galloped down the beach. James knew that the only person he loved more than Bode was Rebecca. James already knew that Rebecca wanted to go to North Carolina, but he knew the discussion with her father would be the difficult one.

To James' surprise and relief, the discussions with Rebecca's father and family about James and Rebecca moving to the colonies had gone well and they were supportive of their plans if it is what would make them happy. Of the fifty original Dragons that had been on this adventure together, thirty-nine had survived the various battles and sicknesses. Of those, twenty-seven wished to return to the plantation and their families in North Carolina. Forty-three of the island-born Black Dragons and several citizens and plantation family members also desired to move to the American Colonies.

James didn't realize it at first, but as he continued making preparations to leave, he was subconsciously avoiding Captain Donovan. True to form, Captain Donovan could always somehow see through his emotions and would not hesitate to address the matters of the heart. One evening, while eating with the other officers, James had quietly excused himself from the dinner table and walked to the ramparts of the main fort and stared out into the harbor. He was thinking about the relationships and friendships that he had made and would be leaving behind, and the ones he was looking forward to seeing again. His heart was breaking and rejoicing at the same time. He heard the steps, but did not turn to see who it was, but recognized the voice and smiled.

"We're running out of time to say our goodbyes my young Captain." Captain Donovan suddenly stated and stood next to him and stared out at the bay as well. "Our shallow discussions and smiles are all good to comfort those around us, but my heart will never heal if I never have a chance to say all that I want to say to you." He continued and James felt a lump of sadness growing in his throat. This was another special friendship that he treasured deeply and dreaded the thought of never seeing him again. James could only nod as he tried to swallow the sadness. "James, God has granted me a pretty amazing life these past fifty-four years. He has given me some amazing friendships that I will remember until my dying days." The Captain paused, "But you need to know and understand before you leave that my friendship with you, these last two years, is the one that I will treasure more than any other. Your courage, your faith, your humor, your humility, and your unfailing belief in me and all of our men, has restored my faith in God and in mankind. I know you don't realize it, but you rescued me from an empty life, and rewarded me with a friendship that I will treasure and will share about all the remaining days of life that God will grant me," his voice was faltering with emotion. "You are the son I have always dreamed of and wanted. I'm so grateful that God has allowed me to pretend to be a father these past few years. I will miss you more than you will ever know James Thornton. I know how much your father must miss you and why I'm even allowing that French frigate to sail out of here with my blessing, because I feel it too." Captain Donovan ended as his voice began to break with the emotion of his words. James could not speak as his heart broke and the tears flowed down his face. James just turned and the two embraced each other.

When the emotions faded enough for James' to speak again, he stepped back while still holding Captain Donovan by the arms. "You have been an excellent father and I strongly suggest that you use your wealth, power, influence," James hesitated as he looked at Captain Donovan, "or whatever it takes to convince a woman to marry you," he laughed, "and have many incredible children. Because they would be blessed to have a father such as I have had these past two years." James ended and smiled and Captain Donovan nodded as if in thought.

"Yeah, well finding one should be a lot easier now that you're leaving." He laughed in response, but James got serious again.

"My dear friend, when you're tired of ruling cities and captaining fleets of ships, when you're ready to settle down, come to North Carolina with your wife and children and live with us. I could think of no greater honor or blessing than to run a plantation and grow old with you." James said and Captain Donovan nodded.

"Agreed."

The day for departure arrived and there was a deep sadness as the Black Dragons, the citizens and families boarded the French vessel, knowing that they would probably never see each other again. James and Rebecca had spent a great deal of time at her family's plantation, saying their goodbyes. When James was not there, he spent his time with Bode. They talked about Bode's new love interest Tamara and the future that relationship might hold, the men and the leadership opportunities that he sees for them and Bode's own dreams and plans. As the departure date had grown closer, their discussions were only about their memories together and what to take back to his family in North Carolina and what memories that they each wanted to leave with the other.

On July 30, 1777 after many tears and hugs were shared between those, from across the island that they had grown to love and respect, James and Rebecca made their way along the dock to board the longboats that would take them to the French frigate. With a smile and a fatherly embrace, James asked Captain Donovan to keep an eye on the Black Dragon Emperor, which the Captain agreed to do. Bode was the last person he embraced before boarding the longboat.

"I would have never made it without you with me." James said to Bode and smiled.

"We would have never made it without you with us." Bode replied and James swallowed hard as he tried to form his last words.

"I will always be with you Bode King." James said to him, choking up at the end.

"Yes, you will and I with you." Bode replied in an equally strained response and James nodded and they embraced as tears filled James' eyes. Then James turned and walked down the ladder and took his seat on the longboat next to Rebecca. James could only bring himself to glance one more time at his friend, who stood on the dock with tears rolling down his face. Rebecca squeezed his hand gently and James nodded toward Bode and smiled and the nod and smile was returned. James quietly thanked God for giving him such an incredible friend.

Several hours later, the big French vessel started to slowly gather the wind and make its way toward the channel that lead to the open sea. A roar could be heard from the walls of the forts, as well as from the docks and banks of the city. At first it was faint, and then it grew to a steady and clear cheer.

"Black Dragons! Black Dragons! Black Dragons!" The heart moving cheer continued well past their exit of the harbor and James was moved to tears once again at the sound of the men cheering. James asked Captain de La Clocheterie if he would fire a cannon as a salute, and the captain made a short bow and gave orders for his men to do so.

As James watched the waving hats and arms fade in the distance, he felt Rebecca slide alongside, reach her arm around him, and then pull him close. She leaned forward and kissed him on the check, leaned her head against his shoulder and quoted from the book of Jeremiah chapter twenty-nine verses eleven through thirteen.

"For I know the plans I have for you," declares the LORD, "plans to prosper you and not to harm you, plans to give you hope and a future. Then you will call upon me and come and pray to me, and I will listen to you. You will seek me and find me when you seek me with all your heart."

As a gentle breeze blew across his face, James recognized the unfathomable kindness, mercy and foresight of God in giving him this incredible woman. God had given him exactly what his heart would need to survive this very moment and so many more too come. With a growing inner confidence, he suddenly looked forward to whatever God had waiting for them and kissed her forehead. She returned the kiss and smiled at him.

"I'm going to go below and lay down." She said and he nodded as she slid her arm out from around him and headed toward the door below decks.

"I'll be there soon." He said as she stepped through the door and glanced back one more time to smile at him before disappearing.

The "Boom!" of the cannon blast made James glance back toward the city and the fort fading in the distance. Instead of heading below, he took a moment to walk over, leaned against the railing, and let his mind drift back to earlier times, his mind filling with the thoughts and memories of his best friend.

###

Other Novels from the Author!

Everything
The untold story of the rich young ruler
(Christian Historical Fiction/Suspense)

"Sell Everything"

Jesus of Nazareth had told the rich young man who had traveled to meet him. *This can't be the Messiah*, Addi thought as he walked away from the encounter. The Messiah would have known he had dedicated his whole life to God, building a deep and powerful financial kingdom right under Pilate and Herod's noses, a kingdom that stood ready to equip and supply the Messiah's army when he returned. The secret organization he belonged to was searching for the Messiah who would step forward as the prophecies of old had foretold, to claim his kingdom, and drive out the armies of Rome. *Therefore, he can't be the Messiah.* Yet Addi could not deny the miracles this Jesus had demonstrated, so surely God must be with him. The man was fearless and bold when he taught the people and his message was powerful and amazing, yet far different from what the Pharisees and Sadducees were teaching; a teaching that had not gone unnoticed by them. *What must I do to inherit eternal life?* Addi shook his head, feeling a little confused. Of all the questions he had wanted to ask the man, that was not one of them. *Or was it?*

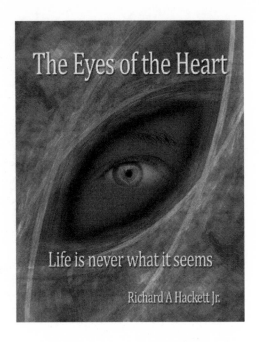

The Eyes of the Heart

Life is never what it seems.

From the time he took the job with Allen Brooke Inc., Luke's life had gone from one incredible challenge to the next. In the blink of an eye they transitioned him from writing training manuals for a new game, to putting his very life on the line for the company. He was quickly realizing that the product was no game at all, and that it had far more uses and dangers for society than he could have ever imagined. Moreover, he was clearly not alone in that understanding.

Secret societies and government intelligence agencies were now looking intently into it, and into anyone who was involved with it. His professional and personal life was suddenly thrust into a deadly battle between two political and religious ideologies that he didn't understand but he needed to grasp if he had any chance to stop the religious genocide that one of them had planned.

He would need to use every resource his body could call upon, including the most important one that he had yet to learn how to use… **The Eyes of his Heart.**

Glossary

Time period of novel: 1750-1777 AD

1625 St Croix is owned by the Dutch and England
1650 120 Spanish soldiers drove off the British
1733 Danish bought the island from the French
1742 264 plantations on St. Croix, 120 cotton, 122 sugar
1749 Fort Christiansted built
1751 Fredricksted resettled by the Dutch
1754 St. Croix became a Dutch colony
1762 Spain & England war over Nicaragua
1765 Stamp Act
1773 Alexander Hamilton left St. Croix for school in the colonies
1773 Tea Act
1775 Colonies, DE, PA, NJ, GA, CT, MA, MD, SC, NH, VA, NY, NC, RI
1776 July 4th, American Colonies declared their independence from England

Key Names:

James William Thornton Jr. – The son of James Thornton Sr.
Bode King – Best friend of James Jr., 2nd
James William Thornton Sr. – Father of James Jr., former Colonel in the British army, where he earned his rank in the French and Indian Wars from 1755 to 1763. He is the husband of Charlotte Rose, the father of James, Cynthia, Madison and Daniel.
Elijah King – Father of Bode, hired to run the plantation in 1758 while Colonel Thornton was away on duty.
Robbie Hanson – Good friend of James and Bode
Captain Ryan Donovan (Merchant Captain, former privateer)
Edward Thomas Edlund – St. Croix plantation owner, former captain in the British army, husband of Elizabeth, father of Rebecca, Edward Jr., Thomas, Allison, and Samuel.
Colonel Stephen Massman – Retired British Colonel living in Christiansted
William Booker – Preacher on St. Croix

Made in the USA
Lexington, KY
13 February 2018